In the Shadow
of Alabama

In the Shadow of Alabama

judy reene singer

KENSINGTON BOOKS
www.kensingtonbooks.com

KENSINGTON BOOKS are published by

Kensington Publishing Corp.
119 West 40th Street
New York, NY 10018

All Kensington titles, imprints, and distributed lines are available at special quantity discounts for bulk purchases for sales promotion, premiums, fund-raising, educational, or institutional use.

Special book excerpts or customized printings can also be created to fit specific needs. For details, write or phone the office of the Kensington Sales Manager: Kensington Publishing Corp., 119 West 40th Street, New York, NY 10018. Attn. Sales Department. Phone: 1-800-221-2647.

Kensington and the K logo Reg. U.S. Pat. & TM Off.

eISBN-13: 978-1-4967-0946-2
eISBN-10: 1-4967-0946-2
First Kensington Electronic Edition: June 2017

ISBN-13: 978-1-4967-0945-5
ISBN-10: 1-4967-0945-4
First Kensington Trade Paperback Printing: June 2017

10 9 8 7 6 5 4 3 2 1

Printed in the United States of America

The heart of this book really belongs to the men and women in uniform who spend their lives protecting us and our wonderful country. Whether their service is recent or in the far past, they have always served despite great personal sacrifice. My grandfather, who was in the navy, served in France during World War I, and was the victim of mustard gas. He returned home with badly damaged lungs that caused problems for him his entire life. My father served in the Army Air Corps, in Alabama, during World War II, and had experiences that changed him forever. We owe every veteran, every policeman, every fireman, and every member of the uniformed services a huge debt of gratitude. My book is a small and humble tribute to all of these heroes.

Prologue

My father was a difficult man, I always knew that. He carried a suitcase of grievances throughout his life, things I didn't understand and didn't care to. He never spoke of his time in the Army Air Force—that's what it was called when he was a soldier. He had served during World War II, and it hadn't been good. I knew that much. But his death left a family of walking wounded, flayed open by his hot temper, shattered to the core by his nasty insults. How my mother bore him for so long was a puzzle, yet she wept when he died.

And now we stood together for his funeral. My sister, my uncle, my mother, and me. We stood listening to the rabbi intoning generic platitudes that meant nothing.

My mother once had a little garden behind my childhood home where white lilies bloomed in the fall, after all the other flowers were finished. Tall plants with complex blooms, they were winter's early harbingers and never lasted very long. They bloomed and they fell apart, spent. White lilies are fragile like that.

We stood, the four of us, listening to the ancient tongue,

while not far from us, off to the side, stood a black woman—respectful, reverential. An elegant black rose among the broken white lilies.

When the service was over, she came over to gently touch my mother's hand. She said she was sorry that her father, who had served in the army under mine, wasn't able to attend. He had been very close to my father, and he had so badly wanted to talk to him about the thing that had separated the two men for an entire lifetime.

And then she dropped a word, so charged, so fueled with anger, that I was compelled to follow it to wherever it led.

Chapter 1

A white horse gives the herd away. That's what Malachi always says. A band of wild, dark horses fleeing from predators into the safety of cut-slate mountains, to seek their refuge inside the brown and violet shadows of twisted brush, can be immediately betrayed by the flash of a white horse.

Malachi's my farm manager, and he always likes to tell me how nature separates dark and white horses. Or maybe, eventually, the dark and white horses separate themselves, he was never clear about that. Still, the white horse is ostracized. Shunned. Becoming an outcast, driven to live at the fringes of horse society, left behind to fend for himself, because his bright color can spell death for the rest. Malachi always squeezes his eyes shut before telling me that part, as though he has to first envision it.

"Funny thing about horses and color," he says, finally opening his eyes and settling himself down with a grunt onto a bale of hay. His fingers fuss through the strands before selecting a thin stalk to slide between his lips. "Horses can't help themselves, splitting apart like that. It's always been that way; it will always be that way. It's nature's rules."

It made sense to me. I could picture a white horse moving across burnt sienna hills like a flash of lightning slicing through a thunderous sky. It made sense, though I've learned not to believe everything Malachi has told me over the years.

Malachi Charge had come with the farm, along with the tractor, the extra motor for the well pump, and six bags of lime—although they were all in better shape than he was. When I first met him ten years ago, I couldn't help but notice the slight tremor in his hands, the barely perceptible drag of his left leg, the pale cast of cataracts in his dark brown eyes.

"I'm seventy-five," he told us then. He was six foot, thin as a tenpenny nail, and wearing clean but faded jeans, a short-sleeved yellow shirt, and a tan newsboy cap tilted back atop his thick white hair. "But I'll do you a favor and stay on, because I been managing this farm for fifty years."

Though the deed showed that our horse farm had only been in existence for eighteen, we didn't quibble with him. We're not farmers by occupation, David and I, only by optimism. And with David working in the city at a large law firm, and me putting in long hours in my home office writing books, we needed this man who seemed to be part of the natural order of farming.

Malachi is black, and we're white, and we felt squeamish "acquiring" a person along with the farm in a sort of package deal, as if he were a piece of farm equipment. It didn't sit right with us, and we were embarrassed by even the thought of it.

"You may as well let me live here," he said, when I told him how I felt funny about it. "I got no place to go." I guess it was that Robert Frost thing. Home is, when you have to go there, they have to take you in. He didn't seem to have family, and so we told him of course he could stay on.

"I won't be any trouble at'al," he declared. "I got my Social Security."

But we insisted on a regular salary and the title of farm manager, and then made things proper and official by naming the place Water-from-a-Rock Farm, because it seemed like that was what we were trying to get. He lived in the small cottage he had always lived in, behind the barn, except that we renovated it for him. And he continued to do what he had apparently always done: gardening, puttering, fixing things, napping the afternoon away, and being bossy.

It's been ten years.

And Malachi, still wearing the tan newsboy cap, insisted on his last birthday that he was just turning seventy-five. Again. If it even was his birthday, since it floats from month to month each year, depending on his mood, needs, and circumstances.

"I could use a new winter coat," he told me in the beginning of November, when the air started to chill. "It's my birthday, anyways."

I couldn't say no to him, because he was my friend, my guide, and my father-substitute, but I couldn't resist teasing him. "I thought your birthday was in May, when you picked out all those new plaid shirts."

He just nodded and spit on the ground. "Yep. May, too."

My career keeps me at the computer, but I make sure I get outside for a few hours every day. I need to feel the changes in the wind, see the sky moving through its expressions of grays and blues, and witness the tangerine pinks that sweep through at sunset in what the old artists used to call the Hudson Valley sky. I like to stand by the barn at night and stare up, looking for the first shift of stars and moon that heralds another gliding change of constellations and seasons.

Spring is the best.

I am always pleased how the flowers know enough to come back on time, how all the grass renews at once, how green things push out of the ground, filling in the dead spaces. The earth lies dreamless for months, brown and empty, then thin emerald blades glide up through the black loam, celadon buds, rolled up like tiny, tight cigarettes, appear on once-dormant sticks, everything obeying a simultaneous choreography. The protocol of brave gold daffodils, followed by an unvarying succession of grape hyacinth, yellow forsythias, pink tulips, purple and white lilacs. I finger the new leaves, gently touch the folded infant flowers, and wonder how they all know when it's their time. How do they strike their annual bargain with the warm spring sun and cool nights? What summons them? The lengthening of days? The rains? Do they hold underground meetings? They come without bidding, they come in their time. I can't figure it, but all these things make sense to Malachi because he knows nature.

"They can't help themselves," he says. "It's in the rules."

He told me once that he was born and raised in Missouri, and had farmed all his life and that's how he knows things. He begins watering and tilling the soil as soon as the ground warms and softens, usually late April. He's "waking the gardens," he says. He prunes bare branches and sows seeds in little paper cups that he leaves on his windowsill and bosses me into buying more plants, more seeds, more bags of fertilizer, more equipment. He'll stand with me a few months later, nodding proudly as I marvel again at small, curled lettuce leaves and tomatoes flowering yellow, and basil growing like a fragrant weed.

"What did you learn?" he would ask me. "What did you learn?"

And like a schoolgirl, I recite his lessons back to him. "Start your seeds early, be patient, make sure they get what they need."

Foals come in the spring.

That is something I understand very well.

I breed horses, have bred them for years, and I understand the swelling promise of equine life that mares carry for eleven months. Though I never wanted children of my own, I think I understand how the mares feel when their bellies bulge out and shift from side to side. When their legs swell as they clumber around wearily, waiting to foal.

"I'll sit up with her," Malachi tells me when a mare begins to bag up, her udders engorging with milk, the area around her tail sinking in. Signs that she is ready to foal. I will watch her for hours, fretting, waiting, until Malachi finally pushes me out of the barn. "Go get some rest and let me do my job." He sends me off to the house as evening falls. "Trust me."

And I do. I trust him more than I ever trusted anyone in my life.

He finally summons me in the very beginning hours of morning, calling me on the intercom to come right now, and I rush to the barn.

A foal dives into its new life, head and neck centered between two small hooves that are sculpted like clay flowers, its long, spindly front legs reaching out for the world. It slips wetly to the ground, knowing what it must do next. An hour later, it's standing.

I have to touch it. Tenderly touch the thumb-size nostrils set into a fine muzzle, the silky mane, the short, curly tail, run my finger over the pink gums waiting for teeth. I look into its dark eyes that know everything about being a horse right away. I am fifty-three, and I still don't know everything about being a person.

"Now, go get some sleep and let me clean them up," Malachi commands me, and I obey him because he has become my father. Because I have long given up on my own father, and I need Malachi's care and management.

As I leave the barn, he'll take a clean old towel and rub the foal down, gently talking into its lily-petal ears, slapping the bottom of its feet. Imprinting it, he tells me. Loving it, like it was his own child, holding it in his big, round arms.

"I made you tea," he'll say when I get off a horse, tired from training it, which is not my real job, only my joy. He'll bring me a cup of steaming tea from his kitchen, holding it in his ever-so-slightly shaking hands, chamomile or dandelion or some other concoction he invented from the plants he grew and dried the previous summer. Or he will bring me whole wheat crackers spread with his favorite sardines—he tells me the best ones come crisscrossed—or sandwiches with tomato and garlic roasted until it's melted, or burdock root and cattail sprouts laid across buttered toast and seasoned with salt. He'll gently brush the hair from my eyes like a loving parent and hand me a bowl of one of his special snacks, shelled walnuts and sugared cranberries mixed with shredded wheat.

I grab handfuls and thank him, and he smiles. "Way back, was a time I used to cook," he explains.

"For squirrels?" I joke, peering at the usual nuts and berries, but I eat it gratefully, thinking how much I love this man.

I stand at the fence that surrounds the fields behind my house and stare at my horses. Sixteen of them, broken up into small herds. The youngsters are in one field. The four broodmares with foals at their side, in another. Then my riding horses, of sorts, because they aren't actually totally broke to ride yet. All of them black Friesians, glowing like seals. Except for Lisbon. He's a Thoroughbred. And he's nearly pure white. I adopted him from a horse rescue about three years ago. He came with a mysterious history that left him head shy and frightened, with nervous, rolling eyes that didn't comprehend. It took almost two years before he allowed me to bridle him properly, without having to take all the straps apart and re-assemble them around his face.

White horses are not considered white, of course. Malachi must have told me a hundred times they are called grays, even though I already know that. He always likes to point out how white horses are born dark, sometimes black, sometimes bay or chestnut. How the white comes slowly, a few hairs that start around the face, then creep down into the coat, more every year, until the horse has turned pure white. I stare at my hair in the mirror sometimes, and wonder when I will be called a gray.

Malachi comes up behind me while I am figuring out the yearlings. We stand by the back fence and watch them together. Four of them, black as the dark side of the moon, their long manes and tails falling in thick, curly tangles. These horses will never turn white; Friesians are forever black by nature. I watch them gallop past me, bucking and playing, legs carved like ebony balusters, tails flaring over their backs, held high with excitement. I bred them to sell, and he comments that they look too thin.

"Feed 'em some arsenic," he announces through the ever-present piece of hay he chews on. "It'll make their coats shine like glass. Plump them up, too, so they'll sell fast. People like fat horses."

"They're well-fed," I say defensively. "They get plenty of good grain and alfalfa. The vet says they look fine. He says young legs don't need so much weight. That youngsters fill out as they mature."

"Is that what you learned from the vet? Ha!" He pulls out the piece of hay and throws it to the ground. "Arsenic won't hurt them," he says. "Years back, we did it all the time. Called it Potter's mixture. Cut your feed bill down. What with the economy, you should be cutting back a little, anyways."

"No," I say to Malachi. "You're talking poison."

"They won't gain weight natural," he says. "You can't trust nature to do what *you* want." He makes a face at my refusal and turns away from me. "Nature has her own rules, for her own self. She likes young horses lean; people like 'em fat. If you want to sell 'em, you can't trust her to do right by you. You can never trust nature. Not ever."

And, displeased with me, he mutters to himself all the way back to the barn.

Chapter 2

Today, the phone rings incessantly. Three times before I finish my morning coffee. The barn phone rings six more times while I am outside with the horses, the jangling old phone sound amplified by the quiet morning air. I know it's my sister Sandra, who is obsessed about being the first to spread news, good or bad, although she specializes in and relishes the latter. I feel guilty, but I don't want to waste two hours on the phone impatiently struggling to be sympathetic.

My morning is spent riding. When I'm finished, I groom Lisbon with leisurely strokes, while Malachi grins at me, his hands on his hips. The barn phone is ringing again.

"Ain't you never gonna call her back?" he asks.

"Maybe later," I tell him, then pause currying mid-stroke to look at him. "You must think I'm awful, not answering."

He shrugs. "It don't make me no nevermind," he says. "I never take calls from kinfolk."

Early that afternoon, I return to the house and sit down at my desk to write. The voice mail is filled with messages from

Sandra, ascending notes of impatience coloring her voice. The phone rings again, but now the caller ID reads *Stanton, Brodie, and Brodie,* and I snatch up the phone. That's where David works.

David is not my husband. Though he has asked me to marry him a thousand times over the years, I have always said no. Getting married and "making it official," as David says, I think burdens love. Taking in love should be voluntary and spontaneous, like air. You can't have "official" air.

"I won't be home tonight," he informs me, and I get the familiar clutch in my stomach. "I have to catch up on some work. I'll just crash in my office when I'm done."

"I see." But I don't. He's been getting home later and later. Finishing briefs, reviewing cases, busy with work, busy, busy, busy. I try to sound good-naturedly unconcerned. "No problem," I say, then force an indifferent yawn. "I have a lot of work myself."

"Talk to ya," he says and hangs up. Not "love ya," not "miss ya." "Talk to ya."

"Yah," I reply to the dial tone. I hunch forward in my chair, dropping my face into my hands. It wasn't what I wanted to hear at all. He used to say, "I love you." He used to say, "I'll be thinking of you," and I liked hearing that. I wanted to tell him to come home. To just come home.

The phone rings again. "Hello?" I grab it before I look and answer breathlessly, hoping it's him again. Oh no, the caller ID catches my eye. The number belongs to my mother.

"Rachel!" my sister blurts. "I'm in Phoenix. At Mom's. Where've you been? I've been trying to get you for a few days now. Dad's in the hospital."

"What's wrong?" I ask calmly. My father has been a frequent flyer at the veterans hospital this past year, so I am not terribly surprised. Or upset. There is no love lost between my father and me.

"His heart," she says.

"Did they call in a geologist?" It's an old joke between Sandra and me that his heart is made of stone.

"He needs a pacemaker," she says, which is old news. His doctors have been suggesting the procedure for nearly a year. "He passed out three times this week alone. Mom wants you to come. Here's Mom."

I doubt my mother wants me to come to Phoenix, but before I can protest, my mother takes the phone.

"What do you want?" she asks me.

"Hi, Mom," I reply patiently. "How are you?"

"My feet hurt."

"Well, do you want to chat for a minute?" She doesn't respond. "You know," I add reassuringly, "it sounds like it's time Dad got his pacemaker. Just like the doctor said."

"We don't trust doctors," she replies. "You know how they are. They just want to get you in their clutches."

"Doctors don't have clutches," I tell her. "Cars have clutches."

It's been a losing battle, trying to get my father to allow them to install a pacemaker. For the past few months, I would call my parents and spend fruitless hours trying to convince them to go ahead with the procedure. I hated calling, because I always had to wait through some twenty-five rings before my mother picked up, then go through the tricky process of defrosting her, because she was always a little angry that, no matter when I called, I should have called sooner. Another half hour would tick by while she summoned my father. After shuffling to the phone, he would abruptly hang up without even saying hello. I used to think it was because he has a hearing loss and wasn't comfortable talking on the phone, but at some point I realized it was just his usual display of antisocial graces.

We called dozens of times, David and I, but after a while, my parents stopped answering. We could never leave a message, because my mother won't have an answering machine in the house, certain that voice mails steal your identity. Nor would she leave a message on mine.

In a final gesture, David even had his best friend, a cardiologist, call from New York to personally explain the procedure. My father remained unconvinced, and even half-joked at one point that we might be trying to kill him so we could inherit his old penny collection. Defeated, I stopped calling them.

I never understood my father. That he had to be so spiteful, he couldn't allow himself to be helped.

"A pacemaker is pretty routine," I tell Sandra, after she gets back on the phone. "They do pacemakers all the time, and the VA's been wanting to put one in at least forever." I glance at the clock, hoping our conversation wasn't going to last two hours.

"Well, Mom wants you to come and help convince him that now's the time," she replies. I know this is Sandra's fantasy, that we are a loving family. I, the voice of cynicism, know better.

"He won't listen to me," I protest. "Besides, you know how he hates doctors. His dying will be their ultimate punishment."

"Well, I just wanted to let you know," she says. "You don't have to come if you don't want to. At least he'll have one daughter here who cares about him."

She does care, that's the thing. She genuinely cares, and I don't get that, either. When we were growing up, our father was always ferociously angry. Angry at everything, angry at nothing. All day, every day. He would make caustic remarks about Sandra's chubbiness, her lack of academic ambition, her taste in friends, as well as her lack of proficiency in keeping the house in order while our mother ran her little gift shop. Sandra was all of seven, I was five. Incensed, I would defend her, until the criticism was turned on me, my relentless waste of time reading, my undeveloped culinary skills, my terrible *attitude*. As things ratcheted up, I would safely duck into our bedroom to weather the storm. Sandra always ended the argument with eyes blazing and a barrage of sharp words.

"Why can't you try harder?" she would scold me when I burrowed under my blankets at night to cry myself to sleep. "Don't get him so mad. Then he'll love you."

I would shrug her off, because I knew that he was angry about things that had nothing to do with us.

I was dimly, primitively aware, then grew certain as I got

older, that somehow my father was broken, too broken to love anybody.

The secret that I had yet to learn was why.

Sandra finally hangs up after half an hour, but I knew she would call me back. She so badly needs to spin our threads together and knit us into the family she always wanted. Plus, she hadn't yet given me her weekly installment of the Sorrows of Sandra, which include complaints about her indifferent husband, her belligerent stepkids, the sloppy dental work she got on her back molar fourteen years ago, and the ungrateful cat she adopted who pees on her pillow. She keeps herself in a constant state of unhappiness, so she is never disappointed with life. Sometimes I think if I were the cat, I would pee on her pillow, too.

Malachi and I are sitting on hay bales in the barn, eating sardine sandwiches and drinking tea. He made the sandwiches for our lunch, along with his old beat-up pale blue thermos filled with tea, flavored with very tiny, sweet figs. We take turns sipping from the metal cup. Of course, I cook for Malachi, as well. I bring him his favorite macaroni and cheese, or bowls of chili, or homemade soup, to make sure he eats something substantial.

"I'm not going to Phoenix," I say defensively, between bites of sandwich and shooing away another enthusiast of his sardine sandwiches, Misha, the barn cat.

"Your father is meaner than a trapped possum," Malachi comments. He had met my father years back, when we first bought the farm and my father was still able to travel. My father automatically hated the farm, calling it the biggest waste of real estate second only to Washington, D.C., and pronounced Malachi a con artist for leading me to believe that a horse farm was capable of making a profit.

Malachi takes a sardine from his sandwich and dangles it over Misha's head. The cat bats at it with a striped gray paw and purrs while his sister, Lulu, sits quietly behind him. "If he's dying, you gotta go," Malachi says in a matter-of-fact tone before neatly dropping the sardine right into the cat's mouth. He tosses another one Lulu's way, and she sniffs it delicately before walking away.

"No," I say. "It'll just lead to more arguments."

He takes a long sip from the cup, then pours out more tea and hands it to me. He looks dapper in his tan cap and blue sweater. Immaculate. But then, he never really seems to get soiled. Even when he's wrestled a horse to the ground to medicate it, or has spent an hour shampooing the mud from its four crusty legs, he walks away without a smudge on him. "You could call him and wish him a speedy recovery," he says.

"He won't talk on the phone."

"Then send him a get well card."

"He rips up cards."

He ignores my remark. "Some of them even play songs now," he adds. "I seen them in the supermarket." He throws his head back and sings off-key, "You are my sunshine, my only sunshine . . ."

"He's not *my* sunshine." I finish the tea in one last gulp. "He rips up cards and he hates music." I study the remnants of a fig in the thermos cup, wishing I could read my fortune in them. "I just can't go," I add. "I've invested a lifetime in being pissed at him."

"Mmm-mm." Malachi stands up and wipes his hands on a napkin pulled from his pocket, brushes off the hay that is clinging to his pants, takes my paper plate, puts it with his, and throws them out in the gray plastic pail we use for trash. Then he carefully screws the thermos back together. He is meticulous about things. "Lissen up! You got to go. You got to do it for you, not for him. Because if he dies and you didn't go, you will spend the rest of your lifetime being pissed at yourself."

I don't answer him, but I know he's right.

Malachi steps out of the barn, and heads toward the big field, before turning to me. "Maja is due any day now," he says. Maja is my prize mare. Well-bred and elegant, and very much in foal.

"All the more reason for me to stay," I reply, grabbing at an excuse.

"I can foal her out, been doing it for the past ten years," he protests. "Don't need you." We've only owned Maja for four years, but I leave his statement alone.

"By the by, you know that colt out of Umberta could use some weight," he says meaningfully. "He's a bit ribby. Gonna be hard to sell if he looks like a skinner."

"All her babies are ribby until they finish growing," I say, then realize what he is thinking. "No poison," I say. "Absolutely no poison."

Later that night I help Malachi tuck the barn in. It is my favorite chore. We feed the cats, top off all the water buckets, rake the dirt outside the barn doors into a pattern of looping swirls, and turn the lights out.

The barn phone rings and I lunge for it, my heart beating hard. But it's only Sandra.

"Rache," she says, her voice pleading. "So, what do you want me to tell Mom?"

"Tell her that I can't come," I say. "That there's nothing I can do for him that she can't do. That I'm on a deadline to finish my book. And I have a horse farm to run. Two careers."

"Did you forget *I* also have two careers?" Sandra's words quicken with indignation. Retired from accounting, she is now a school crossing guard and also sells stuff from yard sales on eBay. "And I put them *both* aside to come here."

"But you're the good daughter," I reply. "They *expect* you to be there." All right, that was a bit too sarcastic.

"You can be a good daughter, too, Rache," she says softly, waits patiently, then tries again to change my mind. "It's not too late."

"Yes, it is," I reply.

"No, it's not." She waits. "Rache?" she says again. "You might not get another chance. You know, at some point, he really will die."

"Humph," I reply. We hang up. But she is right.

Malachi is watching me, waiting in the darkening doorway, the dusky sky draping around his shoulders like an evening coat.

"You worried 'bout more than your father, I 'spect," he says, tilting his head to one side, which he does when he is about to say something I won't like.

I give him a suspicious look. Malachi knows more about me than he has a right to.

"Uh-huh," he says. He grabs the big sliding door and pulls at it. It moves slowly, inexorably across the opening, and I squeeze through before he finishes closing up the barn. "I can keep an eye on David."

I avert my face so he doesn't see the quick collection of tears.

"Hey," he says, and I look up at him. "You forget, or maybe you never learned."

"Forget what?"

He gives me a sardonic grin, then leans over and gives me a kiss on the top of my head. "Lissen up," he says with a half smile, "for the next time he proposes. You gotta tie a rope on a horse, else he don't know you want him to stay around."

Chapter 3

Boarding pass. Wristwatch. Boarding pass. Wristwatch. Ten minutes to boarding, and I am being obsessive, patting my hip, glancing at my watch, patting my hip, glancing at my watch.

It isn't nerves. I have flown all my life. In fact, I spent most of my childhood around airports, because my father worked for American Airlines and frequently took me and Sandra to the airport when we were kids. LaGuardia Field was our playground. Long before airport security locked down those places for good, we would play tag in the lounge, or stand outside on the observation deck and watch the planes fly right over our heads, the wind blowing our curls into swirling knots, the noise rattling our skulls and drowning out our shrieks as we waved to the passengers. And while the cleaning crew readied a plane for its next flight, we were allowed to play in its narrow aisles, scampering in and out of the gray tweed seats, even to sit in the cockpit, where we touched the dials and pretended we were flying. I was once given a small pin by a friendly stewardess—which is what they were called then—a pair of tiny, cheap tin wings with JUNIOR PILOT stamped across, and I thought I was practically crew.

Long ago.

Long before my father had become difficult.

I take that back. He was always difficult, mercurial, sometimes cruel, always explosive. There came a time when he became too difficult to bear, and at sixteen, I finally turned my back on him and ran away.

The boarding pass is in my left pocket. My watch says six more minutes.

I like window seats. The ground rushes past, tilting away at a disconcerting angle, then drops down, away from us, no longer able to comfort us with its proximity.

I stare through the thick window glass as the trees and trucks and yellow ground markings get left behind, miniaturizing, then disappearing behind drifts of white cloud. We are aloft, vulnerable, all alone in the skies. I didn't take out insurance, because I have supreme confidence in the miracle of flight.

But I do have a will. David will get the farm, even though we are not married. I bought the farm with the advance and royalties from my first book and kept it in my name alone. We have been together for fifteen years, and David used to propose to me every night before we went to sleep. *When did he stop proposing?* I try to remember. I guess it was months ago. *Why did he stop?* It was something I needed from him, this guarantee that he still loved me enough to propose, even though I could never say yes. It doesn't matter, it doesn't matter. He will still get the farm.

I am smiling at the clouds. Flight is a miracle. The contest of the plane against its own weight, the subtle tilt of the plane's nose, that enthralling moment when gravity relents and the incomprehensible magic of thrust and lift kick in. I love the race against the air, our speed forcing it to push up against the huge wings, carrying the plane despite itself, carrying it upward and still more upward. It still amazes me that it always works, even though my father spent hours drumming it into my head, how the shape of the wing and the speed of the airflow create forces. He would lapse into lecture mode, and I would try to concentrate, to learn these things, because, really, it had been the only relationship we had. I tried to absorb, assimilate his technical interests, his wonder at how flight had been somehow teased from nature. The Coandă effect of gas attaching itself, then streaming along a surface, Bernoulli's Principle of gas and decreasing pressure, Newton's third law of motion. "As long as birds can fly, planes will fly." He always ended with that. I listened, because I wanted to please him, but I had no interest in the mechanics. I just liked seeing the aircraft chasing along the runway, like a loose horse, fighting to capture the wind.

About five months ago. Right around Christmas. That's when David stopped.

Sky Harbor Airport. We land as smoothly as a swan on glass. I'm trying to gather together all my stuff when my cell phone rings. Sandra. We had made plans for her to pick me up.

"Will you be all right getting a cab?" she asks. "I just don't feel good leaving Mom alone and driving all the way out to the airport."

No problem. No problem to drag an overnight bag and a large suitcase that totals the weight of the *Queen Mary* because it is filled with the requested two dozen New York bagels, three pounds of corned beef resting on an ice pack, six knishes, a certain kind of chocolate marble cake to be found in only one bakery in New York City that David graciously picked up before I left, and six bottles of Skin So Soft, because my mother can't find an Avon rep in all of Phoenix that she gets along with. No problem lugging it all down two ramps, navigating the long, narrow escalator and across the huge lounge, over to the cab station, where, hungry, tired, and cranky, I wait forever for an available taxi because there's some NASCAR meet going on at the big track. No problem at all spending two hours to get to my mother's house, when she only lives ten minutes away.

* * *

The cabdriver recognizes my New York accent right away, because he is from the Bronx. His name is Jerry and he has a gray ponytail, and steel-framed glasses, and he tells me he plays in a rock band called the Dry Gulches. He plans to do it full-time as soon as he saves enough money from driving the cab. I just listen as he tells me about the songs he has written: "Our Love Has Dry Heat" and "The Desert Rocks."

"You get the play on words?" he asks, looking at me from his rearview mirror. I nod. "You like music?" he asks.

"Love music," I answer. "Used to play the piano." Then I stop myself. There is no use talking about the piano.

Finally he asks me what I'm doing in Phoenix.

"My father is dying," I tell him and he grows silent.

"My father died last year," he finally says. "He was in the Bronx, but I didn't go back to see him. We never got along. You know how it is."

"Yeah," I say.

I search my handbag at the front gates of my mother's condo, under a cold, pale lemon puddle of light, and find the key to let myself into the complex, then lumber along the gravel path that winds past the pool, the clubhouse, the laundry rooms. I pass under jacaranda trees, their fragrant clusters strewing delicate lavender lace across the walkway as if I were a bride. Actually, the crunchway, since the plastic wheels of my suitcases are rapidly being consumed by the tiny red pieces of gravel from the little path. First casualty of my trip.

You would think that Sandra could have left the front door open, or at least turned the light on, and be waiting there for me with a warm, sisterly greeting, but the light is off and the door is locked. Typical of Sandra to bolt things down, worried, most likely, that serial killer was coincidentally arriving at precisely the same time I was expected.

I ring the bell—I am never going to find the right key in the dark—and wait. I knock and wait some more. I hear a faint stir inside. I knock again and call out Sandra's name.

The peephole opens with a grating slowness.

"Mom?" I call through the door. "Sandra?"

Sandra cannot bring herself to open the door just yet, without making thoroughly sure that the serial killer isn't imitating my voice.

"Who is it?" she asks.

"Ted Bundy."

"Who?"

"For God's sake," I yell. "Open the damn door. It's me."

The door cracks open, then she fumbles with the screen door, which is also bolted shut. The light is still off. It stays off while she fiddles with the lock. She finally swings the door open, and a puff of stale, superheated air from the dim interior pushes out to greet me.

Sandra's hair is a silver-white pageboy, and she has gotten fat. Very, very fat. I am sad for her, but happy for me, because I had grown up under her constant scrutiny. I never wore enough makeup to suit her. I never wore the right clothes. My haircut gave my head a funny shape. She so wanted me to be the perfect sister, the perfect daughter, so that I, too, could be loved. I give her an appreciative hug. It's like hugging the Michelin Man.

"Well, don't you look *tremendous!*" I say, laughing to myself at the old joke, then I feel guilty. It wasn't very nice of me, and I feel bad about it. Luckily, Sandra doesn't get it.

"I take care of myself," she replies loftily, scanning my jeans and T-shirt. "I would never allow myself to look like a *farmer.*" Heavy meaning, there. I zip open my suitcase and she spies the bagels and grabs them, sniffs at the knishes and corned beef, and admires the cake before whisking it all away into my mother's refrigerator, then disappears without another word.

"Hi, Mom." I poke my head into the kitchen, where my mother is sitting at the small, old gray Formica table with its red and yellow boomerang pattern. She is sipping a glass of milk, her mouth set in a line.

"It's after nine o'clock," she accuses by way of greeting. "I wanted to get to bed early, but I had to stay up for you." Her white hair is pinned up in big, navy blue bobby pins, and there is a slightly wounded tone in her voice. "You always get in late," she adds, as though I was a misbehaving adolescent, taking my sweet time coming home from a date in New York. Out of habit, I almost apologize, then think, it had been a twelve-hour trip, including the three-hour layover in Chicago, due to a bad thunderstorm—as if the city's legendary wind wasn't daunting enough—and an additional hour and a half of praying for a cab at Sky Harbor. I decide against an apology and bend down to give her a kiss on her thin, wrinkled, shar-pei cheek.

"I brought you the Avon you wanted," I say, putting a plastic grocery bag filled with little bottles of Skin So Soft on the table as a peace offering. They didn't fit in my big suitcase, and I had to bring twelve bottles, three ounces each. Even though they were the right size, the quantity had barely gotten through security. I had to convince the guards that terrorists are not interested in dewy skin.

"I asked you for this two months ago," she replies, not even glancing at the bag. "I already bought something else."

I change the subject. "How's Dad doing?"

"He could die tonight," she replies. "At least *Sandra* got here in time."

"So very true," I agree, but I am thinking that if my father hasn't passed yet, then I got here in time, as well, but I refrain from pointing this out.

Sandra returns to the kitchen, now dressed in turquoise flannel pajamas. She starts rolling her hair into big pink foam curlers. "I hope you don't mind if I take the couch," she announces, "because I have a sensitive back. You can have the gold recliner."

"It hasn't reclined since 1975," I start protesting. "How am I supposed to sleep sitting straight up? Why can't one of us sleep with Mom?" I mean Sandra, of course.

"Never mind," my mother announces, rising slowly from her chair. Her frail body has long yielded to the pull of gravity, leaving her spine hunched, like a broken bird. "I'm sleeping alone. I can't fall asleep when anyone is in bed with me." She grabs the bag of Avon and clutches it to her chest.

"What about when Dad was home?" I ask.

"I never slept," she replies.

"You were married fifty-five years and you never slept?" I ask, incredulous, watching her shuffle toward the bedroom.

"Not one wink," she says and vanishes into the dark.

I call home; there is no answer. I call David's office; there is no answer. Then his cell, which is apparently turned off, and I leave a brief message. It is early evening in New York, and I wonder if he's eating dinner. Alone.

Sandra is curled up on the couch with the only extra blanket and watches me set up the gold chair for sleeping. "I'm sorry. I have to take care of my back," she says. "Luckily you're athletic with the horses and all. You can tolerate sitting up and sleeping." She yawns. "And there's always a hotel."

I must admit, the first thing I did, even before booking my flight, was check hotels, but apparently the entire city of Phoenix was booked or grossly overpriced. "Yeah." I snort. "At six hundred dollars per night to start." I open my suitcase and pull out a shortie nightshirt.

"NASCAR," calls my mother from the bedroom. "They always have NASCAR in February." We were at the beginning of May.

"You're going to sleep in that?" Sandra gestures to my shirt. "It's so short. What happens if people see you?"

"That's why they have crowd control," I say. "To keep the paparazzi out of the living room." I point to her flannel pajamas. "Why would you need a blanket if you're sleeping in those?" The air feels even hotter than when I arrived. "Maybe we could put on the air-conditioning?"

"Mom doesn't like air-conditioning," Sandra replies. "That's why they left New York, remember? To get away from the cold? And I'm quite comfortable, thank you, because my body has adapted to heat." She stretches out and yawns.

Her body has apparently adapted to a variety of things, I think, like her intake of several thousand extra calories a day. But is it really possible to adapt to temperatures this high? It's early May, and tomorrow's forecast is for 112 degrees in the shade of what my mother likes to call "dry heat," which means 200 degrees in my mother's apartment as the dry heat keeps accumulating. We are going to turn into sun-dried tomatoes.

"Dry heat" is my mother's favorite expression. It might even be the Arizona state motto, although we all know that "dry heat" is a euphemism for having to open your car doors with oven mitts and then sitting on two bath towels placed over the car upholstery so that your nylon panties don't bond to your ass.

I stuff some of my clothes into a pillowcase, make a futile attempt to fluff it up, then try to settle my body into an old imprint of my mother's spine in the gold recliner that doesn't recline and which should be renamed the Golden Upright. Sandra is stretched out on the couch, her head on the only extra pillow. There are a few cartons stacked right next to Sandra's suitcase. I can't help but notice that some of my father's things are already packed. His shoes are in plastic bags, tucked neatly over slacks, a few old sweaters are rolled into corners. It seems Sandra has already decided what she will take of his, has already taken possession of his memories.

"What are you going to do with all of Dad's things?" I ask her, curious.

"e-Bay," she says. "I think they're vintage. Is there something of his you want?"

There is nothing of his that I want. We drowse in the quiet heat.

"Doesn't Mom look *old*?" I whisper across the darkness to my sister. "Is she okay? She's getting—she seems—a little—crankier than usual?"

"Yeah, well, almost ninety-one," Sandra whispers back. "Besides, she's never been, you know, *June Cleaver.*"

We laugh over this. It's true my mother was born without the regular allotment of maternal nurturing, but I was sensing something else. "She just seems a little"—I wasn't really sure— "maybe—not as 'with it.' She got the month mixed up."

"She thought I was her old hairdresser when I first arrived," Sandra says.

"I'm sorry," I say, feeling guilty that Sandra always visits our parents, faithfully, twice a year, two weeks each time. She really is a good daughter. *The* good daughter.

She plumps up her pillow and settles under the blanket. "Get some sleep, because Mom has the alarm set for four in the morning."

My mother has always gotten up at four in the morning to prepare for the day's outings. Even if it was just to the supermarket.

"I like to get there when the food is fresh," she would always say.

"But hospital visiting hours aren't until eight," I point out to Sandra.

"*Please* humor her." Sandra reaches over to the lamp next to the couch. "She's worried we won't get a chance to see him alive," she says. "She wants us to wake up early so we can be on standby."

"Why do we have to be on standby in the kitchen? Why can't we be on standby right here, sleeping *next* to the kitchen?" I protest, then stop. "How is he really doing?"

"His color was good when we left," Sandra replies, her voice suddenly sounding very tired. "Oh, Rachel, I know how you feel about him, but it's time to forgive and forget. Why don't you go along with things? Just this time. Mom is worried that he'll die alone."

There is a *snap* of the switch, and the room goes dark.

"No, no one should die alone," I murmur. "But it's just that Mom doesn't seem very glad to see me. And he never—oh—I guess it doesn't matter anymore, does it?"

But Sandra's snores already fill the room.

Chapter 4

All veterans hospitals smell the same: of Pine-Sol and sour old men who shuffle the halls in gray bedroom slippers and pale blue-striped robes. This is not my first veterans hospital visit. I am a veteran of veterans hospitals. Before my parents retired to Phoenix, they lived near me in New York, and my father was frequently admitted for tune-ups and tests and minor health skirmishes. I always visited him out of a sense of duty.

"I don't want anyone here." He would wave me off as soon as I walked into his room. "Imagine! They threatened me—if I don't let them do all their tests, they'll discontinue my benefits! Why do I have to prove anything, when anybody can see that I'm a very sick man? I'm signing myself out as soon as I can."

There was an inherent lack of logic in that reasoning, but I never pointed it out to him. I only know that he had considered himself on the brink of death since 1945, long before I was born, although, as far as I could see, there was nothing wrong with him except terminal anger. He was always bitterly complaining about "them": that vast, nebulous conspiracy of government, doctors, motor vehicle clerks, nurses, slow traffic lights, packaged foods, the pharmaceutical industry, and the idiots who couldn't make shoelaces or light bulbs that lasted. I spent a lifetime listening to him grumble, and my hospital visits were spent listening to him contradict his nurses, refuse medicine, and argue over the necessity of every procedure, while loudly questioning both the medical and mental competency of all of his doctors and nurses. I would stare out his window, at the men and half-men who sat in the sun in the garden below, graciously accepting their loss of limbs and minds, and wonder why I had bothered to come.

I am wondering again now why I had come, as my mother leads the way down a blue-gray hallway, really too frail to walk that far with her Quasimodo spine and spindly legs. Sandra, my mother's firstborn, is right next to her, her hair in big, bouffant silver waves, and dressed in a shapeless navy blue Walmart pantsuit, high fashion, apparently, in her neighborhood in Atlanta. She is holding my mother's arm with a certain self-importance. "*I'll* walk with Mom," she had said, sliding her own arm between my mother and me, obviously outranking me as First Daughter-in-Command. I study the back of her head, the cement-perfect silver hair, and think, she needs this. She thinks this is how happy families proceed, the older child with the parent, the kid sister following. So I bring up the rear, wishing the visit was already over and we were heading the other way.

An elderly, skeletal, gray-skinned man dressed in a maroon-striped robe passes us from behind. Every few steps, he leaps the length of a floor tile.

"That's the Jumping Man," my mother whispers. "First he walks, then he jumps. Does it all the time."

He leaps next to us and we watch him. One, two, three, leap. I'm annoyed to find myself counting the tiles along with him: one, two, three, leap.

Another old man, blue-striped robe and black-stained corduroy slippers, comes toward us. He stops and salutes smartly. Feeling gracious, we smile and salute back. He stops and stands there, grinning broadly, and pees in his pants, leaving a pungent yellow puddle that spreads across the floor as we pass. The Jumping Man doesn't even break stride as he jumps the puddle and turns the corner, walking and jumping over invisible land mines from years past. The Saluting Man stands at attention, grinning and saluting and peeing on himself.

My father's room is at the end of the corridor. He is lying in bed, consumed by his bedclothes. He is thin with regulation pallor, tousled white hair. He is wearing his hearing aid, but his thick glasses are on the gray metal stand next to his bed. He is busily trying to pull out his IV, despite the commands of the nurse next to him that he leave it alone. He doesn't look like he is at death's door. He doesn't even look like he is in death's neighborhood. I feel a flash of annoyance. All this way from New York, mares foaling left and right, stuck on a chapter in my new book, all to watch him argue with his nurse. Again.

"I don't want it," he croaks, trying to pull away the nurse's hand, but there is no strength behind his protests.

"Mr. Fleischer," she leans over and says loudly into his hearing aid, "you got to leave it in. That, or I have to tie your hands."

He delivers what used to be his coup de grâce. "Then I'll sign myself out." He coughs hard. "I'll be gone by this afternoon."

"I'm overjoyed," says the nurse, giving us a wink, though I suspect she means it. "They can't let you out soon enough, far as I'm concerned, but the IV stays in." She sails out the door.

My mother goes over and gives my father a kiss on his cheek, which he wipes off. Even now, he garners enough strength for that.

"Hi, Dad," Sandra and I say in unison.

"Have candy." He points to a small basket of hard candy that sits next to his glasses, then his hand drops to his side, weakened by this exertion. Sandra picks up the box to inspect it, then obediently takes a handful of pale pink hard candy wrapped in cellophane, to supplement the chocolate caramels she has been chewing on since she got up this morning. "Hand me one," my father orders.

"Nothing by mouth for you," my mother warns him. "You'll choke again."

"How are you feeling, Dad?" I ask. I'm not sure he hears me. Most likely he has his hearing aid turned off, as he usually does.

"Have candy," my father replies.

"They're from the Jewish War Veterans," my mother explains to us, pointing to the candy. "Only ones to send him anything."

"They're from the Jewish War Veterans," my father repeats. "Only ones to send me anything." I stand by the foot of his bed, wondering if the remark about the candy is meant as a rebuke to me. I hadn't sent anything except myself. I walk to his side and give him a kiss. He wipes it off.

"Ruth, sign me out," he says to my mother, and turns his face away from us. The visit is over.

The nurse is waiting for us in the hallway. "You *have* to convince him," she says to my mother. "He has a pulse of forty-six and it's dropping. He can't live long with those numbers. Everybody gets pacemakers. Tell him that it's not a big deal."

"He doesn't want one, and I won't let anyone force one on him against his will," says my mother, as if she's defending him from evil.

"Mom!" I say, shocked at her words. "No one's forcing him. They just want to help him."

"He's in serious heart failure, and he's going into kidney failure," the nurse warns. "Let me page the doctor. He really wants to speak to you."

"He could die, Mom, if you don't make him get the operation," Sandra says, sucking hard on a candy.

"I don't have to do anything," my mother says, scowling at all of us. "Why should some doctor make a profit on your father's health?"

"You think his doctor is just waiting to buy tickets to Tahiti the minute he finishes operating?" I say, not all that surprised that she has adopted my father's stubborn-over-the-wrong-things approach to life, his paranoia. What do psychologists call this?

Folie à deux? But refusing medical treatment strikes me as the wrong thing to bond over.

"They admitted him because he kept fainting," the nurse reminds her. "And I know for a fact that his cardiologist called him at home every day last week to warn him how sick he was. His heart is barely able to beat."

"You want me to talk to him?" I ask my mother.

"Stay out of this," she replies. "I didn't ask you to come."

"I thought you did." I turn to Sandra for confirmation, but she is staring off somewhere over the nurse's head, her blue eyes vacant and distant.

"He doesn't want a pacemaker," my mother says loftily. "He feels it's experimental. He doesn't want anyone experimenting on him."

Sandra has returned to earth, and I send her an eye signal that tells her I can't believe what I'm hearing. She rolls her eyes and shakes her head in agreement. I am pleased that for this moment, we have connected over something, and I feel the flash of a union with her. Maybe together we can fix this.

"You have to convince him," Sandra says to my mother. "And Rachel is here to help you make the right decisions."

I try to do my part. "Once they fix him up, Dad can be up and around in a few days," I say. "And be back to his old self." Then I wonder if that was really any help, since his old self wasn't all that fun to live with.

"The procedure hasn't been experimental since the fifties," the nurse adds. "Everybody gets pacemakers now."

My mother shrugs. "He doesn't want one." She turns away, leaving the nurse standing there with an incredulous expression on her face. I am embarrassed to be related to such ignorance. Sandra and I follow my mother down the hall, neither of us able to think of anything else to say. We pass another man whose eerie blue-gray complexion matches the walls.

"That's the Blue Man," my mother says matter-of-factly. "Your father says the doctors did that to him."

* * *

The scorching morning sun is crisping my cheeks as we walk to the car. We pass a sprinkling of men in the uniform of old age: white hair, bent bodies, vacant eyes, walking with canes or wheeling their chairs up and down the walkways. Some of them are having meaningful conversations with the jacaranda trees, some of them are napping in the full blaze of sun, in danger of getting more desiccated than they already are. Then there is a contingent of shockingly young men, sleeves or pants pinned up in lieu of a missing limb—bandaged, wounded, metallic structures replacing appendages—with faces that haven't finished maturing but look very old. They talk to each other in loud, joshing voices about their time in the service, but there is underlying pain in their eyes that they do not speak of.

"I don't understand," I say to my mother. "You can make him have the operation, can't you? Don't you have power of attorney or something?"

"He's doing all right without it," she says.

"He's not doing all right. He'll die without it," I reply, startled by the anger in my voice, and I look to Sandra for reinforcement but she is rooting around in her purse for more caramels. She has been taking them, two at a time, like tranquilizers. My mother doesn't answer. We reach the rental car.

"Let's get some lunch," Sandra suggests, having run out of candy. Normally highly opinionated, she is looking sad and surprisingly quiet. Except when I offer to drive. She quickly finds her voice to announce she couldn't possibly let me behind the wheel, because I only have a New York license, then drops into the driver's seat before I can defend myself. Apparently New York drivers aren't as savvy as drivers from Georgia and could never handle the downtown Phoenix traffic.

Okay, I do have two speeding tickets.

Sandra's cell phone goes off during her dessert of chocolate-ripple ice cream covered with a mound of whipped cream, nuts, and chocolate-caramel sauce, the only thing she hasn't complained about during lunch. "Yes," she says, "this is his daughter. I'll tell my mother."

My mother gets on the phone and listens. We watch her expression for some clue to the conversation, but she listens passively. A few minutes pass. "No," she says into the phone. "No." She listens some more. "Oh," she says, "then go ahead," reluctantly giving permission for them to finally try a pacemaker. I know it is a last-ditch, and most likely futile, effort.

We have to return to the hospital.

Dying is not a direct action. Like a plane in turbulence, people dip and dive, maybe hit a smooth spot and recover a little, before the flight ends.

My father has worsened considerably. He has oxygen tubes, more IVs. His eyes are closed. The nurse fiddles with the line going into his arm, then purses her lips in what I feel is disapproval of us, then steps aside. *I am not part of their craziness,* I want to shout, but I just solemnly move next to my father's bed.

My mother takes his hand. There are pinched-looking white scars discoloring the back of his hand that have been there as long as I can remember. They run up his arm, over his shoulder, crisscross down his back, lie in patches that wrap around his legs. He never mentioned where he got them. Now they barely contrast with his pale, pale skin. I stand there, wondering if I really am witnessing his death, and I am afraid. Despite all his claims to terrible illnesses and all his obstinate arguments against getting treated for them, he had reached ninety with nothing more than an age-weakened heart that could have readily been repaired. I stand next to his bed, resenting that he has chosen to die from sheer perverse stubbornness. There is nothing left of him but anger and spite.

Sandra goes to his bedside and kisses his face. "I love you," she whispers, but his hearing aid is on the bed stand next to him; he is beyond hearing. My mother pulls a chair up next to the bed, sits in it, and puts her head down against his face. Reluctantly, I move closer and take his other hand, which is already cold and literally deadweight. The machines show an array of bright green lines, measuring what is left of his life.

The heart line is barely moving. If there was a clock line, it would show no time left. No time at all.

I study his face, still set in angry, obstinate lines. Or maybe I am just reading the past. But he is dying, and this is not the time to think like that. I should say something to him. Somehow, I feel I should exonerate him for being so mulishly enraged at things no one could understand or fix. There is so much wrong between us, but I suppose it doesn't matter anymore. This is my last chance. My very last chance. There are longer and longer pauses between the beeps. What point could I possibly make to him while he lies on his deathbed? It's all over. Death will make the final point.

I bend to him to kiss his face and wonder what I can say, what will mean anything to him. I try to summon something, a feeling. There is nothing inside of me. I do it for my mother, this gesture of affection, and because it's the right thing to do. I do it because no one should take leave of their life feeling unaccompanied and unloved. I do it for Sandra, because she says I should forgive and forget. She apparently has, though I can't and never will. I lean close to his face to kiss it, but stop just above his graying cheek. I take a deep breath, then whisper a lie, for my mother, for Sandra.

Maybe a little bit for him.

"I love you, Dad," I whisper.

And maybe a little bit for me.

Chapter 5

There is a black woman at my father's graveside. She is standing off to the side, her face even and solemn, not showing grief, just attentive. She is well-dressed in a tailored beige jacket and skirt and beige pumps, carrying a brown and black leather Prada bag, in contrast to my mother, who is wearing an orange-and tan-flowered blouse, a turquoise sweater, olive green slacks, and pink canvas shoes, looking for all the world like an envoy from Rainbow Brite.

"Don't you have something darker?" I had asked my mother while we were dressing for the funeral, although I know wearing dark colors in the early Arizona summer is an invitation to instant heatstroke. I really meant, *"Don't you have something dignified and funereal, something that actually matches?"*

"Leave Mom alone," Sandra intervened. "She looks fine. We don't have to dress like we're walking down Fifth Avenue. It's a private funeral." I noticed that Sandra was wearing a black cotton pantsuit that could almost pass for sweats, her face set off by flamboyant Tammy Faye eyes and watermelon-pink lips, and

I wondered where, at what point in our lives, did our fashion sense diverge so drastically. I never wore much makeup and had brought my old standby, a navy Armani suit, a veteran of many client dinners in New York City with David. I thought it would be both somber and appropriate, but Sandra cast an appraising eye over my outfit, scanned my hair and face, wrinkled her nose, and turned to the hallway mirror to run a comb through her gray-white hair.

"You should do something about your hair," she said, and for a moment I thought she was talking to herself in the mirror. But she was directing her comments to me. "You're getting gray at the temples. No wonder David won't marry you. You don't look like a lawyer's wife." I knew exactly what she was referring to. My hand flew to the gray streaks at my temples that I had been debating about coloring. I wish I could make myself pay more attention to these kinds of details, but they always seem to slip past me. I let the remark about David slip by me, too. This is Sandra, she needs to do this. She needs me to be perfect. She released a tornado of hair spray in the direction of her head. "Luckily, I don't have to dye my hair anymore."

"You don't?" I tightened my jaw in an effort to keep it from dropping.

"Look at how perfect the color is. Champagne blond! I stopped dyeing it years ago when I realized that it was keeping the color."

I stared at her hair in amazement. Keeping what color? Her hair was nearly white. How could she see champagne blond where I saw white?

"Yep," she said, giving her hair a final misting. "I'm very lucky." Then she pointed to my face. "Now, what about makeup? I can help you put some on."

"Don't worry about me." I waved her off. "A little lipstick is enough for me. But don't you think Mom should wear something less colorful? She looks like she's ready for a playdate at the Crayola factory."

"It's the grief," said Sandra. She stepped back to give me a last once-over. "I don't know why you insist on no makeup; you look like a farmhand."

I guessed she thought Armani was now designing farm wear, but today was not the day to bicker. I gave her a patient smile. "Well, I do own a horse farm."

"There's nothing wrong in *owning* one." She snapped her large makeup bag closed and replenished her caramels from a newly purchased three-pound bag that was now residing in the kitchen. "You just don't have to look like you *work* on one."

We are waiting at the veterans cemetery in Phoenix. It is on Cave Creek Road. There is only me, Sandra, our mother, my uncle Bob, and this black woman. The sun is burning down on acres of flat, hard-packed pink gravel, reflecting off the small bronze grave markers like lasers. We are waiting for the rabbi, who just arrived, to start. We are wondering whether anyone else is going to pay their respects. David couldn't get away from his law practice, some kind of big merger going on, though I knew that was just a convenient excuse. He was not fond of my father, who is, after all, not even his father-in-law. My father frequently liked to point this fact out to him over the years. They weren't the least bit related, and it was a good thing, my father would add, because he hated lawyers. His anti-lawyer rants were second-favorite only to anti-doctor rants.

Harrison, Sandra's husband, also soured by frequent shouting matches with my father, elected to stay home, as well. He is a businessman who had wisely kept his actual business very vague, so my father was quite thrown off, and hated him only for the sheer pleasure of it.

We are waiting for someone else to come, anyone, to stand with us under the blazing scorch, and share a little in our loss. Not my father's family. His only living sister is in her nineties and speaks exclusively to the goldfish in her bedroom at her nursing home. No one from my mother's family, either, except her brother, my beloved uncle Bob, since my father had alienated everyone else.

"I don't think anyone's coming," I whisper to Sandra. "We should just get on with the service."

She turns one shoulder forward, away from me, indicating that she disagrees, that she wants to wait a little more, because who knows how many busloads of close friends and admirers will arrive any minute now. Our mother is staring sleepily ahead—the rabbi, sweltering in a black business suit, is looking pitifully at us for consent to continue. One hundred and thirteen degrees of dry heat should be reason enough to proceed, I think. My father had been an active member of several veterans organizations, and it appears none of them thought to send a representative. I'm guessing because his personality was legendary. *Get on with it,* I say silently, *before we dry up like tumbleweeds and blow out of here.*

At first I had been annoyed that my father had chosen the veterans cemetery in Arizona. He was a native New Yorker, and his entire family is buried in the ancient, small gnarled cemeteries of Brooklyn. Things could have been arranged. But he had chosen this place, this burnt-out, parched land, with its thick, spiky green saguaro cactuses that resemble giant hands giving the middle finger to the arid landscape. And then I realize—and have to suppress a giggle—that the cactus was the perfect representation of his entire life's philosophy. Embittered, prickly, flipping the bird to the world.

"Go ahead," says my mother, her voice tight with disappointment that there are only a few of us here.

The rabbi looks around and observes aloud that we don't have a minyan, ten people, to officially be able to pray the Kaddish, the Mourner's Prayer, but he raises his book and begins anyway.

> *Yit' gadal v'yit'kadash*
> *Sh'mei raba*
> *May His great Name grow exalted and sanctified.*

We mutter "amen."

A white van pulls up and three people get out. A heavy blond woman in a navy-blue-skirt-white-shirt-blue-jacket sort of uniform, a bugler, and another man, in matching clothing, the patches on their shirts inscribed with *Jewish War Veterans*. They march to the rabbi's side. *You are late,* I think. It's too late for everything.

"So sorry," the blonde says regretfully to my mother. "We had to wait for the van." My mother gives her a wan smile. The rabbi resumes the prayers. The cacti—are they cacti when they are in plural?—continue their irreverence.

> *B'al'ma di v'ra khir'utei*
> *In the world that He created as He willed.*

We are going to die at the graveside from the sun, from the intense, penetrating, broiling heat that is grilling its way through my clothing, through my skin, maybe even bleaching my bones by now. Our brains are going to fry and addle; our faces are going to get twenty years' worth of UV damage in half an hour and we will leave here looking like the Crypt Keeper. The rabbi is interrupted again by a small military bus that pulls up behind the van. He stops and waits. This is going to drag on forever and ever and we are going to melt into our shoes and evaporate à la the Wicked Witch in *The Wizard of Oz*. I don't think I can survive the relentless heat another second.

Seven soldiers march off the bus, rifles at their side. They stand at stiff attention, holding the American flag. Waiting. I smile to myself. Between them and the Jewish war vets, we now have a motley minyan, of sorts.

My mother glances at the soldiers. "Oh, Marty," she whispers my father's name. I think she is remembering him young and in uniform. Suddenly I get tears in my eyes. Suddenly I see my father as one of them, a young soldier, sharp and ready. I focus on his flag-draped coffin, and stare down at the stars. Whatever happened to that young man?

He is dead. My father is dead. I turn the phrase over several times in my mind to absorb its significance.

I try to concentrate on the dull intonation of the rabbi, who didn't know my father, who doesn't know us, and who is sweating profusely while saying something patriotic and correctly comforting without any expression whatsoever. He races through the Hebrew prayers and the black woman is punctuating it with a soft "Mmm-mmm, amen, brother." I don't recognize this woman at all. Maybe someone from the VA hospital? Maybe one of the nurses? I chide myself for first thinking this woman is a nurse. Maybe my father's *doctor*? The one who had called him every day to plead for his life? I keep thinking that she stands out like the white horse in a herd, except it's opposite, the only black person at my father's funeral. Even the seven uniformed soldiers are white. My mother and me and Sandra, Uncle Bob, the rabbi, and the honor guard are all white, white, white.

The guns go off, sharp reports explode against our ears, and my heart jumps against my chest. Three volleys, their shots echo over the flat red-pink gravel, echoing across the open plains, across the flat metal grave markers, over the heads of the fuck-you saguaro cactus, echoing to the mountains, before dying away. In one smooth motion, the soldiers unhook the American flag from the simple pine coffin, flip it into sharp triangles, slip it into a plastic envelope, and present it to my mother with a stiff salute. One of them raises a trumpet to his lips. *No*, I think. *Please don't do that.*

But he plays "Taps." Sandra clutches my hand, and I squeeze her fingers. Though I thought I would cry, I can't. Sandra's eyes melt into black streamers of cheap mascara, my mother's lips turn down in a tight arc of pain, her eyes fill up and spill over, but I cannot join in. My uncle dabs at his eyes with a snow-white hankie. Who carries hankies anymore? But my heart stays empty, and my eyes stay dry like the dust and sand beneath our feet. The final notes sigh away in the heat; the soldiers turn smartly, board the bus, and pull away.

The contingent from the Jewish War Veterans has finished murmuring their sympathies. We each put a handful of dirt on the coffin—a Jewish custom, a symbol of burial—then wash our hands from a small bottle of water, also custom, to wash away death.

It is all over. We can go home now. Without him. Everyone has gone, but the black woman remains, looking toward us, waiting, it seems, to say something. Finally, she approaches my mother.

"Mrs. Fleischer?" She extends her hand, and my mother stares at it, confused. "It was a lot of work to find you." She takes my mother's fingers and gently holds on to them.

"Who are you?" my mother asks.

"Rowena Jackson," the woman replies. "You don't know me. You knew my father."

My mother looks at her, puzzled, searching her memory for the name.

The woman produces a tattered old picture from her purse and hands it to her. My mother scrutinizes the picture. Something crosses her face that I don't understand. She touches Rowena Jackson's arm and nods, the expression on her face softening with recollection. She clutches the picture for a moment before handing it back. "Of course I remember him," she says. "Willie Jackson."

Rowena Jackson's voice fills with regret. "He wanted to come, but, you know, at his age, his health wouldn't permit. I came instead, to pay his respects. I'm sorry I was too late, but my father tried to locate your husband for the longest time."

She pulls a package—square, thick, wrapped in brown paper—from the stylish bag hanging on her arm. "My father wanted you to have this." She hands the package to my mother. "He wanted Sergeant Fleischer to know that he's sorry he didn't do this sooner."

My mother's lips make a tight line; she takes the package, but doesn't look at it.

Rowena Jackson continues. "He wanted Sergeant Fleischer to know that he never really thought he was a murderer. He deeply regrets he ever said that, but he was—you know, so—so—heartsick—and—angry at the time."

My heart freezes at the word *murderer,* and I shoot a look at my mother. This woman couldn't possibly mean my father. He had been surly, bristly, cranky, but that is certainly not murder.

My mother acts like she hasn't heard that word. Or maybe like she has heard it too much before and is steeled against it. "Tell your father thank you," she says evenly, then suddenly remembers to introduce Sandra and me and our uncle. We all shake hands. I like Rowena Jackson. Her handshake is firm; her face is open and forthright.

"Are you hungry?" Sandra asks her.

"Yes, we might go for coffee," says my mother. "Would you like to join us?"

"Thank you, but I have a plane to catch. I have to get back to Boston. I could only take one day off to come here." She shakes my mother's hand again and holds on to it. Their eyes meet.

Please, read Rowena Jackson's eyes. *Please understand.*

"Thank you so much for taking the trouble to come," I interject. "My mother, I know, appreciates it."

"Yes," my mother finally says. "It was a bad time." I'm not sure what bad time she means, the past, or watching my father die.

"My father says thank you," the woman whispers. "He said to tell you that it was in the heat of passion. He wanted you both to know that. He says there are no words to thank your husband for what he had done. I thank your husband, too." There are tears in her eyes. Even she can shed tears.

"My husband tried," my mother says. "He was always trying." Suddenly they embrace, and the woman gives my mother a gentle kiss on the forehead.

I watch Rowena Jackson climb into her car with slow dignity, her face peaceful at having done the right thing, even though I don't know what it was.

Chapter 6

"Anyone feel like eating?" Sandra is driving us home from the cemetery, our uncle following in his rental car; she is chewing on her ever-present candy. I'm sitting next to her, and turn sideways to stare, wondering how she could possibly be hungry. Her eyes are red and puffy from crying; the now-dried Great Lash makes it look like someone has been skiing down her cheeks. "Coffee and cake?" she asks. "Maybe a burger?"

"Nothing for me," I say. How can she be so oblivious to what has just been exchanged? Hadn't she heard—that *word*? But she is concentrating on driving. And chewing. Then I realize, she needs to feed her heart, which is breaking. She needs to pat and comfort herself, hold herself, make it okay. She needs to do this for herself, because in our entire lives, no one else ever did it for us.

"Well, I'm just starving," she says. "Maybe look for a fried chicken place."

I am thinking that if we do stop, we should eat something dignified, that somehow tucking into a bucket of finger-lickin' doesn't seem quite—respectful. Besides, my father hated fast food.

"Mom?" I ask. She has been quiet since we left the cemetery.

"Actually, I could go for a bite," my mother says softly. "I haven't had anything to eat today." She looks lost, shrunken into the backseat, small and frail, a Q-tip, a thin stem with a fuzzy white top.

"Just let me know where," Sandra says, cheerful now at the prospect of food. I scan the sides of the road for something appropriate.

"That looks like a good place," I say, as we come up to a small scenic restaurant in an upscale shopping center. The fresh, bright red bougainvillea that hang in pots, framing a polished oak door trimmed in new brass, give it a cultivated and private club look.

"There's a Church's Chicken on the next corner," Sandra says briskly, ignoring me. "Next to an Arby's. And two blocks down, if I remember from this morning, a McDonald's, which I think I prefer."

"Why don't we get some real food?" I ask. "Something more ceremonial."

Sandra gives me a look, then says dryly, " 'Ceremonial'? I suppose we can pass a cheeseburger around so everyone can take a bite." We both smile at this. "We don't need a white tablecloth to eat lunch, you know," she adds. "It's not really about the food."

The Arizona sky is blindingly blue, and I concentrate on the fluffy white French poodle clouds. My eyes trace where the sky meets the carved rock mountains that surround the city in a steadfast embrace of azure blue and deep red. Phoenix is encircled by landmarks: Squaw Mountain, Camelback Mountain, the Praying Monk, stone monoliths that have been there through the ages. I am not going to fight with Sandra over what to eat.

She drives to the McDonald's. Are hamburgers more decorous than fried chicken? I suppose she is right; it's not about the food.

"McDonald's?" my uncle says with a bemused smile as we emerge from our cars after parking. He is a psychologist and a health nut. "Maybe they'll have salads."

Five minutes after we are all seated and eating, Sandra is complaining about the packet of honey-mustard sauce that comes with the chicken nuggets. Too spicy, it has irritated her tongue. Not nearly as good as the honey-mustard sauce from the McDonald's in Georgia, it has offended her trained palate. She is upset over this lapse in culinary standards.

"They make it all in one huge vat in some factory in China," I start to explain, but Sandra has already gotten up from the orange plastic kindergarten-style chair-and-table combo to speak to the manager. She wants twenty cents back from two packets of honey-mustard sauce, for which she, as a certified school crossing guard with advanced training in rerouting lost pedestrians and parades, had the foresight to deduct the prorated cost from the price of the nuggets themselves before lodging her complaint.

"Why does everything have to be so difficult with her?" I ask no one in particular. "They're just stupid compressed chicken parts. Yesterday morning she complained to the volunteer lady in the VA cafeteria that the wheat toast was too wheaty. Too *wheaty!* What does that *mean?*"

"She has a lot of anxiety," my uncle says softly, picking over his wilted salad with a look of bemusement.

"She was a very fussy child," my mother replies. "She gets nervous."

"She gets obnoxious. Sometimes I feel like I want to just murder her." I realize immediately that this was a stupid choice of words, but "murder" has been on my mind since the cemetery. I look at the brown package from Rowena Jackson that my mother has left out on the table and change the subject. Books?

"Aren't you going to open it?" I ask.

She looks down at the package with some surprise, having absentmindedly brought it in with her. "I suppose," she says.

"I mean, that woman, Rowena Jackson, came all the way

from Massachusetts to apologize to Dad and deliver that. I'd be dying from curiosity."

My mother stares blankly at the brown wrapping paper. Okay, maybe I shouldn't have used the word "dying." It was another stupid choice. I make a mental note not to use "dying" or "murder" anymore today, if I can help it.

"Why don't you open it, Ruth?" my uncle encourages her.

My mother takes her white plastic knife and slips it under the flap, then starts sawing it open. She turns the package around and does the same thing on the other side. Sandra sits down triumphantly, holding twenty-two cents in her palm.

"I know my rights. And I think the manager knew it, too," she explains. "I don't know what they did, but I know my honey-mustard sauce and this doesn't taste one bit like it does in Atlanta." I look up at her to say something, something withering, but I realize that she needs to do this to keep her emotional compass straight. Bickering with the world is a distraction for her.

"Mom is opening the package," I point out. My mother is still sliding the little plastic knife back and forth, sawing through the paper while the knife is practically melting from the friction.

"Maybe you should open that at home," Sandra says. "It might be something very personal. Something you don't want to expose to the public eye." I look around at the public and note that their eyes are focused on their Big Macs. My mother's hand stops.

"No one cares," I reassure her. "And it might be something nice."

Sandra tightens her lips in disapproval while my mother finally lays the paper open to reveal the cover of a very old record album, fat with 78 RPMs tucked into tan sleeves, like pages of a book. The name of the album is *Sophisticated Lady*, with Duke Ellington featuring "Take the 'A' Train."

"Whoa!" exclaims my uncle. "Haven't seen real records in years."

"Are they collectibles?" Sandra asks, putting down a chicken nugget to examine them. "They might be worth something."

"They can't be worth much," I reply, "unless you also collect old phonographs to play them on."

"It's not the *playing* value," Sandra says, going back to her nugget. "It's the *owning* value."

I touch the album; the cover is dry with age. "Were these Dad's?"

My mother shakes her head.

"If you don't want them," Sandra starts, "I can take them." She reaches over and picks a record up with a napkin.

"Maybe that Rowena woman made a mistake and thought he was someone else," I say, taking the record from Sandra. It is bright red with black music notes and a picture of Duke Ellington painted across the grooves.

"That's just it," my mother says, fingering the tattered album sleeves. "She got his name right, but I don't understand why she would come all the way from Boston to deliver this. Your father hated listening to music."

The sun has eased from the sky, but even at night, the dry heat doesn't give up on trying to kill us. My uncle has caught a plane back to Cape Cod, and there is nothing to do. My mother turned the air-conditioning off and the condo is ninety-seven degrees. We sit at the kitchen table, she with a glass of iced tea, me pressing ice cubes to my temples. I want to ask her about the word "murder." I want to ask her why Rowena Jackson specifically used that word, but I don't want to bring up something that might upset her. I am burning up from the dry heat and dying with curiosity—ha, burning up and dying, an Arizona pastime.

David hasn't called me. I've been gone three days and totally expected that he would. I'm angry and disappointed and want to call him again, but my stubbornness won't allow me. I'm the one whose father died. He should be calling me, consoling me. Telling me that he loves me and to hurry home. There are no voice mails on my cell phone. What could be so compelling that he would forget to call me? I don't want to know.

"What on earth are *these?*" Sandra's voice rings out through the apartment, and my mother and I follow it into my father's office. Sandra is standing over a carton of what looks like old radio parts, and holding a small whisk broom with a face on it, the straw bristles pointing upward to simulate hair, a stuffed sock-body wrapped around the handle.

"Where did you find that?" my mother asks, taking the broom-doll and holding, cradling it almost, in her hands.

"Back of the closet," says Sandra. "There's nothing in this box except junk, really. I guess I'll throw it out. Hello! What's this?" She pulls something from the carton, a small white cardboard jewelry box that she opens. It contains a string of tiny silver stones carefully strung together in an awkward attempt to look like a necklace, but it is too odd to be ornamental. There are a few other pieces of electronic flotsam and jetsam also trying to resemble jewelry. The stuff is eccentric, primitive. And ugly.

"Don't touch anything in there," my mother replies, laying the broom-doll on top of the carton and reaching over to finger the artifacts. She looks up at Sandra, and her eyes are watery. "Leave this box with me," she says firmly. "Everything in there was a gift from your father."

Next to the jewelry box is a blue velvet bag. Sandra empties the contents into her palm. There is a gold watch and a gold college ring with a red stone.

"You can have his college ring," my mother says to no one in particular. "But I want the watch." She thinks for a moment. "He had this college ring, but he also had a bar mitzvah ring. I think it got lost."

"I'll take his college ring," Sandra says right away. "If you ever find the other ring, Rachel can have it."

I watch her stuff the college ring into her pocket and the word "murder" comes back to mind.

* * *

We are sitting in the kitchen again, my mother and I, drinking overly sweetened iced tea while Sandra continues to pack like she's all seven of the Santini brothers.

"I've never been by myself," my mother says softly, running her finger around the rim of her glass.

"Maybe you could move near one of us," I suggest, but her eyes widen with horror.

"I couldn't leave your father out here all alone," she says, "with no one to talk to."

"Actually, now you can talk to him from anywhere," I point out.

"He'd want me to stay near," she says, watching me get up to take two more ice cubes from the freezer to make my iced tea icier. "I've always been with him, and I'm not going to stop now."

"You don't have to move right away," I reassure her. "When you're ready. Or maybe you can get some kind of a pet." My father had never allowed us pets. Not anything alive. Ever. "A canary, maybe," I add. "They're easy to take care of."

"No birds," my mother says. "Your father doesn't want birds in the house." I wonder for a moment whether I should point out that there's no way he could know, but remembered that she previously argued how he wants her to stay near him in Phoenix. She gets up from the table and busies herself filling the ice cube trays, concentrating on pouring water into each little square, making very sure they are perfectly filled to the edge. "There," she says, "now you don't have to buy more bags of ice. I never saw anyone go through so many ice cubes. What, are you building an igloo?"

I watch her carefully set the trays in the freezer and decide to ask her about that word. "What did Rowena Jackson mean about her father—being so—angry with Dad?"

"Oh, I don't know," she answers.

If my mother doesn't want to get into a discussion, she deflects the conversation by saying she doesn't know. If she *really* doesn't know something—for instance, where my shoes are—she'll just say, "How am I supposed to know where your shoes are?" but if she's avoiding something, she sighs, hesitates a beat, and says, "Oh, I don't know," dropping her voice on "know." She dropped her voice.

"Did they have an argument?"

"Oh, I don't know, Rachel." My mother drops her voice again and looks away, looks over at the flat triangle of flag from my father's coffin that she had put down on the kitchen table.

My eyes follow hers. "Put that in a safe place," I tell her, meaning, "*It's all you have left of him; don't let Sandra take it home with her.*" My mother carefully pours the rest of her iced tea down the sink drain. The kitchen trash pail is next to the sink and I suddenly notice that she had placed the music album on top of it.

"What are you doing with that?" I point to the album.

"Throwing it out."

"Why?"

"I don't want it," she says.

"Do you mind if I take it home with me?" I glance nervously toward the second bedroom, where Sandra is still busy, keeping my voice soft so that Sandra does not come swooping in to claim them.

My mother shrugs. "What good is it going to do your father? Even if he got it before he died, what was he supposed to do with it?"

"Come on, Mom, what is this all about?" I ask her. "You must know why that woman brought it all the way from Boston."

"I don't know," she says, without doing the voice-drop thing, which tells me that she really doesn't know, and she picks up the folded flag from the table and heads for her bedroom. "I am going to lie down." I kiss her good night and watch her shuffle away like a dispirited dandelion. I look at the album lying on top of the kitchen trash. If it is thrown out, I may never learn what Rowena Jackson's father meant to say to mine. If Sandra sees it there, it will disappear until the records wind up on eBay.

I quickly take the album, wrap it in a plastic grocery bag, and stuff it into my suitcase before Sandra can even know it is gone. Then I go to the freezer for more ice cubes. Sandra hears the freezer door open and is next to me in a flash.

"Don't finish up the ice cream," she says. "I may want some."

"You can have it all." I sigh. "You can have everything."

And, satisfied, she returns to the bedroom.

Chapter 7

I have gained a new appreciation for New York sun. It has variations and nuances that are not found in Arizona sun. New York sun is not your enemy, while Arizona sun is out to kill you. New York sun is bright and cheery, offering comfort in the spring, friendship in the summer, commiseration in the winter. Arizona sun is all about murder.

It's morning and I am back home in New York. The late-May sun feels sweet on my face, warms my back like the body of a lover. David could not meet me at the airport last night, so I took a cab home. Malachi was waiting by the front of the barn when I arrived.

"I'm not glad I went," I told him after he gave me a welcome-home hug.

"Didn't think you would be," he cheerfully agreed.

"But you *told* me to go." I tried not to sound accusing, but I was still upset by Rowena Jackson's words.

"No"—he gave me a teasing smile—"I said you would regret it if you didn't. There's a difference."

I went into the house, brought my luggage upstairs, and unpacked before taking a long, hot shower. David came home two hours later and stayed in the kitchen without coming upstairs to greet me. He could have done at least that, I thought. I mean, my father died. There is a protocol to observe.

There was a clatter of pots and pans. I figured he was probably making his favorite late-night dinner, an omelet. I dried off and went down to sit with him. He acknowledged me with a smile and a nod. *Why not a kiss?* I thought.

He is such a nice-looking man. I sat there, watching him whip the eggs, then snip in fresh chives, the chives courtesy of Malachi. He has straight, light brown hair that gets blond in the summer and is a bit shaggy lately, making him look like I imagine he did in college. Blue-gray eyes and a square face with high cheekbones. And a sweet smile. *What makes a smile sweet?* I wondered. *The length of his lips? The way the corners pick up?*

When he was finished cooking, he lifted the omelet pan and waved it slightly toward me, raising his eyebrows, asking without words if I wanted to share the eggs. I shook my head. "So, how'd it go?" he asked, sliding the eggs onto his plate. I can't help but notice that the bottom is a little browned; it's not as perfect as he usually makes it.

"Not so great," I said. I wasn't being evasive. I was still trying to sort it out. Plus I was annoyed that he hadn't called me. "Hot."

"Well, yeah," he agrees. "Phoenix."

And that was it.

He sat up until very late, working at his computer. I went to bed and waited for him. He finally came in after 1 a.m. and immediately turned over on his side, away from me.

He didn't propose.

The morning sun is comforting as I ride, replacing the cold emptiness that David left with me when he drove off to work. We barely spoke, and I felt a gorge of anger rise. *What is going on? Don't I at least get sympathy points?*

I am riding MoneyTalk, a big chestnut ex-racehorse sent to me for retraining. Training horses is sort of an avocation born of my love for horses, the biggest pets I could find after I grew up. I like solving their problems, replacing their suspicions with trust. I wish someone could do that for me.

The sun hasn't yet risen high against the sky.

MoneyTalk is an off-the-track Thoroughbred, OTTBs as they are called by horse people. Raced as a youngster, done in by the age of three, and sent away to the "sales," where most of the broken-down racehorses are purchased for slaughter and sent to France for meat. He was lucky, though, to be rescued by a woman who saw past his thin, bony frame, his "big knee," his frightened eyes. Even though I breed Friesians, I also encourage people to buy OTTBs, because once the racetrack gets out of their system, they make very fine riding horses.

The trick, of course, is to get the racetrack out of their system.

I am thundering around the riding ring now, at a full gallop that I didn't ask for or want. MoneyTalk has taken off with me in the mistaken belief that he is coming down the home stretch at Belmont.

"He's grabbed the bit," I call out to Malachi, who has become just a dark blur on the fence line. MoneyTalk has clamped his teeth on the bit in his mouth, his back muscles hardening like concrete underneath the saddle, his flanks taut against my legs as he stretches his body long and low to the ground in an effort to gain speed. Of course, if he had shown this talent at the track, he'd still be racing.

"Circle, circle," Malachi yells up at me as he casually opens a tin of sardines, peeling the lid back and spearing them with a plastic fork. "Make a small circle," he calls, then pops a fish into his mouth.

I struggle to turn the horse into a circle, but his jaws are clenched on the metal bit like they are bolted together. It is a little like trying to turn a house around on its foundation using a pair of shoelaces. The wind is pushing into my face, my hands are going numb from pulling, and I have a real fear that I won't be able to stay on much longer. I struggle to bend his face to one side, to break his hold, but he is fighting me.

Malachi is still yelling, but his words are getting caught on the wind and disappearing.

After another tour of the ring, I realize what he was saying, for me to drop my grip on the reins; I push the reins at the horse, loosening my hold, which drops the bit in his mouth. My brain had locked in panic mode and forgotten that racehorses get faster the more you pull back, just the opposite of pleasure horses. It was the signal Money was waiting for and he gives in to me and eases to a slow canter. Then I wiggle the bit in his mouth, sliding it back and forth, and he softens, slows even more, finally breaking to a trot, then a walk. I catch my breath, and, just as Malachi taught me, I ask the horse to canter once again. We canter until I feel him slowing his rhythm. I break him to a walk, let him rest a little, and ask him to canter one last time. His body finally relaxes underneath me as he understands what I want from him, this easy, leisurely gait, and we walk, finished for today.

"Guess he found fourth gear." Malachi chuckles from the fence, spearing the last of the sardines. He delicately blots his lips with a napkin from his shirt pocket. Misha and Lulu meow a duet under his feet, and he gives them the tin to lick out.

"He's strong," I agree and take a deep breath so my lungs can catch up with my pounding heart before I dismount onto surprisingly shaky legs. A few more sessions and MoneyTalk will find his balance and understand that we do not gallop off with our rider, that it just creates more work because he will still have to canter when he is done running away. Horses do not like to do extra work and learn quickly what they should do to avoid it. Malachi takes the horse from me and walks him back to the barn, where he will untack him and sponge him down with Vetrolin and cool water. My heart is still thumping.

"I'm getting too old for this," I say, following them into the barn.

"Yes, you are," Malachi agrees.

Malachi rubs MoneyTalk down with the liniment and sets up his legs in bandages. He does both sets of legs, left and right, passing his hands under Money's left side—old racetrack habits—although Malachi has never admitted to working on a track. Has never admitted to working anywhere, come to think of it, except this farm. He claims no past, no history, as though, like Athena from Zeus, he had sprung, full-grown, from the grassy fields and knotty woods that surround the farm.

"So, I've been thinking about that music album since I got home," I remark to Malachi as he expertly sets up the last bandage, tight and neat, around Money's back leg. "I mean, for what that lady spent flying it to Phoenix, she could have hired a band for my father's funeral."

"You know it weren't about the music," Malachi grunts. He is still neat and clean while I am covered with more dust than a rodeo clown.

"Then, I'm very curious to know what it *was* about," I say.

The phone rings in the house, jangling the barn extension.

"I say, let well enough be." He throws a cooler over Money's back. "It's all ancient history, and history belongs in the past."

He puts Money in his stall and throws him a flake of hay, then brings in the two-year-old Friesian colt. We have a potential customer coming to look him over. It would make David very happy if I sold a horse or two during the coming fiscal year. Or any fiscal year. Malachi begins to groom the colt, trimming off the whiskers, neatening up the hair around his ears, brushing the silky black feathering on his legs. He dabs a bit of Vaseline around the eyes and muzzle to highlight them, an old horseman's trick.

The phone rings again, then stops. Malachi works silently. Thirty minutes later, when he is finished, it rings again. It is Sandra's pattern to call every half hour throughout the entire day until I answer.

"You want to get that?" Malachi finally asks.

"No," I say. "We have a client coming for the colt. I want to help get him ready."

"No, you don't," Malachi says. "You always mess things up."

I do. I don't like selling my young horses; I want to keep them all. I always manage to murmur the wrong thing in front of a prospective buyer, like, "He's a nice horse. Hardly bucks and rears anymore." Or, "Once he stops biting, he should be a safe horse to have around."

Another ring.

"Definitely sounds like your sister," says Malachi. "Go answer it. She might be getting divorced again this week."

"Divorce is so last week," I reply. "This week she's probably disowning her cat and her kids again."

"Did you steal that album?" Sandra asks as soon as I pick up the barn phone. I guess it didn't take long for her to figure out where the album went.

"You mean the one Mom was going to throw out?" I try not to sound defensive. "What makes you ask?"

"Because it belongs to Dad's estate," she says. "And I'm entitled to one half if Mom doesn't want them."

"Actually once Mom put it in the trash, it technically ceased to be part of the estate," I say. "It was an act of—of—uh—*discardation,* which officially removes it from the estate and puts it up for grabs." I'm thinking I probably should have run that terminology past David.

"Don't give me that legal talk," she snaps. "Those records could be valuable collectibles."

"Didn't you take all of Dad's clothes back with you?" I remind her. "And his books and his tools? Not to mention his Air Force pins and his college ring and the gold watch, even though Mom said to leave it in the drawer?"

"I'm keeping it all for Mom for when she moves in with me."

"Actually, Sandra, she said she wanted to stay in Phoenix," I remind her, realizing I should stop, because I don't want to continue bickering. I have always backed away from arguing with her, because she is a human escalator. She brings every discussion to the top floor of anger. "You even took his old shoes," I add. "Plus you took all the old inventory from Mom's shop." Sandra had sat up several nights in a row feverishly packing up ugly faded gift wrap, wrinkled ribbons, mugs that said I LOVE ELVIS, ceramic owls wearing big black eyeglasses and mortarboards on their heads printed with CONGRATS, GRAD. I had watched her whisk the stuff into cartons while wondering whether there was a gene for pack rats with bad taste.

"I might have wanted at least something from Dad," I tell her, even though it's mostly not true. "I still might."

This gives Sandra pause. She hates to give anything up. "You should be more sympathetic," she finally says. "I need things for my eBay sales. I could be divorcing Harrison any day now, and I have to protect myself financially."

"I'm sure there's a huge market for twenty-five-year-old moldy wrapping paper," I say and we hang up.

Malachi has finished with the black colt and has brought Lisbon, my white rescue Thoroughbred, in from the field. Lisbon has gotten into another scrape with Toby, the official ringleader of the three black geldings that he is turned out with. Under Toby's direction, the other horses had cornered Lisbon and kicked him, and now there is blood streaming down his back leg, staining his white hair a menacing red. I turn on the cold water and unwind the hose so Malachi can wash off the blood and check the scrapes.

"Sandra wants that album," I tell him, handing him the hose.

He runs cold water on Lisbon's leg until the bleeding staunches, then goes to the medicine cabinet for antibiotic spray. A few minutes of rummaging around and he comes back with a sheepish look.

"What was I going for?" he asks.

"Blu-Kote."

He returns with a can of Blu-Kote antibacterial and sprays a blue patch on the white hair to seal over the wound before continuing our conversation. "Do you need it?" he asks. "The album, I mean."

I think about it. "No."

"Then let it go," Malachi says. "Your dad is gone. What difference does it make?"

"But my father—that Rowena woman called him a—you

know." I can't bring myself to say the word. "I want to know why she called him that."

"If somebody called my father a murderer?" Malachi says softly. "I would just leave it alone."

He finishes with Lisbon and puts him in his stall. "I guess it's a good thing this horse won't fight back, or I'd be spraying antiseptic on the whole damn herd," he says. "He's a powerhouse of a horse."

"They're all geldings in his paddock," I complain as I slide the lock on Lisbon's stall door. "Geldings are supposed to get along."

"This horse has been abused." Malachi makes a face. "Abused horses get all twisted in their heads. They learn fear—they're afraid to fight for themselves."

"But he's been with me for three years," I counter. "He should be over it by now."

Malachi points a blue-stained finger at me. "I keep tellin' you, you gotta separate him from the others before he gets badly hurt. Toby knows this guy's a coward, and he'll never let up on him." He lets out a long sigh. "Black and white, it's nature, they'll never allow him into the herd. That's the way rules go. If you want to worry about murder, worry about his."

Murder is on my mind. And my father. And I can't reconcile the two. I decide, finally, to find Rowena Jackson, of Boston, Massachusetts, and talk to her.

That night I look for her on the Internet. I find a Dr. Rowena Jackson, who teaches biology at Boston University. I write down the number to call tomorrow morning.

It is my Rowena Jackson.

I thank her for the album, inquire about her father, her return flight, and commiserate about how hot it was at the funeral, reminding her it's a dry heat. Then I ask her.

"You said something," I start. "You mentioned how your father was very angry once and called my father a—" I can't finish the sentence.

"Murderer," she says. "My father says he was very angry at the time. But he's regretted it deeply, *deeply*. That's what he always wanted to tell your father. He wanted to apologize and ask his forgiveness."

"Why would he say something like that, anyway?" I ask, relieved that she knew what I wanted from her.

"Oh, it had something to do with that incident while they were in the army together," she replies. "You know, that horrible bus thing. He thought your father was responsible for getting his best friend killed."

Chapter 8

All VA hospitals smell the same. Of sour old men pungent from sickness and bad hygiene, dreaming old dreams, staring with blank eyes into their past.

We are in Jamaica Plain, Massachusetts, and I am following Rowena Jackson through gray-blue corridors, across stained tile floors, stepping over suspicious puddles and into odd-shaped shadows cast from poor lighting.

I am going to meet her father, Private First Class Willie Jackson. He is ninety, and in frail health. She was pleased that I had contacted her, and had called me back later that night to tell me how eager he was to talk to me.

"His mind is good," she had told me over the phone. "He remembers everything, but the rest of his health isn't so great. He's been deaf since the war. Has high blood pressure, diabetes—lost a leg to it. His heart bothers him, too. I'm sure you understand the heart thing."

No. I never understood the hearts of men.

* * *

Willie Jackson is sitting in his wheelchair, facing the window, and all I see of him, at first, is the back of his head and a steel-gray crew cut. I expected him to be small, diminished by old age, but he is tall, slim, and quite erect, singing to himself while serenely contemplating the clear water-blue Massachusetts sky. As I draw closer, I hear the words.

> You must take the "A" train
> To go to Sugar Hill way up in Harlem

He has a hearing aid tucked into his ear, and it suddenly occurs to me that I don't know how to get his attention. I feel awkward interrupting him. Should I call him Mr. Jackson? Private Jackson? His daughter solves it.

"Dad?" she says, tapping him on the shoulder. "We're here."

The song stops; he turns his chair around and looks at me with dark, dark brown eyes, enlarged from the thick glasses he wears, eyes that I immediately know once flashed with deep rage, once ignited with passion, but now are studying me with friendly curiosity. He is wearing an immaculate, crisp white shirt, a gray tie with red stripes, gray slacks, and a black patent-leather shoe shined to heaven. One pants leg is tucked tidily under him. I realize that he has gotten dressed up just for me, in my honor, and I am embarrassed that I am wearing jeans and a blouse. Even Rowena is wearing a neat pale blue pantsuit and low navy heels. Maybe Sandra was right about my looking like a farmer. Maybe this is *my* expression of the bad-taste gene.

I walk over to him, extending my hand to shake his, but he grasps it with both his hands and holds on to it, still looking straight into my eyes.

"Thank you for visiting an old man," he says.

"My pleasure," I tell him. He gestures to a chair next to him. I see that it was set at an angle, waiting for me.

"What can I call you?" he asks. "You may have to speak a little louder." He taps his hearing aid to show me what he means, and I nod because I know how to talk to someone with a hearing aid.

"'Rachel' is fine," I say and he smiles and nods.

"A nice biblical name," he says. "Second wife of the second son, Jacob, who was described as 'beautiful of countenance.' Do you know the quote?"

I laugh, embarrassed. "I don't know about being beautiful."

"You look like your father," he says. "You have his eyes and nose. His smile, too."

Though it's true that I have my father's almond-shaped brown-green eyes, and his straight, narrow nose, I barely remember him smiling. I don't acknowledge Willie Jackson's remark because I am still thinking how I can't recall my father's smile.

"You like music?" he asks.

I nod, hoping we aren't going to discuss music, waiting for him to change the topic.

"Would you like some coffee?" Rowena asks me, interrupting an awkward pause. "Something to eat?"

"I would, indeed," her father replies. "Bring us both some coffee. With two pieces of cherry pie, thank you. And a little scoop of vanilla ice cream would just make it perr-fect."

Rowena folds her arms and looks at him with mock indignation. "Old man," she says, "there will be no cherry pie for you. You are a diabetic. I will bring you an apple."

"Do you see how mean she is to me?" Willie Jackson smiles and his teeth flash white in his dark face. I have the feeling they have these exchanges frequently. His daughter leaves and he leans toward me, his face turning somber.

"I'm real sorry to hear about your dad," he says. "What was it? I mean, in the end?"

"His heart," I say, and he nods knowingly.

"I have a pacemaker, myself," he says, patting his chest. "But there is only so much they can do."

I murmur something in agreement, but I feel an instant clutch at my own heart. There *had* been something they could do. The pacemaker was that something. My father would still be alive if he had been as reasonable as Willie Jackson. Not that I care, not that I care.

"I want you to know I spent an awful long time trying to find him," he says, almost to himself. "I knew he was from New York, but I lost his address—and by the time I—I—"

"He moved to Phoenix about thirty years ago," I say, leaning toward him so he can hear me. I am used to doing this for my father.

"Saw his name in the *Air Force News* just a few months ago," he says. "An article about him still trying to get that medal. That's how we finally traced him."

I knew my father had been fighting for recognition for some kind of wartime occurrence. He had waged a futile fifty-five-year battle with army bureaucracy, for a medal that never came. I had long ago forgotten what it was all about, if I ever knew. I didn't care much one way or the other.

"How was he, in the end?" Willie asks.

"We weren't all that close," I find myself saying. "He was—a—difficult person to get along with."

Willie Jackson doesn't seem surprised. "Tormented," he says. "Though now they call it PTA?—DDT? KFC—something."

"Tormented"? The word startles me. I would have said "furious," "outraged," "bitter," to describe my father's unfocused, towering rages that leapt from subject to subject like a pinball, his dark silences that went on for days, his distance. Willie Jackson is gauging my reactions to his words, but I am careful to have none. Still, I am turning over this new one. Tormented.

"My biggest regret is not finding him sooner," he says softly. "Not that I might have changed things, but . . ." He stops, and tears fill his eyes. I wonder at them, where they come from. What physiological process releases them so freely in other people? He tries to wipe them away with gnarled fingers.

"Yes," he says. His hands are shaking with emotion, and he wipes his eyes again, then looks around. I get him some tissues from the box on the nightstand near his bed. "An apology. Long overdue," he says. "Long overdue." I'm not sure what he means, and I sit down again, quietly waiting for him to compose himself. He does and sits up straight. "So, what would you like to know?"

I am caught off guard. I hadn't composed any questions, or—

ganized them yet, hadn't thought in what order I would ask him about the "murder" word or the album or how they are linked.

"You probably want to know the whole story," he says. "Why I sent you a music album that never belonged to your father."

But I don't. I don't want to hear my father's story. I don't want to hear Willie Jackson's story. I just want a sound bite, a quick answer, a swift resolution so that I can know it, file it away, give the album to Sandra, and be finished with it. I'm sorry I came. He takes my silence for complicity.

"You're right. The beginning, of course," he says. "We shall start where all things should start. At the very beginning. Like Genesis." He gives a wide smile and stares into my eyes, directly.

He is struggling to pull me in. I don't want to follow. Coming here was a mistake. He is watching me with expectant eyes. I am searching for something to say, to thank him for his time and apologize because he won't get a chance to share some hoary old wartime remembrance.

Because I am terrified.

My heart is trussed together by tangles and knots of bad memories. Of wrecked dreams, of futile longings that never led to being loved. I can't let it all unwind. I will come undone if I do. I will fall through the floor, into the deepest abyss, and keep falling until I am completely gone.

"Looks like he gave you a tough time," he says, his voice gentle, even though I hadn't said a word. I look down at my hands shredding tissues without my permission. "He was a difficult man, even then," he says. "You couldn't tell him anything. That was his best quality and his downfall."

Who is this man? Why does he seem to know more about my father than I ever did? I don't want to hear him out. I don't want to have to forgive my father for anything. It was all put to rest when we buried him.

"Your daughter said you were sorry for calling him a murderer," I blurt out. "I want to know—"

"But that's the *end* of the story," he interrupts me, and leans back in his chair with an expression as though this was self-

evident. "Well, almost the end. But if I didn't tell you the beginning, you would have to hate me in the very end. I wouldn't
want you to hate me." He gives me a sweet, pleading smile,
which I realize is totally manipulative.

I look at him, this old man, and wonder whether that's the
whole reason he wants to tell me his story, that it's really Willie
Jackson's story and he wants some kind of exoneration from
me, for making my father the way he was. He is waiting, and
smiling, and suddenly I know why he wants to tell me. Because
Willie Jackson wants to die in peace. I don't think my father
died in peace, maybe because of Willie, and for a moment I am
resentful.

"I couldn't hate you," I say simply. I couldn't. I didn't hate
my father. I just avoided the emotions he brought out, avoided
the whole subject. I want to leave right now, I think desperately,
but Willie is watching me with the same unwavering, beseech-
ing look.

Don't ask anything of me, I am thinking. *I have nothing to give
you.* When I was young, my sister and I blew notes through
empty glass soda bottles. Long, hollow sounds that came to
nothing, because of the emptiness.

"Maybe just tell me about the album, then," I say. I'll give him
that, and then I'll leave. After all, how much of a story could an
album have?

"Did you bring it back with you?" he asks, glancing down at
my handbag.

"It's home," I answer.

He throws his head back and laughs. "That's okay, the album
comes at the very end, anyway."

"The end?"

"Oh yes," he says. "The end of the story. About a year into it,
long after I met your father." A flash of sadness crosses his face.
"When I wanted to be his friend again. When it was too late." He
reaches over to touch my hand again. "How long you staying?"

"Actually, today. And tonight. I just wanted to—" I start, getting flustered. This is not going at all the way I wanted. "I'm flying back home first thing tomorrow morning."

"Oh no!" He shakes his head. "You stay at my daughter's place and she'll dig out all my old things. I haven't looked at some of that stuff in years."

"I run a business," I apologize. "Horses. And I write books." I usually don't tell people that I write books, because everybody thinks that they're a writer. All of a sudden I'm hearing long, rambling, pointless stories about lives that have come to nothing along with requests that I write it all out for them and then post it on Amazon.

"It would make an old man happy." He tilts his head and smiles sweetly again; now I know for sure I'm being conned. "I don't buy any green bananas," he says, "if you know what I mean. And I can answer a lot of questions." We stare at each other for a moment. He wiggles his white eyebrows up and down to further disarm me.

"I suppose I could call my barn manager and tell him to run things for another day or two," I murmur, although Malachi pretty much runs things without even telling me what he runs. "Just tell me one thing up front," I add. "The album. Why you sent him an old album. I don't recall my father ever listening to music. Ever . . ." It's all I can manage before I think about my old piano and what he did with it.

He laughs heartily and fishes in his shirt pocket for something, enfolds it in his knobby fingers, then holds it in his fist in front of me. "Yes," he says, "I know. He hated music and I'm not Jewish, but—" He opens his hand slowly, with a flourish, like a magician, revealing a gold ring with a blue topaz off to one side, and a gold $\mathcal{M}$ engraved in the middle. "As you can see, I have your father's bar mitzvah ring."

Chapter 9

They looked like kids to him. But nineteen-year-old Private First Class Willie Jackson knew the French government wouldn't have sent a troop of Boy Scouts all the way to Alabama to learn how to fly bombers. The French soldiers were small, child small, and stood at the train station with the other soldiers, puffing furiously on Gauloises, chain-smoking one after another after another, waiting for a commanding officer to show up and direct them to their barracks, or wherever the hell they were going in the stifling, sodden heat of Montgomery.

Alabama sun was really something, Willie thought, it was really something. It battered you, enshrouded you, like it had made a pact with hell and humidity to bring you to your knees.

They stood on the platform, crowding it, the Australians, the Canadians, the Brits, a few Greeks, the French, and the Americans; they stood in tight clusters in the ravaging heat, giving each other wary glances but directing their conversations to their own kind.

Except for the Americans. The Americans didn't all stand together. The white soldiers stood in the middle of the platform, as though claiming it as American territory, joking loudly, ribbing each other, while the Negro soldiers stood at the end of the platform, near a latrine with a sign on it that said COLOREDS. Willie guessed it was their territory, of sorts.

He was from Harlem, New York, and had never seen a sign like that until his train started passing through D.C. He had taken his basic training at Fort Dix, New Jersey, but he had heard about the signs; his grandmother had warned about them. Still, when he first saw them, he was shocked, then sickened, and finally mad. Everything was labeled white or colored. Everything. The drinking fountains, colored water, for Chrissake, the public toilets, even the sections set aside in the shabby little restaurants on the way down, if they allowed you in at all. It was in your face all the time. White and colored. White and colored.

He stood with his new best friend, August W. Randolph, and chatted about the heat, about the jazz music, about nothing, and waited, along with everyone else. August was a big kid in a man's body, probably six-foot-four, and chubby, with a round, sweet, light brown face that carried a sleepily benign expression that gave away his slow-to-understand mind.

Willie had managed to crib a few Gauloises from one of the French soldiers, who hadn't minded sharing, who hadn't minded passing his pack around to the coloreds, because he didn't know yet how it was in America in 1941. Willie and August gladly lit up and took long drags and blew smoke rings that drooped into ovals in the humid air. And waited.

"Hey," Willie said to August, gesturing to the latrine door. "Aren't they nice to give us our own personal shithouse?" His voice dripped with sarcasm, but it was lost on his new friend.

August, a local from Birmingham, looked over at the sign. He knew all about signs. "Not so personal," he drawled softly. "We got to share them with each other."

The train station was just outside Gunter Air Force Base, and the only information Willie had was that it was a major training base to teach the flyboys how to handle the bombers. The big planes. The B-17s, affectionately called the Flying Fortresses. Willie even fancied that he could wind up becoming part of the crew, maybe one of the five gunners who flew in it, or maybe the radio operator. In his more ambitious dreams, he was even the bombardier. He had the required two years of college under his belt.

Yeah.

He looked around at the crowded station and took another drag on his cigarette. Probably everyone here was dreaming the same thing, though not everyone was colored. It made all the difference, he knew.

He had his assignment in his pocket; he had been told not to open it until he reached Gunter. Well, he had reached Gunter. He slid his pocketknife under the envelope flap. It opened easily, and he peeked inside. So. He wouldn't be flying. Why should he feel so disappointed? He knew all along he wouldn't be flying. His papers read Base Security.

The men were growing bored. They gave each other surreptitious glances, eyeing uniforms, ranks, openly eavesdropping on each other's conversations and commenting on them, for want of something better to do.

"What kind of uniform is that?" One of the Americans, a Southerner by his deep accent, looked pointedly at a British RAF cadet who had been complaining loudly about the heat. "Y'all a Yankee?" he drawled.

The cadet, a tall, good-looking man with straight sandy hair and light blue eyes, gave him an incredulous snort. "RAF, mate," he replied, then flashed a disarming grin.

"Naw, I'm certain ya'll are a Yankee," the Southern boy persisted. "That's even a New York accent y'all got there." The RAF cadet made a face and shook his head at this.

A skinny American sergeant with a pencil-thin mustache, curly black hair, and a prominent Adam's apple, took issue with this. "Waddya, stupid?" he snapped at the Southerner. "They're

English. *RAF.* Look at the uniform." Then he pointed into his mouth. "This is a Noo Yawk accent." He motioned to the RAF cadet. "Hey, show this cracker what I mean. Say something in English."

"Lindsey Davies, here." The British cadet extended his hand to the New York sergeant. "And actually, I'm a Welshman." The sergeant gave him a blank look. "Wales," Davies explained.

The sergeant shook his hand. "Marty Fleischer," he introduced himself. "Brooklyn."

"Is that one of your states?" Lindsey Davies asked.

"Absolutely," Fleischer said, then gave a harsh, abrupt laugh.

Half a dozen planes suddenly cluttered the skies above them, small planes, like a flock of starlings. Probably trainers, Willie thought, glancing up at them. They flew through the turgid air, disappearing into the haze, reappearing, dropping down into dives, then turning sharply. Willie noticed some of the men staring up at them, a certain hunger in their eyes. *Those* would be the flyboys, he decided.

A jeep squealed to a halt next to the station, and a major clambered onto the hood, stood up, and carefully balanced himself before putting a bullhorn to his lips.

"I am Major Dugger. Welcome to Alabama, men. Y'all will remain heah," he yelled at them, his languid Southern accent distorted by the bullhorn. "Y'all will remain heah." As though there was anywhere else they could go. "Y'all will be told what to do after I take roll call." He shuffled through a handful of papers and cleared his throat to make a few more announcements about the jeeps that would pick them up.

"I can't quite catch the accent," the RAF cadet commented to Fleischer. "What's he saying?"

The New Yorker snickered. "He's saying, 'grits, grits, grits.' "

"Are we allowed to smoke?" one of the American privates called out. "*We* were told not to smoke." He glared over at the French soldiers who were exhaling smoke like freight trains. So did Major Dugger.

"Y'all can smoke. As far as I'm concerned, y'all can play with yourself," the major yelled back through the bullhorn, "as long as y'all keep it in your pants and stay in this area. I repeat, y'all cannot leave this area until your commanding officer arrives."

Willie waited while the major called out the names of the American soldiers, one by one, going through the list, checking them off as he heard responses.

"Dalton, William J. Staff sergeant." There was no answer. He called out the name again.

"He's playing with himself," the sergeant from Brooklyn called out. "You just gave him permission." There was an explosion of laughter.

"Well, aren't you the comedian!" The major glared at Brooklyn.

"William Dalton, and I'm here," a voice called apologetically from far back. His name was checked; the major continued through the list.

"First Sergeant Martin Fleischer." Brooklyn answered to his name. One by one, they all responded, including Willie, each one getting checked off. A few more names and the major climbed back into the jeep and motored away.

They waited some more.

The air was a shower curtain, sticky, almost slimy, as they waited for someone, anyone, to tell them what to do next. They stood in clusters, wilting, sweating, growing more irritable with each minute.

It seemed to Willie that the actual fight was started by the French. A remark was made, possibly by one of the Southern boys, about the small stature of the French cadets, which got the Frogs a bit touchy. Maybe there was a question about them being able to reach the pedals of the planes, maybe it had something to do with the size of their manhood, as well, but a fight broke out, and before Willie knew it, the station was a small battleground of flying fists and swinging duffel bags, and sweat pouring off the brows of overheated, overzealous soldiers.

Except for the colored soldiers, of course. They knew better than to get involved.

"Didn't think I'd ever get the pleasure of seeing this," Lindsey Davies mused loudly to Fleischer, as they leaned against a wall, watching the fray with detached amusement. "So, the damn Frogs *can* fight."

"Yeah, looks like they fight real good here," Fleischer agreed. "It's nice and safe in Alabama."

The fight was now becoming a brawl of international proportions, attracting several more personnel from the RAF, all of the French, some of the Aussies, and most of the Canadians. By Willie's standards, it was getting quite entertaining, when a jeep wheeled around the corner and skidded sideways in front of the station. A sergeant jumped from the back and screamed the men to attention. Fists were dropped, hats were retrieved, and the men on the platform pulled to a ragged truce. "I'm First Sergeant John Hogarth," he yelled. "Pull yourselves together. The major has ordered jeeps to pick y'all up and take y'all to your barracks. Welcome to Alabama, men."

Another jeep pulled up behind his, an RAF sergeant in the passenger seat. He took his place at the edge of the platform to face his group of cadets.

"RAF—hop into the buggies, get settled in your barracks, and then report to Orientation," he called to his men in a cheery British accent. "And welcome to hell, mates."

Suddenly the platform was surrounded with jeeps and noncommissioned officers screaming orders, capping them with a bellowed "On the double! Two lines. Move it! Move it! Move it!" The men jerked into action, the Americans piling into jeeps, the Frogs scrambling into three more vehicles, the RAF pushing and laughing, gratefully getting into theirs.

The colored soldiers stood at attention and watched the jeeps fill up. Willie dropped his duffel bag, letting it rest on his shoes. August had thrown his over his shoulder, and stood stiffly as they waited to be dispatched. The platform was emptying quickly; the Canadians were gone now, the French driven away, the Australians with their sliding accent, gone. They waited. There was no one left now except the colored men and there was one jeep left. The one that had brought Sergeant Hogarth, and he had just filled it with the few remaining white Americans. The jeep began to back up, readying to turn from the station.

"Sarge," Willie called over. "What about us?"

Hogarth turned around in the driver's seat to face him. He stared at Willie for a full minute before replying. "It's *sergeant*, boy," he said. "Y'all just stand there with your fellow tribesmen." He smiled broadly and the men in the jeep chuckled. "We'll have a colored sergeant take y'all to your barracks in short order. Y'all will have to march there; I'm afraid we've run out of jeeps."

He gunned the engine and screeched away.

"Put your bag down," Willie said to August. And they stood on the platform, with the other men, watching the last jeep disappear into the dust, and waited.

Chapter 10

There is a carton of memories in the bedroom with me. Not my memories; these belong to Willie Jackson.

I am sitting on the bed in Rowena Jackson's guest room. She has graciously allowed me to stay here, in this lovely room, with its pale blue floral and green ivy print climbing the wall and into the drapes. There are pictures on the dresser, of an infant Rowena with her parents; another of a thin, young Willie in uniform with his arm around a pleasantly plump woman dressed in white, in what I realize is a nurse's uniform; of Rowena as a child, big pink bows in her hair, Rowena in a cap and gown. There are no wedding pictures, which tells me that she, like me, has never married.

Or has divorced.

The carton is on the floor, at my feet. There is a thick manila envelope of photos inside, along with an old air force hat; buttons saved from a uniform and stored in a small pink-striped cotton purse with a gold snap; a silk parachute, its delicate, pale material wrapped in a blue pillowcase. One glance inside the case and I knew right away what it was. My father had one just like it, saved for my mother. Yards and yards of cream silk, incredibly fine, flimsy, but strong enough to carry a man to the ground. It had shredded, then turned to dust, while I was still a child; silk does not hold up to time. I reach into the pillowcase. My hands graze against the brittle fabric; it catches on my fingertips, because skin is too rough to receive its fragile tenderness. I recognize the meticulous pleating of the skirt, the drape of the canopy. The way it lay, precisely folded, because improper folding will keep it from opening, one careless line of fabric could mean death. And even though I am pretty sure this parachute, like my father's, was never used, I recognize the lines and feel of the past.

I had spent the day with Willie, though I didn't call him that at first. I addressed him as Mr. Jackson. "Call me Willie," he said, covering my hand with his. "You can call me Willie." But I thought his age demanded a certain respect. He feels, I think, that he knows me through my father. That he knows me through his past, but I can't come to him on those terms.

He had begun his story over lunch, starting it in slow, measured words, each word carefully picked, polished, each, though, an old jewel to bring back into the light, to hold up for a final examination, a final decision to keep or discard. I listened. Impatient at first, for him to get to the point, to the part I had traveled here to learn, but then his deliberate cadence caught me, and I put my thoughts aside, my heart slowed, and I began really listening.

My cell phone rings. It's David. I sit down on the bed and we speak for a while. I've always loved his voice; it is deep and chocolate rich. My mother always said he sounded like a radio announcer; my father always said he sounded like he was selling cemetery plots. His voice seems strained now, tentative. He tells me he has to fly somewhere on sort of a business trip and won't be back for a week. Puerto Vallarta. I sit up.

"*Sort of* business?" I ask, trying to keep the tremble from my voice. "What's a *sort of* business trip?" There is a tightening in my stomach. I can't remember him ever having a business trip anywhere out of the States.

"Well, Harold told us not to bring spouses, they would only get in the way," he said.

Harry is his boss, the senior partner, and has been divorced three times.

"I guess it worked for Harold," I say with some sarcasm. "No one ever did get in his way. When did you find out you were going there?"

"A few weeks ago," he replies.

"Why didn't you tell me?" I ask quietly, trying to push down my anger, which is slowly rising like the morning sun. "Maybe I would have liked to go with you. I could have postponed this trip." I know that before this, spouses from his law firm frequently went on business trips—whoops—I'm not a spouse. . . .

"Didn't see the point in it," he said. "Since you couldn't go anyway. It was around the time your father was—dying."

"Anyone else going?"

"John Ellison and his wife, you met them," he says.

"So, how come John is bringing his wife?" I ask, feeling a bit like a prosecution lawyer.

"Just the way things worked out." He sighs with impatience. "Look, I'll talk to you soon." We hang up. I know in my heart that this isn't a business trip. I don't want to call him back and accuse. I don't want to be like Sandra, who has been married five times. Sandra, who, as David once pointed out, couldn't find happiness if she had a compass pointing to *H* with a smiley face next to it. But I feel empty. It was an empty conversation. No depth, no emotion.

I'm here in Massachusetts, and he's going to be in Mexico. I suspect not alone. Malachi is wrong, I tell myself. I don't need to tie a rope. I don't want to secure someone to me like that. It should be voluntary.

Rowena taps on the door and pokes her head in. "I want to make sure you're comfortable," she says, then sees the carton on the floor, the parachute in my lap.

"He never needed to use that," she says, smiling. "I'm not even sure it was issued to him. A lot of men sort of wound up with stuff after they were discharged, if you know what I mean. I'm surprised he didn't sneak a plane home, too. Have you looked through any of the photos? Your dad is in some of them."

"I haven't looked at them yet," I said, carefully sliding the parachute back into the pillowcase and tucking it neatly into the carton, before closing that, too.

"Come have a cup of tea with me," she invites, holding the door open. "We can look through that stuff together."

I carry the carton to the kitchen, where Rowena takes it from me and sets it on the table. She makes tea, offers me a choice between chamomile and African Rooibus red tea, which is what I choose because I've never had it before. It fits in with the theme of her living and dining rooms, with their carved ebony African masks and intricate beadwork hanging on the walls. There is an old upright mahogany piano with an African robe draped over the top. I am careful not to look at the piano.

"I'm afraid this is all I have to go with the tea," she says, bringing out a package of Lorna Doones. "I never did learn how to bake." We had eaten dinner out, my treat, and we had both decided to pass on dessert as a concession to our waistlines, but now we're making concessions to our cravings.

"Thank you." I take a cookie and she sits down and lifts the envelope of pictures. She lays them out on the table, facing me. Old pictures, faded to sepia. There is one picture clipped to the top of a larger picture. I slip it from under the rusted paper clip and look closely. A young man, in a uniform I don't recognize. His face is startlingly handsome, not even old-fashioned, considering the time, and his light hair is falling into his eyes. He is sitting in the cockpit of a small plane and laughing. The canopy is up and the sun is glancing against his face, his head is tilted back, and he is squinting and laughing into the glare. He reminds me a little of David. The light hair; the long, sweet face and high cheekbones. Laughing. Maybe he doesn't look so much like David as laugh like him; he looks like he has a ready laugh. And a sweet smile. Like he was always prepared to enjoy every second of his life, and then I realize that David hasn't looked like that in a long time. Did I do that, take his smile? Ensnare him in my tangles and knots? I didn't mean to. I was trying so hard, so hard not to. Please, God, don't let me have done that. I was trying to protect both of us. I look at the picture again. This man has an open smile full of goodwill.

I turn the picture over, but there is no name on it. Rowena shrugs her shoulders when I show it to her; she doesn't know who it is, and I return it to the envelope.

The other pictures are faded with age. There is a group picture of a squadron. Thirty-six men, all black, standing shoulder to shoulder, in their army fatigues, their names printed in a small, cramped paragraph below. The heading reads: *823rd Quartermaster Company*. Rowena Jackson points a finger to a face, young, serious, standing in the rear. I recognize the eyes. Willie Jackson.

"Your father," I say.

"Yes." She smiles at his face. "And see who else is there?" The question in her voice puzzles me, and I look down at the picture again. Am I supposed to know someone? Every face is young, so young, expectant, lean with youth. Black. Then, there, in the corner, I see him. A washed-out white dot above the army uniform. A white face among thirty-six black faces. Also serious. Also young. And not yet touched with the anger that I know. He is smiling, in a rueful sort of way. He never liked to be photographed, would not even stand with me when I graduated from high school, our last family portrait. He always stepped out of range. But he is captured here, with an awkward, self-conscious half smile.

"My father?" I say. "He looks so out of place."

"He was their sergeant," she says. "Did you know he was their sergeant?"

"No," I say, baffled that he is standing among them. "Their *sergeant?*" I know little about my father's time in the Army Air Force. He never spoke of it. But surely this is wrong. Was there no black man who could command them? No black sergeant who could lead them? He *is* out of place. Then, I realize, it says 1941. It is Montgomery, Alabama. My father is a Jew. A *New York*

Jew, and he is commanding a platoon of black men. I understand, suddenly, the implications of a white man, this particular white man, standing with thirty-six black men.

"My father was studying to be an engineer," I say.

"So was mine," she replies.

"But—" I am confused, and I point to the paragraph under the picture. "I don't understand," I say. "This platoon—my father—"

"I know," she says. "It says *Housekeeping* Unit. They were cleaners. Ironic, isn't it?"

"That two-year-old is sold," Malachi reports when I call him later in the afternoon to ask him how things are going on the farm. "Seventy-five hundred dollars. Cash."

"Wow," I exclaim. "How'd you get cash?"

Malachi chuckles. "I says to them, it's all cash or I can slap on a little ol' sales tax."

"That's illegal," I remind him, "not to charge tax."

"It made the sale." He sniffs. "By the way, Lisbon's leg looks good. The swelling is gone. And I found a new place to turn him out. A *safe* place."

"Where?" I ask.

He pauses. "Your front lawn."

"*What?*"

"You got that fancy wrought-iron fencing around it," he says, "so he'll stay put. And I gave him extra hay."

"It's not a horse fence," I protest. "And David is a fanatic about the grass and we planted all those flowers. Turn him out with the other geldings." When I mention David's name, I feel an odd sensation in my chest. Like a wire seeking a connection that is capped off.

"Toby is kicking the crap out of him," Malachi says. "I can always plant more flowers, but Lisbon won't grow another leg. We'll get him off the lawn soon as you build a paddock for him."

"Lisbon has to learn to defend himself," I retort. "A gelding belongs with geldings."

I know I'm being stubborn, but Lisbon is a wimp, and I hate that. He has been turned out with several different groups of horses, and he has been the underdog every time. All he has to do is stand up for himself. It's important to me that he learns to stand up for himself against the bullying. Abusive past or not, he has to stand up for himself.

I, myself, am not courageous. I never had the courage to stand up for myself. When I was in my teens, my father would viciously berate both me and Sandra: I didn't help enough around the house, I was useless, who would ever want to marry me? She was dumpy, noisy. I stood there, eyes lowered—like my brain was filled with oatmeal—counting the tiles on the kitchen floor, over and over, one hundred and fifty beige porcelain tiles.

Sandra always argued back. Her courage frightened me. I thought it was going to end the world. I would run upstairs, into my bedroom, and pull the covers over my head while she argued back. I am sorry I didn't stand by her. I have no courage at all, but still—Lisbon has to defend himself. Survive his abusers, or he will be nothing but oatmeal.

"It's nature," Malachi is saying. "They're not going to accept him. And he's going to wind up getting hurt."

"It's not nature," I snap. "He will learn. Give them each their own pile of hay and put out an extra one. That should solve it."

I hear Malachi sigh very loudly on the other end of the phone. "I'll do it, but it's not going to work," he says.

"It'll work," I reply. "Give it time. All I'm asking is that he gets along with the other horses."

"It's been two years." Malachi snorts. "All you're asking for is a miracle."

Chapter 11

The colored barracks were at the very end of Gunter Field, close to the swamp that lay heavy with mosquitoes and snakes and lizards and things that made noises Willie never heard in Harlem. The "colored barracks," they were called, though they were barely more than a row of elongated tents, part of Tent City, the temporary housing the Army Air Force had thrown up for its sudden huge influx of men. Supplies were scarce everywhere, but especially in the colored barracks, which were furnished with old and broken equipment handed down from the white barracks. The bunks were discards, the mattresses were crumbling, the sheets and blankets almost nonexistent. Not that Willie was thinking of using a blanket in that heat. Floor fans stood in corners, but they were motionless; a few men played with the switches in an effort to turn them on, but it was as though the motors were paralyzed by the high temperatures.

"The pool is off-limits to colored servicemen," somebody read from a notice pinned on the bulletin board. "The baseball diamond is off-limits. The airmen's club is off-limits. You will restrict yourselves to the colored PX. You may not enter the white PX under any circumstances. Upper mess hall is off-limits. Lower mess hall is for coloreds."

"Wonder if we're going to get any dinner," Willie mused to the reader, "or is food off-limits, too?" There was a bitter chuckle all around.

The colored men were allowed to sit in the six back rows of the auditorium for Orientation. By the time Willie and August got there, those seats were filled. Willie cast his eye around; there were a few seats vacant in the middle, but he understood the South now, understood standard procedure, that he couldn't sit in the middle of white soldiers, that he had to stand in the back, away from the ceiling fans. He positioned himself by the door. August stood next to him and folded his arms. Rage prickled against the back of Willie's neck.

"There are some empty seats left," he muttered to August. "We should be able to sit down there."

"I don't mind standing," August replied nervously. "Maybe we can catch us a breeze." But any breeze that came through the door felt like the exhaust from a car, and Willie was soaked with sweat in minutes. He wondered whether the showers in the colored barracks were working.

Major Earnest Dugger, who had introduced himself at the train station, welcomed them, talked about the base, told them it was the place the Wright Brothers opened the first training field for civilian flyers, that they could be proud of its important role in the war effort, that in these dark times, the world was depending on their efforts. After an hour and a half, the men were dismissed. The colored soldiers were given a sheet of paper as they walked out the door. Willie scanned it. Nothing new, it basically restated the rules that were hanging in the barracks. They couldn't join the USO club, intramural basketball, or even attend base movies unless they wanted to stand in the back. No, no, and no, the list went on.

"Dispensary is limited for colored soldiers," Willie read

aloud to August, who had barely glanced at his paper, "unless there is a serious problem."

"What's a 'serious problem'?" August asked.

"Verge of death, I guess," Willie bit off. "Try not to get there."

Orders were that newcomers had to report to First Sergeant John P. Hogarth for assignments. Willie and August waited patiently in line, in the melting heat, while the white soldiers went first, two at a time. Willie held on to his orders, Base Security, they read, and he stood in the long queue outside Hogarth's office, wondering whether he would be issued a rifle. He kind of liked the idea of a rifle slung smartly over his shoulder. He had gotten top ratings in basic training for marksmanship. He knew he had a good eye and a steady hand. He thought he might ask August to take a photo of him with his rifle and send it home. He knew his mother would frame it. It would look awfully good on the piano in the living room.

The line was moving. Base Security, he mused. He wondered what part of the base he would be guarding.

"Make sure you go in with me, Willie," August whispered to him. "So's you can 'splain things to me."

Willie nodded. "What are your orders?" he asked.

"We ain't supposed to open them," August said. "I don't want no trouble."

"They said you could open them when you got to Gunter," Willie said patiently. "We're definitely at Gunter."

August pulled the envelope from his pocket and slit it open with his fingernail. He handed the paper to Willie. "You tell me," he said, and Willie realized that he couldn't read.

"Cook," he read off.

August laughed, then stopped. "I hopes they can teach me, 'cause I never cooked nothin'."

The line shuffled along, two by two, until there were only a few left. The colored soldiers, all of them, so far, had come out of Hogarth's office to announce they had been assigned to Fourth Aviation Squadron, whatever that was. Willie wondered what it was, but knew he wouldn't be joining them, because he was heading for Base Security, with probably extra training. Well, he would soon find out. He was next in line.

"Let's go, boys," Hogarth's voice rang out as the two previous soldiers emerged from his office. "On the double."

August and Willie entered together. Hogarth was sitting behind a desk reading some papers. He was a solid man, short and muscular, with a graying light brown bristly crew cut, a slight pug nose, and gray eyes that peered out from under a high, refined forehead. An imposing sign in front of him, made of old shell casings, read FIRST SERGEANT JOHN P. HOGARTH. Mementos from World War I were arranged neatly on a shelf behind, including a steel helmet with a large gash across the front, and a commendation for the Distinguished Service Cross, framed in black. On the wall was a faded photo of Hogarth's old company when he fought at Château-Thierry. Willie waited, quietly looking around, waiting for Hogarth to acknowledge them.

August had stiffened to attention and held a salute; Willie just stood motionless. The sergeant barely glanced at them, but Willie knew he was enjoying August's frozen salute. They waited some more.

"Y'all don't salute a noncom officer," Hogarth finally said to August. August dropped his salute and looked down at his shoes, embarrassed. Hogarth gave him a beatific smile, and spoke slowly, as if to a child. "But y'all do stand at attention until y'all are told otherwise."

August stiffened to attention once again. Hogarth leaned back in his chair and studied the two men before gesturing to his desk. "Let me see your orders. That always comes first. Y'all should know that by now."

Willie tossed his orders onto the desk while August leaned forward and extended his papers, holding them out in front of him. Hogarth glanced down at his desk. "Put them there." He pointed to a spot in front of him. August placed his orders carefully, right on the spot, and Hogarth opened them, looked through them without expression.

"Now, I wonder who's who here," he drawled. "All you colored boys kinda look alike, doncha." He leaned forward. "You're supposed to say your names." The steady gray eyes landed on August.

"August Woodrow Randolph, sir—uh—Sergeant."

Hogarth leaned back in his chair. "And next you say, 'Reporting for duty, Sergeant'."

August got flustered and saluted again. Then repeated, "Private August Woodrow Randolph reporting for duty, Sergeant."

"Y'all finally got it right, boy." Hogarth looked to Willie next.

"Private First Class William Joseph Jackson reporting for duty."

"Good." Hogarth smiled benevolently at them both. "Good for you. I like my colored boys trained up. All right. At ease." Willie bit the inside of his cheek and stood at ease.

Hogarth read through their papers. "William Joseph Jackson? This here paper says you're an *educated* nigra. Is that right?"

"I got some college," Willie said tightly.

"Well, good for you, Willie Joe," Hogarth said. "I like my nigras educated. They don't make too many mistakes that way." He put his hands behind his head. "I got just the right assignment for you. Fourth Squadron. Eight-twenty-third Quartermaster Company. Hangar Five."

"Base Security?" Willie asked, wondering how all the colored men could have the same assignment.

"Housekeeping," Hogarth said.

"My papers say Base Security."

Hogarth leaned toward him, his gray eyes turning hard and cold like the cement in a Harlem sidewalk. "We call it Security, but it's maintenance. You'll be cleaning the planes." He nodded to August. "Both you boys. Housekeeping. That's probably a damn sight better than what most of you are used to. Dismissed."

Willie stepped into the hot orange sun outside, August right behind him, greatly relieved. "Glad I don't have to cook, because that would sure be awful for them that's eatin' it," he said, following Willie to a group of colored soldiers who were being yelled into formation by another sergeant, a white one. "Glad we get to be together."

"Looks like everyone's gonna be together," Willie said. "Looks like we're all going to the same place."

"Suits me fine," said August. "You can't get into trouble when you with you own."

"This is the wash rack, where the planes get cleaned." The white sergeant who marched them there gestured to Hangar Five behind him. "Those are the BT-13s. The Vultee Valiants." He pointed to a small but sturdy-looking plane that was being pushed into the hangar. It had tandem cockpits, one behind the other, and a single prop. Its clear plastic canopy was flipped up like it was hailing them. "Those are the training planes," the sergeant went on. "They teach the flyboys how to handle the bombers. I will be handing out protective gear. You will put it on before you proceed into the hangar."

The men slipped into gloves and boots and goggles and overalls, in addition to head coverings with face masks. They stood like kids waiting to go out into a snowstorm, walking with arms out to the side, legs stiff.

"Watch the steam, boys." The sergeant beckoned them inside.

Willie and August followed the other men into the hangar. Base Security! Willie got it. How would it look if all the coloreds on base were listed as Housekeeping? How would it look in Washington? So the name got changed, some orders said Security, some said Cook, some said Communication. But they were all cleaning men. He got it now.

If hell had a name, Willie decided, it would be called the wash rack. It reeked of benzene and hot wiring and burning metal, the searing fumes made unbearable as they rose into wispy vapors and hung white in the stinking air. Though it was a long, narrow building, it was so filled with steam and noise, of chemical clouds and shrieking tools, it seemed nothing else could fit. Around the periphery were metal grates placed over open trenches, which served as the sewer system. The chemicals and water washed down through the grates into an underground holding tank, which was supposed to be pumped out regularly. It hadn't been and was doing a poor job of containing the fluids from the floor, unfortunately maintaining the reek.

One after another, the Vultees were being pushed inside the hangar, where a team of four quickly disassembled them and sent them on to the next station. Ratchets squealed against frozen bolts, the sheet-metal skin falling away in great clangs. The dynamotor was dropped onto a dolly for special work; the transmitter, receiver, all the radio parts were deposited on rolling carts and taken away to another room, the radio room, where they would be cleaned and refurbished. What remained in the wash rack was just the skeleton of the Vultee, like the metal bones of a dinosaur.

"Just like cleaning a chicken," the sergeant yelled over the noise. "Skin 'em, guts out, wash 'em up."

They followed what was left of one plane to the corner of the hangar. A huge steam generator hissed and spit at them like a livid cat. The hoses that hung from its sides quivered with live steam.

It was all fast work; you had to move fast. The men rushed past the new recruits, running almost, to get things done. Planes were taken apart after every twenty hours of flight time, then put back into service. *There's a war on, haven't you heard? On the double! On the double!* The men rushed the plane under the hoses, spraying it clean, filling the air with more benzene mist, rushing it to the next station, where it was dried.

A figure, dressed in hazard gear, stepped out of the thick steam and walked toward them.

"I'll leave you with Sergeant Shinestone," said their sergeant, gesturing to the figure. "He's in charge here. He'll explain procedures."

"Schoenstein," a voice from inside the protective face piece corrected him.

"Shinestone, Schoenstein. It all sounds alike to me." The first sergeant shrugged. "Here are your new men." He turned on his heel and left the hangar.

"All right, men, follow along." Schoenstein led them closer to the wash rack. The stench was overwhelming, even through the masks. Willie pressed the mask closer to his nose, wondering whether it was even working.

"Live steam." Schoenstein pointed. "There's a valve on the hose, mixes the steam with the benzene solution. Real volatile stuff. Take off your skin in half a second. Stay alert." He walked to the next station; the men followed.

This bay dried the plane with a set of air hoses. "If they don't dry," Schoenstein yelled over the noise, "we can piggyback some carbon tetrachloride into the nozzle. Supposed to dry them better. Just don't breathe it. The heat turns carbon tet into phosgene gas."

"Looks like we don't need to go overseas to die," Willie remarked to August, who nodded vigorously.

"Yep, I'm glad I ain't going overseas," he agreed with Willie, apparently not comprehending what he said.

"I'll be leaving. Going to the front," Schoenstein yelled at them. "Your new sergeant is being processed and will be taking charge at fifteen hundred hours. Should be here in a minute or two."

The men stood at ease, waiting for the new sergeant, watching the escaping sprays of carbon tet misting the air, falling on them like summer rain, the sweet, hot smell penetrating their masks. They watched as a plane was pushed through, dried off, then pushed down to another bay for assembly, only to be replaced by another. Everything moved fast.

"You work in teams of four," Schoenstein yelled. "Two new men will work with two regulars. When you get it down, we'll reshuffle the crews. Scheduling—" He was interrupted by a tap on the shoulder. The new sergeant had arrived, already dressed in the protective suit. He spoke to Schoenstein for a few minutes; they shook hands. Schoenstein walked him through and gave him a thick booklet of procedures before turning the new men over to him. Then Schoenstein left.

"We've seen enough for today," the new sergeant announced. "You start tomorrow at oh eight hundred." He held up the booklet. "I got some reading to do."

They moved to the hangar doors, shuffling behind the new sergeant. He led them out into the burning Alabama sun. Willie didn't think he would ever appreciate being in the sun, but even through his gear, it felt cool to him.

"Remove your mask and identify yourselves," the new sergeant ordered the men, holding up a list of personnel to check off. Willie pulled his mask from his face. The air felt like the caress of a lover against his skin, cool, gentle. He took a sweet breath, then realized the sergeant was waiting for him to speak.

"Private First Class William Joseph Jackson," he said. The new sergeant, still masked, nodded, then turned to the next man.

August also pulled off his mask and headpiece. "Private August Woodrow Randolph, sir."

They went down the line. Each man removing his mask and helmet, each face glistening black under the Alabama sun—

"Corporal Leon Washington Hamilton, sir."

"Corporal Charlie Hobbs, sir."

—until they all stood there, their headgear in their hands, waiting. The new sergeant pulled off his own mask and headpiece, and looked at them. Forty-three colored men looked back. Willie chuckled to himself. It was Brooklyn. Sergeant Martin Fleischer. First *Schoenstein,* now *Fleischer.* He got it right away. A Jew leading a whole squadron of colored men. Leading a *wash rack* squadron. A squadron of cleaning men. After all, it was Alabama. He guessed not a good place for Jews, and certainly not for coloreds. He watched Fleischer's face as he glanced at his new men, glanced at each black face staring back at him, watched Fleischer's expression very carefully.

"Hello," Fleischer said, looking first puzzled, then comprehending, as things began to register. "Welcome to the wash rack, men. Looks like we'll be working together."

Yeah, Willie thought, now they both got it.

Chapter 12

"Know anything about birds?" Fleischer was holding out something tiny and intensely pink in the middle of his palm. The morning sun, not yet raging, sat low in a corner of the sky; the airfield was still obscured by a soft fog that hadn't yet burned off. Fleischer had just taken roll call and his squadron was still at attention, stiffly lined up just outside the wash rack. He suddenly realized this. "Oh. At ease, men." They swung their legs apart and clasped their hands behind their backs. "Birds?" he repeated, looking around. August shuffled forward to study the wriggling pink object in Fleischer's hand.

"That's just hatched, Sarge," he said.

Fleischer gave him a puzzled look. "I thought they got hatched in the spring, not the summer."

August shook his head. "Second clutch, Sarge. Around this time, they lay again. I seen it." They both stared at the creature. Its head wobbled sideways, too heavy for its body. Its black eyes lay just underneath transparent eyelids, pink skin so fragile, you could see its yellow gizzard, its ballooning blue-gray stomach, its heart a black dot, beating just under Fleischer's thumb.

"Prob'ly fell down from somewhere, Sarge," August added. They both glanced up at the roofline of the building, and sure enough, stuffed into the overhang was a strew of small, thin twigs woven with strips of rag, used to wipe down the planes.

"Stupid place for a nest," Fleischer muttered. He looked down again at his hand. "What the hell are we going to do with it?"

August pulled his garrison cap from his head and held it out. "I'm kinda good with birds, Sarge. Give it here."

Fleischer gently lowered the bird into the hat.

"Bread and sugar water," August said. "That's what you feed them."

"Okay." Fleischer grabbed a few coins from his pocket and pointed to the jeep parked next to the hangar. "Get a loaf of bread from the PX."

August hung back and gave him a sheepish look. Fleischer looked puzzled. "I know they sell bread," he urged.

Willie cleared his throat. "It'll take him at least an hour, sir," he said, his words making sharp points in the morning air. "The colored PX is on the other side of the base, and it's not open until fourteen hundred hours." Fleischer took this in, but his face gave nothing away.

"So, go to the white PX," he said.

"Not allowed in the white PX, sir," Willie called out again. Fleischer glanced at the name tag on Willie's khaki fatigue shirt.

"Jackson?"

"Yessir?"

"Are you sure?"

"Positive, sir."

Fleischer looked down at the bird sitting in August's hat and tightened his lips. "Okay," he said to Willie. "Take over." He nodded toward the wash rack. "Get the men inside and started on your first plane. I'll be back."

"You leaving, sir?"

Fleischer jumped into the jeep and turned it on. His face was filled with disgust. "Looks like I got to waste precious Army Air Force *war* time buying myself a loaf of bread."

* * *

Planes in, planes out. It was endless. Maybe it was because of the crashes that their production was doubled, then tripled. *Get the planes out, get them out, get them out. Strip them naked, wash them, steam them, there's a war on and it's going badly.* They needed the planes for bombing training. They needed the planes to get the pilots in the air to teach them how to fly. *Get them out, move it! On the double!* There were fewer planes than ever; the Vultee Valiants were dropping out of the sky, sometimes two or three a week, crashing. Falling from the skies like a shot bird, though no one knew the reason. It seemed to Willie that the crashes were killing their own pilots before the Jerries could. Which meant the brass was up their ass every day. Orders were to find out what was crashing them.

First there was Major Seekircher, who planned to spend the day observing and taking notes. He refused to put on protective gear, and after an hour in the wash rack, left coughing and gagging, tears streaming from his eyes, snot pouring from his nose.

Then there was the team of engineers from Vultee, led by Lieutenant Colonel Chester Fairchild. It ended in a shouting match. One of the engineers had pushed his face right into Fleischer's to make a very vocal point.

"We did some research," he yelled at Fleischer. "Those planes are crashing right after they come out of Maintenance. *Your* men are responsible."

"Is that a fact?" Fleischer shouted back, the veins in his forehead bulging pale blue under his skin, reminding Willie of the baby bird. "We follow everything you wrote in the manual! To the letter! Maybe *that's* the problem!"

"I'm thinking maybe sabotage," the engineer yelled. "I'm thinking—"

"Don't blame my men." Fairchild stepped between them. "We had a problem with the planes crashing before Fleischer was assigned here."

The engineer backed off and looked at the masked figures

who had assembled around them. "Maybe it's because you got a bunch of niggers and a kike working on them," he said snidely to Fairchild.

Fleischer lunged for him, stopped only by Fairchild's sharp command to attention.

Fleischer struggled to bring himself back under control. "My men work hard, sir," he stuttered with frustration. "I won't have anyone talking like that about them."

Fairchild turned to the engineers, who were milling about uncomfortably. "Maybe I approved this model too soon. The BT-13As—not as fancy as the BT-13s. The general will want to run over the specs for it again."

"There's nothing wrong with this plane," the engineer countered. "Maybe you just need to get some competent men on it."

"My men are competent." Fleischer clenched his fists at his sides. "You'll have to prove to me it's not the design."

The engineer clenched his own fists. "I don't have to prove—"

Fairchild stepped between them for the second time. "This isn't solving the problem, and I want it solved." He glared at the two men. "I plan to make brigadier general, and this thing could hold me back. My ass is on the line for this." He nodded to Fleischer and his men. "As you were," and he led the engineers outside. Fleischer spit on the ground, then looked around at his dumbfounded men. "They're all crazy, blaming us. I have an engineering background and I'm washing planes. This whole damn Air Force is crazy."

Every morning landed another baby bird in their laps. August just collected each new addition and put it in with the others, into a nest he had fashioned from clean rags, and which he kept in a box labeled RADIO PARTS. The box was left out on a bench in what served as a corner office off the Radio room so he could feed them the required five or six times a day. The door protected them from the fumes. Fleischer hovered over them almost as much as their mother would have. He seemed almost proud of how well they were thriving.

"Looks like they're bigger than they were yesterday," he would comment to August.

"'Cause they is tough army birds," August would agree admiringly, as he fed them bread soaked in sugar water. The older ones were graduated to canned K-rations, which he carefully pushed down their throats with a soda straw. Some of them had already grown pinfeathers, which stuck out like gray needles from their skin, finally opening to cover their heads with a fluffy gray down. Moses, Flapjack, Big Boy, Little Man, Oswald—August had named all of them. Willie found it pleasant to be greeted by a chorus of sweet, demanding chirps as soon as they opened the doors to the wash rack every morning. It kept some of the war away.

"Fly-shit!" Hogarth was standing in the front of the hangar, with a clipboard of papers and a big grin. He liked creating new and obnoxious variations on Fleischer's name and did it every opportunity he got. "Fly-shit?" His presence meant he was delivering bad news, senseless orders or a denial for a requisition. Willie knew Hogarth enjoyed this particular work, being the messenger of bad news. He could have easily sent a buck private, but he liked to take it upon himself to personally hand the papers to Fleischer as soon as they came across his desk, then stand back and grin like a carved pumpkin. Willie tightened his grip on the steam hose and watched from the corner of his eye as Fleischer walked over to Hogarth, his hands on his hips, his face betraying no emotion. It could only be a problem, Willie knew. Maybe they had to double up production, triple-check the wiring on the dynamotor because of the Vultees falling out of the skies, maybe add another sickening, noxious chemical to the soup they were already using. He watched their expressions as they spoke for a few minutes—Hogarth looking smug and satisfied; Fleischer, a studied indifference—before Hogarth finally handed Fleischer the orders. Fleischer read them without expression, then called out Willie's name.

"Jackson!"

Willie handed off the steam hose to Leon Hamilton, careful to first shut off the nozzle, then point it down and away at an angle, before Hamilton could take it over from him.

"Yessir?" he said, joining Hogarth and Fleischer. He had become Fleischer's right-hand man and he didn't like it. He didn't like being singled out.

"You boys got some extra work to do." Hogarth nodded toward the orders, still grinning happily.

Willie looked at Fleischer with a question in his eyes. He didn't like to talk in front of Hogarth. The less he said, the less he would provoke him, although it didn't take much to start Hogarth on one of his social discourses on nigras.

"New orders," Fleischer said to Willie.

"Salvage," said Hogarth. "Y'all are going to do some salvage." He was nearly pissing in his pants with delight.

Willie had to ask. "Salvage what, sir?"

Just what Hogarth was waiting for. "You boys gotta salvage the planes that crash," he answered triumphantly, rubbing his hands together. "That shouldn't bother a kike and a coupla nigras. You boys, I'm told, are real spiritual, and those planes can get spooky." He giggled at the thought.

Fleischer clenched his fists. "Watch your mouth, Hogarth."

But Hogarth was in too good of a mood to pick up on the fight. "Yessiree. Just came down from the brass today—Y'all got to mop up the planes that crash. Take out all usable parts and clean 'em and catalogue 'em."

"That's not part of wash rack duty," Fleischer snapped. "We're supposed to stay right here. I can't handle it; they already reduced our turnaround time."

"There's a war on." Hogarth shrugged. "We're shorthanded. The other salvage teams are being retrained to serve in the mess hall. They burn out after a while." He looked from one to the other. "You boys can read, can't you? 'Cause I know y'all said you was coll-ege edoo-ca-ted. So y'all got the orders and the manual for salvage operations and y'all should be all set."

A sudden twitter of birds emanated from the radio parts box.

August left his post pushing the planes into the hangar and went into the office to feed them. Hogarth's eyes followed him.

"What's that noise?" he asked.

"Just fixing a bad radio, Hogarth," Fleischer snapped. "You got any other business?"

Hogarth pulled a piece of paper from his shirt pocket. "Just about those wire cutters you requisitioned. I took 'em—I needed 'em for my office. I'll put y'all down for the next set." He gave Fleischer a little shrug and patted the tool that was poking up from his shirt pocket.

Fleischer glared at him for a moment, then gave him a sarcastic smile. "I'm sure your desk job demands a lot of wiring," he said, "but no problem. I'll just resolder the handles back on the ones we have until the new ones come in. Seems a waste of time, but it's easy enough." He jerked his thumb to the door. "Now, take a hike," he said. "I've got a squadron to run and a manual to read."

It was August who found the birds. The next morning. Right after roll call. Right after they rolled back the hangar doors to let the pale peach light of day into the darkness. The night crew had gone home, and the hangar had shut down for one hour between shifts. August went first, with his paper sack of dog food and bread. There was an anguished cry, like the moan of a sick animal, no words, Willie remembered, no words. Just the long, agonized moan. They all rushed to the office. The bench where August kept the box was smeared with blood. The bench was red with it, shiny, congealed blood. The box, too, red. The birds were dead, the whole lot of them, their heads neatly nipped off with a brand-new pair of wire cutters that were left on the bench, right out in the open, right next to the box that said RADIO PARTS. And there was a note from Hogarth.

"Hand-delivered new wire cutters. They work good."

Chapter 13

"That white horse disappeared like smoke."

Malachi had called me on my cell phone from his, which is unusual for him, because he believes that cell phones send out waves that make your brains evaporate. I had gotten him his own phone three years ago, for emergencies, and he'd only used it once before, reluctantly, when he got a flat tire on the truck while he was picking up some extra grain. His voice is filled with concern, telling me about Lisbon, who has apparently vanished from his paddock. I try to concentrate on his words, but my head is filled with the sight of small, bloody, fragile, dead baby birds.

"Where could he have gone?" I ask Malachi, trying to focus. I know Lisbon couldn't have gone far; there are thick woods surrounding my farm, which would make running away difficult.

"Damned if I know," Malachi continues. "I turned him out early, and when I went back to give him hay, he was gone. Spent two hours so far, trying to find him."

"Problem at home?" Rowena Jackson asks me. It is late morning, and she is driving us to the hospital for me to visit with her father again. The plan is for her to drop me off, and continue on to work, then pick me up again in the late afternoon. I nod to her, the phone to my ear.

"Are any of the fences down?" I ask Malachi while nodding vigorously at Rowena. "Gate open?"

"First things I checked," Malachi replies. "He just disappeared like smoke." I can picture Malachi lifting his tan cap to scratch his head, the way he always does when he's puzzled. "Only way out of his paddock is to jump."

"He doesn't know how to jump," I say.

"He does now," Malachi replies. "Fence is four feet high."

There are miles of fields and woods surrounding my farm, and Lisbon could be anywhere. Though he could live off the land for a time, browsing on the undergrowth, drinking from streams, weaving in and out of the shadows of trees, before long his color will betray him; nature can't hide a white horse. Malachi always said so.

"Take my truck and drive along the road," I tell Malachi. "Go real slow—you'll probably spot him. Bring a bucket of grain and shake it out the window. He'll come. He may even be on his way back to the barn by now. They don't like running alone in the woods. Besides, you always tell me they come back."

"Well, the smart ones do," Malachi replies. "But since it's Lisbon, he may need a map. It's better I look for him on horseback. That truck of yours can't get around no trees."

"I don't want you riding!" I exclaim. I am thinking, Maja hasn't foaled yet, the other mares have foals at their sides, the young horses aren't fully saddle-broken, the geldings can barely steer, the only horse available would be MoneyTalk. And the thought of an eighty-one-year-old man combing the woods on a young, high-strung, ex-racehorse that didn't even belong to me, looking for a fancy, high-strung, rescued show horse that did, is making my brain spin. I am thinking of asking Rowena to drop me off at the airport right now. "It's not safe for you to ride."

"Actually," Malachi says slowly, in an I-hate-to-tell-you-this tone of voice, "it's too late."

"What's too late?" I yelp.

"Telling me not to ride," he says. "S'why I called you on my cell phone. The barn phone won't reach this far."

"You go back to the barn right now." I try to sound like I'm in charge, although we both know better. "Wait—what's too late?" Then I suddenly realize what he means.

"Can't go back," he replies. "We're in the middle of a stream—well—whoop-de-doo!"

The phone is silent for a few moments. I know Malachi is fearless. He will grab the halter of a runaway horse that is coming right at him and just pull it to the side. He will stride across an icy barn roof with a broom to sweep off the snow before it accumulates; he will hop on anything that has four legs and is still standing upright. He has even made me feel brave when I was far from it. It's all quiet except for the sound of water swishing in the background.

"Malachi?" I yell. "Malachi!" I am picturing him sprawled, injured, floating facedown. I mentally run through my emergency numbers, hoping I can get someone there to help him. He's a crack horseman, but even he has limits. "Malachi! Are you all right?"

"Ha-ha." He giggles, but I hear a big splash of water and his breath coming in hard pants. "Well, he don't like getting his feet wet. Sucker's got a bit of a buck in him. Don't worry, he's fine."

"I'm not worried about the horse," I reply, then ask what I dread asking. "By the way, exactly who are you riding?"

"MoneyTalk. The only other horse you got that's rideable is the one we're looking for."

"Just go back to the barn," I plead. "I don't want you to get hurt."

"I'll go back presently," he says. "Lisbon can't get far. Not with that bad leg."

"His leg is healed," I say. "You told me that his leg is all healed."

"Not that leg," Malachi replies, and then, "The other leg."

Okay, I think, though I am starting to feel like the straight man in a vaudeville act, *I'll bite.* "What other leg?"

"The leg Toby kicked this morning. Swelled like a balloon. I hosed it, but he was pretty upset. S'why he jumped out, I suppose."

Rowena pulls into the parking lot and drives me up to the hospital entrance.

"Sounds like you got a lot on your plate," she says. "Please don't feel obligated to stay. I've heard my father's stories a hundred times over the years. I can always jot them down, when I get a chance." She gives me a reassuring smile. "And e-mail them to you." But I realize that I want to stay. That part of the stories is hearing Willie tell them to me in his own words. I want to hear his voice. I turn to her. "He told me about the baby birds," I say.

"Oh yes, the baby birds." She reflects. "I was never allowed to have a pet when I was growing up. He never forgot those birds."

I try David on his cell phone; my hand shakes as I push his number. It goes right to voice mail. I take a deep breath and realize that I am feeling a ball of ice in my stomach. I will try him again in a little while. Whatever he had been planning to do, he probably has already done. That part of it is over. My phone call won't stop anything.

Willie Jackson is asleep when I walk into his room. Even asleep, wearing navy pajamas with tiny white dots, he looks dignified. But I see his frailness, his face a dark wisp against the stark white pillows. There's a nasal canula over his mouth and nose, bringing him oxygen; his hearing aid is in his ear, the wire resting on his chest; and a thin, plastic IV line in his arm, bringing him medications. I see the shape of his body under the covers, the outline of his one remaining leg. I sit by his bedside for a few minutes, wondering whether I am intruding. I promised him I would return, but I feel a bit embarrassed to be bothering him. I am not family. I'm barely an acquaintance; I haven't earned the right to be sitting by his bedside watching him sleep. We are too vulnerable when we sleep; it is an act that should only be done in the presence of those we totally trust. His hands grasp the bedcovers in two loose fists, like he's holding reins. It reminds me of Malachi, foolishly galloping through the woods, and I worry that I'm going to be spending the rest of my summer visiting old men in hospitals.

I study Willie's face. It's the face of a gentle and good man. It's not furrowed with lines of bitterness and anger, like my father's. It's the face of a man who has made peace with his life. Who is perhaps trying to bring peace to mine.

I think, he and Malachi are most likely only a few years apart, and there is a world of difference between them. Willie is a frail reed, while Malachi is as strong as a tree. I hope it's more than good genes and physiology. I hope it's the love of horses that makes the difference, the passion that drives me to get up the next morning, because I want to be like Malachi, staying strong and riding forever. I don't want to spend my end years fading to a whisper, hovering between barely existing and dying, and not doing either particularly well.

My worry over Malachi won't quit. Maybe he got thrown by now; I picture broken ribs, a broken leg, a fractured hip. I get up and walk to the window, and despite all the posted signs on the hospital walls, guiltily turn on my cell phone to call him.

"Just got him back," he reports proudly. "He's in the paddock eating hay."

"How'd you manage?" I whisper, so as not to disturb Willie.

"Took a rope with me and lassoed him in, then ponied him home." He pauses and I know what he's going to say. "He needs his own paddock, missy. Toby and the others are out to get him."

"I'm not fencing in a paddock just for him," I say. It's the same old discussion. "Just keep them all busy with extra hay until I get home. And maybe hose his leg. If he was able to run around the woods for a couple of hours like that, he's fine."

"Okay." Malachi sighs. "But by the time you get home, hosing or not, until you get him fenced by hisself, I 'spect he won't have a leg left to stand on."

* * *

I know I'm being stubborn. It's a trait I got from my father. He would set his jaw and not give an inch. Stubborn to the end, literally, to the end. I think about this Lisbon thing, and the on-going battle I have with Malachi, but I don't have the thousands of dollars right now to fence in another paddock, just for one horse. David has offered to pay for it, but this is my farm, mostly supported by me, while David supports the house expenses. I have made sure I can take care of it and myself, that I will always be able to take care of the farm and myself. David has offered to fence in the paddock, to repair the hay barn, to buy me a new tractor. He used to offer to marry me. I try his phone again. Voice mail.

"Why don't you say yes to David?" Sandra always used to ask me. "It's not like men are lining up around the corner to marry you."

She knows about lines, since she has married five times. Maybe six. I can't remember whether Harrison, her current husband, was also number three, or whether that was Donald Harriman. Though we are on opposite sides of the commitment coin, it's the same issue. We both need an escape clause for if somehow the men in our lives wind up acting like our father.

What happens if David escapes through my escape clause?

I decide to let Willie sleep and get some coffee in the cafeteria, maybe take a cab back to Rowena's house and book a ticket home. Willie is tired, spent. He doesn't need to open his heart and reach into the past to retrieve the pain he has kept there. He doesn't need to do that for me. It might be too much of a burden. Rowena can tell me his stories. I brush my hand over his to say good-bye. His skin is cool, soft.

"Don't go," Willie says. He takes the canula from his face, but his eyes are closed.

"I didn't want to wake you," I say softly.

"Wasn't asleep," he says, grinning, eyes still closed. "I was just lying here and thinking about what I was going to tell you next."

Chapter 14

"Bloody hell! The fucker just died on me!" Sergeant Lindsey Davies, of the Royal Air Force, was incensed. The cramped cockpit of the Vultee Valiant could barely contain his hulking frame and huge fury. "It revved properly, then died," he thundered. "What if I had been in the middle of a chandelle?" He gave Fleischer a piercing look, but Fleischer didn't notice; he already had the engine cover open and was hanging into it, puttering around inside. Ten minutes earlier, a messenger had pulled Fleischer from the wash rack to race him across the base and onto the runway where Davies was fuming impatiently in his dead plane. Fleischer had barely enough time to grab a satchel of tools and call out for Willie to come with him.

"Damn thing just came out of the wash rack," he remarked to Willie, as the jeep bounced at breakneck speed along the airstrip.

"Connections can't be dirty," Willie had replied, as puzzled as Fleischer.

"No. And they're tighter than a duck's ass," Fleischer agreed. "There's something else going on."

Willie didn't answer. He didn't like being called out of the wash rack. It wasn't safe, he thought. Not safe at all, to be put out there to solve something that he was sure, was absolutely sure, was going to be blamed on the coloreds, whether it was true or not.

Fleischer tinkered with the wires running to the engine while Willie handed him the tools. Davies, mollified by the sight of the two men sweating in the hot sun and fiddling with his engine, was restored to good humor. He raised his goggles up over his forehead and opened the chin strap of his brown leather flight helmet before sitting back in the cockpit to casually light a Camel, all the while bemusedly watching them.

"Think you'll have it flying before the war ends, mates?" he asked, taking a long draw from his cigarette. "I rather think the bloody thing's run out of coal."

Fleischer straightened up and put his hands on his hips. "You're supposed to keep journals," he said, annoyed. "And turn them over to us, so we know when problems occur. Write everything down that acts funny or even looks funny."

Davies blew a smoke ring over Fleischer's head. "Journals are for schoolgirls," he said coolly. "What am I going to do at five thousand feet with a 109 on my arse and the engine on fire? Send you a love note?" This struck him as extremely amusing; he threw his head back and laughed. "*My dear Yankee Sergeant, I seem to be crashing at this most inopportune moment. . . .*"

Fleischer opened his mouth to argue, but was interrupted by the sound of a jeep screeching to a halt behind him. He spun around to see Major Seekircher jump out, leaving the jeep running, and the door hanging open like a yawning mouth, as he stormed over to Davies.

"Sergeant Davies," he started.

Fleischer backed up and saluted, as did Willie. Seekircher returned the salutes. "Finish what you were doing, Sergeant," he said to Fleischer. "I want this plane flying." He turned his attention to Davies. "You!" he said. "I need a word with you."

Davies blinked innocently. "A word, sir?"

Seekircher took a deep breath. "Our phones have been very busy these past few days with complaints from the good citizens of Montgomery."

Davies raised his eyebrows, but kept the grin. "That so? Sir?"

Seekircher pursed his lips and folded his arms in a show of authority, though they all knew that the American officers had no jurisdiction over the RAF. None whatsoever. "It is a violation of base regulations to stage dogfights over Montgomery or any other part of this state." He glared at Davies. "It is also a violation to bounce on the local highways or to buzz the local livestock. You've been the cause of several recent auto wrecks, and the area farmers are complaining that the cows have stopped milking from the stress. We don't allow American pilots to fly around in our Alabama skies like a bunch of wild cowboys, and we won't tolerate it from the RAF. Any pilot disobeying these rules will be disciplined."

Davies gave Seekircher a broad smile now. "Perhaps another round of calisthenics in your pleasantly sunny climate will improve our morale? We're big fans of your famous discipline drills and formation training. Especially those of my men who've already been in combat. Important for them to know how to stand in a straight line for two hours."

The major's face reddened with indignation. "I don't care," he huffed. "An army is judged by its discipline. We'll see who's running the show on this base."

Davies pulled his goggles off and began to polish them against the front of his flight jacket as the major ranted on. "I knew right away there'd be problems when the RAF sent over flying sergeants, instead of officers who came up properly through the ranks," the major snapped. Davies stifled a yawn. Seekircher stood on his toes to deliver his ultimatum. "I want your entire squadron turning out at oh-six-hundred tomorrow morning for a round of calisthenics."

"Why, Major," Davies replied evenly, "my men wouldn't even be up yet."

Fleischer, struggling to contain his pleasure at Davies's arrogance, stared into the engine. Willie, also trying not to smile, looked down, concentrating on the way his bootlaces were knotted together. The major stormed back to his jeep in frustration, and roared away.

"Intense sort of chap," Davies commented, "isn't he, now?"

Fleischer ignored this remark and continued working on the motor. "Try it again," he finally said, stepping back from the plane. Davies turned on the dynamotor. It rattled to life; the plane sputtered violently and rocked back and forth on its wheels. This was normal for the Vultee Valiant, this wild, eardrum-splitting, bone-rattling shake that worsened in the sky when it hit cruising speed.

"Perfect," said Fleischer. But it only lasted for a moment before the engine died again. "Damn." He pulled on a pair of insulated gloves to protect his hands from the scorching metal, and fiddled with the engine again.

"Glad you're giving it another go," Davies said to him, grinning sarcastically. "I have a vested interest in staying alive. And maybe while you're in there, you can find the cause of the crashes."

"Well," Fleischer replied casually, looking up at him, "we do know what's causing a lot of them."

"And what might that be?"

"The way you Brits are flying them."

Davies raised his eyebrows and studied Fleischer for a moment. "Welshmen," he finally said. "Now, if you lads can impress me with your American know-how and actually fix this kite, I'll buy you both a Fuller's."

"Might be the mixture control, sir," Willie suggested to Fleischer. "The flyboys always have a problem with it."

"That's what I was thinking," Fleischer replied, then gestured to Davies. "Let me in there." Davies jumped out and pulled off his helmet, his light hair drenched with sweat. Fleischer climbed into the cockpit and sat down. He examined the controls, turned a few dials, turned the engine on. The plane shook back to life with a huge puff of smoke before he shut it down again. "Yep," he said to Davies. "Nothing wrong. You must have confused the mixture control with the propeller control, while changing from low to high pitch. The mixture control was in Idle Cutoff. It's a common enough mistake, but it stops the engine." Fleischer gave it a satisfied pat and turned it on again. "All you needed was a little American know-how," he shouted over the roar and gave Davies a sly smile before turning off the plane.

The two exchanged places once again, Fleischer back on the ground, Davies in the cockpit. Davies pulled his goggles down over his eyes and turned on the engine. It shook awake. "Ah yes, the Vultee Vibrator," he yelled over the noise. "I've got a milk shake in me bollucks from flying this thing!" He gestured to Fleischer. "Why don't you check your maintenance work firsthand, Sergeant? Take a spin with me. If you trust it, I guess I can trust it."

Fleischer bristled at this. "I have confidence in my work," he yelled back. Davies simply smiled and waited for an answer to his invitation.

Fleischer looked over at Willie, then back at Davies, back and forth between the two men, before finally climbing into the second cockpit, right behind Davies. "Wait for me, Jackson," he called down just before closing the canopy. "We'll be back in a few minutes. Gonna teach this limey a thing or two about flying."

The plane raced down the airstrip, the prop spinning into invisibility, the silver body swaying from side to side, before it lifted off in a great metallic drone. It climbed to the white clouds; the sun glinted off its shining wings. Willie swallowed hard watching it, a silver jewel slipping through the blue sky, easing in and out of the white puffs that hung high over the airfield. He wanted to fly. He wanted to fly so badly.

The plane went into a steep climb, turning at the same time, a chandelle, then it spiraled back down, only to lift up again. Suddenly it stalled and dove toward earth, and Willie sucked his breath in sharply and waited. The plane banked at the last minute and climbed again. Davies was playing games, Willie realized. The climb was followed by a snap roll, a spin, and a Cuban Eight. A moment later he had to throw himself to the ground as Davies buzzed over him to a landing. Willie got back on his feet and brushed himself off. He walked toward the plane as it rolled to a stop about fifty feet away. Davies lifted the canopy and pushed his goggles to his forehead, still smiling. Fleischer slowly climbed from the rear cockpit and jumped down onto the tarmac, then hunched over his boots for a moment, his face pale.

"Enjoy the ride?" Davies asked him, innocence written all over his face.

Fleischer straightened. "Motherfucking son of a bitch *limey*. Motherfucking *Welshman*," he spat out, then straightened his shoulders and beamed. "I *loved* it."

Chapter 15

The offer of a Fuller's was hard to forget.

"We need to collect our debt," Fleischer said to Willie. "I'm not sure what a Fuller's is, but I think Davies promised us a couple of beers, and I want mine." It was the end of their shift, and Fleischer had just dismissed the men from the wash rack. The September evening felt cloying; the threat of rain hung in the air, collaborating with the flattening heat. They were in fatigues; great rings of sweat rimmed their armpits and made dark shields across their backs. The thought of a cold beer was irresistible. Davies had dropped by the wash rack more than a few times to remind them he would be more than happy to pay up his debt to both Fleischer and Willie.

The problem was, there was no place the three of them could have a drink together. The airmen's club on base was restricted to whites, as were all the USOs in Montgomery. And rarely did the Americans mix with the RAF cadets in the first place.

"I'm not much of a drinker," Fleischer confided to Willie, "but he does owe us."

"Don't worry about it, Sarge," Willie mumbled to Fleischer. He wasn't all that happy to be included. He had his own friends; actually, one—August—and though their conversations were sometimes painfully slow, due to August's limited comprehension, they were safe. Colored and white people didn't mix in Alabama. Not if they didn't want trouble. And it seemed to him that Fleischer just didn't get it. He acted like it was just fine to be friends, like he didn't know or didn't care that there could be *consequences*. But they couldn't mix. Colored and white, they just couldn't mix.

"I don't need to go with you guys, anyway, Sarge," Willie said.

They had finished hanging away their gear, Fleischer stuffing his into the corner of his locker, as he usually did; Willie, more meticulous, hanging his on the hook he had carefully installed inside his locker. He propped his face mask over a wad of newspaper to help dry it out and put it alongside his headgear on the top shelf. The early evening sky was already reddening in preparation for the next day's heat, and he and Fleischer stood together, watching a half moon rising in the distance. "It might be easier if you just met the sarge in town," Willie said, shrugging, the inference being, without him. He just wanted to get back to his barracks; this was getting too complicated.

"Well, I wouldn't mind knocking back a few," Fleischer replied. "But that Welshman invited the both of us."

Willie shook his head. "I don't need to go," he said again. It would be a direct road to trouble.

The squadron fell into formation, ready for their march to their barracks. The mess hall and dinner would be their next activity. Willie looked over, wishing he could join them and get away from this conversation.

"Well, there's a movie tonight," Fleischer continued. "Betty Grable. How about we meet when it's over? I'll find the Welshman and tell him maybe we can grab that Fuller's after the show."

There had been posters put up all over the base about the new movie, *A Yank in the R.A.F.*, with Betty Grable and Tyrone Power. The plot sounded pretty stupid, but at least it was a diversion. Willie had been thinking of going with August. Betty Grable was a real looker.

"Okay, Sarge," Willie said slowly. "Maybe I'll see you there." He didn't hold much hope out for Fleischer's social plans, but maybe the best way was just to humor him and keep watching his own ass.

The audience was impatient for the movie to start. The base movie house, packed with both cadets and servicemen, filled with catcalls as the show started with the Movietone newsreel. Armed Forces were fighting in the Philippines. They were rounding up the Japanese in San Francisco; it wasn't going well at all. But the audience didn't want to hear it. They'd had a bellyful of discouraging news, and they wanted Betty Grable. The news focused on France now, the narrator speaking over a scene of German officers enjoying drinks and conversation at a French café with smiling, obliging waiters.

> *While England fights back, France accepts the Nazi occupation. Officers enjoy summer on the Rue de la Paix—*

This released a barrage of commentary from the audience. "Bloody cowards!" someone called out, which, to Willie, sounded distinctly like Lindsey Davies's voice. "What's the shortest list in the world?" another called out and was immediately answered by a chorus from the RAF cadets, "Frog heroes!"

The newsreel continued:

> *The collaborationist Vichy government orders its troops in North America and other French possessions to resist, to the death, if necessary, any British and Allied land and naval forces, if they attack—*

"Little shits!" a British voice commented loudly.

This was barely spoken before it was drowned out by the booing from the French cadets. Offended by both the newsreel and the audience commentary, they rose to their feet, yelling at the screen in French and waving their fists. This provoked a prompt rebuttal from the RAF. Suddenly, there was an explosion of popcorn and Hershey's bars, followed by fists; it was another riot in the making. MPs immediately swarmed the theater, clearing it out. The loud, wavering sound of the base alarm wailed over their heads.

Willie quickly pulled August outside with him. "We'd better get ourselves back to the barracks," he shouted into his ear.

"Yessir," August agreed. "I think it's gotten too noisy for a movie."

"Hey!" Someone grabbed Willie's arm. He froze for a moment, thinking, but he hadn't been fighting, hadn't been part of this. Bewildered, he managed to turn around.

It was Fleischer. Willie's heart started to beat again. "Not quite the entertainment they promised," his sergeant yelled over the noise. "But I can't say I'm disappointed."

There was chaos all around them, with the RAF and French slugging each other to the ground. Willie just wanted to get back to his barracks, but Fleischer walked over to a quieter spot, near a row of jeeps, with a motion for him to follow. Willie and August joined him there. For a minute they watched as the mêlée spread, more shouting, more fists, sirens screeching across the base for more MPs. The fighting between the Brits and the French had almost become routine by now; it had even been spilling into the streets of Montgomery, and the thought of demotions and punishments meant nothing to the French when they got their tempers up.

"I looked for you before we went in," Fleischer said to Willie, gesturing to the movie house. "Where the hell were you?"

Willie eyed him. The guy was either naïve or stupid; it would take Willie a while to figure out which. "We had to go in through the back door, Sarge, the colored door. We been standing in the rear," he replied in a matter-of-fact tone of voice, fighting to keep the irony from it. "That's where we stand, *sir*. You can always find us standing in the back."

* * *

Davies, neatly dressed in his blue flight uniform, came into the wash rack early the next morning with an official-looking black notebook tucked under his arm. Though there was a cut across his cheek, and his nose was swollen and bruised, he was quite cheerful.

"You Brits had better start calming down," Fleischer greeted him. "The brass is out for blood now."

"Well worth it," Davies replied, giving him a toothy grin through a raw upper lip. "I believe I knocked out a Frog or two." He handed the notebook to Fleischer. "But I came here to hand-deliver this to you. Just like you requested."

Fleischer riffled through pages of pencil sketches. Planes flying upside down, a caricature of Seekircher hanging from a wing, French cadets spinning off the props, a bosomy blonde sitting in the cockpit stroking a huge, phallic-shaped throttle between her legs.

Fleischer was irritated. "What the hell are you handing me doodles for?" he asked Davies, tossing it in the trash with a disgusted flip.

"You told me to put down anything I thought was funny, mate, and I think these are pretty funny." Davies folded his arms and leaned against the frame of a Vultee, still grinning. "Now, about that Fuller's. I can't exactly find them in this lovely state of Alabama, but I do owe you a beer. Just name your brand, and I will make it my top priority to find it."

Fleischer shook his head. "You got to take this more serious," he said. "You're the one up there, flying these buckets. I'm just trying to find out what's going wrong. That's my top priority."

Davies sighed melodramatically. "Leave it to you Yanks to take the fun out of things," he replied.

"It's not that I don't want to indulge," Fleischer added, then gestured with his head to Willie, who was nearby, adjusting the dials on the carbon tet. "But we're gonna have a problem trying to include him."

"Interesting setup the good citizens of Montgomery have." Davies shook his head in disgust as he headed for the doors. "They're awfully concerned about us respecting their milking cows, but don't care in the least that half your servicemen get treated like dogs. Looks like I'll have to take things into my own hands."

It was well past midnight, and the three of them were sitting in the office off the radio room. Fleischer had let them through the outside door, in the back, away from the bustle of the night crew inside the hangar. He had also taken the precaution of locking the door to the rest of the hangar from the inside and turning the lights off, just to be safe from being found out by the night sergeant. The only light came from a radium dial wall clock, and they sat quietly in its eerie green glow. It hadn't been easy to meet here. There had been a few cases of sabotage in local waters, an incident in California and another one up in New York—by Germans or German-American sympathizers, no one was really sure yet—and the place was crawling with MPs. Still, Davies had somehow managed to smuggle several bottles of real beer onto the base, along with a bottle of Scotch. The beer was for Fleischer and Willie Jackson; the Scotch for Davies.

"The beer's warm," Fleischer complained with good humor, as he lifted the cap off his bottle with a pair of pliers.

"As it should be," Davies laughed into the darkness. "But don't blame me for the taste. Wish it was Fuller's. You Yanks make a sorry brew."

"Tastes mighty fine to me," said Willie after taking a tentative sip. He relaxed, leaning back against the wall, then took another big swallow.

"Here's to victory," Davies said, putting his bottle in the center. They all clicked their drinks. "I don't fancy speaking German." They fell into silence over the thought of it.

"It does look pretty grim over there, doesn't it?" Fleischer commented. "Think we'll do okay?"

"I hope so, mate," Davies said softly. "When I was drafted, I was glad to get out of the coal mines, you know, and fly. Poor blokes like me ordinarily never get a chance in the RAF. But the way the war's going, those mines are looking awfully good right now."

"I wanted to fly," Fleischer muttered. "But I'm color-blind."

"I wanted to fly, too," Willie said softly, aware that it was dangerous to share himself, but there was something about the Welshman—he was straightforward, disarming—that made Willie trust him. "They don't let us fly."

"Pity," said Davies. "You think the Jerries give a fig who's shooting at them? An enemy plane is a plane to take down."

He raised his bottle to them. "Well then, lads, I'll fly for the two of you." This was followed by a long swig and an announcement. "To my new friends. Brooklyn and Willie J."

"Hear, hear," said Fleischer, looking pleased with his new nickname. "But we need a name for you, too."

"'Jink' should do it," said Davies. He explained that it was for "jink-away," a British flying term that meant a quick turnaround in the sky. "Just call me Jink," he repeated and they shook hands on it.

Even Willie.

Chapter 16

They met once a week or so, Jink always supplying the liba-
tions. Their evenings wore on pretty much the same every time;
Fleischer double-checked the door to the inner office to make
sure they were secure, passed around the beer, and toasted the
army. Jink usually started them off by complaining how the American brass was treating the RAF cadets, and how the cadets exacted
their revenge by flying in formation, although it was expressly for-
bidden, since it was considered too risky for new pilots to maintain proper spacing. While on duty, they took special delight in
buzzing the men in the airfields below who were drilling in calisthenics, and while off duty, managing an impressive amount
of hard drinking. But their pièce de résistance was panicking
the area's cattle and knocking over outhouses on local farms.

Fleischer and Willie mostly listened, Willie filled with envy
that Jink got to fly. Their own complaints were limited to the
chickenshit orders, Hogarth, and more Hogarth.

One night someone tried the office door and they all jumped.
"Don't know why the day crew locks this damn door," the voice on
the other side complained. The men sat quietly inside, letting

the night fill with the hissing of steam, the shouts of men working outside in the hangar, before their own soft conversation resumed.

"So, you lads working on our little problem?" Davies asked them when they were sure the man outside had left the door. "Had a few near misses last week."

Fleischer groaned with frustration. "I'm changing the pressure settings in the wash hoses," he said. "Experimenting a little. Maybe the connections are just not getting clean enough."

"Funny, I was just thinking how my connections could use a little cleaning." Davies grabbed his crotch. "Hey, Brooklyn, want to join me one of these nights? I got an address from one of the other cadets." He sighed luxuriously at the thought.

"No thanks," said Fleischer. "I got a girl. Trying to talk her into getting married, but no luck yet."

"Tough," Davies said sympathetically, then brightened. "You know, I kissed the Blarney stone once; maybe I can convince her for you."

Fleischer eyed Davies's even, linear features, the sandy-blond hair that fell over his eyes, and shook his head. "Hell, if she meets you, she won't want anything to do with me. She might like blonds better." He ran his hand through his own tight black curls. Davies leaned over and touched it.

"And what kind of hair is this, mate?" he asked solemnly.

"Jew hair," said Fleischer. They both leaned over and touched Willie's head.

"Nappy hair," Willie announced, running his own hand through it.

Davies laughed. "No difference that I can see," he said.

"Nope," said Fleischer, "'cept the heads they're growing on. Hang around with the two of us long enough and you'll be growing a thatch of your own." They clicked bottles.

"I will try to hang around," Davies said solemnly, "but that seems to be entirely up to your American technology."

Fleischer knew what he was referring to. Somehow it always came back to the crashes. They had lost RAF, Americans, a few French, a couple of Canadians. And still no one knew why.

"How about this?" he said. "I can set up a transmitter and receiver right in your plane. If you run into a problem, call me; maybe I can troubleshoot things right from the hangar while you're flying."

Davies nodded. "Sounds all right to me."

Fleischer jumped to his feet and started explaining with enthusiasm. "Good. I'll run a small—"

But Davies interrupted him. "I'm off duty now, laddie, so don't trouble me with details." He burped loudly. "But nothing better go wrong. Not while I'm up there. Or coming down." He reflected on this. "I will tell you this, though, they don't feel right when I bring them in. The ground around here is too soft and cuppy for a decent landing. Damn kites dig a hole for themselves."

"Swamp," Willie added helpfully. "The whole state is swamp."

"No," Fleischer disagreed. "They land hard because they're bigger and heavier than any of the other trainers. You got to fly them like the big planes. That's the whole point of them."

"'Cept the big ones don't turn into lawn darts," Davies said. There was a thoughtful silence.

"I'll find the problem," Fleischer finally said. "And I promise I'll fix it. I'm a man of my word."

They stood up and clinked bottles before polishing off the contents. Except for Davies. He tucked the rest of his bottle of Scotch inside his jacket. Fleischer carefully opened the back door and peered outside to make sure it was clear.

"No MPs," he said softly to the others. "So let's get the hell out of here. Jink, you go first while I spot for you."

"Yeah," said Davies. "The last thing we need is a run-in with the swamp rats." They slipped into the shadows, but then, to Fleischer's consternation, Davies threw his head back and whistled loudly as he marched himself back to his barracks.

A plane fell from the sky the next morning. They could hear it, even in the wash rack, the erratic buzzing over the airfield, the motor cutting out, then sputtering back to life, then cutting out a final, deadly time. The men ran from their posts to the door of the hangar, and watched in horror as one of the Vultees lifted, dropped, lifted, then dropped again, into a deadly spiral, sinking below the horizon of sycamore trees. There was a screech of metal hitting trees and a crash, followed by a high plume of acrid black smoke that swirled ominously up into the clear, bright blue sky. The base alarm wailed to life.

"Jesus H. Christ," Willie said to August. "I hope it's not Jink."

They didn't need Hogarth to tell them they had to salvage what was left of the plane, but he appeared at the hangar first thing the next morning.

"You boys got some work to do," he said, his face split apart by a delighted grin. "Seekircher wants a full report on whatever you find."

Fleischer just stared at him, impassive, quiet, but Willie knew that he was wondering. They were both wondering. They hadn't heard yet who it was, but they knew Davies, who had become a sort of ringleader among the RAF cadets, was fearless, and took more chances than probably any of the others.

"Do you know who it was?" Fleischer asked.

Hogarth suddenly looked solemn, and strangely, they felt relieved by his next words. "It was an American boy," he said quietly.

The plane lay twisted, like a small, glittering, prehistoric animal, broken in two, the oil from the motor spilling across the tan and green swamp grass, wilting it in a dark, wet stain. Willie couldn't stop thinking about the baby birds, when he saw the plane with the wings crooked against the earth, the prop broken off sideways, the canopy cracked in half about thirty feet away, the cockpit smacked off like the plane had been beheaded. Fleischer had taken him and Corporal Charlie Hobbs from the wash rack to salvage what was left, and it took time to carefully sift through the wreckage. Hobbs had done some salvage work on a loan-out to another company, and Fleischer thought it would make him helpful. They had already disconnected the wires from the dynamotor and dropped it into the truck Hobbs had parked behind them. Fleischer was kneeling in the cockpit trying to disconnect the radios, and Hobbs was handing him tools from a kit, when suddenly Fleischer raised his hands and looked at them questioningly. They were covered in a dark reddish-brown oozy film.

Fleischer looked up at Hobbs, then down at his hands again.

"Sorry, Sarge," Hobbs said softly. "They never clean it up too good."

"What is it?" Willie asked. He had never seen anything like it. It was too red for motor oil and fuel was pale yellow; it couldn't be fuel. They both looked over at Hobbs, who shrugged, his lips twitching as he tried not to grimace.

"What?" Fleischer asked. He held his hands up to inspect them again. "What the hell is it?"

Hobbs took a deep breath and looked away. "Pilot," he replied.

Fleischer jumped to his feet, his face contorted with horror as he reeled from the cockpit. Willie stood by the truck, paralyzed. Stood by the truck, holding a joystick that was covered with the same goo. He dropped it to the ground and just stood by the truck, with no place to look as Fleischer kneeled down, kneeled onto the swampy earth, next to the broken plane, and puked his guts up.

Chapter 17

What am I to make of this process that transfers memories from one person to another? These murmurings, these old images that are being pulled from some distant circumstance, half-remembered, half-felt, shaped into words, and whispered across a hospital bed for me to hear and reflect on, until they settle themselves in like bedfellows alongside my own.

I hear Willie's voice in my dreams at night; I hear the wasplike buzzing of a Vultee climbing over the skies, its screaming complaint, then fatal silence as it loses its grip of air and clouds. I feel the heart-clutching horror of the pilot when he knows that nothing can help him, nothing can help him, nothing, nothing.

I hadn't planned for these memories, have no room for them, but I still sit by Willie's bed and listen, with the fascination of someone driving past a car wreck, not wanting to look or know, but directed by some primal force, compelled to stare and acknowledge that something terribly wrong is happening to another human being. I pull myself from a restless sleep in the middle of the night, my heart beating rapid-fire, and sit straight up, just before the plane hits the ground.

I reach over to touch David, but he is not next to me.

Puerto Vallarta, I remember.

And I know for sure.

He is next to someone else.

And I mine my heart, my chest, for some deep, wrenching pain. There is a hollow where the pain should be, and there is a knowing, at arm's length, a certain twinge, that I should feel more.

"Would you mind terribly much to bring me up some tapioca pudding?" Willie asks me as soon as I greet him in the morning. He is out of bed, and sitting in his chair at the window. The newspaper is opened in front of him, a cup of tea next to it. He twinkles me a smile. "The cafeteria makes good tapioca pudding," he says. "Every Thursday."

I stand there for a moment, trying to think whether tapioca pudding is okay for him. What do they put in that stuff? Whom could I ask?

"Is he trying to get you to bring him some tapioca?" The nurse comes in right behind me, rolling a blood pressure cart. "He knows he can't have it. Last week he tried to bribe me." She sets the cart near him and wraps the cuff around his thin arm.

Willie snorts. "I gave you a dollar forty-five. What kind of bribe is a dollar forty-five?"

She rolls her eyes and starts to pump the cuff.

"If I was going to bribe you, I would have given you a million dollars," Willie continues. "Now, that's a good bribe." The nurse shushes him. We hear the hiss of the cuff as she releases the gauge. "Nice," she says. "One-ten over sixty-two." She writes something in his chart and puts a thermometer under his tongue. "Did they check your sugar today?" she asks, then riffles through his chart.

"And I don't recall you returning my money, neither," Willie says thickly, the thermometer bobbing with his words. "One forty-five."

"I'll bring your money back later," the nurse replies. "But not even a million dollars is going to get you tapioca pudding." She adds his temperature to his chart and reads through the morning entries. "Fasting sugar was one forty-two. That's a bit high."

"I will not go to my grave without ever eating tapioca pudding again," Willie says adamantly. "Write that in your notes."

"You know you can't have it. Your blood sugar will climb to the moon." The nurse heads for the door, where she pauses. "You want to give me more grief by putting yourself into a coma?"

"Damn!" Willie slams his fist on the table, and his cup clinks against the saucer. "I'm eighty-nine. A man of eighty-nine has a right to tapioca pudding, if he wants it," he declares, but the nurse is finished arguing. "I'm a veteran. I *fought* for the right to have tapioca pudding."

"Can't they make it without sugar?" I ask her.

She raises her eyebrows and gives me a weary shrug. "Don't look at *me*, honey," she says. "I ain't running home to cook it."

I rented a car. I can't ask Rowena to drive me around anymore; I can't intrude on her life, even though she promises that I am no trouble at all. I have even rented a room at the nearest Best Western, which has orange hot water flowing from the showerhead, stale bagels for their continental breakfast, and an air conditioner that stays on one temperature no matter how you set it. But I can sit in the bathroom late at night and read the newspaper, or lie across my bed and eat a bag of chips with the television loudly tuned to *Cops*, without worrying about keeping Rowena awake. I can release her from the burden of having to again explore and absorb these memories that are being given to me, word by slow, careful word. I can spare her that.

I am eating sour cream potato chips, which don't taste like either chips or sour cream, and watching a musical video on the hotel television station about the hotel swimming pool, because I couldn't find *Cops* on any of their three channels. The pool, according to the dancing mermaids, is closed for drainage repair, and will reopen in three weeks. Sadly, I won't be here for that grand moment; I don't know how much longer I want to remain.

It's been nearly five days. I am assuming that David is still in Puerto Vallerta. He never called to let me know that he got there safely, I don't know where he's staying, and his cell phone always goes to voice mail. I keep thinking of Malachi's words about tying a rope around a horse's neck so that it will stay, but I can't do that. David has to stay because he wants to be with me.

I hear Malachi's voice in my head, arguing. He is asking me how David could know I *want* him to stay with me if I never told him. I argue back—what if I ask him and he says no? What if I allow my heart to commit and David's love is temporary? What if my father had been right all along, that in the end, no one would ever really want to be with me?

Even proposals can be taken back.

I finish the whole bag of chips while staring at my cell phone. I can't call him again.

I drive to the hospital, trying hard not to get lost. I am thinking about Willie. Nothing he has told me so far has changed the way I think about my father. Perhaps I understand a little more about not being allowed to have pets, but that really doesn't matter, since I've more than made up for it. Over the years, I've adopted, and seen through their dotage, perhaps a dozen cats and dogs, four guinea pigs, a three-legged lamb, an ex–Easter duckling that someone had discarded with their trash, and several deaf chickens. The chickens were Cochins—they had long, graceful white feathering on their legs, and when I rode my horse around the farm, I had to carry a pocketful of tiny pebbles to toss at them to get their attention, since they couldn't hear me coming. But they kept the duck company. I still have the duck. He's an Indian Runner, that stands upright like a brown and white bowling pin, and runs after us, squawking for treats, while ferociously attacking our shoelaces. It satisfies me greatly to stand by the back door and watch the duck chase the dogs, which are two rescued pit bulls, the dogs chase the cats, and the cats chase after Malachi for sardines. And Malachi, restoring order, shooing them all back to where they belong. All is well, I think, when I see this chain of command, this natural order of my farm and family.

Why am I staying here and listening to Willie? It won't make much of a difference, and wasn't that why I came? To make heads and tails of the relationship with my father? I can see him in his uniform, thick black hair and pencil mustache. I can still hear his voice. But I am seeing him through a filter of time and the knowledge of the man he became.

My therapist once told me that everything in your personality is pretty much fixed in place by the time you are six. "The cake is baked," she told me. "The ingredients are set. There's very little changing who you basically are."

It was many years ago, and I trusted her. I had started with her because I felt I couldn't love. Just didn't know how.

"What does it *feel* like?" I had asked her when we started. "Is there a sensation that I can look for? Like hot? Or hungry? Or—needing to burp?"

She stared at me for the longest time, then looked out the window as though plumbing the depths of her own heart. "I suppose it sometimes can be hard to identify, but soon you recognize it," she finally said. "It *is* knowable."

I was twenty-eight at the time, and had never cared much to have a man in my life, and it was starting to bother me, mainly because I didn't care that I didn't care. I had a boyfriend in high school, another one in college, but I was pretty much indifferent to them. I thought maybe I was into girls, but I was indifferent to them, too. Then I realized, it was love I was indifferent to.

"*I* don't know it," I said to her.

"Why do you think that is?" she asked. And I knew the answer, though I didn't tell her. I had never felt love. My mother was always working long hours in the little gift shop she owned; when she was at home, she was preoccupied and distant, busy coping with my difficult father. And my father was preoccupied with being difficult. I cared about Sandra, although she didn't make it easy, and I suppose that was love of a sort.

"I don't know what to look for," I replied.

"It's something visceral, that springs from inside," my therapist tried to explain. "There's a portion of loving that makes you want to take care of someone and be with them. Worry about their welfare. Think about them when you're away. Miss them. They become part of you."

"Oh yes," I said to her, the light suddenly going on. "That's just how I feel about my dog. I—I—I *love* my dog!"

Willie talks to me all during the afternoon, and then we watch *Cops* together.

"Whooee, would you look at that?" he exclaims as the criminal is pursued across a highway median after getting his tires blown out by strips of nails.

"I like it when they chase them up on the sidewalk," I add.

"That's good, too," he agrees.

I leave him at the end of the day, after I have lifted the silver lid from his dinner tray, and opened his juice container, and poured him his tea. After I have folded back his newspaper for him, and made sure his curtains are closed. After he has gotten into bed and drifted off to sleep. I whisper good night and leave the hospital, and a thought occurs to me. I get into my rented car and drive to the nearest supermarket and buy him a six-pack of sugar-free tapioca pudding.

Maybe *that* is love, of a sort.

And maybe that's all I can hope for.

Chapter 18

What surprised Willie most about Alabama winters was how cold they were. The shut-your-lungs-down cold that he expected in New York caught him off guard here.

"I thought the South was supposed to be hot," he said accusingly to August as they marched to Hangar Five in formation, shoulder to shoulder, braced against the ripping wind that stalked across the open base like a fierce animal. It didn't help that there was a shortage of winter gear. Sort of a shortage. The white soldiers had been issued cold-weather jackets a month before; the colored units were informed that they had to wait on supplies. They had to wait on wool blankets, too, for their bunks, as the wind peeled under the canvas tents that were being used for their barracks and blasted them in their beds.

"The South *is* hot," August said through chattering teeth. "In the summer."

Ice had frozen across the base in thin gray sheets that cracked like hard candy under their boots. New ice froze on top of it. But there was never ice around Hangar Five, because each day sent another small tide of rainbow-colored chemical-water through the doors, water that oozed in glistening purple and iridescent red puddles no matter how cold the weather got.

Inside, the air was warm and banked around them in lazy clouds of sweet gray steam. The men worked up sweats as they "turned and burned" the planes, hard, fast work that rushed the plane inside the hangar, stripped it, gutted it, sprayed it clean, dried it, assembled it. All they could think of was the next plane. Next plane. Next plane.

Though the rules stated that he didn't have to, Fleischer worked alongside the men, lending a hand where it was needed. Otherwise he could be found fiddling around on something or other. He constructed odd little crafts for his girl back home, made of strands of thin metal conduit and string and bits and pieces of aircraft material, soldered and twisted into necklaces or funny-shaped animals or puzzles. He possessed a wiry energy, a drive that kept him constantly busy, an enthusiasm that puzzled Willie, who wanted nothing more than to finish his tour of duty and get back home. Fleischer always had ideas to improve the cleaning protocol, the hangar, even the tools they were using. He wasn't going to win the war by himself, but he acted like he could if he wanted to.

This time he was working on a large wooden plaque that took him days to finish. Then he hung it inside the wash rack over the front doors. HOUSEKEEPING UNIT, it proclaimed, with a mop and broom crossed like swords underneath and a small model of a wash bucket under their center. Willie hated it. Housekeeping Unit! As if Fleischer didn't mind at all that they were cleaning planes. Didn't mind at all that the other squadrons were called "The Tigers" or "The Eagles" or "The Flying Warriors" and that his men were cleaning planes like scrubwomen. Didn't seem to mind at all.

The green canteen truck slowly rolled from hangar to hangar, dispensing coffee and doughnuts every day. The brass had just initiated it for the winter, for morale, a coffee break every day from ten hundred to ten thirty hours, announced by the "Big Voice," as the base PA was called, as the newest morale booster. The door to the wash rack was opened and waiting, while the men kept a hungry, watchful eye for the truck. A good strong cup of coffee and a doughnut or two would be just the thing to clean the taste of kerosene and carbon tet from their mouths. Fleischer stood at the door, watching as the truck stopped across the road at Hangar Six, where worn-out plane parts were replaced, then at Hangar Seven, where the planes were inspected. Men clustered by their hangar doors, sipping fragrant, steaming hot coffee, grateful for their coffee break. He watched as the truck rolled right past Hangar Five and disappeared across the base.

Fleischer straightened his shoulders. "They run out of coffee?" he yelled to the sergeant standing in front of Hangar Seven. The man shrugged.

"Not that I know of," he yelled back.

It took Fleischer all of a minute to understand. He turned to Willie.

"You're in charge," he said. "I'm gonna get us a coffee break."

Hogarth was in the next morning, beaming. "So, I'm hearing y'all went to the brass to get yourselves a cup of coffee. All the way to *Seekircher* for a goddamn cup of coffee, if that don't beat all."

Fleischer said nothing.

"Well, I'm in charge of setting up the canteen truck," Hogarth continued. "Seekircher told me to pencil you in, and I'm penciling you in for Good Friday next year."

To Willie's surprise, Fleischer said nothing.

The next morning, promptly at ten hundred hours, Fleischer wheeled in the small table from the radio room office. On it was a large Air Force–issue coffee urn, along with a pile of Air Force–issue paper cups, metal spoons, sugar, milk, and a platter of fresh Air Force–issue doughnuts.

"Anyone want a cup of coffee?" Fleischer asked, pouring himself a cup. The men gladly joined him.

At fourteen hundred hours, Hogarth visited them again.

"You are in illegal possession of a coffee urn," he announced loudly. "My orders are to seize this urn and return it to the mess, from which it was removed without authorization."

Fleischer belched in his face. "There are a few doughnut crumbs you can seize, too," he said, pointing to the hangar floor. "Just make sure you do a good job cleaning up. I suggest you use your tongue."

Hogarth poured the milk into the floor drains, snatched up the doughnuts, utensils, and cups, and carried them out to his jeep. He triumphantly lifted the coffee urn. "I am returning this, forthwith, as ordered, to the mess. Any further infractions will be cause for punishment, even a possible court-martial."

"Good thing there's a war on," Fleischer replied. "Otherwise there's no telling what kind of chickenshit you people might worry about."

The next morning at ten hundred hours, the canteen truck rolled past Hangar Five. Willie saw it pass out of the corner of his eye, just shrugged to himself, and went back to work. He would wait for lunch. At least they got lunch.

"Coffee and doughnuts," Fleischer announced, wheeling out the small table from the radio room office. There sat a brand-new, shiny silver urn steaming with hot coffee, alongside the usual paper cups, utensils, sugar, and milk. And doughnuts. A big plate of doughnuts.

The men just stood at their stations and gaped.

Fleischer poured himself a cup of coffee and took a doughnut. "Anyone?" he asked, looking around. The men took off their headgear and looked at each other. Was it a joke? A *trap*?

Willie decided to hell with it; he wanted a doughnut. He stepped forward. "Is that Air Force–approved, Sarge?" he asked, grinning. He always used "Sarge" when he addressed Fleischer in front of the men.

"It's wash rack–approved," Fleischer replied, taking a big bite of his doughnut.

Willie hesitated. He was reluctant to get in the middle of a pissing war between two white men.

"I bought everything at the PX last night," Fleischer explained. "With my own money. They can't tell me how to spend my own money."

The men looked to Willie; he had become their spokesman, of sorts. He smiled. "Let's get ourselves a cup of coffee, men," he said, and headed for the table. The men gladly followed. August poured himself a half cup, filled the rest with milk, and stirred in five sugars. Willie took a doughnut, and was about to take a bite when Hogarth sauntered into the hangar.

He stood by the doors and looked around, his mouth finally settling into a line of fury. Willie quietly put his doughnut down.

Hogarth glared at Fleischer. "Y'all think you're a wiseass, don't you, *Fly-shit!*"

"You have no jurisdiction here." Fleischer stepped up to face Hogarth.

"I have jurisdiction to check this base for safety violations," Hogarth replied, "and I'm checking this urn." He poured the coffee out, unscrewed the bottom, and checked the wiring.

"If it doesn't pass inspection," Fleischer said coolly, "I suppose I could complain to the supply sergeant that the Air Force is selling defective items in the commissary."

Hogarth studied him for a moment, then glanced at the urn. "You got this in the *commissary?*"

"Our very own commissary, on our very own base," Fleischer replied.

The urn passed. The paper cups passed, the milk passed, the doughnuts passed. Hogarth stood there for a moment, pondering his next move.

Fleischer moved closer to him. "Get the hell out of here," he said, his voice low and deadly.

"I don't take orders from you," Hogarth started, but Fleischer suddenly snatched a doughnut from the table, grabbed Hogarth's hand, and squashed it into his palm, squeezing the man's fingers around it in a hard grip.

"Pulleeze don't leave without a doughnut," Fleischer said. The men crowded forward, forming a semicircle around Hogarth and Fleischer, standing shoulder to shoulder. Hogarth's eyes took them in, and his face turned to chalk. Fleischer grabbed his arm, bending it behind Hogarth's back, and marched him to the hangar doors.

"Let's see if I get this Southern hospitality thing right," he hissed into Hogarth's face as he pushed him outside. "How's this? Come back again real soon, *you all.*"

For some mysterious reason, Fleischer's weekend passes were cancelled for the next two months.

"It's that bastard, Hogarth," he complained to Willie, who knew better than to reply. He knew Fleischer was right, but there was nothing either one of them could do. Things had their own protocol in the South, and nothing they could do would ever change it.

The coffee and doughnuts story didn't surprise me at all. I can remember my father championing the underdog many times as I was growing up. He loved challenging authority and took a malevolent glee in winning. He started petitions to get the cop on the beat where our house was, special orthopedic shoes because the guy's feet hurt in his uniform shoes. He got the city to put a No Afternoon Parking sign outside a neighborhood store belonging to an elderly butcher, enabling him to have a clear path for delivery trucks. All that relentless energy, boundless and burning, ready to turn a cause into a case into a victory.

And when he came home, the light dampened in his eyes, the vitality drained, the cold, distant anger returned. He set his lips into a tight line and locked himself in the basement to tinker with his electronics and tune out his family and keep the pain at bay.

Chapter 19

It seemed to Willie that Fleischer spent most of his time in the radio office, bent over the small workbench, either tinkering with sketches that might fix the Vultees, or working hard on one or another of what he liked to call his "projects." This time he was twisting fine, hair-thin silver-gray tungsten wires around tiny pieces of galena crystals, the polycrystalline semiconductors he had salvaged from the dozens of old crystal sets that had been discarded on base after somebody was finished experimenting with them. The galena crystals were suspended from woven strands of tungsten, their gray metal shining against the silver wires in a strikingly delicate pattern.

"What is that for, Sarge?" Willie pointed to the array of sparkling crystals that were gathered on the bench.

Fleischer picked up a few crystals and wiped them against his shirt to polish them. "It's a gift for my girl. A necklace. She loves it when I send her stuff like this. Just loves it."

Willie shook his head over the electronic jewelry. "Mmm-mmm," he replied with a mild sarcasm that was lost on Fleischer. "I'll just bet she does."

* * *

Better than the radio stations that played country songs filled with heartbreak all day long was the special station that carried the talks between the pilots on their training flights and the control tower. Fleischer had illicitly wired the wash rack radio to a loudspeaker so that they could pick up transmissions and hear what was happening in the skies above them. He took notes— he was always taking notes—trying to match performance and complaints with the problems he found on the planes when they cleaned them.

A week earlier, he had put a requisition in to advance the pressure on the benzene hoses.

"Maybe the pressure isn't strong enough to knock off all that oil," he had explained to Willie. But the brass held firm. Seekircher even made a special trip to Hangar Five to tell Fleischer that the pressure gauge was set by Vultee, approved by Colonel Fairchild, and that there would be no deviation. Just concentrate on cleaning the planes, he said, and send them back out. Solving the crashes wasn't part of the job description.

"They're not worried, because they're not the ones flying," Davies commented darkly to Fleischer one night during a drinking session. Fleischer had been complaining about Fairchild's resistance to any change of wash rack procedure. "They can always order up a new set of planes."

"Maybe you should put in for something else," Fleischer answered. "Until I figure things out, Jink, maybe you shouldn't be flying."

Davies's head jerked back in indignation. "Not fly?" He gasped. "I love to fly! I love it. Besides, it got me out of the mines. Do you know how many in my family have died in the mines? I'm ever grateful it got me out of the mines."

Fleischer looked down and shrugged, embarrassed. "I just don't want anything to—you know—happen—to—" There was an awkward silence.

"I guess like my trombone playing got me out of Harlem,"

Willie broke in. "I played professional for a while. It got me out of a life of trouble."

"Trombone! You don't say!" Davies's voice rose with enthusiasm and relief at being able to change the subject. "I play the valve trombone, myself!"

"No kidding!" Willie was pleased that he and the Welshman had something in common. "Ellington is using the valve trombone, you know. You can get those quick changes from B flat to B natural that you can't get on the slide."

"It *is* a challenge." Davies nodded.

"Before I got drafted, I was trying a plunger on my slide trombone," Willie said. "You know, like 'Tricky Sam' Nanton. Only I can't get his 'voice'."

"He's sure one of a kind," Davies agreed.

Fleischer gave them both an impatient look. Music talk bored him; he'd rather discuss the new radar technology. He leaned forward. "Jink, you probably don't know this," he casually dropped into the conversation, "but I, myself, play the flazoo."

"The what?" Willie and Davies chimed together.

"The flazoo," Fleischer said evenly. "It's a toilet paper roll, and you cut holes and hum through it." He pulled another cap off a bottle and took a deep drink. "Now, let's stop wasting time talking and slide some beer down our throats."

They heard the French boy go down not long after that. Heard him in the radio room, his voice coming out of the illegal wash rack radio in a wild, frantic staccato French. They didn't understand what he was screaming, but one of the men, from Louisiana, spoke a sort of bayou French.

"He says the equipment is going crazy," he translated for Fleischer. "He's trying everything. Doesn't even have time to open his chute."

It ended in a crash of angry static that echoed across the hangar and stopped the men in their tracks. They had to clean him up, too. The next day.

Seekircher dropped by the day after that. August was, as usual, the lookout. His job, of pushing the planes into the wash rack, gave him the advantage of being outside most of the time. His second and most important job was to give Fleischer enough warning so he could turn off the receiver in the radio room.

"Visitors," August yelled, just the way Willie had taught him. It was hard for August to understand things, but if you told him slowly and carefully what to do, he did it well.

As soon as Fleischer heard August's warning, he flipped the radio switch from intercept to its regularly scheduled country-western heartbreak, silencing the tower voices and leaving nothing but the sound of the smoke and steam and clanging of planes along with the Delmore Brothers singing about how they were Layin' Down Their Old Guitar and Tellin' the World Good-Bye. Just in time, too, as Major Seekircher stepped into Hangar Five.

"Fleischer," Seekircher started, "remember your plan to change the pressure in the wash hoses?"

Fleischer nodded. "Yessir."

Seekircher made a face. "Well, to hell with Vultee, vary the pressure. See if it helps. At this point, we'll try anything. Just don't mention this to Fairchild. He's afraid to piss, since he's been bucking for general. It's just between us."

"Yessir." Fleischer saluted, then pulled out a clipboard filled with notes to show Seekircher what he had been planning. Seekircher took it from him and looked it over carefully. There were pages filled with pressure graphs, sketches of the Vultee, and modifications of wash rack procedure. Seekircher ran his thumb up and down each page, quickly scanning the contents.

"You put a lot of thought into this," he said.

"Yessir." Fleischer nodded. "And if these ideas don't work, I have another approach."

Seekircher handed back the clipboard. "Proceed," he said grimly. "Try these changes, and then send your reports directly to me. At this point, we have nothing to lose."

Nothing more to lose except the three or four pilots whom they were already losing almost every week.

The Brits were on the flight line today. Fleischer had the radio turned on; the men were working hard, but their attention was on the broadcast chatter. They liked listening to the British pilots as they flew, because for all the commands and injunctions and reprimands, the RAF cadets still did pretty much what they wanted once they got into the sky. They had been ordered to perform regulation maneuvers today, but things were sounding more and more like a dogfight.

"Coming in tight. Show me a big smile." Willie recognized Jink's voice.

"You can do better than that," a second Brit replied. They could hear the whining pitch of the engine as it complained its way higher into the sky.

"Flatten out, flatten out," yelled a third voice. "You damn near hit me."

"Gonna do some hedgehopping," said the second pilot, meaning he was bringing his plane in low.

"Check your six," the third voice warned. He meant that he was close on the other's tail. The men in the wash rack listened to the pilots taunt each other, listened to the engines humming, the laughter at near misses. Fleischer was smiling with satisfaction. He had fine-tuned these planes like Swiss watches, and he liked hearing them being put to the test.

"Angels four," Davies reported, meaning he was four thousand feet up. "Nice view." His tone of his voice changed suddenly. "Bloody hell," he suddenly yelled. "She's not responding. I can't keep her nose up."

Fleischer stiffened. Willie handed his hose off to the man next to him and immediately joined Fleischer in front of the hangar.

"That's Jink," Fleischer said to Willie.

"I know," Willie replied. "But if any flyboy can pull it out, he can."

"Bloody hell," Jink was yelling. "Bloody hell." The engine went quiet; the men shut down the hoses to listen. You could hear a pin drop in the wash rack.

"Looks like I'm going to get a faceful of your special swamp," Jink yelled. "Bloody hell!"

There was an earsplitting roar, the *twang* of metal. Several minutes of silence.

"Oh God," said Fleischer.

"Amen," said Willie.

Then Jink's voice again, first dazed, then strong, followed by a loud laugh. "That was a bit of a dicey-do. Landed in some treetops. Sorry, mates, I think I pranged your kite."

Chapter 20

"Pranged?" Fleischer kept repeating. "*Pranged?*"

"Enough now, mate." Davies took a long, soulful drink from his ever-present bottle of Glenfiddich. "I've had my fill of flak from my CO. Broke? Smashed up? What *do* you Yanks say?"

"Busted," said Willie.

They were sitting in the office, zero hundred hours again, in the dark again, and drinking. Again. They had become an odd trio, different accents, different colors, different personalities. Fleischer was wiry, quiet, and serious, Davies, brawny and fair, was a cutup, while Willie, dark as a Hershey's bar, was suspicious, worried. Not friends exactly, but drawn together by their interest in electronics and planes and flying and the war, and where it was all going, and a little bit of music even, thrown into the mix.

"Pranged!" Fleischer snorted. "You'd think they'd teach you Brits real English."

"Welshmen," Davies corrected him.

"Well, pranged or not," Fleischer said, "what the hell happened up there?"

"I don't know." Davies grew uncharacteristically somber. "She just started pulling from side to side as soon as I started cruising. I hit about two hundred twenty-five or so knots. The brass hats are blaming it on me, you know, that I was buggering around, but I swear, I was just cruising when the stick went dead."

"You scared of going up there again?" Willie asked him. "You know, after this?"

Davies snorted. "I'm keen as mustard to fly again." His voice went soft, his words coming out in a reverential whisper. "It gets in your blood. It's like—the plane is your body, though your mind, your mind is flying ahead of the plane. You got to fly ahead of the plane."

Willie leaned forward, almost like he was going to pray. "I know what you mean," he said reverentially. "Like music—you got to see the notes that are coming ahead, all the while you're playing the notes in front of you. You got to be ready."

"Yes, music." Davies nodded enthusiastically. "You got to fly like you're playing music. Your body does it, automatically, but your mind is way ahead."

After that, all they talked about was music. They were drawn together by the music.

At least Davies and Willie were. Davies liked the jazz that was coming out of the States, his favorite song being Ellington's version of "Take the 'A' Train," though Willie mentioned that he preferred the one by the Delta Rhythm Boys. They talked about Count Basie, Jelly Roll Morton, and Jack Teagarden, who also played the trombone. They always talked music until Fleischer would go crazy and tell them to shut up. He had a tin ear, he said; all music sounded the same to him.

Fleischer became obsessed after Davies's crash. He changed the pressure settings for the hoses practically every day; he took notes. He had the men send the planes through the drying procedure twice before they got his okay to reassemble them; he crawled up and down every inch of every plane, balancing across the forty-two-foot wingspan, climbing the eleven-foot frame, testing the bolts on the round barrel of its Pratt and Whitney engine, running ground checks by revving the engines on the bench. Finding nothing. There was no hydraulic system—the large flaps were operated by a crank-and-pulley system—and no retractable landing gear, so he focused on the engines. And by every standard, the engines looked fine.

"I don't get it," he confided to Willie one morning after the second crash in as many days. "Okay, it was another Brit and he was buzzing a few cows, but they do that all the time."

"He didn't pull up fast enough," Willie replied. "Smacked right into a tree."

"That shouldn't have happened. Those throttle jockeys are fast." Fleischer's eyes looked haunted. "And the planes should be sharp," he repeated. "They tell me that sometimes the rudders feel mushy, or the gauges go off, or they lose the radio. Sometimes the transmitter cuts out, but okay, they can deal with no transmitter until they land. But when the engines go? How can the engines just stall?"

"Gremlins?" Willie offered. That's what the Brits always blamed their problems on in their journals. The ones who kept journals. *Gremlins,* they wrote in big block letters, *Gremlins in the engine today.* Gremlins in the transmitter. Gremlins holding back the landing flaps. Gremlins in the engine. Fleischer was starting to believe that just maybe the imaginary creatures were real. Sabotage? For months there had been reports of Jerries infiltrating waters off the coast and he'd thought it was confined there, but now he was starting to consider there might be someone right there on base, maybe even a few someones, like a secret bund sabotaging the training . . . he was ready to believe anything.

"Could be that guy from Vultee was right," Fleischer continued, more to himself than Willie. He ran his hand through his hair with exasperation. "They're crashing right after they leave us. Within twenty-four hours. How can that be possible? We're cleaning them exactly to specs."

Willie didn't know. He was starting to believe something that made his skin crawl. That maybe there was someone *in the wash rack* who was an infiltrator. Someone they were working with every day.

They were going to modify the pressure settings on the hoses again. Fleischer had handed Willie a sheet of paper filled with yet another set of numbers. "It *has* to be something to do with the connections," Fleischer said. He had been sitting up all night, staring at the plane in the wash rack, as if it were going to speak to him personally. The men had found him sitting in front of it when they reported for duty early in the morning, sipping a cup of cold coffee, his eyes half-closed, muttering about the connections. "They shoot off a lot of oil. It's got to be gumming the connections," was the way he had greeted Willie. "I really think it's the connections."

When Willie raised the pressure settings, the hoses took on a life of their own, snaking violently from side to side, lifting the men off their feet and jerking them like a bucking bronc across the floor. They held on for as long as they could, before one of the hoses finally wrenched itself out of their hands, spraying carbon tet all over the hangar, and knocking a few men against the walls.

"Never thought I could get wounded just cleaning a plane in Alabama," one of the men commented to Willie.

"I know," Willie agreed. "If things get any worse, we'll be putting in for Purple Hearts."

It took them three hours to clean it all up. Three hours wasted, of precious time. Three hours when they could have turned and burned at least two more planes.

Seekircher came in at the end of the shift and blew a fuse.

"Where are the goddamned planes?" he demanded.

Fleischer looked at him, bewildered. There was one in the wash rack, one being dried, one being reassembled. "They're right here, getting serviced."

"And that's the problem. Fairchild's been on my ass all week," Seekircher snapped, then pointed outside, to the sky. "They're in here getting serviced and they should be up there. Flying."

Orders came down a week later, to change the solvent. Hogarth delivered the news with gusto.

"Gasoline," he announced. "Looks like you guys are going incendiary."

Willie knew what he meant. The flash point of gasoline was dangerously lower than kerosene. That meant it was more explosive; even the fumes were prone to ignite. Vultee, unable to come up with any solutions, had issued the change in solvents.

"Gasoline?" Fleischer repeated. "That's crazy."

"Yep," Hogarth agreed, stepping through the doors of the hangar to the fresh air outside. "Real tricky stuff." He pulled an opened pack of cigarettes from his shirt pocket and tossed it to Fleischer. "Why don't y'all have a smoke on me."

Maybe it was the fumes. Maybe it was the gasoline—slick, silken fluid, its scent that insinuated itself inside their safety suits, the voracious fluid that left the planes clean, grease-free, and gleaming silver. Maybe it was because, no matter how careful they were, it got on their hands, their clothes. Inside their mouths and nasal passages, like they were drinking it. Maybe it was the fumes, but Willie was as sick as a dog.

He was sitting next to one of the steamers, doubled over in a cold sweat, when Fleischer noticed him.

"Jackson, what's wrong?" Fleischer peeled up his face mask and yelled to him.

Willie just sat there, holding his guts. Fleischer tapped him on the head.

"Are you okay?"

"I'm not feeling so good," Willie managed. Fleischer studied him for a moment, then gestured for him to go into the radio room office. "You can sit things out," he said.

Willie walked there slowly, painfully hunched, holding his innards, and sat down on a carton of airplane parts. He sat there until the pain tore at him, slicing through his stomach like a razor blade. He let out an involuntary moan, then another. Fleischer poked his head in.

"Worse?" he asked.

"It's bad," Willie managed.

Fleischer watched him a moment more. "Report to the dispensary. I'll have Randolph drive you."

Willie shot Fleischer an incredulous look. "It's against rules," he whispered. "They don't want coloreds to report to the dispensary."

"You're too sick to sit here." Fleischer signaled to August, who handed off his hose and joined them.

"No," Willie managed. "I don't want trouble. Give me a few more minutes."

"They don't like us to go on sick call, Sarge," August explained. "I think they too busy."

Fleischer looked from one to the other. "Get in the jeep, Jackson," he ordered. "I'll drive you myself."

They weren't happy; the nurse at the base hospital dropped her papers when she saw Willie follow his sergeant into the hospital. Maxwell Field Army Hospital was set up for the servicemen and their families.

"Let me get the—let me get—let me get someone in charge," she stuttered and left them. Willie pressed himself against a wall for support.

They waited. Others came in and were treated, but they waited.

"Take that man to the dispensary behind the hospital," someone shouted from a doorway. It was a sergeant. He rattled the clipboard he was carrying meaningfully. "Take that man behind the hospital. There's a place back there for him."

Willie could barely walk, but he made it to the jeep. Fleischer drove around back, drove to the colored dispensary, a small office behind the hospital. It was bare, except for a few cots and cabinets. And an orderly who was sitting, half-asleep, his chair tipped back against the wall.

"Get the doctor," Fleischer barked as soon as they entered.

The orderly stood up, flustered.

"Get the doctor," Fleischer said again.

"He comes in later—" the orderly started.

Fleischer pounded his fist on a table. "Get the doctor!" he yelled. "Get *a* doctor! Get *any* doctor!" He was screaming now. "Get the doctor! Now! On the double. On the double! The doctor. The doctor. The doctor!" The confused orderly rushed from the room.

It wasn't the gasoline after all.

Willie's appendectomy took place in the hospital, the proper hospital, an hour later.

Chapter 21

The gold lights below me suddenly angle, then thrust into a sharp vertical, piercing the horizon before straightening into the familiar Boston coastline. The plane climbs away from the city. Pale clouds stand in bas-relief against an indigo sky, and we fly through white wisps that leave beads of water along my window. The lights drop behind us, becoming obscured by the darkening night, disappearing into a fog of thickening lavender clouds. We are airborne. We are above the city, then above the ocean, flying from the day, from the past, flying on, as the night reaches and overtakes us.

It is such a miracle, this reaching into the heavens, grabbing just enough of it to stay aloft. This miracle equation of engines and wings and flaps and thrust that keeps us balanced on a ridge of air. One failure, one deletion in the delicate equation, and the sky will immediately betray us, letting us fall, spiral down to an unforgiving earth. But I will not think about that. I need to trust in the miracle once again.

* * *

I put my head back against the hard upholstery and dim the overhead. The engines drone, the plane rocks like a cradle, and it lulls me. I close my eyes, but I see Willie, young, already embattled. I see a white horse struggling to find his place in a herd of black ones who will not have him. I see Malachi, waving to me, his expression unfathomable. I hear my father, "*If you tried hard enough, you might actually get good at something.*" The sound of the engines fade away as I drowse, wondering whether or not David will be waiting. He once promised that he would always be waiting for me, and now it seems that it had been true. He was always waiting for me. But I hadn't heard from him at all this time, and I won't allow myself to think about it. I close off my valves, my pressure valves, and take a deep breath. It's peaceful now. Why hadn't I thought of that before?

I had been gone for six days, and it was time for me to return. I'm not sure whether I will ever come back to Boston; I can't think of that now, either. The pursuit of his story may never be completed, and I'm not sure it is okay. All I know for now is that Willie needed his rest and I was needed at home.

I have to get a taxi because no one is waiting at the airport. David's phone went right to voice mail and no answer from the house phone. Maybe he's asleep. There are no messages on my cell phone.

Everything is in order at home. Even though it is eleven at night, the first thing I do is drop my suitcase on the driveway and visit the barn and my horses. I need to see them, touch them, to stroke the soft muzzles, and playfully squeeze big, rubbery horse lips as I push my face against the hard bones of their foreheads. I kiss each horse good night, then turn out the light before stepping outside into the cool night, to stand under the set of stars that had just been my nearest companions. The ground in front of the barn is raked, every scrap of errant hay is gone, every footprint, except my new ones, scraped away. There are wavy patterns on the ground, made by the tines of the rake. Malachi always rakes like that, like he is weaving the

sand and dirt together, weaving a lock into the earth to keep in-
truders out. All the paddock gates are closed, the wheelbarrows
are neatly turned on their noses, handles up, the rakes are
hung, everything is in order and I let my breath out in a long
sigh. There is a dim light in Malachi's little house. I won't
bother him.

David is not home. I make myself a cup of tea and sit at the
kitchen table in the dark and sip it. I always fancied that if
things changed between David and me, I would know. Like
knowing in advance whether your horse is going to spook. They
tighten their muscles and raise their heads, maybe snort. I sift
back through the past weeks. Nothing. I saw nothing.
  Oh.
  Right.
  He had stopped proposing. My heart drops like a plane in
free fall.
  He had stopped proposing.

Malachi is waiting for me outside the barn early in the morning, wearing his tan cap, tan slacks, and a light blue shirt. I hug
him, and give him a mug of hot cocoa that I'd made before I
left the house, and one of the two bagels that I pulled from the
freezer and toasted and buttered for us. He takes a long sip
from his cup, and stays quiet. We go inside the barn and settle
ourselves down on two bales of hay.
  "I need to tell you something," he says suddenly. "I need to
leave."
  I am speechless for a moment, not sure I heard him right.
"Why? Where on earth would you go?" I finally ask, my voice
quaking. I am more than surprised; I am astonished. I thought
he would stay with me forever. I thought I would give him the
spare bedroom in the house when he wanted to retire, and
then hire someone to take his place running the farm. "I need
you," I say, trying not to let feelings of betrayal color my voice.
  "There is places I got to get to," is all he says.

"But why? Is there something I can do to change your mind?" I ask. "Raise your salary?" I know enough about him to know it's not about money.

"Hell no, missy," Malachi says. "I was gonna leave it all to you anyway."

I smile because I know he doesn't have anything. We're always giving him extra money, but I never cared about the money.

"What is it, then?" I ask.

"Family," he says. "I heard from my big sister, Minnie. She says it's time to come home."

I am surprised. He has never mentioned that he had a sister, never mentioned that he had family at all. He always told me he never took calls from kinfolk. I feel a little jealous.

I can run the farm. I know I can find someone younger, stronger to help me. Someone who won't slap his thighs and laugh at me when I am unceremoniously dismounted from a horse. Someone who won't pull a candy bar from my hand and tell me that my horse would grr-eatly appreciate it if I ate an apple instead. But no one else will make me fig tea, with the sweetest of figs mashed in the bottom, and orange calendula flowers delicately floating on the surface, and hand it to me at just the right moment, without asking whether I need it or not, to calm me down.

I can't imagine this place without him. He did tell me once, a long time ago, that he had "itchy feet" and that he liked to keep on the move. He had also once told me that he had lived on my farm for the past fifty years. What to believe? And more importantly, where could an eighty-one-year-old man go, when he doesn't have anyplace else?

"Why?" is all I can manage to say. "Aren't you happy here?"

"Happiest I ever been in my whole entire life," Malachi replies. And his eyes get a little red and watery.

I turn to face him. "Are you sick?" I ask. "Because I can take care of you. We can get you medical care. I always promised you that."

He shakes his head and grabs a handful of hay, long strands that he weaves into a braid. But he says nothing.

"Why won't you tell me anything?"

He gives me a sharp glance and stands suddenly. The conversation is over. "I don't tell anything, missy, because there's nothing to tell."

I stand up and walk out of the barn to a paddock. I don't understand. He has been with me for so long, I thought I knew him. Or knew most about him, of what he wants me to know. He never spoke to me about his past, but it didn't matter. I had recognized his easy familiarity with horses, his competence, his gentle patience, and that had been enough. And I cared so much for him. Suddenly I need something to do. I grab a horse, just holding the side of his halter, and lead him from the paddock to the barn. It's wrong; Malachi always yells at me to "learn something" and then reminds me to use a lead rope, but I don't care. I can do things any way I want to. I spend a useless day grooming all the young horses. I can barely look at Malachi.

David comes home the next morning. We greet each other somberly.

"Did you find what you were looking for in Boston?" he asks me as he lifts his suitcase from the trunk of his car and carefully locks it up.

"Did you find what you were looking for in Mexico?" I ask, more pointedly. He gives me a sharp look.

The valves are staying closed for both of us.

Now that I am paying attention, I can see it had all been getting too much for Malachi. I spend the next few days interviewing barn help and settle on a young woman named Danielle. She has ridden her whole life, had a pony when she was a kid, can ride anything, just loves horses, blah, blah, blah.

Danielle comes every day to clean the stalls. When she arrives, Malachi pulls a bale of hay outside the barn, returns with a saddle and a small bucket filled with water and a little tan sponge floating on top, and starts cleaning, though the saddle looks pretty clean to me. I lean against the fence and watch. Danielle waves to us, and disappears into the barn. I don't know what to say to Malachi about leaving, and he offers nothing.

Danielle steps from the barn flanked by two horses, one lead line in each hand. I don't like her leading horses like this; it's not safe if one of them decides to spook. Malachi just raises his eyebrows.

"One at a time, please," I call out to her. She nods and puts them in their paddock, shuts the gate, and goes back into the barn.

She comes out with two more black horses, one being Toby, who looks particularly innocent this morning as he gets put in a paddock with his henchmen.

"It goes faster this way," she says, by way of passively arguing with me, then returns to the small barn and comes back out with Lisbon.

"Where do you want him?" she asks.

"In the paddock with the others," I say at the exact same time that Malachi tells her, "By himself. I roped off the far end of the paddock for him."

Sure enough, I see that Malachi has put in temporary wooden stakes, with thin ropes strung across Toby's paddock.

Danielle nods and leads Lisbon to the small, roped-in area.

"It's too small for him," I complain and Malachi nods in agreement.

"But it's as safe as I can make it," he says. "You didn't want him on your lawn."

We watch as Danielle releases the snap from Lisbon's halter and he wanders over to a pile of hay. She clips the rope barrier back onto the post. Toby immediately picks up his head and pricks his ears, and trots the rope line, back and forth, his eyes and face in full alert. Before we can say anything, he jumps the rope, catching it in his front feet and dragging the posts down. He races toward Lisbon, the ropes dragging behind him before falling away, menacing the white horse with bared teeth, ears pinned, and comes to a halt atop the hay pile. Lisbon trots a circle around him, a futile, dispirited trot, before he drops to a walk and heads to a corner of the paddock. He stands there, neck lowered, defeated, far from the hay. I can almost hate him for being such a coward.

"Damn," says Malachi. "I would have sworn it was gonna work."

"Take the ropes away before the whole herd gets tangled," I yell over to Danielle as I run to help her. Together, we pull the posts out, one at a time, and drop them into a neat pile of lumber outside the paddock.

"Poor Lisbon," she says to me, puffing under the exertion of carrying a wooden post. "He better grow some balls, 'cause Toby can eat him for breakfast and still have room for hay." She drops the post and returns to the barn to grab a wheelbarrow and duck inside to clean stalls.

"You're expecting him to do what he can't do," Malachi says, giving a little hoot. "Lissen up: Hardest thing in the world, to do what you can't do."

We sit on hay bales for most of the morning without saying much more to each other. He's cleaned four saddles that didn't need cleaning, and took apart and put back together as many bridles. This tells me that he wants to talk without words actually passing between us. Sometimes we can sit for a whole hour like this, just taking in the sky and the sweet smell of hay and the sight of the horses grazing, in a companionable silence. But today we sit and say nothing, because I don't know what to say. For the first time since I've known him, I don't know what to say to him. Finally I let out a long sigh.

"Where are you planning to go?" I ask.

He gazes at the sky. It is bright blue, and clear as lacquer. "I'm thinking Wyoming," he says. "Or Montana. Someplace I can still work with horses." I am beginning not to believe him.

"I don't believe you. You're going to leave me to work somewhere else with horses?" I tell him. "Besides, do you think someone out there is going to hire an eighty-one-year-old cowhand with a bum leg?" He gives me a goofy grin. "Where does your sister live?" I pursue. "She can't be living in both Wyoming and Montana!"

"She lives far away," he answers without answering.

"So, it's settled," I say. "You should just stay here. We'll keep Danielle on as your assistant."

His mood darkens, and he looks down at his shoes. "Can't, missy," he says. "It'll just be a mess."

"What kind of mess?"

"A personal kind," he says.

"I'll help you with anything," I promise him. "If it's legal, David's a lawyer."

Danielle throws a few squares of hay into Lisbon's corner of the paddock. We watch Toby mosey over, and Lisbon trot away, to the first pile of hay. The two horses go back and forth between the two hay piles, Toby not letting Lisbon rest at either one, exactly the way Malachi and I are going back and forth in our conversation. None of us, equine or human, are getting anywhere.

"Why won't you tell me what's going on?" I ask. I am fighting frustration and tears because I don't want to lose Malachi. But he is resolute. He shrugs and stares at the green and brown mountains off in the distance, the Catskills that surround my farm.

"I just gotta go," he says. "My ghosts have caught up with me."

"You and Lisbon," I say, standing up and brushing the strands of hay from my jeans. I tell him a truth I have only recently learned. "You both have to know this—running away from your ghosts only makes them come after you faster."

Chapter 22

The new foal is windswept.

Maja's foal is a black Friesian filly, with sturdy legs, a stout barrel, and a face delicate as lace. She is the last foal of the season, and Malachi foaled her, even though he said he had to leave right away, even though he said he was running from ghosts.

"You don't have to stay," I had told him dispiritedly, meaning the exact opposite, as we watched Maja fretfully pace back and forth in her stall. "If you have to leave, I understand." Of course, I didn't understand at all.

"I signed on to foal out all the mares, and that's what I plan to do," he said firmly, and I smiled inwardly at this. He hadn't actually signed on for anything.

We stood at Maja's stall door and watched her paw at her straw bedding, then lift her tail and press her butt against the wall. Indications of impending labor.

"She'll probably go tonight," I said. "And then I suppose you'll be leaving."

"A distinct possibility," Malachi replied. "Both a very distinct possibility."

* * *

I leave the barn monitor on; the camera is sending a grainy picture to the small monitor in the kitchen, but since Malachi is sitting up with the mare, I barely glance at it as I make myself dinner. He is an old hand at foaling, and has never required my help, although I have always insisted on standing there to hand him things he doesn't request or particularly need. I couldn't sit with him tonight, though. I could barely look at him, I felt so betrayed.

Maja started to foal sometime as the night slipped into dawn. David had long gone to bed after a nearly wordless dinner, and I was slouched over the kitchen table, with my head resting in my arms, dozing off for the third or fourth time. At various times throughout the night, I had brought Malachi a bowl of tomato soup, a cup of coffee, a can of cola with a cheese sandwich. Just in case he got hungry. Or wanted to talk.

"That mare's going to foal, and I'm going to put on two hundred pounds," he said appreciatively as he took a small plate of shortbread cookies with his tea the last time I went out to the barn.

I glanced past his shoulder into the stall where Maja was making a nest out of her straw. "Do you need anything else?" I asked.

He sat down on a hay bale to relax, balancing his tea and the cookies on his knees. "Don't even need this," he said. "Go to bed."

"Missy, you got to come see this." Malachi's voice booms from the barn monitor, waking me up, and I rush out to join him. "It's a filly foal," he says as I walk toward Maja's stall. "Big one, too. With a big problem."

I look in and catch my breath. She looks deformed, twisted, barely able to stand and nurse. "Oh no! What's wrong with her?"

"Windswept," he says. "The foal is windswept."

I had never seen this before. Instead of arrow-straight, she stands grotesquely curved to the right, like a foal in fetal position. Her neck and back are rotated to the right, her head is cocked, her legs and hips shifted, blown to one side, as though she had literally been caught in a windstorm.

I burst into tears.

"What are you crying over?" Malachi asks.

"She's broken," I barely manage to gasp out. "She's brand-new and she's broken."

"I can straighten her out," he says calmly. "Just let her get some colostrum for now. I'll fix her in the morning."

"What can you possibly do?" I ask through tears. "Look at her! Besides, I thought you had to leave in the morning."

He gives me a steady look; his expression doesn't change. "I s'pose I can hang around 'til I get this done," he says. "I can't leave you with a windswept foal. I'll leave after I put her to rights."

"Where did you learn to do this?" I ask Malachi later that morning as he sits in the stall with the new foal, massaging her tight, misshapen body.

"Oh, here and there," he replies, picking up one of her small hooves and bending it back and forth.

The vet has finished examining both the filly and the mare, giving them shots, checking the placenta to make sure it's complete. Under his direction, I bury the afterbirth so the coyotes don't come for it.

"Windswept," the vet announced as soon as he saw the foal. "Just keep her in a small paddock. Could be a problem." He ran his hands over her body and shook his head. "She might end up being clubfooted. Or with angular limb deformity. She'll be unrideable, if she doesn't straighten. Time will tell." He packed up his equipment and got into his truck.

"Vets!" Malachi snorted after the vet left. "What do they know! I'll have her straight before you can say Johnny-jackrabbit."

"How?" I asked. "When will you get the time—I thought you were running from ghosts." He just flapped his hand at me and went into the stall again, where he sat in the straw, next to the foal. He took her into his large, sensitive hands and began to massage her body.

"Leave us be," was all he said. "You got horses to ride."

Malachi has been sitting on the stall floor with the foal in his lap for three hours, murmuring to her, bending her neck, rubbing her tight little muscles. "You be a good girl now," he says into her ear as he pulls on her crooked legs. "Or we'll have to name you Pretzel."

I am sitting outside the stall on a bale of hay, watching. "How do you know she'll be okay?" I ask him. "How do you know what to do?" I am hoping for a few words from him, something that will tell me about him, let me in. In all the years he has been with me, he hasn't told me much of anything. I don't really know where he's from, or where he'd been. He had mentioned family, but in all the years on my farm, no one has ever visited him. I need to know it all before he leaves me.

He doesn't answer. His hands just slowly knead the filly's back muscles, adjusting them, stretching them, counter-bending her to the left, adjusting her some more.

Suddenly I smell something acrid, foreign. A curl of noxious hot plastic wends its way into my thoughts, even before my nose detects it. Even before I realize that the smell is something burning. I spin around to look down the aisle; nothing. But it is there. I sniff the air like a spaniel. The smell is growing stronger. Black smoke spirals from my tack room and I run toward it.

In the middle of the floor, the coil of the portable water heater has burned through the bottom of a water bucket, burned right down into the rug underneath. I unplug it, grab the smoldering bucket, and throw it out the back door of the barn. It flies into the air and lands sideways in the dirt, displaying a black hole in the bottom that allows a circle of daylight to shine though.

"Totally forgot I plugged it in," Malachi apologizes behind me. "Wanted some warm water to relax her back muscles." I am shaking. He walks back to the tack room and stamps on the still-smoking rug, then carefully pours water on it. I say nothing, but in my mind I am seeing a raging barn fire. The hay, the shavings, the wooden stalls, the horses. My breath is caught inside my chest and I can't speak. Another minute. Another minute, and it would have been too late.

I check on the barn throughout the day, because I am scared to leave it. Malachi has never forgotten to turn off the heater coil before. He has always stood over it until the water was hot, then unplugged it. And now I am checking, checking, all day, nervously eyeing the barn, sniffing the air.

I take Malachi lunch, although it is just an excuse to check the barn again. He is rubbing the filly with a wet, hot terrycloth towel, and I watch him scrub big, strong circles against her body. "Watch how I do this," he says, "and learn something."

I excuse myself and check the tack room. In the middle of the floor is another bucket, filled with warm water; the water heater has been neatly replaced on its hook on the wall. Relieved, I return to him.

"How do you know what to do?" I ask him again.

He shrugs. "Oh, I picked up some techniques here and there." He flexes her joints, one by one. The fetlock, the knee, the shoulder, pulling against them, rubbing them, his muscular hands working deep into her body to take out the spasms. It seems to me that she looks a little straighter.

"You're going to disappear out of my life, and I'll know nothing about you," I say softly, then start to cry. "It's not fair!" I want to tell him that my heart is being bent and twisted, windswept with grief, that he must stay.

His hands stop for a moment, and his dark eyes search mine. "Aren't you a Nosey Parker!" He says it with humor, and affection, I know. I hear it in his voice. But there is a wariness there.

"It's just that—just that—" I can't finish my sentence. I can't tell him that if I could love anyone as a father, it would be him. I just stare at the filly, blinking tears away.

"Worked on a big breeding farm in Kentucky," he suddenly says. "Seen racehorses born like this. Fixed them up, too. A few went on to win some mighty big races."

The thing with Malachi is that sometimes you can believe him and sometimes you can't. "Is that where you were born?" I ask him. "Kentucky?"

He shakes his head. "Mississippi," he says. I am trying to lead him, like a horse getting halter-broken, one step at a time. Or is he leading me? "I was born in Mississippi," he adds reluctantly. "Then I drifted to Kentucky." He pulls the filly to her feet and she stands. Almost straight.

"She looks better." I sniffle.

"You never know what you can do," he says, "until you get it done." And the words remind me of my own father's philosophy, which was so opposite. Cynical and angry, he had always thrown his hands up and said, "*The world doesn't give a crap about anything you do, so why bother?*" and then, to ratchet up the pressure, he would gleefully drop every obstacle he could think of in my path. And I would struggle and strain until I accomplished what I wanted. College, first job, first apartment.

But the memory of my father was becoming more and more of a puzzle. There was Willie, telling me how hard he had fought for his men, yet the man I knew was a defeatist. Willie remembered him as a man full of compassion, battling for what he thought was right. What could have happened to him that turned him so around, like a windswept foal, twisted back on itself; distorted, broken?

I see the foal is standing before me now, her legs straighter, her little hooves pointing forward. I can't help but wrap my arms around her. She is slowly healing. But was there anything that could have healed my father? Straightened his soul? Restored him to the man Willie remembered, the man I never knew?

"I knew I could fix her," Malachi says with obvious pride. "I know all the tricks."

"Did you learn them from your family?" I ask. "Did they own horses?"

He laughs out loud and slaps his thigh at the idea, startling the filly. "Missy, my family didn't even own the dirt we lived on."

* * *

I decided, when I grew up, I would be a writer. I got accepted into college when I was fifteen, having skipped a few grades, and immediately sat down to plan a program that would lead me, at the very least, to the Pulitzer prize in literature. Until my father informed me that I would be paying for my own education.

Fifteen is a little young to have accumulated a college fund, and so I was stuck. I think I had about 150 dollars in a savings account, having spent most of my babysitting money on classical music records. I loved piano music, and couldn't wait to own a copy of Glenn Gould's *Goldberg Variations* or Barenboim's Beethoven sonatas, in which all the reviews said his technique overpowered, and which I thought were just *fervent*. I played the piano, torturously learning "Moonlight Sonata," a few simple Bach pieces, Liszt's "Ständchen," and then "Les Preludes"... wonderful pieces. And though I played them clumsily, they enfolded me, calmed my heart, and lifted me to heaven. My parents didn't see a reason to give me lessons, as my father had no use for music. It served no purpose, he used to say; it doesn't save the world from anything.

I taught myself to play on the old upright that came with the house. I played all the time, the piano becoming my companion, my best friend, my diary, my solace, my passion. Every note was a new word; every passage, a thought. The music would surround me, sometimes so strongly that I almost forgot that I could still be seen by other people when I played. It made life bearable.

Until I came home one day from school and the piano was gone. My piano. My heart. No explanation, no apologies. I stood in the living room for a whole hour, staring at the spot where the piano had been. I didn't cry. I just stood there. And then I swore that nothing would be that important to me, ever again.

"If you can find money to buy music, you can find money for college," my father announced when my first acceptance letter came in. "And don't look to me for help." I wouldn't have dreamt of it.

I did find money for college. I worked three jobs.

"If you're working, you can pay us rent," my father announced. "No one gets a free ride." I wouldn't give him the satisfaction, and so I ran away. At the age of sixteen, I lived secretly and illegally in the gym locker room of the city college I was attending. My mother, busy with her shop, barely noticed I was gone.

And I didn't become a writer for a very long time. I became a teacher first, only because they had a better chance of earning a living.

"She looks almost normal," I marvel to Malachi. And the little foal does. We are out in the paddock, where he's tied Maja to a fence post. The mare watches her baby with anxious eyes as Malachi hand-walks the foal back and forth, a halter on her tiny, deerlike face, and a lead line wrapped around her pumpkin-size butt. Her legs are straight, her neck arches out at the correct angle from her shoulders, her back is almost straight. Her steps follow in a neat line, hind hoof into the print of the front hoof. Perfect. The mare nickers softly, and the baby answers her with a tinny squeal.

"She's going to need a few more sessions," he declares, as he gently leads the filly forward.

"Okay." I move to his side, ready to take over. "Show me what to do."

"Missy, you need the touch," he says and flexes his fingers proudly. "I got the touch."

"But you're leaving," I remind him, hoping it'll make him open up. "Unless you leave your touch behind, you got to show me what to do."

"I ain't leaving nothing behind," he says dryly. The two of us take a few more steps with the foal.

"Afraid the ghosts will find you?" I joke, but he looks at me sharply and I feel bad for saying it. I try another tack. "What if someone asks me about you?"

"You'll know where I'm going after I leave," he says.

"Okay," I say. "How will I know?"

He thinks long and hard about this statement. We are at Maja's side, and her baby stretches her long, elegant neck forward to nurse.

"You will know," he answers. "My sister's coming for me. Minnie."

"How long has it been since you've seen—Minnie?" I ask.

He watches the foal nurse. "They sure need their mama," he says, "but they never care who their daddy is."

"That's horses," I tell him. "People are different. Or should be. How long has it been since you've seen your sister?"

He doesn't answer me.

"Whatever went wrong," I say, "she must still love you if she's looking for you."

There are clouds scudding across the sky, making purple shadows on the ground. We watch the earth and hay in the paddock fall under the weave of dark and sun as the clouds pass. Danielle is singing to herself in the barn while she cleans the stalls.

"She wants to bring me back to the family," he replies. "I don't mind it, missy. It'll be a good thing. She says they'll take care of me, and truth be told, I kind of miss them, too."

"Why didn't you tell me you had a sister? We could have made arrangements for you to see her sooner. Don't you want me to meet her?"

And he turns his face from me, and stares off into the graying sky and the blowing clouds with sad eyes and says nothing more.

Which is an answer, of sorts.

Chapter 23

"We were boys, really," Willie is saying. "Boys."

He had called me from his hospital bed to "chat me up a bit," as he put it. Rowena is working and he was lonely. I was at my desk, working, too, on a new novel, and I reluctantly turn away from my computer screen to talk, but I am annoyed. Doesn't he understand that I work, just like Rowena works; doesn't he understand that at all? Does he call her in the middle of her workday to tell her stories? Does he interrupt her day with pointless memories as he tries to relive the old days?

He wants me to come to Boston.

"I've run out of tapioca," he jokes. "And Rowena is tired of my stories."

"I've got to take care of my farm," I remind him. "My manager is leaving."

"If I could come to New York, I'd help you," he says. "I'm a bit indisposed at the moment, but I used to be good on ladders if you need anything painted." Is he being ironic? Just in case he isn't, I diplomatically refrain from pointing out that ladders might be a little difficult for him to negotiate, since he is ninety and has only one leg.

"That's very kind of you," I reply, "but I think I can manage."

"Well, it's just that I would really like to see you. I don't buy any green bananas, if you know what I'm saying." His voice is full of meaning. "I want to finish my story. So, come soon. *Soon.*"

Is he warning me that he is ill? I know old men talk in code. And before I realize it, I've promised to go.

Two days later, Malachi has partitioned the big pasture with some post and rail we had left in the garage, so that Maja and her windswept filly can graze in peace. I insisted that he at least put Lisbon in with them.

I am leaning on the fence and watching Maja browse through her hay. Suddenly, as though cued by an unseen ghost, she pins her ears and raises her head high to swing at Lisbon, threatening him, telling him not to come near her foal. He just stares. The foal regards him with big, blinking, trustful eyes, before mincing a few dainty ballerina steps toward him. I hold my breath as she stretches her neck out and makes a chewing motion with her mouth. Mouthing, they call it. She is telling him that she is a baby and poses no threat. His eyes are fixed on her, his face alert, ears pricked, his neck rigid. She suddenly retreats behind her mother, only to peek out at him again.

"Pretty soon she'll be arrow-straight," Malachi predicts. "You'll never know she was windswept. But we got to get Lisbon out of there before Maja kicks him to little pieces."

"She won't kick him," I reply. "She knows that he's just a friend."

"She could break one of his legs." Malachi seems not to hear me. "Or he could hurt the filly foal. A protective mama is a force to be reckoned with."

"They'll be okay," I insist. "They know the rules. You know how you always talk about the rules and how horses are full of rules." And I cross my fingers behind my back because I'm not sure what the rules are anymore.

It seems there are rules made by nature. Tomatoes bloom around the same time; cherries grow on trees. Spring always brings new buds and baby animals. There are rules for when lilies grow and die. Rules that keep planes in the sky, and rules that turn vibrations into music.

I understand all that.

But the other rules, the rules made by humans, don't seem to be rules at all. They are just decisions, passed along, like the decision that kept Willie from sharing quarters with the white soldiers or that kept him sitting on a hot train while the rest of the men ate in a restaurant. Those aren't rules; they are whims and notions that spring from hateful ignorance.

When Lisbon decided not to fight back because of the humans who had beaten him, he had made a rule for himself.

And then I realize. *Not all rules have to be followed.*

David and I are talking in code.

He is home and looking tired and a bit rumpled. Even like that, he looks so good to me: straight, sandy-brown hair falling across his eyes; full, arched lips and high cheekbones that make him look a little like a blond American Indian. I need to touch him, to run into his arms and kiss him until we can't breathe, but I remind myself of Puerto Vallerta. And how many times his phone went to voice mail. Wasn't it his choice to end our relationship and start another? Instead, I let him peck me on the cheek and hate myself for my silence. His words are guarded. Mexico was good, work was good, the farm looked good. It was a good idea to hire Danielle. How was Boston?

"Good," I reply.

"Would you be open to a discussion this weekend?" he asks me.

"If there's something you want to tell me, tell me now," I reply, trying to keep the edge out of my voice.

He is a little taken aback by my brusqueness. "I thought we might talk out some issues. Really talk to each other. We've both been preoccupied lately, but I thought we could *talk.*"

"Don't apologize for being busy," I say, then blithely add, "I'll be busy, myself. I'm leaving for Boston again day after tomorrow. Plan to stay for a few days. Maybe we can pencil in a talk after that." There is sarcasm in my voice, which is the way I handle anger.

"I see," he says. There is a tone in his voice that I haven't heard before. "Well, I guess I'll be seeing you around. Let me know when you get back."

"Will do."

He cocks his head to one side but says nothing more. For some odd reason, I feel relieved. Like I haven't betrayed my true self, haven't broken my own rules. And then suddenly I feel awful. Have I hurt him enough for trying to love me? I didn't want to. I don't want to. Yet I can't stop it. How do you make new rules?

That night I reach out and touch him, but he wraps the blankets tightly around his body and turns away, leaving me to lie awake and hate myself all over again. I think back to when I was fifteen, just before I ran away to college. I never dated. My father used to take aside every boy I brought home, hoping for a night out at a movie or miniature golf.

"Why do you want to take my daughter out?" he would ask. "What do you *see* in her? She's nothing special, you know. Why would you want to go out with her? I think you just want to get in her pants."

Mortified, horrified, I would die inside a thousand times over, and embarrassed, the boy would leave. Sandra would always lie that she was going out with a girlfriend and met her dates around the corner. She managed to have quite a few boyfriends and got a lot of action that way. I envied her skills. And her courage.

Maybe my father was truly curious when he questioned my dates. Maybe he was filled with concern for me, but I feel like I am still waiting for the boy to answer. Maybe I am answering for him, but the answer is never good.

David and I have coffee together the next morning and make no reference to the previous night. I ask him to keep an eye on the farm while I am in Boston, because I am getting nervous about Malachi. Danielle has informed me that several times she found the water pump left on because Malachi had forgotten about it. It's more important than it first sounds. If the pump is left on, the hoses could burst and flood the barn.

It shouldn't be all that difficult to keep an eye on things, I tell David. I have Danielle, to feed the horses and put them out into their paddocks in the morning, and to clean stalls and be my eyes during the day. David just has to supervise. Make sure that the horses are all upright before he leaves for the city, and still upright, in their stalls, when he comes home at night. He nods, grabs his briefcase, and leaves for work.

Later that morning his grandmother calls to ask me how I liked Mexico. She is eighty-eight and in an assisted-living facility. "I called to congratulate you, dear."

"For what?"

"Oh," she says. "David mentioned that he was planning to get engaged in Mexico. I sent him my mother's garnet and diamond ring. He was very excited about the trip when I last spoke to him."

"I didn't go," I tell her.

She is surprised. "He sounded so definite." She sighs. "I would love for you kids to get married while I'm still alive."

"Well," I joke, "you saw his brother get married twice. That should make up for David."

I am riding Lisbon. On every side of me, there are woods. The deer slip in and out of ocher trees like whispers, brown against brown; their gray chests, tan legs, upright necks, and dark brown backs look like strips of bark, blending into the cloak of trees. Nature hides them well. Lisbon and I glide easily along the path, my scent disguised by the scent of my horse. The deer continue to eat undisturbed, even though Lisbon is such a contrast, a slash of white against the warp and weave of brown and ocher. His stark, glistening silver white plays counterpoint against the harmony of the woods. Rabbits scutter and zigzag in front of us, unconcerned. I talk to him while we ride.

I tell him that I love him and ask him to trust me. It took me almost two years before I was able to brush his face, touch his forelock. He had been beaten across his head with a pole before I got him; there is still a dent in his skull from his early brutal training, and he would bolt backward every time I tried to touch his face. It was two years before he was able to drop his head and let me touch it. Two years of torturously slow work. And when I thought I had finally gained his trust, he would reel back as soon as he saw my hand move toward his face. I cursed those people who had done this, who had betrayed the innocence of his soul.

"Back off," Malachi would tell me. "Back off. Let him figure things out himself. Let him miss your touch for a while."

And though it hurt me, though my hands craved to touch Lisbon's head and ask him to stretch it down to me, I left him alone. Grooming him, I slipped him treats, talked to him, waiting so long for the day when he would believe in me.

And then, one day, he just dropped his head on command, and let out a long, relieved sigh. I pulled his head to my chest and wept into the soft velvet hair that covered his face, and kissed his awful dent, and held him for a long time. I whispered to him, how brave he was to let me touch him. How brave, how brave, how hard love comes to some of us.

His trot has evened out to a glide as he reaches into the bit. His white ears flick back and forth, listening to the warning snort of a deer. His white, white neck stretches into an arc of submission in front of me. And I am thinking, Lisbon's wondrous flash of white is needed among the dark green leaves and brown trees and russet weeds. You need white to see the brown, to realize the contrast. You need the intrusion of light, so you can see and understand the dark. One defines the other. One needs the other.

Malachi is waiting when Lisbon and I return. His brown leather satchel is packed and standing outside his front door, as if to say "*I mean it. I really am leaving.*" There is a little tag attached to the handle. But Malachi himself is in the paddock with the new foal, wheedling her into walking.

"Why don't you just unpack and stay?" I call over him while I unsaddle Lisbon.

"Just getting things ready, missy," he calls back. "I always like to be ready."

I study him, patient, and gentle with the foal. This is the man who will pick up a live wasps' nest with a stick and drop it into the woods so as not to hurt them, who walks across the barn roof in lightning storms to clear the drains of leaves, who catches mice in one swoop of a brown paper bag to let them loose, away from the barn. This is the man who, when I took a horse in for retraining because he wouldn't stand still for saddling or mounting, leapt onto the animal's bare back and stood straight up with his arms out to the side like he was a circus act and declared, "I don't think you'll have a problem with him."

"I always thought you were the bravest person I know," I say, as he snaps a soft rope through the foal's halter and jogs off. The mare raises her face from her hay and trots close behind him. "And the kindest." He looks over at me, surprise in his face. I take another breath. "You're the one who sent me to Phoenix, to my father. You gave me the courage to do it."

"Why was you so afraid to go?" he calls back, puffing now from the exertion, then coughing hard, but the foal is trotting pretty straight.

"I was afraid to watch him die," I reply, which is true. I had never seen death before. And I had already tried to make peace with my father by swallowing his bitterness and making it my own, so we would have something in common. It didn't work. It only poisoned me.

"Besides," I remind Malachi, "you made me go."

He considers this.

"Stay," I add. "It's my turn to help you."

He caresses the foal's back as though she were his child, too. "Please?"

"You can't help me," he says softly. "But I'll stay as long as I can."

"When is your sister coming?"

He adjusts his tan cap. "Don't exactly know. And that's all I aim to talk about it." He leads the foal away. The conversation is over.

"Well, I need to go to Boston for a few days," I call after him. "I'm taking a night flight day after tomorrow. How about you call me when your sister arrives and I come home right away?"

He stares at the foal as she nurses. He watches me as I deliberately take Lisbon and lead him into the paddock with the mare and foal and turn him loose. Lisbon walks to a pile of hay. The mare raises her head and pins her ears at him, then takes a step or two, pretending to charge him. He pins his ears back and I hold my breath, but it all comes to nothing. Malachi's eyes meet mine.

"I would like you to stay if you can," I say. "I can't trust anyone else."

"I suppose you can't," he agrees softly. "I'll do my best."

Willie calls again to make sure that I am really coming as promised. "I am waiting for you," he says.

"I'll be there, but for now, I need to get some work done."

He sighs. "We had such baby faces," he says, trying to engage me. "You know?"

I think back to the old pictures in the box and agree. The faces are all too young, black faces, cheeks and foreheads reflecting white from the flash of the camera, their eyes holding a moment of blaze. Young faces that are somehow not youthful; the eyes are too closed off, too guarded.

"Did you see your dad's picture?" he asks. "He was in there." That's why he really called.

"Yes, I did," I say with forced enthusiasm. "Yes, I did."

"And Jink," he adds. "We took a picture of him in the plane." I have a quick flash of the picture Rowena had tucked away, of the laughing pilot with sandy hair. Willie stops talking for a minute, and I draw a breath, hoping it's the opening I need to tell him I can't talk right now.

"They were all going out on night navigation training," he continues.

"Who were?" I ask, thinking, *Here we go again.*

"The Brits," he replies. "They had to get certified on night flying. You're flying blind at night. Nothing but the sky and the stars."

Despite myself, he is drawing me into his world again. I can picture it. The black night sky above, with not nearly enough light to steer by. Only an interminable length of darkness, a void, stretching out in front of you, without end.

"Is this near the end of your story?" I suddenly feel impatient. I don't need to hear all of this winding, endless loop. My father's gone. This is the history of old men. My first mistake, really, was to go off to Boston the first time, and now I see myself as a captive audience whose purpose is simply to keep an old man amused. I have to draw this to a close. This time when I get to Boston, I will tell him my time is limited. And I can't come back.

"Yep, flying blind," Willie adds. "It's tricky business."

"Yes," I agree. "By the way, I'm taking a night flight to come see you. We can talk when I get there."

"Sorry you're flying at night," he apologizes. "The night sky keeps its secrets, you know. You can't trust the night. Tricky business."

And I think about Malachi wanting to leave, me wanting David without the risk of loving him, Willie needing to tell me things that maybe I need to hear.

All those needs.

It's tricky business.

Chapter 24

I'm not crazy about the way Willie looks. I came right from the airport to see him. He is in his wheelchair, waiting for me, thinner, his movements slower. I put the package of tapioca I had brought from home on his lap.

"Thank you, darlin'," he says, looking eminently satisfied. "You made an old man very happy. Is there a spoon?" There is. I give him a plastic spoon from the plane.

He smiles. "Don't tell the nurse. This is our little secret."

"The nights are too quiet." Jink put his bottle of Scotch on the ground next to where he was sitting, pushed a piece of hair back, clasped his hands behind his head, and leaned into them. The pale green radium dial on the wall clock gave the office a ghostly look. Its luminescence played across his face, sharpening his cheekbones and cutting worry lines into his forehead. The men sat in the emerald shadows and drank quietly. "I don't trust quiet nights."

"Are you complaining?" Fleischer asked him. "You need a couple of Messerschmitts over the base to liven things up?"

They were drinking with high hopes of getting "blotto," as Jink had optimistically put it. A few weeks ago, Fleischer had prevailed upon Seekircher to write up extra duty orders so that he and Willie could work on the Vultee problem, though the orders mostly served to make them look industrious while getting them out of the barracks at night. They were risking court-martials, they knew, if they were caught drinking, but it was worth it. It was the only time Fleischer could allow himself to relax, and it gave Willie the opportunity to talk music and Jink to talk flying.

The sound of planes overhead rattled the hangar. "Canadians," said Jink, looking up at the metal ceiling, as if he could see through it. "They're getting qualified on night navigation."

"Got a craptogram that you guys are on the line for tomorrow night," Fleischer commented, making reference to a rumor whose source was the latrine.

"None too soon." Jink's voice had a catch of excitement. "Soon as I qualify, they'll be sending me home to fight."

"Welshland?" Willie half-jokingly asked. He wasn't all that sure where a Welshman actually came from.

"Wales. Swansea," Jink explained, his voice softening with memory. "Twenty-two Graiglwyd Road, that's my address. I hope my family's still there. With the bombings and all."

"They all talk like you?"

Jink laughed. His voice echoed against the metal walls and fell off into the darkness. "Worse. They speak *Cymraeg*—Welsh." He pronounced it *Comrye-eeg;* Willie made him repeat it four or five times because he couldn't get it. Jink took another swig from his bottle and belched. "Wish I was home, for sure."

Willie had never known anyone like Jink. He was everything Willie wanted to be, and knew he never would—could be—independent, free, indifferent to authority, indifferent to criticism. Lindsey Jink Davies was his own man. Even in the skies, he was his own man. Especially in the skies; he defied the skies.

"Either one of you miss home?" Jink asked.

"No," Fleischer replied right away. "I have nothing there except Ruth, who may or may not be my girl." His voice was low, heavy with thought. "My parents sent me to New York to live with an aunt when I was eleven. They're still in Poland. Most of my family is still in Poland."

"Well, I suppose I miss New York," said Willie. He missed Harlem. The knots of people who walked in the streets, who strolled along without watching to step off the curb, people who said things he understood. He missed the African Methodist Episcopal Church his mother attended on Wednesdays and Sundays wearing her big pink hat, and he missed the restaurants where a man, even a colored man, could sit wherever he wanted and eat.

"Wonder if I have a home left," Jink added ruefully. "I haven't had too many posts from my family. They were getting bombed pretty badly when I left." He sat quietly for a few minutes. "Last I read, me mum was worried. Thinks I got too thin." He patted his stomach. "She should see me now, after eating all this Yank food."

"Too bad you can't send her a picture," Willie said, and Jink shot him a thoughtful look.

"I would," he said. "If I had a camera."

"I have a camera," said Fleischer. "Got it in payment for fixing a radio. It's pretty old, but I tinkered with it and got it working. We could set you up in one of the planes."

"Brass hats will put me on jankers if I get caught doing something wrong again," Jink replied glumly. He already had been disciplined a few times for infractions.

"As I was saying"—Fleischer seemed not to hear him—"right after it comes out of the wash rack. We could use someone to rev the engines, so I could do some diagnostics. I'll write up a request for a pilot. Come by tomorrow around seventeen-hundred." He leaned over and clicked Jink's bottle. "And don't forget to smile."

Night training always started out from Montgomery. The cadets would fly from Maxwell Field to Jacksonville in broad daylight, then back to Montgomery under the blanket of night. It was a simple trip, even flying blind; the Americans had breezed

through it, followed by the Canadians and the Greeks. And
Fleischer had been right; the Brits were up on the schedule,
twenty-four of them scheduled to fly the next night. A simple
trip.

Hogarth bounced into the wash rack early the next afternoon, cheerful as a Christmas display.

"Looks like you get to use that technical talent y'all keep
bragging about." He waved a set of orders over Fleischer's
head. "The rest of us will be tucked nice and cozy in our bunks
while y'all get all the fun of pulling night duty in the swamp."
He giggled at the thought, his upper lip pulling back to reveal
large white teeth, which, with his pug nose, made him look like
one of the guard dogs.

Fleischer looked over the orders. He, and one assistant of his
choosing, were being assigned to support the RAF radio spe-
cialists in setting up and monitoring the field radios during the
Brits' return flight, which was scheduled for twenty-one hundred hours.

"Don't know where you're gonna pull an assistant from."
Hogarth made an exaggerated effort to scrutinize the men
working in the hangar. "You know how the nigras get spooked
at night."

"I'll take any one of my men over a piece of Southern shit,
anytime," Fleischer snapped.

Hogarth drew himself up to his full five-foot-five height and
pushed his face into Fleischer's. "I've got a fist with your name
on it," he snarled. "It's just aching to fix your big Jew nose."

"I think I hear your wet nurse calling," Fleischer growled
back. "Her titty is getting cold." Hogarth pulled his fist up, so
did Fleischer, and for one raging moment, Willie thought they
were going to slug each other. He quickly looked away. It was
safer.

The men were faced off like two bull terriers. "You ain't
worth the three seconds it would take to lay you flat," Hogarth
rasped.

"You ain't worth the piece of toilet paper they would need to wipe you up," Fleischer replied.

Their bodies arched in fury, faces red, veins standing out like maps in bas-relief.

"You ain't worth a court-martial," Hogarth finally declared, and after a final glare at the entire platoon, left.

The tension in the wash rack dropped about thirty notches. Fleischer straightened his shirt and readjusted his pants. He ran his hand through his curly black hair as he watched Hogarth pull away in his jeep. Then he turned to his men, who had stopped working to stare at him like a group of cats.

"Back to work," he ordered. "Back to work. There's a war on, don't you know?"

Willie practically threw himself against the side of the Vultee they were cleaning, hoping he'd blend into the gray paint, but it was too late.

"Jackson," Fleischer called Willie over. "Don't want you to think I'm getting romantic, but we got a date for tonight."

Chapter 25

Orders were to set up a small radio tower in a deserted cow pasture about two miles from Maxwell Field. The pasture, really a desolate swamp of dried sedge and saturated peat, was strategically located. Since the radios on the planes were not powerful enough to reach the base as they flew up from Jacksonville, the tower's job was to relay radio transmissions from the planes to the main control tower in Montgomery, and to relay orders back.

Four men were assigned: Fleischer, Jackson, an American corporal who looked to be about twelve, and an RAF sergeant from Scotland whose speech was totally unintelligible to everyone. "Sergeant Parker" was all they caught when he introduced himself; maybe he said it was getting darker.

November nights were wretchedly cold; that part was predictable. What wasn't predictable was the rain that started moving into Montgomery during the early evening. A sudden sweep of north winds dropped the temperature to thirty-three degrees and turned the cold drizzle into stinging sleet. The frozen drops glistened in the yellow glow of the truck headlights, clung to the yellow stalk weeds, then turned to vapor as they rose from the hot metal flood lamps like ghosts.

The men managed to ignore the conditions as they assembled the portable tower under a large black tarp, then secured it to a wooden platform. Willie's job was to illuminate the operation from several angles with the flood lamps on the back of the truck, while Fleischer wired the transmitter and receiver together. The baby-faced corporal was in charge of running the generators still in the bed of the truck, and Sergeant Parker "oversaw British interests," which meant that he offered useless suggestions and mostly got in everyone's way.

No one was particularly worried about the rain. Planes could fly in rain, flew in it all the time, their wings slicing through wet gray clouds like fish gliding through a pond. The men just pulled their ponchos up around their necks and dug in, anxious to get the work finished.

"Base to Field Station One." Colonel Fairchild's voice boomed over the radio as soon as Fleischer connected the generator. "Formation left Jacksonville at twenty-one hundred hours. They should be over Hurstboro by now. Are you getting anything yet? Over."

"Nothing, sir," Fleischer replied into his microphone. "Over."

"We have twenty-four planes up there." Fairchild sounded exasperated. "There's got to be something coming in, over."

The men looked up, searching the sky for incoming lights. As if in reply, the rain and sleet grew heavier, sheets of it streaming against their faces and into their eyes. A white tear of lightning illuminated the black clouds. A burst of wind blew their small tower sideways. As Willie walked to the truck, the wind lifted the corner of the tarp he was carrying and plastered it across his back. He peeled it off and draped it over the equipment, then searched the truck bed for any wire, thinking he could sling up two corners of the tarp to the back fender and fashion a protective tent.

"Witzic wit' t'bloody wither? S' Baltic," Parker complained from the front seat of the truck.

"What?" Fleischer asked. Parker repeated himself.

"Baltic," Willie yelled over the wind. "He said Baltic."

"Aye," said Parker.

"Poor guy, sitting and complaining from inside the truck," said Fleischer, his voice dripping with mock sympathy. "Hope he doesn't get his tonsils wet from the rain."

The baby-faced corporal laughed, but Willie only gave a tight smile. He wasn't going to laugh at a white man in public. And white was white, no matter where they came from.

Another strong gust of wind whipped the tarp straight up in the air, where it flapped wildly for a moment before settling on their heads. There was a loud crackle from the radio.

"Any word?" Fairchild's voice boomed over the noise. Fleischer handed off the mike to the Scotsman in the cab. "Here. Your job is to stay in contact with the colonel," he said, then thought better of it. "Wait, we need someone who speaks English." He turned to the corporal, who had been checking on the fuel levels of the generators. "Corporal, stay in contact with the colonel while we secure this thing. The Scot here can roll up the windows and keep the seats dry."

The corporal took the mike, and Fleischer grabbed the end of the flapping tarp. He and Willie pulled against it, fighting the wind, leaning backward until their full weight brought it again to the ground so that Willie could secure it with the wires.

The sleet grew heavier, torrential; hail big as eggs bounced across their ponchos and cascaded down their sides, creating slippery piles around their feet.

The radio squawked a few more words, then went dead. Willie scrambled onto the bed of the truck and adjusted a spotlight to illuminate the back of the receiver, as Fleischer squatted in the mud in order to tighten the connections.

The Scottish sergeant rolled his window down to complain that the coffee in his American-made thermos had gotten cold. He complained about American technology in general as he emptied the coffee out the window with a look of disgust. It blew back against the truck.

Fairchild's words broke and fizzled from the radio. The lightning split the sky like Morse code, bolt upon vicious bolt, flashing out deadly rhythms around them. They couldn't hear what the colonel was saying through the thunder.

"Try to keep in contact," Fleischer roared at the corporal, who looked scared of the lightning.

"Base," shouted the corporal, "this is Field Station One. Can you read me? Over."

"Read you," the colonel shouted back. "Over." The lightning reached across the sky, trying to grab at them with crackling fingers. "—contact—" Fairchild's words were coming in pieces. "Make contact, one thousand feet. Keep this channel—"

Willie could barely make out Fleischer's form in the driving rain. The tower was slipping sideways, floating on a sheen of mud and marbles of ice. The men righted it, dug it deeper into the slick ground, and secured it with ropes Willie had found in the truck bed. Fleischer took the mike while the corporal and Willie secured the tarps to the back of the truck, pushing the radio tower under them. The sleet grew more furious; the headlights from the truck barely made a path across the field, into the night.

"Divert them to Birmingham," the colonel was saying. "Maxwell's socked in."

"Naw!" The Scot suddenly came to life, shouting over Fleischer's shoulders, toward the mike. "Ay new hoo mooch they kerry. T'won't have enough petrol." Somehow Fleischer understood that.

"There's an RAF cadet here says they won't have enough fuel," Fleischer yelled against the thunder.

"—checking that," Fairchild yelled back. "Stay at your stations." There was a long, noisy pause filled with static. The men waited. Willie rechecked the knots in the ropes, then, with aching arms, used all his strength to hold the tarps in place as the wind tried peeling them from the truck. Fleischer was still kneeling in the mud, rolling on the ice balls, scanning the receiver.

"—less than a hundred-feet visibility," Fairchild's words finally broke through again. "We're adding extra emergency lights on a makeshift runway. If you can reach them, order them to Gunter."

"Those Brits probably won't listen to orders anyway," Fleischer muttered under his breath, and the Scotsman laughed at the truth of this. Fleischer wiped the transmitter clean with a small corner of his shirt that was still dry.

"Sarge." Willie nudged Fleischer a few minutes later. "Look." Flickering along the horizon was a feeble, glittering line of yellow dots moving together, two by two. They stared at the apparition, trying to figure it out.

"Trucks," Fleischer yelled through the rain. "Headlights. Looks like they're setting up a runway out there." But there was no way to confirm it; they had lost radio contact again. Fleischer pointed to the receiver. "Pull the tarp directly over the back of this," he ordered Willie, "and jam the spotlight real close; maybe the heat will dry the wires."

Willie pulled hard at the tarp, but it fought like a man, blowing sideways through his fingers. Fleischer pulled his poncho up around his head, hunching forward, to cover the front of the receiver and transmitter, and picked at a few wires, wiping them under his armpit before pushing them back into the radio. There was a loud hiss of static.

"Field Station One to Bee Tee Squadron Leader," Fleischer yelled into the mike, hoping to raise an answer from one of the planes. "Do you read me?" He waited, then tried again, to no avail. Willie held the tarp in place for what felt like hours. He was soaked, beyond soaked; his blood had become cold rain, his breath gray clouds, his heart the towering thunder.

"I might redo the wires," Fleischer yelled, pulling some strands together with his fingers, weaving them into a knot, and pinching them tight.

"Sir, gi' me that." The Scotsman leaned out of the truck window and pointed to the mike. Fleischer gladly handed it up to him.

"'Tis's Field Tower One to ana Royal cadet. We wont a bloody ahnswer." The Scotsman yelled into the mike. "Over. Over. Over. Can y'rid me?"

There was a faint crackling that slipped between the shrieking wind and the loud gashes of lightning.

A voice burst through the static. "Aye, laddie, I read you."

It was Jink. The four men cheered.

"Hope you're not wearing your kilts on a night like this," Jink said. "Your arse is going to freeze. Over."

"Tell him to stay on this channel," Fleischer shouted from behind the transmitter, huffing on his fingers, then flexing them to warm them up before he pinched the wires together for another try.

"Stay on tis chennel," the Scotsman relayed his words.

"He is to proceed to Gunter," Fleischer continued, forcing his voice over the wind. "Tell them there's a makeshift runway out here, if he can't make the airfield. Base'll talk him in through us."

"They want'ye t' proceed t' Gunter," Sergeant Parker repeated Fleischer's words. "But tere's a runway oot in t' swamps. When you're ten miles from t' field, Base will talk y'and t' others in."

"There aren't many others." Jink's voice came back. "Twelve down so far. Navigation went all right, the bloody planes—" His voice was lost to the crackle.

"Jesus Lord Almighty." Willie gasped. "Did he say twelve planes down?"

"Naw, can't have," said the Scotsman. Fleischer pulled the mike from his hands.

"Jink, Jink, can you read me? Repeat what you said. Over."

"I said what I said," Jink answered grimly. There was a long pause of static and drone, then, "I see lights. That you, mates?" The men looked up, and the sleet stung against their faces. They strained to see through the low-blowing clouds. Was there anything there? They strained to find something, anything visual in the godforsaken night.

They finally saw a glint. Flying through the storm, bouncing on waves of sleet and thunder with flashes of lightning illuminating its silver body, the Vultee was almost overhead.

"There he is," Willie shouted into Fleischer's ear. "Directly above us."

"He's off course," the Scotsman yelled and jumped from the truck. "T'ere's no place for him t' land 'ere."

"Jink! Where the hell are you going?" Fleischer roared into the mike. "Thirty degrees left! They set up a strip."

"I won't make it," Jink replied. His voice was calm, flat.

"It's only three miles," the Scotsman yelled behind Fleischer.

"Can't get enough airspeed. She's dying on me."

"I'm patching you through to the colonel." Fleischer's fingers pulled at wires, pushed little black pins into dark spots in the back of the receiver. He turned dials frantically until there was a soft hum.

"I can't even see me bloody wings," Jink said, his voice sounding flat, desperate. "Can't maintain airspeed. What the hell good is the colonel? Jesus, I'm going to hit those bloody trees."

The Scotsman jumped from the truck and ran like a madman toward the careening silver body above. "No," he was screaming, waving his hat at the plane. "No, no, no. Pull up! Y'ive got t'pull up! Oh God, *no!*" He sank to his knees into the mud and dropped his palms to the ground, his head between them, as the plane swung by him, swaying in the wind like a wounded bird. It tipped sharply to one side, then lay across the rain before nosing hard down.

The men watched helplessly. The engine screamed in protest as the plane veered in a crazy angle to the ground, maybe an attempt to turn around, Willie couldn't be sure. The wind seemed to blow the nose up for a moment, before the plane suddenly fell to the earth, like an elevator with its lift gone, the speed continuing to push it across the mud and slip of ice marbles into the waiting trees. They could hear Davies gasp from the radio, then his last words. "Say a prayer for me, laddies, looks like I'm going to die in bloody Alabama."

There was the sound. Willie knew he would never forget the sound, the crush, a different kind of thunder, the deadly, ugly pounding of metal against trees, a splintering crash, the sound of swamp grass ripped from its roots and moaning under the burden of a broken plane as it fell to earth, slid across its slippy face, and embedded itself in the trees. And then nothing. Just the deadly drumming of sleet that ended the night.

Chapter 26

They were draped in Union Jacks, thirteen coffins. Thirteen coffins carried down through a line of RAF cadets who were standing at rigid attention. A formation of crisp blue uniforms, their young, undeveloped, boy faces looking stunned, not ready for death, not ready to lose to death like this when they were all getting ready to fight at home. The boxes were carried down through their ranks, and they could barely look at them, their mates, dead, thirteen in one night.

Everyone was attending, the French cadets, the Canadians, the Greeks, the Americans, all of them somberly paying tribute to the casualties of war. Except it wasn't war. They didn't know what it was. Planes flew in miserable weather all the time; could it really have been the weather? Wars didn't stop for rainstorms. Or sleet and snow. It couldn't have just been the weather. Could it?

The chaplain stood up to deliver the eulogy.

"Our sons are to be interred here," he intoned. "We did not intend to bring them here to lose them like this. . . ."

* * *

His words were blown by the November wind, and Willie could barely hear him at all, because the colored Americans, the colored American *soldiers,* had to stand in the very rear, even behind the foreign cadets. Even here, at Oakwood Cemetery, on this consecrated ground, this old historical place, as consecrated as church ground, they had to stand in the rear. Willie wondered where they would have buried him, had he died. But then, he wouldn't have died, because he wouldn't have been flying.

The Lord is my shepherd . . .

The rows of men were praying together now, a deep chorus of male voices, but Willie didn't join them. He hummed to himself to keep it together, because his friend was in one of those boxes. He knew Fleischer was standing up front, and though he couldn't see him, he knew Fleischer would be paying respects for both of them. Still, he wanted to pay his own respects.

"Take the 'A' train," he sang softly. It would be his own personal tribute, because Jink Davies liked the song. Willie preferred "Solitude," but this was for Jink.

Melodically, it was a difficult song to sing, the words slow at first, then coming fast, to fit into the beats. The Delta Rhythm Boys sang it best, he thought, every word sweet and clear. He forced himself to concentrate on what they sounded like.

But the Twenty-third Psalm was scattering Willie's music.

Surely goodness and mercy shall follow me . . .

Willie didn't recite the prayer along with the rest of the men. He didn't trust his voice. Besides, he couldn't hear the chaplain very well, could barely see him over the lines of hats. No one would know whether he was praying or not.

"Why you hummin'?" August whispered to him. August was standing next to him, his hat over his heart and praying, like the prayer meant something. Like he was important enough to pray with the rest of them.

"I'm just praying my own way," Willie replied.

"No, you ain't," said August. "You hummin' ' "A" Train.' That ain't no prayer."

"It is to me," said Willie, then turned away, so that August wouldn't see his face.

"You better stop your singin'," August cautioned. "The Lord is back here, too, you know. He knows whether you prayin' or singin'."

The bugler played "Last Post," which was what they played for Brits instead of "Taps," and then they were all dismissed. Willie waited by the gates, staring down at his shoes, because to look any of them passing by in the eye was to invite trouble. General Chase, General Markham, Colonel Fairchild, Major Dugger, down to the sergeants, Sergeant Hogarth, all filing past him. They liked their coloreds in their place, these men, so he stared at his shoes and waited. Fleischer came up to him. The veins were standing out across his forehead.

"It wasn't right—" Fleischer started. "It wasn't—" He shook his head and walked away. No, Willie thought, it wasn't right. He lost a friend, but he would never be able to say a proper good-bye.

The next morning was brand new and blameless, with the sun shining bright yellow, the air cold and clear as though it had never been anything else. The clouds hung in a blue sky, in thick white clusters, like soft pillows, like Jink could rest his head on them. It was all innocent. Planes took off, announcements were made by the "Big Voice," planes landed, like nothing at all had ever happened. The men from Willie's squadron marched across the field to the wash rack, marching to Hangar Five, ready for duty. Except the doors to the wash rack were closed. Strange, Willie thought, because they were never closed, the work never stopped. Day and night, the planes were rolled in and taken apart and cleaned and put back together and rolled out. This morning the doors were closed, even though there was a Vultee waiting right outside. He could hear some kind of racket coming from inside. A thumping, slamming sound. Shouting.

The squadron came to a halt and then stood at ease in front of the doors, waiting for orders.

"Give a hand," Willie yelled to August, who stepped forward and pulled against the hangar doors to roll them apart. Several men got in position to grab the plane, ready to push it in. They stopped and stared. The reason for the noise was obvious now.

Fleischer was inside, kicking the shit out of the plane in front of him. "Goddamned piece of crap," he was screaming. "Goddamned piece of crap . . ." He was oblivious to the men. He was oblivious to the night crew, who had gathered around, or the night sergeant, who was pulling at his shoulder and telling him to cool off. He just kicked and screamed, like he was possessed. The night sergeant finally ordered his crew to leave, and left with them. Fleischer was even oblivious to the fact that his own men had arrived.

"They had no right to approve it!" Fleischer screamed at the shell of the Vultee. "No right at all!"

He gave the plane a final kick. It slid backward, then spun into the metal walls, knocking into the hoses and gauges, scattering tools with a splintering *clang*. Willie stood frozen for a moment, then stepped to Fleischer's side. He lifted his hand to touch Fleischer on the shoulder, then thought better of it and dropped it.

"Whoa, Sergeant," he said carefully. "The men are here. The men are here. Your men are here." He turned around to order the men to wait outside. Fleischer, panting from the exertion, squatted down and hunched there for a few minutes until his breath returned. Then he stood up. "Have them clean this up," he croaked, gesturing to the array of tools and plane parts scattered across the bay. He strode toward the radio office and snapped the door shut behind him. Willie turned to the men.

"You heard the orders," he said. "Let's get this place cleaned up. Get this plane out of here. August, set it up."

"Yessir." August grabbed a wing with his huge, meaty hands and righted the plane. "That man sure got hisself a bad temper," he said, shaking his head. "One mighty bad temper."

They never mentioned Jink's name after that, though Fleischer and Willie still met a night or two a week. First, they drank near beer, which was all Fleischer could find in the PX, and later, Cokes, because they realized that neither of them were really drinkers. The beers had always been Jink's idea.

They had little to talk about, but they persisted meeting, supposedly to work on the Vultee problem, though neither one of them had the heart to even talk about that. There was nothing they had in common; Jink had always been the lubrication that got the conversations going. Fleischer and Willie sat in the office, in chairs now, lights on, with the Vultee specs laid out in front of them, all blue-penciled by Fleischer, like it meant something. They didn't talk about it; they didn't talk about anything. It was a ritual neither one of them could give up, even though it meant nothing anymore.

One day Willie saw a newspaper, *The Montgomery Independent*, lying on the worktable, opened to an article about the recent World Series. Later, in the office, Fleischer was reading it and sipping a Coke. There was another Coke on the table waiting for Willie. He picked it up and, using the edge of the table, snapped the cap off, glad to see Fleischer was interested in baseball. Willie loved baseball; they could talk baseball, he thought. Something to talk about instead of sitting and thinking about Jink and not talking at all.

"You like baseball?" he asked Fleischer. "'Cause, you know, I play for the Colored Flyers." The Maxwell Field Colored Flyers and the Gunter Black Tigers were the two teams made up of all colored soldiers, since they weren't allowed to play on the white teams.

Fleischer looked up from the paper with interest. "Are you any good?"

"Just last week I made a great play on a fly ball for the final out," Willie said proudly. "I had to run back twenty feet and nearly broke my back to reach it, but it fell right into my glove." He demonstrated his move. "Smooth."

"Well, they sure could have used you last month when Owens dropped the third strike," Fleischer said, flipping the paper back onto the table. "Wish I had been there to see it. Dodgers fan?"

"Yankees," Willie replied, wondering, *Dodgers?* Was there nothing they had in common?

"But we got PeeWee Reese! Pete Reiser!" Fleischer retorted. "Great players."

"You don't have DiMaggio," Willie said, then hoped that he hadn't sounded too uppity. He liked Fleischer, but he still felt like he had to watch everything he said. He had felt that way ever since he had come to Alabama. The worry, the wariness, was something he wore, like it was part of his uniform. The worst thing was to come off uppity. It meant trouble. But Fleischer merely grinned and clicked their Coke bottles.

"Yeah," he said. "I got to give you DiMaggio." It was the first time he had smiled in weeks.

If anything turned out to be the key to solving the Vultee problem, Willie guessed, it was the jeweler's loupe.

Fleischer's girlfriend, Ruth, had sent it from New York because Fleischer wanted to make her some kind of special engagement ring out of tiny pieces of pyrite he had harvested from around the airfield. He was even planning to take a weekend furlough up to Hog Mountain in Tallapoosa County and maybe mine some gold flakes to melt down. He did things like that, cobbling together rags and dust and plane parts to make gifts to send to his girl. Proud of it, too. What she did with the stuff, Willie couldn't imagine, especially when they sold perfectly nice little diamond rings you could pay off, right in the PX. Even the colored PX had them. But Fleischer wanted something unique; he called it "unique," though Willie thought it was just cheap crap.

Ruth had dutifully sent Fleischer the requested jeweler's loupe, and Fleischer being Fleischer, he used it to examine every part of the radio room, peering at dead spiders, crumbs from the coffee cake, his own fingernails, a piece of hair from his head.

And the wire connections of the plane.

"Jackson!" Willie heard him suddenly exclaim from inside the radio room. "Get in here! Look at this! Jackson!"

Willie handed off his hose to Corporal Hobbs and stepped into the radio room. Fleischer was holding up a piece of wire from a plane radio, the jeweler's loupe clipped over one side of his glasses.

"Know what I got here?" Fleischer asked, his voice rising with excitement. Willie shrugged. "Take a look." He removed the loupe and held it out to Willie, who nervously took it and the wire. Not sure what he was doing, he held the loupe to his eye to peer through. It took him a minute to find the focus, but when he did, he was astonished. The metal end of the wire looked like someone had chewed it.

"What's wrong with it?" He glanced back at Fleischer, who was practically leaning over his shoulder.

"Corroded," said Fleischer, his voice breathless with shock. "The solution we're using to clean the planes is dissolving the connections. That's why the fucking planes are crashing. The connections melted; that's why they can't hold! It's been our own damn fault, the whole time."

Chapter 27

My father had that jeweler's loupe until the day he died. He was always peering through it, captured by some microscopic invisible world on the other side. Sandra and I found it again, alongside his gold high school ring from Brooklyn Tech, class of 1939, a thick gold watch with its Flex-O-Band, an onyx tie tack, and a blue and gold aviation pin, all of them stored inside a little handmade wooden jewelry box tucked in the front of his sock drawer. It had been a day or two after the funeral, and our mother, after setting aside what she wanted to keep, gave us permission to divide my father's possessions.

Sandra packed up most of his good sweaters for her husband, while I folded the rest of my father's things into a carton for Goodwill, old slacks and shirts I remembered my father wearing, a few leather belts, some pajamas still in cellophane. Sandra managed to fill a large carton to be shipped home to Atlanta: a new robe, shirts that had hardly been worn, the cellophane-wrapped pajamas she liberated from the Goodwill box along with two pairs of special orthopedic shoes.

"What on earth are you going to do with the shoes?" I asked, as she carefully enfolded each one in plastic bags. "They're custom-made for Dad's feet."

"They cost over two hundred dollars," she said indignantly. "Harrison can wear them."

"Good thing you're not taking Dad's glasses," I said, "or poor Harrison could wind up going blind from eye strain." I paused what I was doing. "You're not, are you?"

"Don't be ridiculous," she said. "Did you see the frames?"

When we got to the sock drawer, we both stared at the jewelry box for a moment. "You can keep the socks," she said in an uncharacteristic gesture of generosity, grabbing fistfuls of old socks and handing them off to me.

"What am I supposed to do with old socks?" I asked, dumping them into the Goodwill carton.

But Sandra was already lost in the contents of the jewelry box, jeweler's loupe firmly planted against her eye, while she turned over each item to see if it was real gold, the watch and tie tack having been already examined, and immediately stored in her pants pocket.

"You'd think that they would have made this out of fourteen carat," she complained, holding up the gold aviation pin. She put that in her pocket, as well, then thought twice about it and held it out to me.

"Would you like this? A memento from him?"

I barely glanced at it. "No." I didn't want anything from my father.

"Let me know if you ever change your mind," she said, and put it back in her pocket. "Just the pin, I mean. Not the other stuff."

I knew my father made his own peculiar jewelry, working meticulously on the most unlikely of materials, and so the presence of the loupe in his jewelry box didn't surprise me. He'd crafted a necklace for my fifteenth birthday, of tiny, tiny polished silver nuts and bolts hanging from a braided copper wire, taken from an old transmitter. The copper made a green circle around my neck and I threw the necklace out.

"You'll have a school ring," he promised me in my senior year, after I pleaded for one. And one day he appeared at my bedroom door with an odd little box fashioned from the slats of an orange crate. I lifted the rough-hewn lid with great anticipation. "No one else will have a ring like this," he said. And he was right.

Lying against a bed of cotton batting was a ring. In lieu of the traditional gold high school ring with its carved emblem and blue stone, he had fashioned one out of the brass shim stock used to patch planes, cut and rolled down to fit my finger, and engraved with my initials.

Biting back savage disappointment, I put it somewhere in the back of my underwear drawer, never to look at it again until it finally just disappeared.

We weren't poor. It was just his way. He held a good job with the airline; my mother owned a little gift shop. When she admired a crystal chandelier, and remarked that she would very much like to have one in her dining room, he made one out of old pale green Coke bottles, turned upside down, the bottoms cut off to allow for wiring, with tiny, flame-tipped light bulbs inside. Her coffee table was made of orange Teflon landing gear from a small plane, set on four legs. She hated it, I knew she hated it, but she never said anything that was less than complimentary to him, and I never understood that. And, of course, she also kept that box of ugly junk jewelry he had given her over the years.

"I remember his jeweler's loupe," I tell Willie Jackson as his nurse helps him back into bed.

"He was never without it," he replied. "He always said it gave him a different view of life. How things really are."

I remember that speech, the reality speech. The speech when he cleared his throat and told me that whatever I saw, there was a different and equivalent counterpart. Another dimension to things that inhabit their own reality. That an atom was as big in its own molecular world as I was in mine, and no less important. He meant for me to be humble. I think he meant for me not to brag, not when I was skipped two grades, or finished all the badges in Girl Scouts, or was elected to the Honor Society and accepted to three good colleges when I was fifteen; he felt compelled to downplay it.

He shrugged. "You and fifty thousand other people," was his standard reply. I think he meant to put it into some kind of perspective, so I would remember that though we may feel very big in our own universe, we may be very small in another. He wanted me to remember that we are all equal, that in the great scheme of things, no matter what I accomplished, the world was indifferent to it, that I was no more important than anyone else. It was a noble philosophy.

But I took it to mean that I wasn't important at all.

Willie is napping now, his breath purring softly through his lips, and I take the opportunity to make a quick trip to the bathroom, grab a cup of coffee and a late lunch in the cafeteria. Then I check in with David and Malachi.

David is sitting in on a big business deal and can't speak for long, but he does manage to tell me that we need to talk. Soon. "I don't want to hurt you," he says. "And I don't want to be hurt, either."

"How does a piece of paper make a difference?" I ask. "How does it prevent anyone from getting hurt?" It is my eternal answer and has always worked for me before.

"It makes all the difference," he replies. "It makes it official. It lets the whole world know that we are important to one another. It is the one unique gift we can give to each other. A commitment in front of the world. It's something that I need from you or . . ." His voice trailed off.

"Or?" I repeat.

"Or—we're going to have to make some changes." His words undo me. I promise to give him an answer when I get home.

Malachi tells me over the phone that he is still waiting for his sister. "It's going to be my Judgment Day," he laments.

"You think she's coming to judge you?" I ask. "I'll bet she just wants to see you."

"I don't know," he says ruefully. "I didn't live with them for much, never learned 'bout being with family."

"I never learned, either," I say and give a half laugh. "And I did live with mine."

There is a storm moving across the area. Low-slung, black-gray clouds needle each other with lightning as they move swiftly toward us like sports cars. I want to leave early for my motel, before Willie's dinner arrives, so that I don't have to drive in the pounding rain. But he awakes and smiles sweetly at me when he hears the tray cart rolling down the hall.

"Won't you join me for dinner?" he asks, and bats his eyes. I know I'm being manipulated, but I say yes, keeping a wary eye out the window. I watch as he cuts into slices of gray-colored Yankee pot roast, samples the dollop of brown-crusted mashed potatoes and tired string beans. There is a small salad of iceberg lettuce with orange dressing drizzled across the limp leaves, and diabetic strawberry Jell-O for dessert, along with a container of skim milk and a vanilla zwieback.

Willie looks the tray over. "Mmm-mmm-mmm," he says sarcastically. "We're going gourmet tonight."

"I can get you something from the cafeteria," I offer. He shakes his head.

"Don't need it," he says, flashing all his charm. "Your company will make it a wonderful meal."

He is the slowest eater I have ever seen. He takes minuscule bites and chews them into subatomic particles, swallows, takes a sip of unsweetened tea that he has slowly squeezed a lemon into. Another tiny bite. Another sip.

Rain is washing hard against the window now.

"I think I should go," I offer, watching him cut the pot roast into crumbs. "I don't want to drive in this."

"I'll be done in a flash," he says, taking another bite. He suddenly looks up at me. "You been pretty quiet. Are you okay?"

My heart jumps in my chest, and I can't catch my breath. "I don't know," I say with a shaking voice, and I am surprised at my sudden emotion. "I can't figure my life out. I don't know what to do. I don't know where I'm going."

"Child." Willie reaches up for my hands and holds them in his cool, wrinkled, delicate fingers. His eyes search mine; I see the pale graying of cataracts across his dark eyes. He shakes his head and gives me an ironic, sweet smile. "Child, you're just flying blind, and it's okay. That's how life is, darlin'. We're all flying blind."

Chapter 28

All that rushing around. All that worry about cleaning them just right. All that stink about keeping journals and reporting funny noises. All those nights of speculation over them crashing. And it looked like they were destroying their own planes, right there in the wash rack. The inside of Willie's head felt like it was twisting, like someone was playing tricks with his mind, spinning his brain like a top, one way, then the other. His stomach plummeted at the very idea of it; he thought he might even vomit. Could they really have been responsible? But it was there, in front of him. Proof. Dozens of small bubbles and pockmarks that made the ends of the wires brittle and useless.

The loupe dropped from his hand and spun, clinking across the cement floor, coming to a stop at Fleischer's foot. Fleischer left it there. He looked to Willie as though he was lost somewhere. His eyes looking inside himself, maybe watching the skies, maybe watching Jink slide to his death into the trees.

"Sergeant?"

Fleischer's eyes met Willie's, and Willie thought he might have been waiting for something, some kind of response, to help him sort it out, put it all into place. But Willie, who always had a snappy answer, because that's what street kids from Harlem always had available, had no answer at all.

"How do you like that?" Fleischer finally managed.

"Sure looks like you're on to something," Willie agreed.

"We got to report this," Fleischer said softly.

Willie shook his head. He could smell problems before they were born. "You gonna tell Vultee they're wrong?" he asked. "You gonna tell them they don't know how to clean their own planes?"

"I'm not gonna tell those jerks from Vultee anything," Fleischer replied, bending down to pick up the loupe and put it safely in his pants pocket. "Gonna tell the colonel himself."

"Good luck," Willie said, thinking now he would just sort of slip back into the work bay because this was starting to sound tricky. "Colonel Fairchild is one tough bas—uh—colonel," he ended lamely. "'Course, I hope you let me know what he says."

"Won't have to," Fleischer said, "because you'll be going with me."

They took the jeep. Willie drove while Fleischer excitedly expounded on his discovery. It would be the end of planes and men falling from the skies to their deaths. It would be good news for the base. For England! For France! Maybe earn them commendations, for he was planning to include Willie in his report, as a tribute to all those beers they'd shared late at night. Maybe it would be enough to get them both out of the Housekeeping Unit and doing something they were actually trained to do.

Willie thought Colonel Fairchild was going to have a stroke. His face was crimson; his veins made a map of blue lines against his temples. "I'm in line for brigadier general," he screamed at Fleischer. "You think I'm going to call General Markham and tell him that I approved the wrong cleaning protocol?"

"It's corroding the connections," Fleischer repeated for what seemed like the fourth or fifth time. He held out the loupe and a few wires, holding them out to Fairchild to see for himself, but Fairchild wouldn't even look down at Fleischer's hands. For once, Willie was glad he wasn't in charge of anything. Glad he wasn't the one who had to pass news along.

"Do you think the United States Army Air Corps is going to tell all those families that their sons died because we made a mistake *cleaning the planes?*" Fairchild slammed his fist down on his desk, his eyes still avoiding the wires. His mug of coffee bounced and sprinkled the papers next to it with brown dots. "British families? *French,* who don't understand half of what we tell them, to begin with?" He stood up and began pacing next to his desk, his face agitated, his hands gripping each other behind his back, as if to reassure themselves.

"I don't think we have a choice, sir," Fleischer said patiently, blinking disbelief at Fairchild's reaction. "But I'm sure I'm on to something. The wires hooking up the engines, the controls, sure, we replace them regularly, so they're not wearing out, but after only a couple of thousand miles, they're all corroded. It's got to be the solutions." But Fairchild was already shaking his head. He stopped in his tracks, to face Fleischer.

"Get that shit out of my sight," he said.

Fleischer put the loupe back in his pocket, but left the wires on Fairchild's desk.

"And take this with you," Fairchild said, grabbing the wires and tossing them to Fleischer. "As far as I'm concerned, I didn't see anything."

"Sir?"

"And not a word, hear me? Not a word," Fairchild added. "You will carry on with the same protocol, until I can think of some other way to get this past the general. Now, get out of here."

"If that don't beat all," Willie exclaimed as he drove them back to the wash rack. "You'd think he would have handed us medals on a platter." He pointed to his chest. "I was getting a spot ready right here."

"He's looking for a way to cover his ass," Fleischer muttered.

"In the meantime, we have to find another way to clean them. Maybe something less corrosive."

Willie took the wires from Fleischer, and ran his thumb and forefinger up and down their sides, feeling the insulation. The black rubber insulation had a funny feel to it. Spongy. The ends felt crumbly with corrosion; the wires themselves were brittle. "I don't know how we gonna do it," Willie mused. "But I don't think Ivory soap is the answer."

Hogarth was waiting for them the next morning, before they even started their shift.

"What do you want here?" Fleischer snapped at him as the men began their work, rolling in the first plane of the day, double-checking the pressure settings on the hoses, washing down the reeking gasoline from overnight into the gutters of the scrub bay.

"Some Housekeeping Squad. I hear you boys can't even run a simple cleaning operation," Hogarth said, rubbing his hands together. "Fairchild sent me here to check things out. All on the QT, you understand." He placed himself by the front door and folded his arms. "One of you bring me the cleaning manual, so's I can go over it with y'all."

"I don't need anyone babysitting me," Fleischer growled.

Hogarth bent toward him with the eager look of a dog that had just been offered a piece of meat. "I'd hate to report to the colonel that you won't cooperate. With the war on and all. You seem pretty jumpy about me watching things."

There was something in his choice of words that made Fleischer stop in his tracks. "What's that supposed to mean?" he asked.

Hogarth shrugged. "You wouldn't be the first one to try to sabotage this base." He gestured to Willie. "I have on good authority that you and this nigger been having some late-night meetings with that RAF fellow who was killed." He raised his eyebrows at Fleischer. "I just might suggest an inquiry. If I have to."

Fleischer's body nearly lifted off the ground with anger. Willie thought he was going to rise right up into the ceiling of the wash bay and fly around Hogarth's head like a demon.

"You don't know what you're talking about," Fleischer yelled, but Hogarth just smiled at his fury. He had the advantage and he knew it. "I hope I don't find even one little change from the manual," he said airily. "You never know what the problem could be. And you just might wind up getting court-martialed."

"You won't find anything," Fleischer roared, tossing the manual at Hogarth. "Check anything you want; we follow every damn thing that was written down." Willie dropped the hose he was holding and glanced over at the gauges. Had Fleischer forgotten that Seekircher had approved the changes in the pressure settings? Nothing written down, no initialed change of orders, no amendments to the manuals, he had done it casually. Fairchild probably had never been asked to approve it, and apparently Hogarth knew all about it. Because now, just as casually, he was going to screw them to the wall.

Fleischer ordered his men to stop working as Hogarth made a slow tour of the hangar. He checked every tool, every piece of equipment, every work order against the manual while Fleischer followed him, watching over his shoulder. Every piece of plane that had been disassembled, every nut and bolt. They moved together, station by station, one determined to start some trouble, the other determined to avoid it.

Finally, they made their way to the wash rack. Hogarth checked the composition of the cleaning solution, the angles of the hoses. Then, with a smug smile, he started to check the pressure settings on the gauges while Fleischer hovered over him like a nervous groom.

It took Hogarth over an hour to check and recheck the pressure gauges. He seemed disappointed that they checked out exactly according to the manual. He stalked to the front of the hangar and threw the book at Fleischer's feet.

"Just try something," he warned Fleischer. "I'm watching and I'm waiting." It was only over for this time, Fleischer knew. There was another shoe out there somewhere that would be ready to drop.

As soon as Hogarth marched through the doors, Fleischer was at Willie's side. "What's the story with the gauges?" he asked Willie, his voice shaking with relief. "How come they're back to their old pressure?"

"Shit, Sarge, August and I changed them back while you and Hogarth were chewing on each other's faces," Willie replied casually.

Fleischer leaned against a plane, before extending his hand to Willie.

"Thanks, Jackson," he said. "You may have just saved my ass."

"Maybe this time," said Willie, shaking Fleischer's hand, "but I got a feeling you're gonna need a spare ass or two before this is over. Sir."

Chapter 29

After Pearl Harbor, Willie didn't think there was going to be much of a holiday at all. Maxwell Field, like the rest of the country, was grim, nervous, and worried. All leaves had been cancelled; all but emergency passes were frozen; guards were stationed around the base in case of sabotage; everyone was ordered to wear their uniforms, stay alert, be ready for another attack.

But there is something about soldiers and Christmas.

The week before the holiday, the "Big Voice" announced that the ban on passes would be lifted and fifteen hundred passes would be given out. The USO had asked the citizens of Montgomery to open their homes to the servicemen on base, to give them a place to go for the holiday. Someplace to share a good Christmas dinner and perhaps even open a little gift or two, and the response was overwhelming.

But Christmas came to Maxwell Field, as did every other event and holiday. In two colors, black and white. Because there was no USO for the black soldiers. Because there was no one in the great city of Montgomery who would reach out and offer them a holiday. No home-cooked meals, no lumpy knitted sweaters or platters of home-baked cookies. Nothing, until the black citizens of Montgomery got together and arranged for a joint Christmas party to be held with the men from Tuskegee.

"Do your people celebrate?" Willie asked Fleischer as they made a last-minute adjustment to a transmitter to be replaced on the Vultee being cleaned outside the radio room.

Fleischer shrugged. "Nah, we have Chanukah. Besides, I just proposed to my girl. I'm hoping she'll come down on the train so we can get married during the holidays. I already sent her a ring."

Willie remembered the pyrite and copper-wire ring that Fleischer had been working on. "You mean the one that was so—unique?" he asked.

Fleischer straightened up with pride. "That's the very one!" he said enthusiastically. "I'm hoping she'll say yes."

"Right, Sarge." Willie smiled. "If anything's gonna convince her, that ring will just be the thing to do it."

The PX featured a small tree trimmed with glass balls, and all kinds of modest gifts for the holidays underneath its branches. Cartons of cigarettes with red bows, big packages of Hershey's bars with red bows, Wrigley's gum, shaving kits, extra canned food, stuffed dolls to send home, red bows. The mess hall was hung with wreaths and tinsel and red bows. There was turkey on the menu and announcements that members from several Montgomery church groups would be arriving at the base on Christmas Eve to join all military personnel for a stroll around the grounds and a night of Christmas caroling. But Christmas Eve brought a cold drizzle and the carolers had to take refuge in Hangar One, which was dazzling with decorations. The Montgomery Ladies' Guild had spent days fixing it up, making preparations for a big Christmas Day party. Everyone was invited.

Everyone, except the foreign cadets who were left to wander the streets of Montgomery to entertain themselves.

Everyone, except the colored soldiers, who were left out of everything.

"What are *you* doing for Christmas?" Fleischer asked Willie, the day before. Fleischer had managed to buy a big box of Hershey's bars for the holiday, to share with the men. They were taking a coffee break and enjoying the chocolate: August breaking his into little pieces before savoring each one, Fleischer dunking his into his coffee and letting it melt. "You got any plans?" Fleischer peeled back the wrapper and dropped in another piece, swirling it around with his finger.

"I think August and me are going to try and find a colored church somewhere in Montgomery," Willie replied.

"Yessir." August nodded happily. "Some place that'll serve up a big old Southern dinner." He licked his lips. "Maybe ham and black-eyed peas. And chitlins. And my aunt Lily's fried peach pies."

Willie laughed out loud at this. "You think they're gonna know your aunt Lily?" he asked.

This puzzled August. "My mama always say she's *famous* for her peach pies," he said. "They little hand pies, all fried up, and you eat 'em with vanilla ice cream on top. Yessir, my mama always say that Aunt Lily was famous for her fried peach pies. And famous means everyone knows her, don't it?"

Willie patted him on the back. "Well, then, maybe we'll find them." He turned to Fleischer. "You can come along, if you want. Since you being of the Hebrew persuasion, you probably have nothing to do."

Fleischer grinned broadly and dropped in a large piece of Hershey's, then polished off his coffee, now a thick, dark brown syrup. "By the time I see you guys again, I should be a married man. Ruth said yes. I plan to get hitched on Christmas Day."

They all ran into each other in town. In Montgomery, the day after Christmas. Though there was a chilly rain, Willie and August had decided to go see the Christmas Lights Festival in town. They walked along, admiring the decorated trees that lit up the businesses, the glitter and brightly colored balls that hung in the windows, always mindful to step off the curb when they passed white folks, to let them go by.

"We don't do this shit in Harlem, you know," Willie said to August as they stepped into the street.

August wrinkled his brow to consider this. "They don't got streets up there in New York?" Willie just shook his head at his friend's innocence. August had never been out of the South, had never known anything else.

Someone, a couple, was strolling toward them, and instinctively, without looking up, Willie and August stepped into the street again.

"Hey!"

Willie startled. It was Fleischer.

"You don't have to do that," Fleischer said, gesturing to the curb.

August did an embarrassed shuffle and looked around. White folks didn't talk to coloreds in the streets just like that. Just like they were friends. Even if they were soldiers.

"This is my new wife, Ruth," Fleischer proudly introduced the woman at his side. She was petite, Fleischer's new wife. Blond, blue-eyed, pretty, in a soft, round way, with a round face, almost like Betty Grable, and Fleischer was looking at her with total adoration. She couldn't take her eyes from his face, either. Willie felt like he was intruding, just by standing with them. "We got married in Corpus Christi. Only place we could find a rabbi."

How Fleischer managed to find himself a rabbi in Corpus Christi, Texas, take the Greyhound bus to get to him, and get married, all on Christmas Day, was something that Willie could never figure out. But married he was, and happy about it, too.

Ruth gave them a warm smile and extended her hand.

"Marty told me so much about you," she said. "He says that you're his closest friend down here."

Willie touched her fingers quickly and dropped his head, while August tipped his hat. "Yez'm," he and Willie murmured together.

"Hope you men had a merry Christmas," Ruth said.

"Yez'm," August replied. "But we never did find those fried peach pies." Ruth gave him a puzzled look.

"His aunt Lily makes them," Willie tried to explain.

"You mighta heard of her," August added.

Ruth shook her head.

"Well, anyway, we sure had a bang-up dinner at one of the churches," Willie went on. "Turkey and macaroni and cheese, and beaten biscuits and ham. All you could eat."

"Pecan pie," August added. "No peach—"

"Well, we gotta run," Fleischer interrupted. "Got to find a place off base to live, before my two-day pass runs out." He took Ruth by the arm and led her toward the bus stop.

"Merry, *merry* Christmas," August called enthusiastically as they parted. Ruth waved back.

When they were out of earshot, Willie poked August in the ribs. "*Merry, merry Christmas,*" he sarcastically repeated August's words and then laughed out loud. "Man, you don't know nothing! They don't celebrate like us. They're Jewish! They celebrate—*Chramininakah.*"

There were three more crashes during the holiday season. Three more families who wouldn't be getting their son home at the end of the war. Three men who had died for nothing, as far as Fleischer was concerned. "It's murder, that's what it is," he muttered to Willie after each crash. "Fairchild ought to be tried for murder."

"Murder," Willie agreed. He rolled the word around in his head. *Murder.* It was the worst thing, he thought, that you could do to someone. It meant your personal right to die in your own way and your own time was taken from you, ripped out of God's hands and changed forever. Fleischer was coming to work looking dog tired. Married two whole weeks now, he was sitting over a cup of coffee in his office and struggling to keep his eyes open.

Willie almost hated to bother him, thinking a man should be left alone on whatever honeymoon he could piece together. He was probably up all night making sweet love. Yeah, he would leave the sarge alone as soon as he got the sign-off sheet initialed. He rapped softly on the office door before walking in. "Hey, Sarge," he said, dropping the paper on the desk in front of Fleischer. "You sure do look sleepy." He couldn't contain a knowing smirk, though.

Fleischer sat up and rubbed his eyes. "It's those damn chickens, Jackson."

"Chickens?"

Apparently Fleischer and his wife had managed to find a room to rent in an old farmhouse just outside of town. The cows were kept in a barn down the road. The pigs in a sty in the back. And one hundred and twenty two baby chicks were being incubated underneath the house.

"Do you know how much noise one hundred and twenty-two chickens make?" Fleischer asked.

"I'm from New York City, Sarge," Willie said. "I don't know much about chickens."

"Hell, me neither." Fleischer yawned. "I thought they came in pots. You know, with carrots and celery and matzo balls."

"Sounds about right to me, though I don't know nothing about matzo balls."

"Know what else?" Fleischer rubbed his eyes. "These chickens don't appear to have much interest in sleeping late."

"No, sir."

"They're up before I am," Fleischer continued gloomily. "Every morning. One hundred and twenty-two chickens." He sighed. "What is so important to a chicken that it has to be up by four in the a.m.?"

Willie tried to look sympathetic. "Can't you find someplace else to live?"

Fleischer shook his head. "It's only two bus rides away. We can barely afford this, even though my pay was raised to twenty-one dollars a month. Ruth is eating mashed potatoes on white bread to fill up."

"Probably better than what we get in the mess hall," Willie observed.

"Yeah, well. The only good thing is at least we get a free

chicken thrown in every two weeks when we pay the rent." Fleischer signed off on the paper Willie was holding, then brightened. "But this idea came to me out of the blue. I was thinking about the plane crashes, you know? And for some reason, I thought maybe we can put something on the tips of the wires. Some kind of protection."

"Just came to you out of the blue?" Willie said with a sly smile. "To slip some kind of *protection* onto the *tips* of the wires? Just came to you, *on your honeymoon?*"

"Yep," Fleischer said in earnest, not getting the reference. "So I came up with this invention. Ruth and I been making dozens of them. Little sacks. I'm going to bring them all in and test them out."

"And you spent your whole first married week on that?" Willie repeated.

"Yep."

Willie shook his head. "You sure know how to show a girl a good time, now, don'tcha!"

Chapter 30

"They almost good," August declared after downing six little
fried peach pies. He took a big gulp of very light, sweet coffee.
"'Course, my aunt Lily's are better."

Fleischer had brought in a shoe box full of peach pies earlier
that morning for the coffee break, after an hour's commute on
two buses and a very close inspection by the guards posted at
the front gates of the base.

"Got a treat for you guys," he had announced as soon as he
walked into Hangar Five, setting the box down on the office
table and proudly pulling off the wax-paper covering. "I fixed a
record player for that sergeant in Requisitions, and he paid me
in canned peaches. Twenty cans. We were up all night making
these."

The men dug in right away. Willie ate as much as he could
hold. Clyde Sanders thought the crust a little thick, Charlie
Hobbs thought they could use a little more sugar, and of course,
August politely mentioned how they fell short of Aunt Lily's, but
in less time than it took to offer them, they disappeared.

"Where'd you learn to make fried peach pies?" Willie asked, helping himself to the last one.

"I asked my landlady," Fleischer replied. He poured them another round of coffee, more like a dinner party host than a sergeant in an airplane hangar. "Glad you boys finished them off. For some reason, Ruth said she doesn't want to see another peach as long as she lives."

Twenty huge army-size cans of peaches. Fleischer always had deals like that. Always after fixing someone's radio or record player or steam iron or even washing machine, anything, as long as they could haul it to his apartment. He set aside one night a week repairing things for the locals in order to earn some extra money, though he mostly got paid in pork pies or pots of cheese grits or bottles of moonshine that smelled suspiciously like antifreeze, or, as in this case, twenty gigantic cans of peaches.

Many mornings he brought the extra food in; the men were always hungry, since food in the mess wasn't particularly tasty, and they appreciated the supplements to their regular fare. They wolfed down all sorts of local oddities, and gladly accepted the blankets or cast-off sweaters or extra woolen underwear or mismatched socks.

It had occurred to Willie more than once that he really ought to give something back to Fleischer. Maybe some kind of wedding gift. But Willie had no money; the only thing he kept in his barracks locker was a pearl-handled shaving kit with a silver comb and matching brush. He figured his mother must have saved for months to buy it; it was all he owned besides his trombone, which was still safe at home in Harlem. And he certainly wasn't handy enough to make unique items the way Fleischer was fond of doing, so after some deliberation, he finally pushed the matter to the back of his mind.

A week after the peach pies, Fleischer came in with another surprise. This one a chicken feed bag filled with, well, Willie didn't know what they were exactly. Made from white oilcloth with little pink roses, that Fleischer and his wife had purchased at the local five-and-dime, they were small, odd-shaped pouches, hand-sewn with tight black stitching and shoelace drawstring tops. These were the sacks Fleischer had been talking about, and Willie guessed they looked as plain as their name, though the roses gave them a nice touch.

Sacks. Fleischer showed the men how to slip the whole thing around the ends of the wires and pull the shoelace tight. They were shapeless, slippery, awkward to use; the men struggled to make sense of them.

"Dumbest thing I ever did see," Charlie Hobbs complained to Willie. "We're supposed to increase productivity, and he gives us these damn things to slow us down."

Willie nodded sympathetically. "You know how to solve that, don'tcha?"

"What?" Hobbs asked.

"Put 'em on faster."

Fleischer made sure they were always in use. He reminded his men, exhorted them, brought in dozens of new sacks when the old ones cracked from the chemicals. They soon became part of wash rack protocol.

Unless Hogarth came poking around. Then, courtesy of August, who was excused from wash rack duty to be the lookout because of his deep, penetrating voice and his inability to do much else, the sacks would be whipped off and tucked out of sight. Fleischer didn't want anyone to know what they were doing until he had proof that it was making a difference.

"Visitors!" August would call out, initiating a flurry of activity. By the time Hogarth came through the doors of Hangar Five, the men were deeply engrossed in hosing down the floor, sharpening already-sharp tools, rolling planes back and forth, or elaborately tightening nuts and bolts that had been tightened just moments before.

It amused Willie that Hogarth never noticed that while the hoses were officially bubbling and hissing and steaming away, and in general, filling the entire hangar with the usual acrid, foul-smelling, gasoline-laden steam, there was never actually anyone washing down the planes while he was around.

Once Hogarth left, it was a different story. Sacks were pulled out from under armpits, from behind benches, from lunch boxes, from empty coffee mugs, and carefully placed back on the connections, ready to do their jobs.

"It's like a scientific experiment," Fleischer explained to Willie. "I have to prove they work. The brass won't believe anything unless the whole procedure is written down, in black and white." To that effect, he kept a daily journal. He replaced every wire with new ones so that they would have a fresh start, squinted over the connections before and after cleaning, examining every wire, the jeweler's loupe wedged firmly in his eye, and wrote endless notes in his constant companion, a little black book. Notes and notes and more notes.

By the end of February, there hadn't been any more crashes. Not one. Not one American boy or French or British cadet was lost to a Vultee falling from the sky. It was all the proof Fleischer needed. He gathered his papers, and the carton of sacks, new ones made fresh every two weeks, and decided to file a request for another conference with Colonel Fairchild.

"You'll come with me," he said to Willie, as they pored over the request form lying on the table in the radio office. "We can tell him together how we did this. I'll make sure the whole squadron gets credit." He scribbled a statement at the bottom of the paper and pushed it toward Willie to witness.

Willie was reluctant. He didn't care so much about getting credit, or even a medal, so much as he cared to be left out of the fray. Fleischer had disobeyed orders, and that was tricky stuff. Willie didn't fancy spending his remaining army years in prison.

"It's really *your* invention, Sarge," he said, gently trying to ease the form back to Fleischer.

"You guys did the cleaning," Fleischer replied, sliding it right back to him. "I want to be fair."

And Willie pursed his lips and signed his name to the paper.

* * *

The reply came two days later. A base messenger brought an official-looking envelope to the hangar addressed to First Sergeant Martin Fleischer. Fleischer slit the envelope with a letter opener he had fashioned from a shard of broken propeller and read through the contents. He pulled off his face mask and stormed into his office, where he immediately kicked his chair across the floor.

Willie handed off the steam hose to Charlie Hobbs and made his way across the slick floor to the radio office.

"Sarge?" he asked.

Fleischer waved the letter over his head. "What is this shit?" he was screaming. "Proper channels?" He let out a stream of invectives that Willie thought were both highly creative and explicitly vulgar.

"I gotta go through channels," he roared, crumpling the paper in his fist.

"It's probably just a formality," Willie said, trying to calm Fleischer down. "You know how the army does things."

But Fleischer was beyond reason. His eyes bulged with anger, and there were flecks of white spittle flying from his lips with every word. The other shoe had dropped. The other shoe had dropped, and it was a direct hit.

"It's Hogarth," he yelled. "Now I got to go through *Master Sergeant* John P. Hogarth. He outranks me! That motherfucker got himself another rocker."

Chapter 31

Horses aren't all that complicated. They eat when they are hungry and sleep when they are tired. If they are frightened, they run. Yet, they have gestures and signals that are exquisitely complex. A whole world of communication exists that determines who will be in charge, who will wait for the second bite of hay, who will watch over the others, who will no longer be part of the herd. The flare of a nostril, the flick of an ear, the merest suggestive raise of the head, all part of a code they worked out eons ago. It keeps everything in order. Every horse, no matter where it comes from, no matter the breed or color, obeys the ancient rituals. Ancient rules, you might say. I envy the clarity of it. I wish humans were as easy to read as horses, because we rarely get it right.

Willie is feeling strong today. I find him dressed and hopping around his room on crutches, packing his personal items into a tan canvas satchel. He announces that he has cleared it with his doctors to get discharged. He had been brought in to get his diabetes back under control and now it was. Discharge is to be Friday morning. Except that this is Wednesday afternoon.

"Does Rowena know?" I ask him.

He looks up from the little black grooming kit he is packing with an old-fashioned razor and hairbrush. I can't help but notice that they have matching mother-of-pearl handles.

"Not yet," he says, tucking the grooming kit into the satchel. "But she'll be happy about it. She's been talking about getting some projects done." He puts a few unused tea bags from his bed tray into the satchel, then picks up a pile of newspapers, sorting through them and discarding the ones he has finished reading. The unread ones also get packed. He looks up and smiles at me. "She's so busy all the time. There's a lot of things I can get done for her." His face is full of optimism. I can read it easily. He really believes that he is going home to help Rowena with her house.

He swings his crutches in front of him and gracefully slides his body forward to reach the windowsill, where he has a philodendron and a small framed picture of his late wife. He puts the plant and the picture under one armpit and glides back to the bed, to pack these, too, into his satchel.

"Work," he repeats. "A man likes to be useful. I'm pretty handy. And Rowena needs me." Now I see pride play across his features.

But I am wondering how Rowena will take the news. She works long hours, and taking care of her father will be very difficult. His medications, his special diet, his strong need to be relevant. I wonder whether I should caution Willie that Rowena might not be able to bring him home today. Or that he would certainly find he isn't physically able to do much work around her house. Not wanting to hurt him, I say nothing. I just nod agreeably, hoping my face won't betray my doubts. We sit together in his room and wait.

Rowena comes by later to deliver several flawlessly pressed shirts hanging in a row, like men waiting for a train. "Anything you want me to bring home to wash?" she asks, rolling his old shirts into a ball and tucking them into a plastic grocery bag.

"Nothing," Willie says. "I'll be doing my own laundry."

She stops in her tracks. "What?"

"My numbers are all good," he tells her. "They're letting me go home today."

A fleeting look crosses Rowena's face in spite of herself; it's scarcely there, but I see it. I can read it. She feels frustrated and burdened.

"I thought you were coming home this weekend," she says levelly. "Today's only Wednesday." I hear the unspoken part. The exasperation.

I'm sure Willie hears it, too, but he chooses not to acknowledge that he might not be wanted. "Thought I'd get a jump start on things," he replies.

"A jump start on what things?" Rowena asks suspiciously.

"Well, did you ever get your kitchen ceiling painted?" Willie asks. His voice is filled with a plea to be needed.

Rowena puts her hands on her hips and shakes her head. "Old man," she says, "do not think for one minute you are going to paint my kitchen ceiling."

"We'll just see," he says, drawing himself up. "I'm feeling real good, and I got plans."

Rowena says nothing more, just takes his crutches and helps him into his wheelchair. They ring for the nurse to let her know they're ready to leave, and she appears a few minutes later.

"I got to wheel him to the front door," the nurse declares, taking over the handles. "Insurance regulations."

We follow behind, carrying Willie's stuff. "He gets like this every once in a while," Rowena whispers to me. "His numbers go crazy and he goes to the hospital. Then he feels good, comes home, wants to do everything. Eats what he wants. Thinks he's seventy-five again."

We make an unlikely caravan crossing the parking lot: Rowena pushing her father's wheelchair; Willie Jackson, dressed in navy slacks, a pale blue shirt, and yellow tie, riding like a sultan, his satchel on his lap; and me, following along, carrying plastic bags filled with laundry and medical supplies.

"We can pick up two gallons of semigloss super white on the way home," Willie announces as Rowena lifts him into the car and begins dismantling the wheelchair. She grunts with the effort. It's an old-fashioned chair and won't fit in the trunk, so she has to grip the bottom center and pull it up hard to collapse it, then lift it into the backseat of her car.

"I'm not picking up paint," she huffs, struggling to get the castors over the door sill. I help her, then squeeze in next to it. "I have to drive Rachel back to the motel to pick up her rental car. That'll take up the rest of the day."

"When she gets her car, Miss Rachel can drive me to the paint store," he says, gesturing to me. Rowena's eyes and mine meet. I give her an invisible smile that says *"No, I won't."* She gives me an invisible smile of relief back. Just like horses, I think. The secret code between me and Rowena is working almost as well.

The next morning I am making Willie breakfast. Rowena had asked me to stay over and spend the next two days with her father, since he can't be left alone, his health aide isn't available, and in his haste to come home, he had forgotten that Rowena works all day. I don't mind helping. Rowena has already left for work, and I am nervously fumbling around her kitchen. I've never cooked anything for a diabetic before, and I am absolutely paranoid that I might use a wrong ingredient and get him sick. Willie, himself, is not to be trusted with his own menu.

"I can have waffles," he tells me right off, as I dice some green pepper for the one-egg omelet allowed on his menu sheet. "Two. With maple syrup, and a slice of ham." He points to the refrigerator. "Rowena always keeps maple syrup on the bottom shelf in there." I look at the menu hanging on a cabinet door. Along with his egg, he can have whole wheat toast, one slice, but only if his blood sugar is below one hundred.

"What was your blood sugar this morning?" I ask.

"Perfect," he replies and uses his crutches to pull himself over to the kitchen table, to sit down.

"'Perfect' is not a reading," I say, whisking the egg and carefully sliding it over the peppers. "It has to be a number."

"I know what I can eat," he scolds me. "And I want waffles. I been a diabetic for twenty-three years and I been doing just fine."

I try not to look over at his one leg, lost apparently, because at some point he didn't do all that fine.

"No waffles, no syrup," I tell him. "I made you a nice omelet." His face registers disappointment as I serve him breakfast and tell him he can also have a helping of cottage cheese, and canned sugar-free peaches for dessert.

"Canned peaches," I say ironically, handing him a dessert dish filled with fruit.

He touches them with his spoon. "Canned peaches," he repeats. "Your father made the most god-awful fried peach pies I ever ate. The dough was like cement." He pronounces it "*seement.*"

"But you told me you ate at least seven," I remind him. "You sounded like you enjoyed them."

He squints his eyes as if to look back into the past. "As I recollect, that's all I had to eat for the day," he says. "Sometimes the food was awful bad in the colored mess and us boys skipped it entirely."

Willie and I go through the pictures in the bedroom carton. He gently lays the folds of the silk parachute aside and lifts the pictures from the box and spreads them across the kitchen table. I hand him the photo of the laughing sandy-haired pilot.

"Jink," Willie says. "I told you about him." He touches the face in the picture with a thin finger. "We promised each other after the war was over, we would jam together. You know, have a little blow session. That's what we musicians call it, when you play together."

"Yes, you told me." I examine the picture closely. Lindsey Davies was very handsome. Long, almost equine face, aquiline nose, high cheekbones. I can hear the strains of his Welsh accent, the clip and swing of his words.

Willie finally puts the pictures aside and sits at the table, then points up to the ceiling. "Let's get that paint," he says, but I detect something in his voice. Maybe worry.

"Are you really sure you want to?" I ask. "It's an awfully big job. Looks like it's going to need two coats."

He studies the area above him, pondering the work. "I suppose not," he says slowly. "Maybe in a few days." His face fills with relief. He suggests a game of cards. The only game I know is double solitaire.

We play for a few hours, and Willie beats me every time, playing to the foundation cards until he wins. I look up and am happy to see that his face is filled with innocent pleasure. I am glad to be here, but there is an impatience welling up inside of me, to get home. I need to do things at home.

Rowena calls a little later. "How's it going?" she asks.

"We've been busy," I tell her. "Going through those old pictures, playing cards."

"Great," she says. "I can't thank you enough for staying with him while I'm at work. I called for a home health aide. She should be coming in a few days."

"No problem," I reply. "We're having fun. He's a wonderful man."

"Yes, he is," she agrees, then laughs. "Just watch him during those card games. He'll cheat your socks off."

Breakfast the next morning goes well. Willie has a bowl of oatmeal and some pineapple chunks and a piece of wheat toast. I am relieved that his sugar has been right where it should be. I haven't poisoned him.

"Today I want to go downtown and renew my driver's license," he announces as I clear the table. He hobbles his walker to the front hall closet and grabs his sweater and fedora, then gets his wheelchair and lowers himself into it, parking his walker in a corner. "I plan to buy myself a car."

I look at this frail man, sitting in his wheelchair, clutching his hat—because in his day, gentlemen wore hats—waiting expectantly by the front door. I open the door and stand beside him. The sun is sweetly yellow and melts into a flawless blue sky. The clouds are white and high, the wind calm, like a movie set.

"I don't even know where the Motor Vehicle is," I say.

"Washington Street."

"I don't know how to get there."

"I'll drive," he says. "I'm a real good driver. I drive everywhere."

"Today isn't a good day for driving," I tell him.

"You think I can't do it?" he asks. "I'm a very active man."

I get a sudden sad stab of pain in my heart. I am afraid that Willie is failing mentally, that he is lost in the past. Then I wonder if any of what he has told me is even true.

"The rental car isn't fitted for you," I say, trying to be diplomatic, trying not to disappoint him again. "You'd need hand brakes or something." But I can barely look at him, because I know my face is full of information I'm afraid he'd mistake for pity. And Willie Jackson is not a man who would stand for pity.

He looks down at his leg, the neat tuck of pants under his body, then looks up at the sky.

"We can take a nice walk," I suggest, my voice becoming gentle. "I'll push you. I don't mind at all, pushing you." And I realize immediately that was wrong. Willie Jackson is not a man to be pitied or a man who would sit in a chair to take a nice walk.

"You think I'm soft in the head," he shouts, suddenly rolling his chair away from me. "Because I want my life back! Well, Miss Rachel, I am in full, clear possession of my mental faculties, thank you! You will not humor me. I know what I'm doing. I know what I'm saying. I *know!*" His eyes flash with indignation.

"I believe you," I say, and I do, again. There is too much Willie present for me to have even doubted him. He rolls to the front door again and stares up at the sky for a long time, as though he was trying to will his chair to fly through the heavens.

"Perfect day for flying," he says. "Just enough wind to lift your wings. Good WX. That means good weather, you know, good WX."

"Did you ever fly?" I ask him. His face crumples into sad lines.

"I wanted to fly commercial planes, you know, after I got out of the service." He looks down at his hands. "But you got to have flown in the service and there was no chance of that."

"Did you become a musician?"

"No," he says softly, touching his hearing aid. "Lost the music. Lost the music in the war."

"How?" I ask him.

"Explosion." He stares out at the sky, then suddenly looks up at me. "Listen to me," he says. "Listen to an old man. Don't let anyone take the music away from you."

I can't answer him; I just nod mutely, thinking, *It's too late for that.* "Okay," I finally manage to say.

We stay at the front door for a while, feeling the soft breeze rustle over our arms. "So what did you do for a living?" I ask him.

"Oh, I went to school, got a degree in education. Became a high school shop teacher," he says. "Was the first black teacher to work in Brookfield. Nineteen fifty-four." I am glad that we can talk again. That we got our rhythm back, but his choice of words puzzles me.

"'Black'?" I ask. "But you've been saying 'colored.' 'Colored' soldiers. 'Colored' mess . . ."

He takes my hand and looks at me, looks me in the eyes. "Darlin', I called myself colored, so you would know that back when I was in the service, I was colored. I was just a colored man when it wasn't good to be a colored man." His eyes fill with tears at the pain and the memories. "Then I got out, times changed." He sits up in his chair. "I'm a black man now." The tears slide down his cheeks, and he nods his head with each proud word. "I live in a world that is led by a black man and I am a black man. You know what that's like for an old man like me?" He gives me a triumphant look, but he is still weeping.

I reach over and caress his face; his tears wet my fingertips.

There it is.

Tears.

The strongest symbol between humans, no matter where they are from, no matter what color they are. The one gesture that cannot be anything but pure. The one that even horses cannot share.

And I reach down and pat his hand and wish I could weep with him.

Chapter 32

It seemed Hogarth got himself a new personality as well as a new rank and a new office. He was now in charge of Hangar Security, and was friendly, amiable, even, to Fleischer, though Willie might as well have been invisible, standing there.

"What you got there, Fleischer?" Hogarth leaned forward and reached out to the carton of sacks Fleischer had thrown on his desk.

"I was ordered to bring these in," Fleischer said carelessly. He hadn't saluted, hadn't said anything else. Just walked in and threw the carton on the desk. He had resigned himself to going through Hogarth, because there was no other way to save the pilots. And saving pilots was what it was all about.

Hogarth picked up one of the sacks, turned it over in his hands, slowly, carefully, examining every inch of it, as Fleischer explained what he had been doing. He pulled out his ever-present loupe and showed Hogarth how to look through it, showed him a sample of the old wiring, a few pieces of new wiring, how the sacks worked, his enthusiasm finally overtaking his initial suspicion.

"Made these yourself, didja?" Hogarth asked, opening and closing the little drawstrings. "Where'dja get the idea from?"

Fleischer explained about the connections, how he always thought it had something to do with the connections.

Hogarth held up his hand. "Wait just a second," he said, and pulled out a pad and pencil. "Connections, eh? What are we talking about here?" And Fleischer continued to outline how he changed the pressure settings, how he got a hunch, how he finally decided that it was how the wires were hooking together.

Hogarth listened to every word. He reminded Willie of a bull-dog puppy he had when he was a kid, listening with his head cocked, one ear tilted toward Fleischer, nodding with every word.

"Who paid for the materials?" he asked, when Fleischer finished.

"I did," Fleischer replied, explaining that it came from his twenty-one-dollar-a-month salary that left barely enough money for groceries for him and Ruth. "My wife worked on them, too."

Hogarth chuckled. "If that don't beat all," he said cordially. "Now you got the little woman working for the U.S. Army Air Corps." He tossed the sack into the carton, and leaned back in his chair.

"The colonel mentioned you might be coming in with something," he said. "And this is a doozy."

"It was challenging," Fleischer said.

"Challenging," Hogarth repeated and jotted the word down.

"And I want to mention that all my men worked on it," Fleischer added, gesturing to Willie. "They should get credit, too."

"I'll have to write this up, you know," Hogarth said. "Gotta go through channels. But I'll get right on it."

Fleischer dropped his notes on the desk. "It's all there," he said. "We can save a lot of boys."

"I know we will," Hogarth agreed heartily. He stood up and extended his hand, without even one glance at Willie. "The United States Army Air Force thanks you for your hard work," he said. They shook hands. "And," he added, "the colonel is going to be very, very impressed."

* * *

Two weeks passed. Three. The men continued to use the sacks; Fleischer continued to take notes, make small modifications, scan the skies anxiously, all the while waiting to hear from Fairchild. There hadn't been any crashes since they'd started using the things, and Fleischer was happy, buoyant, that his invention was making a difference.

"Throw out the old ones," he said to Willie one morning as he carried in a box of replacement sacks, now patterned with yellow daisies, the five-and-dime having run out of pink rosebuds. He was still making them at home with Ruth, still waiting for some kind of acknowledgment.

"They're probably sending the specs to a private firm to have them made properly," he explained to Willie. "Gotta stamp 'U.S. Air Force' on them or they won't use them." He sighed. "I would give anything to have thought them up a month sooner."

Willie knew what he meant. They'd still be sharing warm beer with Jink Davies.

"My mother always says, things happen when they're supposed to happen," Willie tried to console him. "Anything yet from the colonel?"

Fleischer shook his head. "You know how careful they have to be," he said. "I'm sure it's just a matter of time."

It got a big write-up in the *Stars and Stripes*. A commendation and a medal. A raise in rank and a United States savings bond that would be worth one hundred dollars in twenty-five years. The thing was, it was awarded to Chief Master Sergeant John P. Hogarth, and his country was proud of him for being instrumental in saving the lives of all the young men who were stationed at Maxwell Field Army Air Force Base for bomber training. It had been challenging, Hogarth said in his interview, *challenging*, to finally figure out what was causing the crashes and convince the men in the Housekeeping Unit to help.

Fleischer let out a roar of fury and a string of curse words that could have scorched the paint off the plane in front of him. Willie had never seen anyone's complexion turn that purple.

"That prick took my idea and signed off on it," Fleischer screamed as he waved the newspaper over his head. Willie took the paper from his hand and quickly scanned the article.

"He takes a nice picture," he said, but Fleischer was in too foul a mood for levity.

"Get in the jeep," he barked to Willie. Willie's heart dropped into his boots. He left the paper on the office desk and followed, but only as far as the hangar doors. He stood his ground there.

"I don't think you should see Sergeant Hogarth at the moment," he said. "Maybe go through channels." This was going to get ugly, he just knew it. He could smell ugly a mile away.

"Don't worry," said Fleischer. "You won't be involved. That's a vow."

"Then what do you need me for?"

Fleischer started the jeep. "To call the medics," he replied.

"Medics?"

"Oh yeah," Fleischer replied. "'Cause—between me and Hogarth? After I finish with him, one of us is going to wind up dead."

Hogarth's office was at the end of a long, low-slung building that housed airfield maintenance equipment, and Fleischer drove there like a madman. Personnel were jumping out of his way, thinking it had to be some sort of base emergency. Willie thought he could hear the siren of MPs in the distance.

They stopped right outside the door. Fleischer jumped from the jeep and paused. He wasn't a fighter, Willie knew.

"I'm going in," Fleischer said, but didn't move.

"You don't have to," Willie reminded him. "You could file something—go through channels. Everything goes through channels."

"This went through channels," Fleischer said grimly. "And look what happened." He clenched his fists, but stood there. "I'm going right in," he said.

Willie studied the sky. Clear blue, clear for takeoff. A few Vultees were disappearing into the clouds overhead. "Yes, sir," he said.

Fleischer faced the door, then suddenly turned around, pulling something from his pocket. "Take this," he said and held it out. It was a gold ring with a large blue topaz stone on one side, and the letter $\mathcal{M}$ engraved next to it. Willie took it into his hand and stared down at it. It felt heavy and smooth and cold. He rolled his finger across the stone.

"What is it?"

"My bar mitzvah ring," Fleischer said. "I don't know what's going to happen to me, and I don't want to lose it."

The fight only lasted a minute or so. Fleischer had gathered himself, kicked open the door to Hogarth's office, and given him a roundhouse punch before Hogarth could get out of his chair. Willie could see that much through the door. Hogarth answered with a well-aimed slug and Fleischer flew backward, out the door.

"You're a dead man," Hogarth shouted after him. "You will burn in hell, if I have to light the fires myself."

An alarm sounded somewhere, the MPs surrounded them all like an angry swarm of wasps, and Fleischer was handcuffed and taken away.

Willie gave a statement that basically he saw nothing, knew nothing, wasn't involved, was just the driver. They dismissed him. Though it was the literal truth, he felt very bad over it, but it could have been ugly for him. He touched the ring in his pocket with shaky fingers and drove back to the hangar.

Fleischer was released a few days later, by order of Colonel Fairchild. It seemed that Hogarth didn't want to press charges over the punch; in his statement, he said he was more interested in the war effort than to prosecute a delusional crank soldier; it had all been a misunderstanding. Hogarth let it be known that he would drop the charge of striking an officer, if

Fleischer would let the matter of who actually invented the sacks quietly disappear. Fleischer felt he had no choice.

"I shouldn't have punched him like that," Fleischer explained to Willie. "I should have just killed the fucker outright."

Though the charges were dropped against Fleischer, it wasn't over. Hogarth had his supporters, who were urging him to prosecute the "little Jew." Remarks about returning Fleischer to Jerusalem were passed around the mess; remarks about "Ikie— the kikie" were whispered behind his back; salt was dumped over his food when he wasn't looking; he was pinned to the wall in the latrine by a burly sergeant he didn't recognize. It left Fleischer nervous and short-tempered and chronically worried.

"It's not fair," he complained to Willie. "I'm getting hung by the balls for nothing."

"I know, Sarge," Willie agreed. "Things ain't never been fair."

It wasn't long before Fleischer completely stopped talking about Hogarth. And then stopped talking about the sacks. At Ruth's urging, he submitted receipts for his expenses, to help buy more oilcloth, but it came back denied because they were unauthorized. The wash rack made do with the ones they had.

"That savings bond would've made a nice surprise for Ruth," was Fleischer's only reference to the whole thing.

But in late January, the Air Force took over the manufacturing of the sacks, except that they weren't sacks anymore; they were tight little rubber fittings that snapped onto the ends of the wires. The men had to remove their gloves to work the fittings on and off; the chemicals burned their fingertips and it slowed them down. But the little rubber caps did the job, Willie supposed, even if they couldn't compare to the beauteous rose designs of the oilcloth. Turnaround time for getting the planes clean slowed to a crawl, but for some reason, no one came in to complain. Colonel Fairchild, it seemed, had decided to leave them alone.

The whole matter was dropped as though it had never happened.

Chapter 33

Willie and I spend a whole day playing Double Solitaire and Rowena was right. He cheats. He slips cards from his pocket onto the table, returns his cards, and reshuffles the deck when he isn't happy with the hand he gets, forgets it is my turn and plays a second time, adds the numbers wrong after insisting on keeping score. I didn't care. I was listening to his reedy voice reach back and pull up the past.

The Alabama spring came in February, soft and misty for a week or two before dropping back into winter again. The pale sun and tender air slid across the base with promises of warmth and gentle rains, then rescinded with cold nights, before settling, finally, into a damp gentility.

It was a dark spring.

McArthur was fighting gallantly in Bataan, the RAF was desperately and unsuccessfully trying to sink a key German battleship, the *Tirpitz*, Japan had pretty much conquered all of the Pacific, and the U.S. War Relocation Authority was interning Japanese-American citizens.

It was an uneasy spring.

The mercurial weather only made Fleischer more jumpy; he saw enemies everywhere. Hogarth was insidious, he had friends, and there had been small incidents. Or maybe not. Fleischer was never sure. He didn't trust the system, he didn't trust his superiors, he didn't even trust the weather. He constantly wore a thick dark green sweater that Ruth knit for him, even on the warmest days, like it was going to protect him.

It was a spring of longing.

August yearned for his family and the farm at home.

"I always help my mama plant," he told Willie. "She be planting beans and collards and corn 'bout now. I turn over the soil for her, 'cause it has to be just so."

Willie could picture the big man pushing against a till, moving the dark loam, softening it for planting. August was a farm boy, and Willie knew nothing about farming. August could look up at the sky and tell what the weather was going to be the next day. He could sniff the air and predict rain within an hour. He knew the feather and call of every bird that flew overhead. His mother sent him seed packets, and he planted tomatoes and pansies in the hard-packed dirt outside the barracks.

"Gotta have some flowers, too," he told Willie. "My mama always says that collards is good for the stomach but flowers is good for the eyes."

As for Willie, spring made him nostalgic for his music. When the weather was good in Harlem, he used to sit on the fire escape outside his bedroom window and play. He missed the feel of the trombone against his lips, the shudder and vibration of the music coming from his breath and fingers. The way the air curved itself into songs as he played. He decided to ask his sister to send him his old trombone. It would be nice to run his hands over the smooth brass, almost like caressing a woman, coaxing a response. He missed his music very much.

"Look at that sky." Every so often Fleischer would stop at the hangar doors and comment on the horizon. The sky was all innocent blue now, without a hint of malice. Only the Brits were crashing, mostly because they were still "bouncing" on farms, a quick touchdown and up, buzzing cars on the highways, playing fiercely with each other against the backdrop of fleece clouds. They still pissed off the helpless brass, but it would make them crack fighters when they returned to the UK. Fleischer stood in the morning sun and studied the sky above. His arms were folded, and his face held no expression at all.

"What you lookin' at, Sarge?" August asked him. August was still in charge of pushing the planes into the hangar to be cleaned. He stopped to look up at the sky, too.

"It's what I'm not looking at," Fleischer replied with a certain grim satisfaction. "I'm *not* looking at planes falling."

But he was restless. The sacks had served to challenge him, absorb his energy, direct it. And he had nothing to preoccupy him anymore. He paced the floors, made a doll out of a small corn dust broom for Ruth, invented a joke—a flashlight battery stuck inside a carefully hollowed-out light bulb, so it lit up without being plugged in. He was still fixing broken appliances one night a week in his apartment, but mentioned how Ruth was annoyed with the tiny rooms getting cluttered with radio tubes and extra plugs, and boxes of screws and tools laid out across the kitchen table. And the chickens, which always seemed to sneak in from their pen under the house into the bedroom, but it was mostly the clutter that was driving her crazy.

"Can you imagine?" Fleischer complained to Willie during coffee break. "I'm trying to earn some extra money and she's not happy." It was a real problem, he went on to say, and she wasn't going to sleep with him until he solved it.

Corporal Charlie Hobbs had a suggestion. "Why don't you use my church?" he said. "I can ask Pastor Booker if he would mind."

Charlie, like August, was a local boy and faithfully attended services off base every Sunday, since he wasn't allowed into the chapel on base.

"I don't have any money to pay for the use of the church," Fleischer said. "I'm trying to *make* money. I can't pay any kind of rent."

Charlie thought for a moment. "The church has a lot of things that need fixin'," he said. "Maybe you could trade work for space. Maybe the good Lord means for you to do a little church work."

Apparently He did.

Pastor Booker was delighted to offer the trade. One day a week, staying into the evening, Fleischer visited the First Baptist Church of Montgomery and fixed all the things that Pastor Booker, a man not much older than himself, brought him. He fixed things for believers and things for nonbelievers, record players and radios and clocks, even wristwatches, and irons and toasters. He fixed the boiler for the church, and the pump on the organ. He even fixed Mrs. Booker's pressure cooker and took back a huge metal pot of ham hocks and chitlins, which the men happily ate as soon as they returned to base. A few of the men regularly came with him and worked at the church, painting, repairing, cleaning, planting, weeding, a never-ending list of the Lord's needs. It was all working out pretty good, Fleischer told the men, pretty good.

"Maybe the good Lord did have something to do with it, because the church was surely in poor shape, and no money to fix things," Charlie Hobbs replied. He put his hands together and looked upward. "Thank You, sweet Jesus."

Fleischer was taken aback for a moment, then gave a rueful smile. "Well, maybe He did," he said softly. "'Cause I never thought I'd be going to *church* on a regular basis."

Fleischer had finished the last of the jobs. A sewing machine. The bobbin wouldn't let the thread out evenly, and Fleischer got it to run. Its owner was a seamstress and offered to pay Fleischer off over the next several months. The machine was her livelihood, he knew. He also knew she didn't have a dime to spare, since being poor in Alabama seemed to reach below the depths of plain poverty. He handed her the machine and told her to forget about paying him. He had done that with a lot of his other clients; one more didn't matter.

Evening was near, the sun was drifting downward, and a soft half-light was falling over Montgomery. Fleischer and the rest of the men—August and Charlie Hobbs and Leon Hamilton and Willie—were tired. They had carried boxes of clothing for a clothing drive into the basement, tarred a portion of the roof, changed light bulbs in the twenty-foot-high rectory, painted a small bathroom, and fixed some tile.

Pastor Booker gratefully accompanied them to the door, where he blessed them. "And maybe the Lord Jesus will lead you back to us," he said to Fleischer. "Maybe you will find Him in your heart and return to the flock as a faithful follower." He made a blessing over Fleischer's head and leaned forward to kiss his cheek. "Thank You, sweet Jesus, for bringing this man to us." Fleischer looked embarrassed.

"Thank you, Pastor," he mumbled, then signaled his men. "We'd better go. We got a bus to catch."

I had just finished serving Willie his lunch. A waffle with sugar-free syrup, a spray of butter-flavored something or other, and a slice of turkey bacon, which I thought would make him very happy. He loves waffles, but he only glanced at his plate.

"What's wrong?" I ask, taking a sip of my coffee.

"You're not going to like me much after today," he says quietly.

I jerked back in my chair with surprise. "Why do you say that?" I asked. "I do care about you."

His lips moved without words. "I will tell you the bus story now." He sighed "It's the story you really came for."

Fleischer and his men would have to take the bus from the church and change to a second one, for a long ride back to base. The first bus was late, but eventually pulled into the stop and the doors flipped open. The second one was waiting at the curb, and because it was dinnertime and a bus headed for the outskirts of Montgomery, where the base was located, it was empty. The men climbed on and settled into seats. Normally, servicemen in uniform rode free, but Fleischer knew that courtesy didn't apply to his men, so he paid for all of them. Leon Hamilton headed straight for the back. Willie sat just past the middle, toward the back, next to Charlie Hobbs. Fleischer sat one seat in front of the middle; August looked around and yawned.

"You can sit here," Fleischer said to him, gesturing to the seat across the aisle.

"It ain't in the back," August replied.

"It doesn't matter," Fleischer said. "There's no one on the bus. And I don't think anyone's going back to base with us."

August flopped down in the seat and stretched his large frame out in front of him. Fleischer had some paperwork to do in the wash rack before he could go home; the men were hungry and tired and actually looking forward to the mess hall. They leaned back in their seats; August yawned. Willie closed his eyes, hoping for a quick nap.

"Wake me when we get to the base," he said to Leon.

"We better get Charlie to wake us both; he's reading something," Leon answered and leaned his own head back. The men started to drift into a sweet reverie.

Willie thought he heard a shout and opened his eyes. It was the bus driver. "Move to the back," he was yelling. He was seated and looking at the men through his rearview mirror, looking directly at August. "Move way to the back, or I ain't drivin' this bus."

Fleischer stood up. "These are United States servicemen," he said.

"You tell that nigger to move to the back of the bus or we ain't going nowhere," the driver snapped back. He had turned around in his seat now; his large girth straining against the steering wheel. He pointed to August. "That nigger right there is out of order."

Flustered, August stood up. "Yessir," he said.

"Just wait there a minute," Fleischer said to August, then

turned to face the driver. "There's no one else on the bus. These are servicemen. We're going back to base."

"You tell that nigger to move to the back," the driver repeated, his voice growing louder. Fleischer stood there, getting angry. He wasn't in the mood for crap. He was tired of Alabama. He knew this happened, he'd seen it before, but not his men. Not his men.

"Hey," he started to say, but the bus driver grunted to his feet and stood with beefy hands on his ample hips.

"Y'all startin' something here?" the bus driver rasped, tilting his chin up.

"No," said Fleischer. "It's just that there's no one on the bus and these are United States—"

"Y'all startin' a *incident?*" The driver's voice rose in fury. "Y'all planning to break the law?"

August put his hands out in front of him, palms up. He was confused. He never broke the law, and he didn't understand what the screaming was about. He would move to the back. Right away. Right now. He stepped into the aisle. He would move. He didn't want trouble. He stepped into the aisle so fast, he stumbled forward.

The bus driver misunderstood. He saw August lurch toward him. "You stay right there, nigger," he screeched, "Don't you come at me."

August froze in place for a moment. "No, sir," he said. He would never break the law. He knew his place.

"Did you just say 'no, sir'? Did y'all just tell me you *ain't* movin'?" the driver yelled at him, his fury rising. He slammed the door open to prevail upon bystanders to summon the authorities. "Get the police," he screamed. waving his hand out the door. "I need help! We got a incident here! We got a incident!"

Some of them waved down a patrol car, which turned on its flashing red lights and pulled over. Two policemen jumped onto the bus, their guns drawn. It was all confusion, and screaming and movement and misinterpretation. It was all attitude and agony.

"I didn't do nothing, sir." August stepped forward to apologize. His large frame filled the aisle.

"That's him," the bus driver screeched, backing up. "He was comin' at me. He was threatening me. Get him!"

"Stop right there!" the officer commanded, but August was even more confused. He wanted to move to the back. He took another step to turn around.

"Get him," screamed the bus driver. "He's runnin' away." August turned to see who they were going to get.

"Stop right there," the officer shouted, then fired off a shot. It hit August in the chest. His body lifted a foot in the air from the impact before he slumped across the back of a seat and slid to the floor.

"*No!*" Fleischer screamed, running to August's side and turning him over. The bullet had gone straight into his heart.

"What did you do?" Fleischer screamed at the officer. He was incredulous, grabbing August and propping him up against a seat. He frantically pulled off his own sweater and pressed it against the wound; the dark green wool turned red-brown from the blood. "What did you do?" he screamed again, his eyes nearly popping from his head as he stared up at the policeman. The officer was standing there, confused, his gun still in his hand. His face went slack as he looked at August, then Fleischer, then the bus driver.

"He threatened to kill me," said the bus driver.

Willie jumped to his feet. "Murderer!" he cried in anguish, not caring who was there, or who heard him, or even whether he was going to be shot next. "You *murdered* him." He wasn't even sure who he meant, Fleischer or the cop, or the driver, or maybe all three.

The policeman looked down at August, at his uniform, as though the deed had finally registered in his own mind. "He's a soldier," he said. He looked stricken. The bus driver mumbled something and got off the bus, to be greeted by a small crowd just starting to gather outside, speculating on what had happened.

Willie dropped to August's side and took him from Fleischer, who walked to the front of the bus.

"Somebody call an ambulance," Fleischer yelled through the door. "Hurry. Call an ambulance. I've got a man down."

Willie pulled August to his own chest and called his name. There was only a bubbling sound from August's mouth, a whisper of death. Charlie Hobbs and Leon Hamilton stood in frozen shock as Willie looked down the aisle at Fleischer in disbelief and fury.

"Look what you fucking did," he croaked, not caring about ranks or protocol or much of anything. "You got him *killed*. You ordered him to sit in the front. You *murdered* him. You're a goddamned murderer!"

"No," Fleischer started. "No, no."

Willie couldn't look at Fleischer. Old rage, plumbed from depths of old pain, filled him. Fleischer was just another motherfucking white man screwing it up. What had been the point to push things? To push until it came to this? He cradled August in his arms and called to him, "August. August!" as if, if he made his voice loud enough, he could summon him back from the dead. He pressed his ear to August's chest. The blood wet his face and seeped onto his clothes. He cradled his head and wept over him, his own body shaking violently

Fleischer was near-hysterical now. "How could you shoot a man like that?" he kept screaming at the policeman, who moved as though in a dream. "What did you do? You killed him. You *killed* a U.S. soldier!" He was moving back and forth, between the policeman and August, his hands pressed on the top of his head in disbelief and rage. "What the fuck did you *do?*"

Sirens called from blocks away, coming closer, bringing more men, more confusion. It was too late for August. It was too late for anything. Blood was everywhere, blood and noise and lights and confusion. The police swarmed the bus and arrested Fleischer and Willie and Leon and Charlie for disorderly conduct and inciting a riot.

* * *

The news spread like a drop of ink in a water bottle, curling its way through the streets, swirling across the city in streams of information. Everyone had an opinion. The whites thought it was justifiable: The police were supposed to enforce municipal codes. The blacks were filled with rage: This was more proof, another incident in a long history of brutality.

Crowds gathered outside the police cars, watching as the men were being driven away, raising their fists and screaming. Willie looked out at them from the window. All he could think of was that he hoped he'd be safe in jail. That Montgomery had gotten dangerous and ugly and that it didn't take much to turn perfectly ordinary people into a lynch mob. And it wouldn't surprise him at all to get lynched for nothing.

Chapter 34

Even now, I can't summon tears. Willie's face is filled with anguish; he bows his head, letting his own tears fall onto his plate. All over his waffle. Perhaps I understand, now, my father's rage. He was well-intentioned, he was a champion of sorts, for the men he cared for, and he was rejected summarily, harshly, brutally, even. And I feel immensely sorry.

We sat together quietly for a few minutes.

"You have to eat something," I tell Willie, standing up and removing his spoiled food. I scrape his waffle into the trash and open the freezer to get him another.

"I'm so sorry," Willie says through soft tears. "I was angry."

"It was a time for anger," I say, popping his new waffle into the toaster. When it's ready, I put it on a fresh plate and place it in front of him.

"You have to eat," I remind him. "Or your sugar will drop too low."

"Yes, ma'am," he says and picks up his fork, then sighs. "You know, there's a time for anger, and a time to let it go."

I suddenly reach out to touch his hand, compelled to say something. "It's a poison."

"Yes, ma'am," Willie responds and tilts his head at me. Suddenly I sit back to sort through what I'd just said.

We poison ourselves and we poison each other. A cruel remark, the turn of a shoulder, the indifference to someone's pain. I remember how often I flinched under my father's comments, but I never realized how much it could fester, infiltrate in its insidious, toxic way, through his life my life, a family.

A culture.

A furious General Markham was notified right away that four of his men had been jailed. He was known as a fair man, forward-thinking and protective of his base, and he was not about to have any of his soldiers incarcerated. He immediately called for a conference with the police commissioner that very evening. The commissioner admitted that perhaps the policeman should not have been following the orders of a bus driver, but really, it had been necessary to keep law and order. "This is my city," the commissioner said, and he ran things the way he saw fit. The soldiers belonged on base, General Markham insisted, and he wanted them to be given over to his custody or he would take legal action against the policeman, against the entire Montgomery Police Department, with the full support of the United States Army Air Corps behind him. Maybe even the president. He was in the middle of a war, and he didn't have time to play with a chickenshit police department. It was an ultimatum the Montgomery police couldn't refuse.

The men were released.

Willie never thought he'd be so happy to see the MPs come for him.

"I want a full report," General Markham said to Fleischer as soon as he and the men arrived at the base. He had ordered them into his office for a debriefing, and they had lined up at stiff attention in front of him. He settled himself into a brown leather chair, ready to take notes. He was a tall man, slim, with silver hair and silver-framed glasses, and the way he uncapped a gold pen and waited for Fleischer to speak reminded Willie of a high school principal. Willie could barely steady himself, he was so spent with rage.

Fleischer cleared his throat, but no words came out.

What are you going to say, motherfucker? Willie thought. *August is dead.* He stood stiffly at attention, his back hurting from standing so stiff, so tight with anger, his hands clenched into fists. He waited for Fleischer to speak.

The room was silent; they could hear planes outside, flying over the base. Night training for someone. Jeeps rolled by outside; voices called out.

"Sergeant Fleischer?" the general repeated. "I'd like to hear what happened. Your own version."

My own version is that this is just another white man with no feeling for the way things are, Willie thought. *August is dead. He didn't have to die today.* He stole a sideways glance at Fleischer. The motherfucker had pushed August into the arms of death. Had risked the life of a man to make a point. What kind of point was this motherfucking—*Jew!*—going to make in *Alabama,* for Christ's sake? In *Alabama!* What was he going to change? *Who* was he going to change?

"Yes, sir," Fleischer began, but still said nothing. He seemed to be trying to sort it all out, maybe trying to figure out in his dumb-shit white-man mind how it had turned into *that.*

What can you say? Willie thought.

"Go ahead, Sergeant," the general said.

Fleischer swallowed. "We were coming back from church, sir," he started, seemingly unaware of how the words sounded, the odd juxtaposition of a Fleischer who looked like, well, like a Fleischer, coming back from church.

The general apparently thought so, too. "Church?"

"Yes, sir," Fleischer said, sounding relieved that he could say something that made sense. "We go every week to help Pastor Booker." Then he stopped talking, lost again on the bus.

"Sergeant?" the general said.

"Yes, sir." Fleischer's brows knitted together, and his eyes looked watery. His voice was shaky. How could he have lost a man coming back from *church*? This wasn't Germany. Or war-ravaged London. How could he have lost a soldier in *America*? How was it possible to shoot an American soldier for sitting in the wrong place on a *bus*? He started to speak, but Willie stopped listening; the furious, screaming words were exploding from his heart, filling his head now. *You got a man killed, mother-fucker. Killed one of your own men with your pigheaded, asshole stub-bornness, thinking you were going to fix the world.* But he stood at rigid attention, because that's what the rules were; you had to stand at attention.

Fleischer was talking, explaining for probably the hundredth time in four hours, his voice gone flat, his face blank, getting blanker each minute.

Willie just forced himself to concentrate on the wall picture behind the general. It was a picture of the American flag and the face of the Statue of Liberty superimposed over it. He didn't want to hear Fleischer talk. They were all the same, these white men; every one of them was guilty and responsible; you couldn't sep-arate them out. Willie should have remembered that.

Fleischer finished, and the general took off his glasses and held them in his hands, opening and closing the arms.

"I believe you," he said to Fleischer, "and because I believe you, I put the full authority and support of the United States Army Air Corps behind you. This was a terrible tragedy. A need-less loss."

Fleischer blinked hard. "Private Randolph—he wasn't, you know—all that sharp, sir." He tried to explain. "He moved slow, if you know what I mean. But he tried hard to do the right thing."

"I see," said the general.

"He was a good man," Fleischer added, his voice cracking. "August was a good man."

Don't you be using his first name, like you was his friend, Willie thought furiously. *You got him killed.*

"I see," said the general.

The men shuffled in their places. They didn't want a speech

on how good August was. He was dead. It was too late for a speech.

"Let me ask you," the general said, putting his glasses back on and leaning forward. "Do you think this could have been prevented?"

"Yes, sir," said Fleischer.

Willie felt his face get hot. *Yes, sir,* he would have answered. *It could have absolutely been prevented.* If Fleischer had just let August move to the back of the bus, they'd all be reporting for work first thing tomorrow morning, all doing their jobs.

"How do you think it could have been prevented?" the general asked. He seemed sincerely interested in Fleischer's answer.

Fleischer licked his lips. He looked over at Willie.

Don't be looking at me, motherfucker, Willie thought. *Don't be looking at me for answers.*

"Maybe some kind of training—maybe for the police," Fleischer started. "On how to treat a United States soldier."

How to treat a colored soldier, Willie added in his head, *'cause white soldiers get treated with respect.*

General Markham gave a half smile. "You'll be glad to hear I already recommended that, Sergeant," he said. He looked at the rest of the men. "You men have anything to add?"

The men drew their shoulders up even more; their eyes stayed straight on the wall behind the general. What was there to say? That the whole world was fucking screwed up? That things were never going to be different? That talking to a few cops would do shit? They had nothing to say.

"Thank you for your time, men," the general said. "Dismissed."

They stepped out into a very different day than they had stepped into that morning. Night was drawing upon them; the sky was filling with stars. Planes flew overhead, gliding onto the field in smooth landings; trucks rolled past, jeeps drove up and down the base roads, the "Big Voice" made a few lackadaisical announcements, it all looked normal, it all sounded normal, but it was far from normal. The three black soldiers had seen something, shared something they knew was just a matter of time coming, for any of them. That's the way things were. If you were colored in America, you would never be safe. Even in the *army*. The three men marched to a waiting jeep and got in, leaving Fleischer behind.

Early the next morning, Willie stepped from the barracks out under a torturous and unapologetic sun, standing in its burning rays and looking up at the sky, then across the path to a small, patchy garden. The one August had planted. Tiny tomato plants were uncurling, beginning to stand up next to what he guessed were pansies. He walked over to them. This was what spring was about. Promises. It was all about promises. It was all about promising that this year, things would be better. But it was a terrible lie. The plants would come to nothing, because August would not be tending them. They were sending his body back home for burial. For planting. August did not know that he would be part of the earth this spring instead of these small, struggling plants. Willie stood there for a moment, wondering about spring, and how it comes to nothing sometimes. How these plants would come to nothing, how friendships come to nothing. A breeze shuddered through the small green frills, and they bent their tendrils down, as if in grief. He didn't know how to care for them, he was not a farmer, but he would not watch them twist in the sad Alabama wind and punishing sun and die from neglect. No. He stood over them for a moment, then picked up his foot and trampled them under the heel of his combat boot.

Chapter 35

It was the wash rack as usual. But it was the wash rack with one terrible difference. Despite the daily work, the ratcheting of metal, the hissing of hoses, the squall of planes being shifted from one bay to another, there was an unseemly silence that permeated the air. The men worked as usual, but said little, A few gestures here and there to get the task at hand finished, but little else. No one called out, no one made jokes, let their laughter mix anymore, with the heat and gray-white steam. Losing August was like losing a tooth from the front of your mouth, a huge, painful gap that everyone could see. They didn't mention his name, never talked about that *incident;* it was off-limits. Conversation was for the barracks. Where they were safe.

They shunned Fleischer.
Oh, they were unfailingly polite to him, called him "sir," or "sergeant," but the informal friendliness was gone. They avoided his eyes when they spoke to him, ate their lunch in little clusters outside the hangar, looked down when he passed by.
He slowly changed. Became a loner. He'd always had few friends

on base, mostly because he was always involved in his projects, but now he had nobody. Especially not Willie.

Willie was torn into pieces. What to think? How do you pull out the good and the bad from someone? Things had always been a balancing act between them, a white man and a colored man, caught in a puzzle. Which pieces do you put together and which do you throw away? Willie was angry all the time, and confused. Things had become too difficult to figure out.

Fleischer rarely spoke to his men now, except for issuing orders or discussing a particular problem with a plane. He no longer laughed with them, no longer brought in extra food, didn't stand with them when they had their coffee break, though he continued to bring in the coffee and supplies, just dropping things off in the radio room, grabbing a cup of coffee after it was brewed by one of the men, and then retreating to his office, shutting the door behind him. At the end of the day, he dismissed his men without an extra word, and headed for the bus that would take him home.

Ruth came to the wash rack once in a while, when she visited the PX. But the warmth was gone from her manner; she gave the men polite nods, then would speak in low tones with her husband before she left. She never said good-bye.

Everything had changed in the wash rack. Everything and everyone.

A few weeks passed and Fleischer called a meeting. "I've been ordered to a follow-up with General Markham," he said. The men stared at him impassively. Willie hoped that he wasn't included; he had nothing to add, nothing to say. His anger toward Fleischer had kept him up for nights; he raged against him in the privacy of the barracks, despised him, the anger feeding on itself until it had become the most essential and biggest part of him.

"I plan to bring up the sacks we worked on," Fleischer went on. "He needs to know that those sacks came out of this wash rack, and that you men deserve some kind of commendation."

He held up a copy of the *Air Force News*. A small article in the lower left-hand corner stated that the rate of Vultee crashes was down nearly ninety-two percent in the past three months. The men just stared at him, their eyes dead. Fleischer looked at Willie. "I'll need you to go with me," he said.

General Markham looked tired. The Japanese had become unstoppable and the Pentagon was ramping up the pressure to get more men ready to fight. It was the perfect time to bring up the success of the sacks, Fleischer had said to Willie as they drove to the general's office. But Willie didn't answer him. Frankly, he didn't give a shit what kind of time it was. He was planning to finish his tour and get the hell out of the army. Alive. Yes, it would be very nice if he got out of the fucking state of Alabama alive.

They spoke a few minutes, Fleischer and the general, about how the program was going with the Montgomery police. The commissioner had actually instituted a training program on how to deal with soldiers, especially colored soldiers. General Markham had high hopes for its success. Willie stood, arms and legs at ease, ignoring the conversation, filling his head with something tolerable.

Take the "A" train.

He concentrated on the words to mask the polite conversation, to contain himself, to keep himself from screaming out that it was all motherfucking bullshit.

"I wanted to talk to you about something else, sir," Fleischer finally said. "The sacks."

The general looked puzzled. "The—what?"

"The sacks, sir," Fleischer said, with a little more courage. "You know, the new addition to the wash rack cleaning protocol. To keep the planes from crashing."

General Markham squinted his eyes, trying to remember, then nodded wearily. "Oh yes, seems Colonel Fairchild mentioned something about capping the wires. I believe he and

Sergeant Hogarth came up with that solution. Brilliant idea. You're both from the wash rack, aren't you? What do you think about them?"

"It was my idea," Fleischer said. "And it's working very well."

The general stared at him. "Your idea?"

Fleischer drew himself up and glanced over at Willie.

Willie met his eyes. *I'm not backing you on this, motherfucker.*

"I kept all the records, sir," Fleischer said. "I have all the records. I discovered the wires were getting corroded by the chemicals, so my wife and I made these sacks—"

"Your *wife*, Sergeant?"

Fleischer nodded, then finished eagerly. "Yes, sir. To cover the ends of the wires. I mentioned it to the colonel, sir, and he ordered me to turn them over to Sergeant Hogarth."

"You were ordered to turn what over to Sergeant Hogarth?" the general asked patiently.

"All my notes, sir," Fleischer replied. "How we made them. I still have the original notes." He explained how he had mailed himself copies of his notes, and how the United States Post Office could serve as his witness because the dates on the envelopes, along with the daily newspaper clippings tucked inside, would document that his idea was formulated long before Hogarth had claimed it for his own.

"My men worked hard on it, too, sir," Fleischer added. "They had to put them on the wires without losing production time. They even suggested some modifications so it worked better." He turned to Willie. "Isn't that right, Private Jackson?"

Willie looked at him coldly, and barely assented.

General Markham leaned back in his leather chair and made a bridge with his fingers as he reflected on Fleischer's words. "Bring those records to me, Sergeant," he said. "Bring them to me immediately. I would very much like to see them."

It created a small stir on base when Hogarth was issued an official reprimand. Fleischer had presented all his notes and self-addressed envelopes, his sketches, a few samples of the original sacks done in the white oilcloth with pink roses, convincing the general that Hogarth had pirated the idea. An official warning was put in both Hogarth's and Colonel Fairchild's permanent records, and Hogarth was demoted to corporal. The one-hundred-dollars-in-twenty-five-years savings bond was cancelled and reissued to Fleischer, though as far as Willie knew, he never received it. All the men in the 823rd Quartermaster Squadron were issued commendations, that, in the privacy of their barracks, were joked about and demoted to the status of toilet paper. Fleischer received no other recognition for his efforts. What he did receive, though, were a lot of new enemies who felt he had done both Hogarth and Fairchild a major disservice.

It had all come to nothing, Willie thought with some measure of satisfaction. Screw him! All Fleischer's efforts had come to nothing. Today had been another long, hard, sweaty day in the wash rack and it was over. He sat on his bunk and took a deep breath. The fury he felt for Fleischer wore like a gall, like a rock in his shoe. How could he ever have thought there could be a friendship between them? How could he have been so stupid, so fucking stupid, as to think they could be anything? They were living in two different countries. They would always be living in two different countries: the United States for White People, and the United States for Colored. He stood up, ready to take a shower, when he remembered Fleischer's ring. He felt around, deep inside his pocket. It was still there. He took it out and looked at it. The stone was hard and cold under his fingertips; the gold band sparkled in the light. His first impulse was to toss it in the trash, but he felt funny about that. He walked to his locker and pulled the door open, and stood in front of it for a long time, turning the ring over and over in his fingers. He went off to the latrine to get a wad of toilet paper and returned, wrapping it around the ring and stuffing it into his shaving kit, right under the brush with the mother-of-pearl handle. When the time was right, he might return it. It just wouldn't be right now.

Chapter 36

Cruelty is so simple, really. You just turn your back on your own humanity. It's a blindness of the soul, really. You see symbols instead of the life in front of you. The pastor saw the chance to bring a Jew into the fold instead of a man simply repairing broken items to supplement a meager army pay. The bus driver saw a big black man looming toward him, instead of a confused and flustered young soldier trying to figure out the right thing to do. Willie had seen a white man who screwed over his men, instead of a man so indignant over their treatment that he was misguidedly driven to do something about it.

You have to look with your heart. It is really the vision from the heart that matters. After Willie told me this part of his story, he had to rest a bit; the story took a piece out of him. There was nothing I could give him, no exoneration that he could accept from me, that would make it all right.

For days after Willie told me about the bus incident, I saw nothing except the slow-motion fall of a gentle giant, clutching his chest, his face puzzled, his last moments spent trying to understand an unspeakable act. I didn't want to talk about it anymore with Willie after he told me the story; his eyes had taken on a glitter of rage and then inexpressible sadness when he spoke and it worried me. I didn't want to lose him as a friend, but I didn't want to listen to my father get maligned. He was still my father. I didn't mention it to Rowena. I played it over and over in my mind, like a private horror movie. I hear the vitriol in Willie's voice when he spoke about the bus, the bitterness he harbored toward my father, and I am flustered. I didn't know what to say to him, since I see both sides. I know my father and I know he never had a prejudiced bone in his body. He was just trying to do the right thing, but it was at the wrong time.

Willie and I spend the rest of the day playing checkers and talking about the weather and my farm and general things, avoiding the pain and hate and plunging remorse that had once filled Willie's heart.

"You like music?" Rowena asks me after dinner. We are relaxing in her living room, talking politics and religion, agreeing and disagreeing, enjoying a bottle of white wine and each other's opinions.

"I used to play the piano," I tell her and regret it immediately. I never tell anyone that I used to play the piano. She glances over at the piano, black ebony elegantly draped with a green, yellow, and ocher dashiki, then walks over to it, slides the robe away, and opens the cover to reveal the orderly array of black and white keys.

"Please play something," she says. "I haven't played in years, but I would love to hear something." She steps away from it expectantly, her hand still resting on the robe.

My heart pounds with embarrassment. "Oh no, I haven't played since I was sixteen. I taught myself to play, so I don't really have any technique."

"Oh, that's okay," she coaxes. "My father taught himself to play, too. Won't you just play something?"

I approach the piano like it's a place of worship. The keys are cool under my fingers, familiar as if they were my own children.

I sit down and close my eyes. I know what I crave to play, something I used to play from memory, "Les Preludes, Part Two," by Liszt, an exquisite symphonic poem. I start, and at first get only a few hesitant notes, dysrhythmic, quarreling with each other about who goes first, who will take a turn. I am impatient with my hands, clumsy, awkward, there is no music in them at all. Then slowly, like a fawn approaching from the woods, the music comes; I hear it, my fingers summon it, notes fall upon themselves, upright and triumphant, it flows, it flows and I can only listen, as much a bystander as Rowena and Willie. I know it without thinking; my fingers play like they were sixteen years old again, lyrically, ferociously, the way they played before my father gave my piano away, right before I ran away forever. I play it with anger, remorse pushing away the broken phrases and sour chords. I play with fury, fury over a young black man who died for nothing, fury for the hollowness that I carry; my father never stopped once, to listen to me play. I play for my heart, which beats in agony, struggling to help me find a way to tell David that he is loved, loved, loved. I play until my arms burn and my fingers ache and I have to stop, breathless.

I look up at Rowena. "Oh my," she says, comes over, and kisses me on my cheek. I excuse myself and go to bed.

The moon is full, iridescent white in a black sky, an alien pearl lighting the room. I slip from bed and take the carton of pictures from the closet and carry a handful to the window. I find the one that matches August Woodrow Randolph. He has a round, good-natured face, with eyes that remind me of a deer, dark and dreamy. I can envision the look of surprise that crosses his face as the bullet tears into his heart, the light fading from his eyes, the full lips grimacing in pain before going slack. A cloud crosses the moon and the room darkens. I need to cry. I want so much to untie all the strings and let the knots fall away, but I am like the earth in the winter. Dead. Covered in a mulch of memories. I slip back to bed and quietly grieve for the music I had lost, for the love I might lose, for my ancient piano, and a young black man I have never met.

* * *

"I am sorry," I tell Willie the next morning. "I'm sorry that August died. I'm sorry that my father was involved with it. I guess that's why you never returned his ring."

Willie looks surprised and holds up his hands to stop me. "Oh no!" he says. "You don't understand at all. I *was* angry with him. But then, as time passed, I realized he couldn't have known what was going to happen."

"He should have known," I say. "Those were bad times. He should have known that it was going to lead to something bad."

I had fought this journey

I had just wanted to pay my respects to Willie, pick up a sound bite, and move on. I knew my father was a smart man. He could reinvent electricity, if he had to. He was flawed. But was he redeemable?

Willie puts his hand on mine. "Only the good Lord knows what is going to happen."

I look away from him. If the good Lord knew what was going to happen, why couldn't He have stepped in and prevented August's death? Willie and I sip our coffee in silence, thinking. Finally, I stand up.

"I have to go home soon," I tell him and lean down to kiss his cheek. "I'm needed at home."

"You have to come back again," he says. "You know, you have to hear the end of the story to understand any of it, at all."

"Call Mom," Sandra says. She had called me almost as soon as I walked in the door, home from Boston. There is something in her voice, and so I immediately call my mother. She answers on the thirtieth ring.

"Oh, it's you," she says in a low, defeated voice. "If I knew it was you, I wouldn't have answered. I was expecting Sandra." I'm not sure what to say, but I know I won't apologize for not being my sister.

"How are you doing?"

"I don't know what to do with myself," she answers. I don't know what to advise. I know so little about her. After I left home as a child, we barely saw each other. She was not a nurturer; every bit of her maternal energy had been directed at my father to keep him calm.

What might she like to do? Travel? Join some kind of widows' group and make friends and do crafts?

"Are you eating? Make sure you eat." It sounds lame and shallow right after I say it.

"Not much. I miss your father," she says. "I think about what his voice sounded like and I miss him."

"He screamed at you all the time," I feel compelled to point out. "How can you miss that?"

"You don't remember him the way I do," she replies. "He used to make me laugh. He was always being silly."

I can't imagine my father making anyone laugh. I'm trying to summon a picture of him being silly; it doesn't come.

"Don't you remember the little poems he used to write?" she asks.

No.

"He used to write me little poems," she says dreamily. "With little drawings. Don't you remember those little pictures?"

No.

"I don't remember anything like that," I say. "All I remember is his anger."

"Oh, that was after he got out of the army," she says. "The army did that to him. He was different before." I don't say anything for a while, letting her remember.

"Do you remember the sacks he made?" I ask. "For the planes?"

She is quiet for a moment. "We sat up every night for weeks, making them," she finally replies. "I didn't have a sewing machine. Made them by hand out of oilcloth. My fingers got all raw."

"What ever happened?" I ask. "When Dad showed his report to the colonel?"

She doesn't seem the least bit surprised that I am familiar with a story my father never told us; she shows no curiosity, no interest. "Oh, I don't know," she replies, dropping her voice on *"know."* "He had been all excited at first, and then never mentioned it again. I don't remember if those things happened before or after."

"After what?"

"That explosion," she says. "When they all got killed."

My heart slams to a halt from the shock that jolts through my body. I take a sharp breath. "When who all got killed?"

"Oh, I don't know." She drops her voice on the last word again, and I know it'll be useless to try to push her for more information. "It's all in the past. I'm tired of talking." There is a pause, then she adds softly, "In fact, I'm tired of living."

When you look into a mirror, you are not seeing things as they truly are. The reflection is backward. A parallel vision perhaps, but it is all reversed.

I didn't like at all the way my mother ended our conversation, and I call Sandra right away. She and I have never seen the same thing, even in the same situation. We see mirror images. I see my mother secretive and stubbornly rejecting help, insisting that she wants to stay in Arizona; Sandra sees an elderly woman failing in health and memory who needs someone to step in. I see my mother trivializing the ravaging damage done by my father; Sandra sees a normal family with a few issues. But my mother's last words have stayed with me. I don't want her to feel that way. My heart breaks from those words.

"I think I'll just fly out there, pack her up, and bring her here to live with me," Sandra announces after we talk for a few minutes. "She needs to be supervised."

"You're probably right," I say unhelpfully.

"She is frail. And I don't think she's taking care of herself," Sandra continues. "We need to step in."

"I don't think she wants us to." But I am thinking, she doesn't want *me* to.

"It isn't right to let her live alone like that."

I am immediately stricken with guilt. Sandra is the good daughter. The good daughter for thinking of my mother's welfare, for making sure my mother spends her last years being taken care of by family, for taking over the reins. And she *is* a very good daughter. I would have dutifully obeyed my mother's wishes and left her in Arizona and called her once a week, worried about her. Discouraged and hurt by her constant rejection, I wouldn't have even thought to bring her to my home.

"No, no," I begin to insist, in a redemptive bid. "Why don't we bring her to New York? She can live with me."

"Don't you think it's a bit strenuous to bring her to New York?" Sandra asks.

"She isn't going to be flapping her arms to fly the plane," I retort. "And it's just about as far as flying to Georgia."

Sandra pauses. "Are you sure you want to do it?" she says. "I know you don't feel very close to her."

And I realized this. Cruelty is turning your back on those who, even though they have rejected you, need you for their survival.

"I'll take her," I tell my sister. "It's my last chance with her."

Chapter 37

Malachi's bag is still packed and standing outside his front door. While I was gone, he restrung ropes in another area of my yard. They are very tenuous; all Lisbon has to do is push against them with his chest and down they'll go.

"Order fencing," he tells me. "Before there's a catastrophe."

Danielle has pretty much taken his place as barn manager, but she doesn't actually manage anyone. I have promised to find someone to help her, because she is doing all the stalls now, plus stacking hay and grain and taking care of the horses. She is competent and pleasant. More than competent, she is highly efficient. She feeds the horses breakfast, pulls out a few bales of hay and spreads the flakes around the paddocks, cleans out the buckets and fills them with fresh water, then leads out the horses, and mucks out the stalls, all before ten in the morning. I realize, with a wrench, that Malachi would have gotten half of it done around noon. Maybe 2 p.m. After his second nap. She gives me a cheerful wave as she pushes the wheelbarrow past me.

"I put Lisbon in his new paddock," she says. "So he and Toby don't fight."

"Thanks," I say, but I am a bit annoyed that the stupid rope paddock was put up without anyone consulting me. "But I really want him turned out with the other geldings."

"I know," she replies, "but no one wants the responsibility of watching over him."

"Malachi can sit near the intercom," I say. "He can beep the house if there's a problem."

"He sleeps too much. Naps most of the day. You know, I'll miss Malachi after he leaves," she says wistfully, "but he is getting so forgetful. He kept leaving the gates open while you were away. The horses were always getting out. And lots of times, I had to double-check the water buckets. He never remembered to give them water. I am always reminding him of things."

This takes me by surprise. Malachi was a stickler for details like that.

There is a white picket fenced–in area by the garage that was going to be a vegetable garden for "proper vegetables," as Malachi called them. He wanted to plant tomatoes and corn and peas and raise a few chickens for eggs. He had even started to build a henhouse. Now it all lies fallow.

"My sister, Minnie, is coming for me soon," Malachi says. "I spoke to her last night. I don't want to start a garden I can't finish."

Now Lisbon is staring over ropes at the rest of the horses, whinnying to them and now and then, pushing against the barrier with his face. Oddly enough, they are all whinnying back. It's a separation call. If only Malachi could hear the one from my heart.

"What is your emotional goal?" my therapist had asked me once.

"My what?" I blinked at her words. Were we supposed to have emotional goals along with academic goals, financial, weight? I laughed at the idea. But she was waiting for me to answer, pen poised over paper, forever taking notes, a perennial secretary to the psyche.

I wasn't crazy about her office décor, and many times, when I was supposed to be sitting there and doing what she liked to call "emotional work," I was really doing emotional decorating, redoing her place in my head. Get rid of the sculpted dark green carpet already, I would mentally scold her, so outdated! And put down a nice oriental floral. Okay, maybe you can leave the walls their monotone school-hall green, but take down those white plastic Venetian blinds and hang some kind of print window treatment. Maybe toile. I like toile. I would run my fingers along the brown leather couch that I was sitting on, with the tan denim throw pillows, and think, maybe a hunting scene, a toile hunting scene, since we always seem to be hunting for answers, but then that might clash with—

"I see this is a difficult question for you," she would prod gently. "That you are struggling. Close your eyes and lean back and think of what you would like to achieve. Close your eyes and go to your happy place and describe it to me."

My "happy place"? Could anything be more trite? Well, it wouldn't have been her office. I closed my eyes and all I could see were those ugly tan denim pillows that were supposed to look like envelopes with big brown buttons to fasten the flap part, and I thought, okay, maybe keep the brown leather sofa, but please, toile pillows. At least, toile pillows.

"Rachel?" She wasn't going to let it rest. Okay, what kind of place could possibly make me happy? A room filled with sweet whispers and loving arms to hold you like you've fallen into a mound of hay? A bare room with my old upright piano standing against a wall? A barn full of horses on a bright morning, turning their faces to me when I walk in? I couldn't answer her. Where she saw possibilities for emotional advancement, I would always see enclosures, walls.

"Do the work, Rachel," she would chide. "What is your goal? And where do you want it to bring you?"

It was exasperating. I looked at her smiling at me, full of

eager, goal-fulfilling joy, when I finally came up with the perfect answer. "My goal is to drop forty pounds by next Tuesday."

The light went out in her eyes and she shook her head. "You need to find out," she said. "You need to stop fighting yourself. Not for me. For you."

It was my last session, ever.

David carries my mother's suitcases up to the spare bedroom before we realize that there is no way we are going to be able to carry my mother up there. The bedroom is on the second floor, along with the full bathrooms. We make some rapid provisions and rearrange the den for my mother. She can have the sofa for tonight, but being able to bathe is going to be another problem.

"You should have thought of this before I came here," my mother snaps. "Sandra would have thought everything through."

"You're absolutely right," I say.

"She's a good daughter."

"You're right again," I say. In the meantime, Sandra is in Phoenix packing up all my mother's antiques and moving them to Georgia.

"She can use the den until Malachi leaves," David suggests. He sees a soon-to-be empty cottage that would make a perfect home for my mother, and I reluctantly agree, though I see her moving in there as the final curtain between Malachi and me.

"I want to sue all those doctors who killed your father," my mother announces the next morning over breakfast. David drops his English muffin.

"Martin died of heart failure," he says.

"Rachel should have protected him." She is actually sounding indignant. "All he needed was a pacemaker. It would have saved his life. Somebody should have told us." My head is swimming from the contradictions. I look at David, and he is just buttering the rest of his muffin, staring at his knife. I can imagine him thinking this isn't officially his family, and how lucky for him it isn't.

"Do you remember us telling you that he should get a pace-maker?" I remind her. "For months we begged him."

"Don't *you* remember?" She shakes her white hair fiercely. "They *did* give him one. They called us at the restaurant? They gave him one and then he died. So much for their advice."

"It was too late by then," I try to explain. "They gave him one when it was already too late."

"Why did they give him one if they thought it was too late?" She folds her arms, then adds triumphantly, "Those doctors just like to experiment."

All I see is my mother's anger, but David immediately sees my mother's guilt. "It isn't your fault," he says gently. "You couldn't have helped him. He didn't want to be helped. You tried, but he didn't want to be helped. You have to agree that sometimes he could be very difficult."

My mother's voice is filled with relief. "That's right," she says. "He was difficult." Her expression fights back from confusion and she stares down at the table.

I look at David with appreciation. He always knows what to say. He has always known what to say. I am ashamed of how little I give him for it. My mother takes a sip of her coffee and agrees again with David. "You couldn't tell that man anything at all."

We are looking into a mirror, my mother and me, and we are seeing two different sides of the same picture. She sees the distortion, like the glass in a fun house, wavy and indirect and deformed. And I see a straightforward medical decision that she made too late.

I am standing by the paddocks under a dark sky. The night is falling, dropping across the farm like an arm, encircling us all. The windows in Malachi's cottage are lit; pale yellow squares glow within its dark frame. His bag is still outside his front door, waiting.

My mother is in the guest room. David helped her go upstairs in slow, slow, wavering, wobbling steps. We made her promise to wait in her bedroom until we can help her downstairs tomorrow morning.

I peek in on her later. She is sitting on the bed and staring at my father's picture.

"Why don't you get some sleep, Mom?" I tell her.

"I can't sleep without your father," she replies.

"I thought you said that you couldn't sleep *with* him."

"I couldn't," she agrees. "He used to scream during the night from the nightmares. I used to sit by him and tell him it was okay. I always made it okay for him, and then I sat in the gold recliner until I fell asleep."

Her face is filled with grief and longing, and I go to her side and give her a hug. She is certain we all failed her. And perhaps we did. Perhaps I should have gone to Phoenix sooner, even before Sandra thought of it, even before my father died, and wrested the medical decisions from them, like Malachi's sister, instead of waiting for disaster. Perhaps I should have been a better daughter. She will always think I failed her.

I will always think I failed everybody.

Chapter 38

"We need to talk," David whispers into my back. We are in bed, and I am rolled onto my side away from him. I suddenly awake and sit up.

"What do you want to tell me?" I ask with dread.

He doesn't answer me at first, just draws in a long breath. "You know, you can't hurt your father through me. You can only hurt me. Is that what you're trying to do?"

"Oh God, of course not!" I jump out of bed and stand next to it in quivering outrage. "Why didn't you invite me to Mexico? I would have gone! Because you wanted to bring someone else!"

"Living with you is lonely," he says, not denying my accusation.

"Luckily you fixed all that." My voice is filled with sarcasm, which is how I get angry.

"Did you ever feel anything for me?" he asks.

I can't answer. I want to, but the first thing I think of is that I can't allow myself to become that vulnerable, especially now.

The second is, *Foolish, foolish, foolish girl, how many chances will I be given?*

"I want to tell you about Caroline," he says, his words falling quietly in the dark room. I vaguely remember her name, Caroline M. Erikson, LLD, vivacious brunette, pixie-cut hair, serious curves, junior partner.

"You had an affair with her in Puerto Vallarta," I say. He doesn't answer right away, though I am waiting for him to say no, to exclaim that I got it all wrong.

"Your grandmother called to congratulate me on getting engaged," I say, my voice freezing over each word. "I guess you gave that ring to *her*. Should I be shopping for a wedding gift yet?"

"We're not engaged." He says nothing more, just quietly gets out of bed. We are each standing next to the bed.

"When were you going to tell me?" I am trying to keep my voice from shaking. "Or are you waiting for her to pick you up at the front door in her wedding gown?" My breath is banging against my lungs. He is just standing and listening. I close my eyes and allow myself to breathe, slower, quieter. You can't catch a horse by running after it and screaming. I keep my voice calm. "I would like to know at least what you wanted to tell me." He sits back down on the edge of the bed. There are long minutes of silence.

"It was a trip with a few partners from the firm," he finally says to the night. "Half business, half working vacation. Things are going good at the firm, and I guess Pete Stanton wanted to celebrate a little. I didn't bring Caroline; she was invited just like I was." He pauses and takes a wavering breath and I wonder if he's crying. I can't see him for the dark. "I wanted to ask you to come, but you were so preoccupied, your father and then going back and forth to Boston."

"You still could have asked me."

"I suppose," he says.

I wait for him to finish, but he is just sitting there.

"So?"

"My grandmother sent me the ring," he adds. "It was for you. But then I thought, What's the point?"

"The point?"

"You take such pride in saying no." I could hear his sigh across the dark room. "Things lead to—things. I slept with her. I was lonely."

My heart freezes the next beat, skips it entirely, then lurches forward in a sickening jump.

"I wanted to give the ring to you," he chokes out.

"Please leave." I am acidly polite.

He gets up and crosses the room to find his pants and shirt, which are neatly draped over a chair, his shoes nearby, as though he had been planning this escape all along. "Maybe we can talk," he says. "Really talk."

"What for? You need my advice on—what?—dating tips?" My words come out like knives, and I am breathing deeply to keep myself under control. Inside my head, a little voice claims how right I was all along.

"I don't want to fight about this," he says. "I will call you in a few days."

I keep my voice casual. "Oh, let's not make promises we can't keep."

He heads downstairs, two steps at a time. I want to cry. Where are my tears? My chance is gone. It hadn't been my fault, I think in a bitterly triumphant voice that exonerates my behavior. I hadn't been able to love him because somehow I knew, somehow I had always known, *sooner or later, he was going to hurt me.*

My mother had just finished breakfast, oatmeal, fresh-squeezed orange juice, buttered toast, and sour complaints, before she retreated to the living room to sulk in front of the TV. I bring in a second cup of coffee for her. She loves good coffee. I am sick over last night.

"Sandra would have found me a civilized place to live," she starts.

"Actually, Sandra thought it was a good idea for you to come here," I say, forcing myself to be patient when I want to scream. I can barely concentrate on her words; all my thoughts left with David. "But I'm glad to have you." It's a lie; maybe she senses it, maybe not, but she doesn't answer me. And then I ask her, "Mom, I was wondering, remember my old piano? Why did you give it away?"

"Piano?" She looks at me, confused, then tilts her head to sift back through time. "I think your father sold it to pay for a lawyer."

"A lawyer?" I ask.

"Oh, you know," she says vaguely. "He was trying to sue the army to get his medal."

"I loved that piano," I tell her, and suddenly fully realize how much I really did love that piano. "I loved it." Was suing for a medal for creating a bunch of sacks twenty-three years earlier worth taking the music out of their daughter's life? "I loved playing that piano."

She walks over to the window and presses her finger against a pane of glass. I am waiting for her to tell me something more, so that I can understand things. So I can understand why my father took the music from me, but she only runs her finger across the windowsill and says, "There's an ant on your windowsill. Maybe you should pick up ant spray when you go out today."

Lisbon is in his new paddock, pacing back and forth and nickering to the other horses. I bring him some extra hay and look at him with different eyes. I am trying to see past the symbols, past the assumptions. Trying to see past a cowardly horse who won't fight off bullies to a gentle horse that just wants to live in peace; past a man who hatefully sold the one thing I loved, a man so desperate for recognition that it ate like a worm through his soul; and another man—David—who had probably never been mine to love.

Malachi is drowsing in the sun in the lawn chair I had gotten him. It is tilted back; there is a cup of fig tea on a hay bale that he is using as a table.

"Hey," he says, then coughs hard.

"I don't think you can travel with your sister until you're better," I say to him.

"Heard a car and peeked out my window. Saw David leave," he says through a series of bubbly coughs.

"He is interested in another woman," I say, irony ringing in my voice. "I could have tied him up with all the ropes I wanted, but he would have untied them in the end."

He starts to answer me but is racked with another series of wet, ominous coughs.

"I want to ride Lisbon today. He needs to get away." Actually, I need to get away. I need to concentrate on something equine. "But I'm going to take you to urgent care first."

"I won't say no," he wheezes. I call for an appointment right in front of him. They will see him later that afternoon.

I make my way to the house and stand on the back porch watching Lisbon eat his hay, and then I get my car keys and my purse, to buy some groceries, a can of bug spray, and maybe, just maybe, after I drop Malachi home from urgent care, I'll stop at the music store at the mall and look at pianos.

The urgent care doctor checks Malachi thoroughly and takes an X-ray of his lung. There is an outline, a gray cloud, a storm cloud hovering on the horizon of his lung. The doctor thinks it could be pneumonia and gives him antibiotics. I gasp at the sight. I don't know what cancer looks like, but this looks like a good bet.

"I ain't been feeling quite right," Malachi tells him.

"We'll do some tests," the doctor reassures him. "You need a CAT scan. We'll get to the bottom of it."

"He plans on traveling," I tell the doctor. "His sister is supposed to be coming for him."

The doctor raises his eyebrows. "Where does your sister live?"

Malachi drops his head and doesn't answer him. I don't understand why. I try to cue him. "Mississippi?"

"It's far," he says. I raise my eyebrows at the doctor as Malachi pulls on his sweater and makes his way through the door. "The elderly can get forgetful," the doctor says to me in confidence as I follow him out.

* * *

When I get home, there are four messages on my phone. One from Willie, one from Sandra, another one from Sandra, and a third one from Sandra. The phone rings a few minutes later, and I pick it right up, expecting David, but it's Sandra.

"Mom called me. She wants me to rescue her," she informs me.

"From what?"

"She's not happy," Sandra carefully replies. "Couldn't you have tried a little harder to get along?"

"I thought we were getting along."

"She's unhappy."

"She's impossible," I retort. "She says the oatmeal's better in Phoenix. I can't please her."

"Make her eggs next time," Sandra suggests. "Or let her make her own meals. She's always been a complainer, but you could find things to make her happy. I mean, it was your suggestion that she come to New York."

"She won't cook for herself; she's afraid that the stove is going to blow up," I add. "It's *electric.* She doesn't like the taste of New York water, and she hates my food."

"Things worry her," Sandra says. "She told me she's afraid that the horses will go crazy and stampede her. I'll try to get up to you as soon as I can, maybe I can smooth things over."

Lisbon is spooking at rabbits, which he has never done before. I wonder whether the tension in my body is making him nervous. We are riding through the woods, through shadows of soft ocher, stepping into pale brown patterns, stepping carefully over lacy gray-green ferns and small purple wildflowers that poke through the leaves and lay across the flat rocks like they've been sacrificed. I had to get away from the farm for a while, from my mother, from everything that she is turning sour. Sandra will be coming later today, and I need these woods to comfort me. The trembling leaves play music as compelling as Liszt, and I close my eyes and let Lisbon take over, walking us through the brush and trees while I listen.

Maybe I was meant to be single. I had never been truly loved by anyone. I am grieving for David. Why don't people send sympathy cards when a relationship ends? It's as hard as death. Maybe I was expecting too much from life. It's all right not to be loved, if you don't think about it. If you don't build up your expectations, if you allow the woods and the flowers and horses and dogs to fill you up. It's enough. You can thrive, even.

Then it strikes me. *That* should have been my emotional goal. To thrive.

A mirror only tells half the story.

It echoes back what is held in front of it. The reflection is impartial, not the final, perfect truth. It's all about context. You have to take a big step back and look carefully, because the glass reflects the opposite of life, balancing the image of what you see around you.

I know I can be stubborn like my father, and see only what I want to see. Maybe David needed more from me than I owned. Maybe my mother and I will never find a place where we can meet. Maybe Lisbon can never be with the other horses. Maybe they would have fought him forever and he would have paid a terrible price for my stubbornness. I am paying a terrible price now for my stubbornness. I am not thriving at all.

And then I know. I *know!* My stubbornness is not from being convinced I am right; it is my protection, so that I don't tumble over the precipice. It is the wall that keeps me safe. If I let it go, I will evaporate, disappear into the chasm below. I am breathless from knowing this. I stop Lisbon in his tracks and lean forward and throw my arms around his neck.

"Lisbon," I whisper into his ear. "I'm sorry. I'm sorry. I'm sorry."

Chapter 39

Some families belong together and some will forever prickle against each other. Sometimes you have to cobble your family together from people who have dropped into your life here and there and because you realize that you love them. I tell Malachi that I plan to move him into my guest room so he can recuperate and ask his permission to show my mother the inside of his cottage. He nods sleepily, sitting in the sun, drooping like a flower without water. I can still hear the wheeze in his chest. I am hoping my mother will like the cottage enough to live there.

"My sister's comin' for me anyways," he mumbles.

"You'll stay with me until she gets here," I say.

My mother follows me into the cottage with a look of disdain. "How am I supposed to cook a twenty-pound turkey in there?" she asks as she opens the oven door to the little stove in the kitchen.

"When is the last time you needed to cook a twenty-pound

turkey?" I ask her. She draws her hunched body up to her full kyphotic four-feet-eleven and looks indignant.

"I may want to have someone over for dinner," she huffs, then points to the top of the stove. "And look, there's no clock on it. How do I tell the time?"

I point to the microwave sitting on the counter right next to the stove. "What's wrong with the clock on the microwave?"

"And where's the TV?"

"Malachi never watched TV, but we can get you one, first thing."

But she doesn't hear me. Her eyes are darting around, looking for further proof that I am not a good daughter by making her live in this house. A horse whinnies outside and her head jerks back.

"Oh my God!" she gasps. "I won't be able to hear myself think because of all that noise."

We returned to my house without speaking. Where I saw a cute cottage, an adorable home that could serve my mother well, she saw a small shed behind a horse barn surrounded by dust and animals and noise.

It was all mirrors.

Sandra arrives later that afternoon, sailing right through the front door as soon as she gets out of the cab and heading straight for the living room, where my mother is staring at the television. Sandra's out to get the real story, I suppose.

"I want to talk to Mom alone, please," she says by way of greeting. Her purpose is to find out from my mother how awful I've been to her. I can see Sandra sitting on the couch, shaking her silver hair as she clucks with sympathy. She spends about an hour in there, until finally, the two of them make their way into the kitchen, where I am putting out platters of food for lunch. Sandra has her arm protectively around my mother's shoulders as they slowly walk through the door. The position of her arm says to my mother, *Don't worry, I'm here to take care of you now. I know how you feel, I know how Rachel failed you, and I am here to make everything better.* Sandra, the good daughter, is riding in on the white horse to rescue her.

My white horse.

"Sandra!" I say when she comes into the kitchen, giving her a hug. She smells like baby powder. Then I realize that there are no suitcases anywhere. "Where are your bags?"

"I only brought a small overnight bag," Sandra replies. "It's in the living room. I plan to leave tomorrow right after breakfast. I'll share the bed with Mom tonight; she doesn't want to sleep alone."

"Because I heard coyotes howling last night," my mother explains. "The Discovery Channel says they prey on the weak."

Sandra suddenly stands back from me and wrinkles her nose. "Horses," she says. "You always smell from horses."

"You think that's bad?" says my mother. "She wants me to live in the barn with them."

"It's not the barn," I correct her as though it mattered. "It's a little cottage next to the barn."

"It's really no place for her," Sandra says. "She needs to be with family. Harrison and I have a room ready. A real room. I'm taking her home tomorrow."

"The cottage has been totally renovated; it's a very nice place," I protest. Wait, did she say my mother needs to be with *family?*

"I'm starving," Sandra says, sitting herself at the table. "What are you making? All this country air has made me hungry."

"Sandwiches," I tell her while putting out platters of cold cuts and bread and bowls of salads. I begin setting places for us around the table. Sandra makes my mother a turkey sandwich, then reaches for the liverwurst and forks the entire half pound onto two pieces of bread.

"The bread isn't as good as it is in Phoenix," my mother points out after taking a bite of her turkey sandwich.

"It's the same brand you always get," Sandra and I say in unison, then look at each other. There is a nano-moment of silence, then I crook my pinkie finger and hook it up with

Sandra's and shout, "Jinx, jinx." At first, her face registers surprise, and then the two of us suddenly laugh.

"I'm glad you girls are having a good time," my mother says. "I haven't been able to eat a thing since I got to New York." She leans back in her chair, trying to look weak and emaciated, but is not quite pulling it off.

"You eat with me every day," I remind her.

"But I don't cook it," she says. "It's because your stove is trying to electrocute me. I got a terrible shock from it yesterday."

"Static electricity," I say. "From shuffling across the floor in your socks."

"My socks don't shuffle," she says. "It's my knee. It's from my old football injury."

Sandra and I give each other looks. "Ma," she says, "you never played football."

"I was an athlete," my mother says, making her hand into a fist and holding it up to show off a thin, wrinkled arm with a shriveled, flaccid bicep. "I played football during recess in the third grade. It just shows, you don't know anything about me."

And maybe we don't. My mother has never really talked to us, never really told us about her life, or our family, never said that she loved us. She just raised us, the way one would raise a plant. You feed it and water it, and put it somewhere so it can get on with the business of growing. At some point, it either blooms or dies. I'm not sure which one applies to me and Sandra.

Sandra finishes her sandwich and makes herself another.

"How are things going for you?" I ask her as she takes a big bite. She chews for a few minutes, looks up at me, then looks away. Her face clouds; she clears her throat.

"Actually, Harrison and I—"

"I need to see a doctor for my knee," my mother interjects. "The only doctors who come around here are horse doctors."

Sandra drops back to the business at hand. "I'll make an appointment for you when we get to Atlanta," she says briskly. "We have some very good doctors." We continue eating our lunch. My mother complains about the potato salad, the tomatoes, the coffee. Sandra has finished her second sandwich and gets up to scan the kitchen. "You have anything for dessert?"

"I need to see a dentist," my mother says. "I thought the tomatoes were slippery, but I think my dentures are loose." She is wearing one of the necklaces my father made, handmade brass links with a pendant made of tiny clock parts. If it was a little more graceful, it could almost be steampunk.

"Did Dad make that?" Sandra points to the necklace.

My mother nods. "He was so proud when he made it. Said no one else in the world would have anything like it." She strokes the piece with her fingers. "He liked making special things for me."

I remember Willie's words and picture my father huddled over a workbench, carefully picking up little pieces of metal junk to turn into jewelry. "It's nice," I tell her.

"Cake?" Sandra asks.

I take the white bakery box from the refrigerator and put it on the table. She cuts the red string with a knife and opens the box with the expression of someone opening a wonderful gift, then cuts a huge slice of chocolate cake for herself. She pours more coffee and sits down with her plate.

"Everything's going just fine," she replies to my earlier question, and smiling happily, takes a big forkful of cake. I feel bad for her.

"I have an announcement," I say to her and my mother. "I finally bought myself a piano. Just today. I haven't played in years and I decided to play again." My mother stares at me as I sit there, excitement filling my heart. And I wonder what David would have said.

"That's exactly why your father got rid of that old piano," she says. "All that stupid pounding was giving us a headache."

Families who prickle, families who try to love. I have them both.

Chapter 40

With its carved cherrywood, shining brass pedals covered in green felt, the next morning my new piano arrives incognito under white quilts, like it's trying to slip back into my life without making a fuss. A baby grand, with silken white keys, interrupted by neat pairs and trios of black. The deliverymen unwrap it, assemble it, promise me that someone will stop by tomorrow to retune it, and then leave me alone, to run my hand over the sleek, glossy wood, run my fingers across the keys and contemplate all the music buried inside. It begs me to play it. My mother says nothing during the entire delivery.

"Your books must be doing well," Sandra murmurs.

Sandra has relented and plans to stay a few days more. That night, after dinner, she and my mother decide to take a little evening walk around my farm. The house is dark and quiet. David hasn't come home or called, and I allow the shadows in the house to fill me as I sit down at the piano, almost shy. I rub my hands together, then clasp them, almost like I'm praying. What to play? What to play? I had also bought some books, filled with wonderful music, transcribed down to my level. I'm sorry I have to bring this lovely piano down to my level.

Bach. I pick out a simple Bach piece and stumble through it twice. *I will get better,* I promise the piano, *I won't disgrace you.* I play it a third time.

I am suddenly aware that my mother and Sandra are in the doorway, watching. They must have slipped in through the back door. My mother asks Sandra to help her upstairs to bed, and they leave without another word.

I start to play again. My fingers find what they need and Bach sputters from them before settling into real music. Oh yes, I remember this passage. I remember how these notes move together, find each other. How the melody leans on the bass, supported by it, before sailing lyrically away. I wish David were here. He has never heard me play the piano, and suddenly I wish he could just know this part of me.

I finish and decide to check on Malachi one last time before I go to sleep. He doesn't answer his door, but I can peek in through his living room window and see that he has left the night-light on and that he is asleep on the sofa, in his pajamas.

Through the shadows, I can make out the bulk of a figure walking toward the barn. It is Sandra. "Mom is asleep," she calls out to me. "I told her to put a suitcase behind her bedroom door until I got back. I told her I'll give her three and a half raps to let me in."

"She's safe here, Sandra," I reply, not even questioning how she's going to do half a rap. "Honest."

"Serial killers can come to horse farms, too, you know," she says, then pauses on the path, unsure of what to do next.

"Want a cup of tea?" I ask.

"If it's not too much trouble," she replies with what sounds like relief, then waits a beat. "Is there any cake left?"

"One piece, I think." She follows me back to the house and into the kitchen. "Are you sure you want to take Mom back with you?" I ask. I don't want Sandra to think I'm dumping our mother on her. I want to do the right thing by both of them.

I pour boiling water into a china teapot and start to steep a tea ball of chamomile. Malachi always made me chamomile tea at night. "She's so difficult," I add. "You'll never be able to make her happy."

"She's always been easier on me, because she knew I would fight back. That I would stand up for myself," Sandra says matter-of-factly, taking the white box from the refrigerator. "I can shut it all down. I won't mind her at all."

I stare at her for a moment. "You really are a good daughter," I say. "She doesn't deserve you."

Sandra's lip quivers for a second, and then she catches herself, shaking her head, shaking off my words like a dog shaking off bathwater. "Look," she says, pulling a slip of folded paper from her sweater pocket. "I went over a budget with her. She hated the idea, but she'll need to budget her money. That's why I decided to take rent from her. I'll put it into a secret account so that when the—the time—comes, she can be cared for properly in a decent nursing home."

When the time comes. I know what time she means. "You think she's getting— worse?" I ask.

"I see it even more now than when Dad died." She helps herself to the last of the cake. "So, we have to make a budget," she says and sits down at the table, the slice in front of her. "And me being good in math, I know she has to budget things so that she'll have enough left over. It's very important to have enough left over for the end."

We sit silently together with our tea. Sandra stirs in three teaspoons of sugar and takes big forkfuls of cake. She looks peaceful sitting there and eating. I watch her, aching to really talk to her. She finishes her cake and scrapes the plate clean with her fork, getting every last crumb, serene satisfaction written all over her face, and suddenly, I understand her. She needs to get every last crumb, from everything, because nothing, nothing will fill her up, nothing, nothing, will fill up the hollowness, the aching loneliness, the need for loving attention and just as suddenly, I feel very bad for her.

Her irritability, her ridiculous snide remarks, I see it all differently now. It keeps her from being so nakedly vulnerable. She has that, and her food.

And I have my horses.

Plants grow funny when they don't get enough light.

"I really tried to take care of Mom," I say.

"Actually," she admits slowly, "the cottage is a cute little place."

This surprises me. "Thank you."

"I'd live there myself, if I had to," she adds. "I might still, if I divorce Harrison."

"Is it that bad that you would really divorce him?" I ask.

She takes a deep breath. "Oh no," she says. "But I'm always waiting. You know. For the shoe to drop."

I know too well.

We finish our tea. The idea of both my mother and Sandra living with me gives me pause. "The cottage isn't *that* cute," I say. "Sometimes there's a strong draft that blows in from under the front door."

The cake is all gone and Sandra finally relaxes over our second cup of tea. "Why don't we sit someplace more comfortable?" I tell her. We carry our tea into the living room and she stops abruptly. "Why did you get a piano?" she asks, drawing to it. "Now, after all this time?"

She sets her tea down on an end table and rubs her fingers gently over the piano's gleaming wood, then sits on the bench and lightly touches the keys. I used to teach her little songs when we were young, when I had the piano. When we were children. I used to sit with her and teach her how to play. It was the only time we weren't arguing. She picks out "Heart and Soul" with one finger.

"Remember this?" she asks softly. I put my tea down and sit next to her. "You taught me this," she says. "Remember?"

"Of course I do."

She touches the keys again and starts the melody of "Heart and Soul," then stops, embarrassed. "Don't stop," I tell her.

She sits at the piano and stares down at her hands. "I always loved our little lessons," she says. "You were the only one who really cared about anything I did."

"I liked the lessons, too," I tell her. "You were the only one who cared about what I had to say." I start to pick out the bass, then stop. "I'm glad you came," I say, and mean it. She starts the melody again, we sit close to each other, and slowly, stumbling over the keys, giggling at our mistakes, fingers banging into fingers, we play our songs from the past until long into the night. Heart and soul.

Chapter 41

Malachi is admitted to the hospital. We had all gone together to drive him to the emergency room, my mother and Sandra and me. His color had been awful that next morning, his breath coming in choking whistles.

The doctor meets us there, puts him on oxygen, and decides to call in a pulmonologist. The three of us discuss Malachi's case while my mother and Sandra spend the time at Malachi's bedside. They are talking like old friends. The doctors and I decide to aggressively treat whatever it is with an initial round of stronger antibiotics before we proceed to a lung biopsy.

"His sister, Minnie, is supposed to come for him," I mention to my mother and Sandra as I drive them home a few hours later. "But I don't know how to get in touch with her."

"You don't know anything," my mother says. "You don't know old men. I asked him if he had any family and he said no one is left. His sister, Minnie, was the last one and she's been dead for twenty-two years."

A shock rips through me. Oh, I suddenly realize, stricken.

Oh. Why didn't I get it? He was talking to me in that code of old men. He was trying to tell me that he was dying. Oh.

"I didn't know," I say.

"You never listen," says my mother.

The night is falling differently than I ever remember. The shadows are harsher, striking the light from the day. The stars look distant and uncaring. The moon is only a sliver, like a tiny prayer. It's late summer but the air is unseemly chilly, pulling all hope and warmth from my bones. It is reminding me again of a lesson I learned when I was young: not to love, because love is not a boomerang, it does not come back. It is not an investment, because it does not pay. Sandra can take my mother home with her; I won't mind. My mother is an entity unto herself. Maybe it was because she poured so much into taking care of my father, there was nothing left; maybe it was because he couldn't give her anything, and so to make sure that someone paid attention to her, she nurtured herself, getting lost in a world of self-absorption. In any case, there is no love lost between us. She is just unable to give it, and, as I spent a lifetime learning, unable to receive it, either.

I will not lose love anymore, like a bird lost to the night sky, except for Malachi. I love him and I know I am going to lose him, too. I think about him and my throat tightens. He anchored me to my farm and my horses, to the earth that grew things in its own sweet time. He was my source of common sense and strength. How will I bear not having him in my life anymore?

My love for him surprised me. It grew like one of his vegetables that pushed through the fallow ground, a tenuous, pale sliver, then a small plant, then a bush, upright and vital, and finally—tomatoes—ripening full red. I am a tomato. *Please,* I pray into the darkness, *don't take Malachi.*

It seems there is an answer from the wind. It blows a chill through me, and I pull the sweater around my shoulders and feel very alone.

I miss David.

David, whom I always knew was the most dangerous love of all. The one that could annihilate me.

I close my eyes and force myself to stand very still under the indifferent crescent of the moon. Losing David would be like losing the moon. My life would go dark.

I just wish I had told him. I suddenly understand how he had stood in the shadows, waiting for me. How lonely it had to be for him, waiting there. What was I fighting all these years? What have I done? What have I done?

I can't lose him.

I have to tell him.

David's cell phone takes my voice mail. "Please call me back," I tell him. "I'm sorry. I'm sorry."

"Do you ever watch the clouds?" Willie was asking me. He was home, at Rowena's, discharged from the hospital, less from the fact that his condition was stable, than the Veterans Administration trying to cut costs. "Did you ever watch the clouds, and they look like nothing, and then they shift together, and all of a sudden, you see a picture?"

"I suppose," I said, wondering what point he was trying to make. This would be my last trip to Boston. Willie had promised his story was almost at the end. He promised. He had called and used that old green banana line on me again, then promised he would finish his story. My sister had taken my mother back with her to Georgia; David was not answering his voice mail; Malachi was getting chemo in the hospital and was spending most of his days and nights sleeping. Danielle was proving to be pretty competent. I figured I wouldn't be missed much for a few days.

"When I finish my story, it will be like vapor coming together into a cloud," Willie promised.

Frankly, I was grateful it was coming to an end. Perhaps I would understand a little more why my father was the way he was. Why he never had friends. Why he raged with suspicions, his anger rolling like a loose bowling ball, knocking everything down in its path. He had been blamed for losing a man, a life, and though it hadn't been entirely his fault, it had been entirely his responsibility. Maybe I would understand that a little more, though it wouldn't have made much of a difference in our relationship.

There are no white clouds today, just a gray wash of sky. The Weather Channel on the television has been predicting thunderstorms for the entire Boston area, and there's a moist breeze blowing down from the north. Willie has a blanket wrapped around him as he sits on Rowena's little back porch in his wheelchair.

"We're gonna get some weather," he announces, pulling the blanket tight up around his chest. "WX."

"Would you like to go in?" I ask. I wonder whether the rain is going to travel down to New York, whether Danielle will bring the horses in early, whether she will keep an eye on Lisbon, who has taken to ripping down his rope paddock on a regular basis. Did I remember to close the bedroom windows? Is David standing by a window somewhere, watching the rain wash the streets dark gray and thinking about me?

I wonder about something else, as well.

"How come you didn't just return my father's ring to him?" I ask Willie. "Why didn't you just stick it in an envelope and send it to him?"

"Well, I was," he says. "I was planning to find him and call and apologize, and surprise him by sending him the ring, but Rowena found out at the last minute that he passed away." His face reflects his disappointment. "I had spent a long time looking for him."

"Poor Rowena," I say, "flying all the way to Phoenix on a wild goose chase. At least my mother would have understood you returning the ring. What she didn't understand was why you sent her an album."

He shakes his head. "Your mother would have tucked the ring away, and said, 'Well, here's this fella that had this ring for some reason, and just found it and returned it to me.' And she would have sent a polite little thank-you card, and that would have been the end of it. She was awful mad at me for calling your father a murderer back then."

"I suppose that's true," I agree. "But what was she supposed to do with the album?"

"I wanted someone in your family to get curious. I wanted someone to get in touch with me and say, 'Why did you send me this stupid old album? What is it all about?' " He crosses his arms in triumph. "It had to be the right person. I knew that old album would do the trick."

"Did you really?" I wasn't sure whether I was annoyed or pleased to be manipulated.

"Oh yes," he says. "I didn't even tell Rowena what I had in mind. She would have said, 'Old man, mind your own business.' "

"I guess your plan worked," I say, though I still have no idea what his plan was.

He turns his face to the sky and answers my unspoken thought. "My plan was to set things right," he says. "Before I go to my final rest, I have to set things right."

Fleischer and his men had come almost full circle; spring was gone, summer was just starting, and the heat was pushing hard at them. It had been one year ago, when they had come here; you'd think by now they would have gotten used to the Alabama sun. You'd think by now, they would have gotten used to life in the wash rack.

But every day, the chemicals were a fresh assault. Gasoline, carbon tetrachloride, both potent solvents, burned their throats and noses, joining with the smell of wires and steam, and sweat and metal. The heat was unbearable, like they were using a piece of the sun to burn the planes clean, and the racketing noise split into their skulls, day after day.

It had been almost two months since August died. The men had made peace of sorts, with Fleischer, grudgingly resuming a working relationship. They weren't friendly, they weren't unfriendly; they spoke to each other with a wary neutrality.

* * *

Midmorning was still the best time of day for the wash rack. The coffee break, followed later by lunch, made the day feel shorter, made it more bearable. Today was no different. They had already turned and burned several planes this morning, and a new plane was being swung into the bay. They finished their coffee reluctantly and swarmed toward the new plane, to work in a rhythm of sweat and steam, degreasing the wings, pulling out the dynamotor with its wires waving, like the legs on a giant centipede, dismantling the radio and pushing it across the floor to the radio room on a dolly like it was a king being brought into court. The assembly crew was almost finished with the plane that had come in before this one, Willie was near the front of the hangar, making last-minute adjustments on the cables that worked the wing flaps, and Fleischer was in the radio room, repairing a transmitter. Earlier that morning, they had given each other a brief hello, said nothing during their coffee break, and just went back to work.

Maybe it was the flash that caught Willie by surprise, the stunning burst of white light; he turned his head around to see it better. Maybe it was the immediate, thundering throb of noise that blew hard against his body. He was never sure what came first, although thinking back over the years, it had to be the light. All he knew was that his ears felt like they had been blown from his head, that he heard the screech of bells, a ringing so loud that it shuttled his brain from one side of his head to the other. His first notion was that they had been bombed, that it had been sabotage, the Germans had attacked, and the base was being blown up. Or maybe the sun had finally fallen into the hangar, its fiery surface eating them alive. Always their savage enemy, maybe the Alabama sun had grown impatient with its slow sear, and, its appetite more voracious than ever, had plunged to earth in a final effort to devour them.

The hangar was all raging light, fire, great orange walls, bending and swaying and roaring, alive with fury and appetite, accompanied by the never-ending ringing—no, it was screaming. He was screaming; everyone was screaming with pain. The sun had fallen, the walls had fallen, fire, fire was everywhere, and his body was burning. He was going to burn like Sunday morning bacon. His hazardous-materials suit was nothing against this. His clothes were melting. Oh, the pain! He was going to die! Right now! He would never see New York again, never see his mother, oh, his mother, in her Sunday-going-to-church hat, the yellow one, with the big yellow flower, yellow fire flower, just like this, in this moment, like Jink, he was going to die in fucking Alabama. He was going to burn to death inside the ringing and the screaming, with the pain streaming out from the orange walls, flame arms reaching for him. Now orange, now red, now white-star blue, they were yellow, yellow flames everywhere. The noise was pain, and the light was noise and pain, a devouring roar, a blood-cooking, bone-searing, flesh-burning inferno-roar.

Something was grabbing him; maybe he was hooked on a shard of metal, no, arms, arms were pulling him and he resisted, pushing them away, trying to move himself someplace away from the pain, although he couldn't see anything but fire. What if it was one of the men, pulling him backward into the heart of the storm? He tried to squirm out of the grip, but the arms pulled him, and he fell into them, and suddenly he was outside of the hangar, lying on blackened, smoldering grass, black, he had never seen black grass, he thought stupidly, but it was black, and then he looked at the hangar, billowing furious streams of flame behind him. Fleischer was standing above him; the arms had belonged to Fleischer. He had pulled Willie from the hangar and then he was gone, disappearing into the smothering smoke, then reappearing like an apparition, emerging from the devouring gold-orange with another man, and another. Willie forced himself to stand, forced his legs to take him away, standing up on bare bloody feet with the skin shredding like pulled pork because his boots had been blown off.

He tried to call out, but the inside of his mouth and throat were rags, rivers of snot poured from his nose, his eyes were hot, all his words were burned away. He fell again to the ground and raised his arms to the sky, a plea, a surrender. "Oh, dear Jesus, please save us," he tried to say, but the words were burned away.

Huge globes of black smoke and orange flame roiled from inside of the hangar, sending hell up into the heavens. White flames rose in concert with his arms, into the sky; it was the arrival of Armageddon—it was the beginning of the end, it was the end of the end—until one furious blast, a summoning of the damned, a heralding of death to everything in its path, a thundering, consuming detonation that pierced through the strident ringing in his head, that finessed the pain to an even higher plateau and brought the entire hangar down to a pile of molten metal.

Had it been days? Weeks? Willie wasn't sure. The ringing filled his ears, day and night, its constancy crying throughout the blank hours, into his sleep, numbing his every thought. His eyes were bandaged; his arms and hands were bandaged; he could feel his body still burning. His mouth was burned, his nose and throat were raw, and he lay in the blackness of his own mind wondering whether the world was still there.

He tried to sleep, but the flames were waiting for him. The men were waiting for him to return to his dreams so that they could die again in front of him, so that they could scream for him to save them, *come back, save me.* He heard their screams even as he struggled to wake up and flee them.

"Try to eat," the nurse was saying to him, but he turned his head away. The ice cream she brought him burned his mouth with its chill. Even the warm soup was too much. He turned his face away and mumbled that he wasn't hungry.

She brought him toast, but the crumbs were like broken glass, harsh against his tender tongue. She brought him soft bread and butter and he managed a few bites, but the butter tasted like airplane grease, the eggs tasted like gelatin, and he gagged, until he vomited. Fruit juices burned; bananas stuck like paste to the new skin inside his mouth.

"You have to eat something," the nurse said. The bandages were still on his eyes, and he pictured her looking like his mother when he was five, when she gave him honey and tea for his sore throat. The nurse would be plump and cocoa brown and have her hair done up in big, soft curls. She would be wearing her best yellow dress, with the sunflower print and ruffles around the neck. And the Sunday-go-to-church hat set triumphantly on her head.

"You have to eat something," the nurse said, and he turned his head away. There was nothing he could tolerate.

"Try this," she said one afternoon. She thought she had found something he might eat.

It was cool and sweet, and his healing mouth could taste the subtle flavor of sugar and vanilla and eggs. She fed him spoon-fuls and it was okay; he could tolerate it. It slipped down his throat, and settled nicely in his stomach. He wanted it every day and the nurse brought him bowls of it. Every day. The only thing he could, would eat.

"Thank you," he said to her, opening his mouth like one of the baby birds in the wash rack. And she fed him little spoon-fuls and he ate it gratefully. He grew to love it, depend on it. It was all he wanted.

For two months, for two months, three times a day, a grateful Willie stayed alive on tapioca pudding.

Chapter 42

"Where are the men?" Willie asked again, and the nurse averted her eyes and pulled at his pillow to smooth out the wrinkles. "The men?" he rasped. "Where are they?" The bandages had been taken off his eyes, and he could see her now. She was plump, but young, with a beautiful, round cocoa-brown face, skin like a baby, and thick, tight curls pulled up under a ruffled white cap with a black band around it. Her name was Mildred, she said, she was from Philadelphia, and part of the army's quota of fifty-two black nurses.

"How are you feeling today?" she asked him every morning, smiling with perfectly even white teeth that made her face light up like heaven. But her voice was low; he could barely hear it through the ringing.

"Where are the men?" Willie asked again, more urgently. He knew she understood him; his tongue wasn't swollen anymore, and they had reduced the morphine, so he was making sense. He could form the words, and he knew she understood what he meant.

"Why don't you rest, Soldier," she said softly, smoothing his covers.

The men were all gone, he knew, without her answering. They had to be gone. There was nothing left of the hangar; they had all been taken up in a roaring conflagration of pain and smoke and great thundering orange-gold flames. Leon Hamilton and Charlie Hobbs, and LeRoy Davis and Grover Jones, and Milton Chalmers, and Clyde Sanders, all of them, all of them.

Okay, he thought, he would put his question another way. "How many are left?"

Mildred winced. "Eight."

Eight. Eight out of nineteen. Like some crazy kind of math puzzle. What is eight out of nineteen? What is nineteen divided like that so it makes eight living, eleven men dead?

"And Sergeant Fleischer?" he asked.

She inclined her head toward the hall. Oh. Of course. Fleischer wouldn't be in the colored ward. "He's still sedated," she said, the ringing nearly masking her words. He put his hands to his ears to shake the ringing away. There was something sticky on the side of his face, and he looked at his fingers, puzzled. Something yellow.

"What is this?" he asked, holding his fingers up to show her.

"From your eardrums," she said. "Serum. Your eardrums were blown out." He could hear her, but her voice sounded far away. "I can put some cotton in, so that it doesn't get on your face." He said okay.

He tried to talk to her, but always, there was the ringing. "When will it stop?" he asked. "The ringing, I mean," and she looked down at his blanket, and her lips quivered.

"Maybe it'll go away when your ears heal," she replied, but there was a question in her voice.

"And maybe it won't?" he asked, and she didn't answer. He wanted to cry, but he wasn't going to cry in front of a pretty nurse. The army had taken everything from him; his time, and his spirit and his dignity, and now, of all things, it had taken the one thing that might have restored everything else, the ability to hear his music.

* * *

Fleischer was still sedated when Willie, with Mildred's help, rolled his wheelchair down the hall, and into the ward. The sergeant was bandaged like a mummy, the bandages yellow with boric petroleum. An IV of plasma was flowing directly into one arm, and he lay as still as a dead man. His ears, too, were stuffed with cotton.

"He doesn't say anything, even when we debride him," Fleischer's nurse confided to Mildred. Mildred gave her a knowing look. Debridement was the most painful procedure in the world. The men screamed and cried like babies and begged the nurses not to do it. Even the morphine didn't help.

"It's like he's not in there," his nurse continued.

Willie pointed to Fleischer's ears and looked up at Mildred. She nodded.

"Eardrums. Blown out," she mouthed. "We think he's totally deaf."

Willie sat by Fleischer's bed for a long time while Mildred waited, standing quietly next to his wheelchair. Neither of them spoke.

"Is he gonna live?" Willie asked.

"We don't know," said his nurse.

Willie sat by Fleischer's bed for a while, not knowing what he felt. Triumph that a man he hated was going to die? Guilty for hating a man who had saved him? Did he really hate him? It was all mixed up in his head, and he didn't know what he felt at all. People were ciphers, pieces of good, pieces of bad, and you had to put it all together and figure out what you saw. Or maybe it didn't matter. Maybe all that mattered was that Fleischer had done this for him, pulled him out of hell. Maybe all that mattered was intention, and Fleischer's intentions had been good. Even on the bus, he had meant to do good. He sat by Fleischer's bed and stared at him, the bandages, the IV line, and wondered whether Fleischer even knew he was there. He turned his face toward his nurse and gestured for her to take him back to his room.

"Well, his ears better heal," he finally said, as she rolled his wheelchair toward the door. "Because I got things to say to him."

He visited Fleischer every day after that, sitting by his bed, trying to puzzle it all out. Things were so complicated. Willie was full of remorse, then anger, then guilt. Fleischer was either a hero or a fool or something else, something indefinable, that left Willie confused and anguished. He was sorry he had screamed at Fleischer, called him a murderer, yet when he thought of August lying dead in the bus, he wasn't sorry at all. He was grateful, yes, *grateful* was the right word, for being alive. Fleischer had saved him, risked himself to save him, and Willie felt indebted.

Can you feel grateful and angry and sad all at the same time? For the same person? Why was it so hard to find the answer, the balance, the solution to the puzzle?

He sat for days by Fleischer's bed, wanting to talk to him, but there was never any indication that he even knew Willie was there.

Sometimes Ruth was there, sitting quietly and reading, or stroking her husband's arm. She greeted Willie with reserve, and always asked politely how he was doing, then looked away, her lips set in a straight line. He guessed that Fleischer had told her about the bus thing and how Willie had called him a murderer, which added to his agony even more. One day he came in when she was in the middle of arguing with two doctors and a nurse.

"No more," she was saying. "He's too sick from it. I want the treatment stopped."

"It's the best we can do," one doctor was saying. "Tannic acid treatment is experimental, but it's all we have."

"He's getting sick from it," Ruth repeated firmly. "He told me so."

They all looked over at Fleischer, who remained immobile. "He *told* you?" the other doctor said, his voice filled with doubt. "He hasn't talked to anyone since he came in here."

"He talks to me," Ruth said. "When no one is around, he

whispers to me. And he said to leave him alone. He doesn't want you to experiment on him like an animal."

Weeks wore on. Sometimes Pastor Booker was there, up for a visit and a prayer. He left a Bible and a plate of homemade lemon cookies from Mrs. Booker. Sometimes he brought a few members of his prayer circle and they swayed and praised the Lord over Fleischer's bed, but he never acknowledged them. He never acknowledged anyone.

Time passed; the swelling and redness was gone from Fleischer's face, and his hair, which had been totally singed off, was growing back. So were his eyebrows, and every once in a while, Ruth would gently shave his face. His eyes were open and staring up at the ceiling. He made no attempt to communicate, even though his bandages were slowly being removed. One day both his arms were finally bare, pink and tight and shiny new–looking; a few days later, his legs. The asbestos in their hazardous-material suits apparently had saved his life, both their lives, but Willie wondered whether anything could have saved his mind.

"You'll be going home in a few weeks," Mildred informed Willie. "The doctors think you're going to be okay." Except for his hearing, of course. His ears still oozed a little, and the ringing had grown fainter, like he was hearing something from outside the window or down the hall, but it was always there.

He took her hand—Mildred's hands were as soft as angel wings, as cool as a stream of water—and his eyes met hers. He had fallen in love with her. She was tender and sweet, and gentle. She was the most beautiful woman he had ever seen. He couldn't picture life without her.

"I'll go home only if you go with me," he said. She flushed and said yes.

He pointed to his ear. "I can't hear you," he said, and she laughed, and said, "Yes, yes, yes," so loud that a passing nurse poked her head into the room to see what the shouting was about.

* * *

Willie had expected some kind of an inquiry long before this, but there was none. Careless, the brass said. Someone in the hangar had been careless with a cigarette and it had ignited the gasoline. But Willie knew that it wasn't true. No one smoked inside Fleischer's hangar. He was a stickler about safety. A pain-in-the-ass stickler. He wanted to talk to Fleischer about it, but Fleischer just lay there, his eyes dead, never saying anything. The nurses turned him from side to side so he wouldn't get bedsores; the plasma IVs were eventually removed. Ruth fed him every night, since she now had a job working in a gift shop in Montgomery to help earn some money and couldn't come up in the day. She came every night, and fed him Jell-O from his tray, or some soup, and he opened his mouth like a baby bird and ate from the spoon, and swallowed, but never said anything, not even good night to her, not even when she bent over to kiss him long after it was time for her to go home.

Willie was bored. Occupational therapy consisted of making pot holders out of brown and maroon and yellow strips of corduroy cut from old bathrobes. Willie made twelve pot holders and sent them to his mother and his sister. He made five more for Mildred and three for Mabel, Mildred's sister. Then he refused to make any more. Parts of the hospital were off-limits; the swimming pool on base was off-limits, even though the doctors had told him that swimming would be good therapy for his skin and to build up his arms and legs. The trouble was, the color of his skin was the trouble, even in the hospital. He sent a letter to New York and asked his mother to send him his trombone. He would sit in the colored lounge and play his trombone. He didn't hear all that well, but he knew he could pull some kind of music from inside his head.

The package arrived a week later, wrapped in brown paper and cardboard. Willie recognized it as soon as Mildred brought it in to him, along with his mail and a box of sugar cookies cut into stars from his grandmother. He and Mildred shared the cookies and she admired the smooth, golden curves of the trombone. She wheeled him down to the lounge, and he sat by a window in the golden sun and put the trombone to his lips. It was like kissing a woman; it was that sweet. He played it softly, a few notes, then a few bars. It sounded far away, dampened; the ringing in his ears was still there, but he could hear the notes through his head. It wasn't the same, it wasn't the same at all; it was muted and trembly and he knew it would never be the same again, but at least he had some of the music left.

Fleischer was sitting up now, and they wheeled him to the window every morning so he could see what the world was like outside, but he never looked out. He stared straight ahead, barely blinking. They wheeled him into OT, but he never even looked down at the table where the long strips of corduroy were waiting to be made into pot holders. He ate with some help from either his nurse or Ruth, and didn't do much else. He never spoke; he never even indicated that he recognized Willie, who had cut his visits down to twice a week. Willie had run out of things to talk about, and he didn't want to tell Fleischer how the brass thought the explosion was caused by the carelessness of the men in the hangar. Willie knew why it happened. He knew it was somehow caused by Hogarth. It was revenge. One day maybe he and Fleischer could talk it over. One day, maybe the brass would straighten it all out, but he knew Fleischer wasn't ready. He just kept staring off somewhere. Maybe he was home in New York. Maybe he was lost somewhere in the hangar pulling out his men, though Willie hoped not. Wherever he was, Willie hoped that Fleischer could pull himself back out.

Night fell; it was lights-out. Mildred came in and gave Willie a lingering kiss on the lips.

"My mama is planning for us to have a big church wedding," she told Willie, who could think of nothing he wanted more. "Soon's you get discharged." She kissed him again and left to make rounds.

He sat in his bed and looked across the ward. The men from his platoon were getting better. Two had been sent home; the other five were healing. Their faces were puckered and drawn, melted, with their mouths or their eyes pulling to one side as the burns turned into contractures and made their faces look like drama masks Willie had seen once in a theater. But they could shuffle along the ward during the day, to OT, to make pot holders, and they could eat by themselves, so the army pronounced them cured and was sending them home.

Willie slipped out of bed and pulled on his robe. He took his trombone from under his bed and slipped it from its case. He would be going home in three weeks, and he wanted to leave something for Fleischer to remember him. If Fleischer ever came back to his senses, Willie wanted him to know that he had been there, and that his anger and fury had been debrided from his heart, that he was renewed, that he could see that sometimes color gets in the way, both ways, and that all it boiled down, in the end, to the fact he was just grateful that Fleischer had saved his life.

He slipped into Fleischer's room. The other men in the ward were sleeping, but Fleischer lay in his bed, his eyes open and unseeing. Willie sat next to his bed and rubbed the trombone on his sleeve. It gleamed golden in the soft light from the hall. "This is all I got to say," he whispered softly and pressed the trombone to his lips. His ears were still stuffed with cotton, to keep the fluid that dripped from his ruptured eardrums from irritating the skin on his face. He wouldn't be able to hear it all that well, except through the bones in his head, but he hoped it would be enough to say thank you. Fleischer just lay there, his own ears stuffed with cotton, saying nothing. Willie took a deep breath and gently blew a note. He could feel the music in his head; it echoed back into his skull. The two of them were wrecked, and he wanted to put that in his music along with his apology and his gratitude.

"Take the 'A' Train," he played, soft as a whisper. The other men in the room gave appreciative grunts and turned to listen, and he sat by Fleischer's bed every night for the next two weeks and played music. After a while, the men made requests for him to play some of their favorites, and he played "Sophisticated Lady," "I'm Gonna Sit Right Down and Write Myself a Letter," "Mood Indigo," and then he played his own personal favorite, "Solitude," playing into the night. Playing until his arms got tired, playing through the dim ringing, all from memory, hoping, in some way, to reach the man lying in front of him, who never seemed to hear him at all.

Chapter 43

Willie sent his trombone back to New York the week he was going to be discharged from the hospital; his medical discharge from the army came soon after. He took Mildred with him and married her one month later, telling everyone at the wedding that the army thought so highly of him, they sent him home with his own private nurse. It was a church wedding, at the African Methodist Episcopal Church in Harlem, and her family came up from Philadelphia. They didn't have any money, and Mildred wore a simple white silk blouse with an orchid pinned to her shoulder, a borrowed pale blue taffeta skirt, and a short veil. Willie wore his uniform. They invited Sergeant Fleischer and Ruth, in care of Maxwell Field Army Hospital. But Fleischer had been discharged, and the invitation was returned without a forwarding address.

Willie had to find a job, though he knew it wasn't going to be with music. The army had taken his music; he had to find something else. The trouble was, there weren't any jobs for blacks beside the usual maintenance man, especially since he was listed as having done that kind of work in the army, and possible employers always wanted to know what he had done in the army.

The next year Mildred got pregnant; his mother got diabetes. The year after that, Mildred's father had a stroke. It was all on Willie's shoulders now, and he got the only job he could, mopping floors for the phone company. He wanted more; he'd had some college years before and decided to try again. He went to school every night for his teaching degree. It took him ten years, and in 1954, he was finally able to put his mop down and get a job teaching shop. Mildred brought nine-year-old Rowena to his graduation ceremony and they sat right in the middle row, fiercely proud of him.

Before Willie knew, the years passed, like water running through his fingers, and Fleischer was pushed somewhere in the back of his mind. Someday he would find him, he promised himself. Someday he would straighten it all out. Every few years, he became ambitious and wrote a few letters to the Veterans Administration, but nothing came of it, and before he knew it, he was an old man, closing up his apartment, giving it a final cleaning, because he couldn't take care of it all by himself with Mildred passed on, and him being eighty-seven, with one leg. He had been packing up his desk when he found Fleischer's ring, wrapped in toilet paper, stuck in a corner of a drawer. Gold, with a blue stone, as clean and shiny as the day he had packed it away. He held it in his hand, feeling its heft, running his thumb over the monogrammed *M*, and remembered. The years had painted them all with the same brush. They were both old men now; it was time to let the ring make peace between them.

Dusk is falling, softly graying the rooms. The rain has come, and the house is sitting in a pocket of thunder. A flash of light startles me; a loud *clap* catches a beat of my heart unaware, and makes me jump. I am still caught up in the explosion in the hangar.

Willie and I are sitting in the living room; it had grown dark around us without us much noticing or caring. We can barely see each other now; Willie's voice has dropped to a lull, then to nothing. His story has spun itself out and is retreating back into the past, and there is nothing left but the sound of rain, and thunder. I am trying to think of my father as a hero, bravely forging through flame to rescue his men. I can only see his angry face, hear his angry voice. All I can think of, and I am sorry about it, was that he was no hero to me.

We sit quietly for a while, listening to the bustle in the kitchen. Rowena has found a home health aide to care for Willie, since the VA informed her it has no beds left because of the new war, and won't let him return. He has officially become an outpatient, even though Rowena is working and can't stay home to care for him. Salary for the health aide comes from his meager veteran benefits and Rowena's paycheck. The aide flicks on a light to dispel the dusk and comes in to take Willie's sugar level by pricking his finger with a lancet. She apologizes for hurting him, but he just smiles up at her.

"Didn't hurt me one bit," he says gallantly.

"I'll start dinner," she says. Willie wheels himself to the back door and opens it. The air is moist, like tears. I stand next to him and we watch the rain.

"So, who do you think did it?" I ask Willie. "The explosion, I mean."

"Hogarth," he answers softly. "There's no question in my mind. We all knew it was Hogarth. He hated your father. He hated all of us. Besides, he had made threats."

"What did the army do about it?" I ask. "Because my father never said anything about an explosion."

"They said it was a careless cigarette." He gives a bitter laugh. "But none of us were smokers. Then they said maybe it was some kind of industrial accident, but we knew."

"Is that what my father thought?"

He shrugs his shoulders. "He still wasn't talking when I got discharged, so I never knew what he thought."

I think back to old conversations I had heard between my parents. "I remember he tried to get total disability for his hearing," I say. "And some kind of medal." I never cared enough to ask either one of them about it, and the matter had been long dropped. But I remembered the tortuous patches of skin on my father's arms and legs and back, an uneven quilt of pale, pinched, textured skin that he took great pains to cover. "They wouldn't give award benefits to him, because he couldn't prove anything was service-related."

"Oh, I know," Willie says. "I tried for it, too, for my ears." His hand reaches up to gingerly touch his hearing aid. "But after a while, they said that all the records got burned in Ohio in 1957, and then, after a few years, they denied that there had been any explosion at all. They said I made it up just so I could get benefits." He sighs, but it's more like a shudder. "Like I was imagining I was deaf." Another bitter laugh, and he rolls up his sleeve to reveal a twin arm to my father's, with white and pink-tan skin mapping a agonizing route, up past his elbow. "Imagining I got burned. Does this look like my imagination?" He shows me his scars, and the lightning illuminates his face, and it is all pain

By the next morning, the streets are washed clean from the overnight rain. Soon I will be flying home to New York. Willie and I are eating breakfast together.

"I'll have waffles and syrup and a couple of sausages," Willie tells the health aide. She is a large black woman in her sixties, with red hair, and her name is Rita.

"This ain't a restaurant, darlin'," she purrs in a silken Jamaican accent, and puts a bowl of Cheerios on the table. "Skim milk, one piece of bread, sugar-free jam. And what be your glucose this mornin'? You shouldn't even get this 'til I know your numbers." She gives him a strict look.

He beams at her. "You remind me of my late wife," he says, pulling the Cheerios across the table and picking up his spoon. "My number was ninety-two."

She smiles and slices a corn muffin for him and spreads some sugar-free jam across the surface. "Guess you can be havin' this, then, 'stead of the bread," she says, putting it in front of him.

He bows his head a little. "I think you're gonna work out just fine," he says and picks up a piece of muffin.

I watch him eat, then sip the coffee Rita has put in front of me, along with a muffin.

"I brought the album with me this time," I tell Willie. "It's in my suitcase."

"I'd be glad to have it back," he says, licking jam from his fingers. "We'll do a little exchange before you leave. One old album for one old ring."

It is a solemn ceremony of exchange. Willie is sitting in his wheelchair dressed in a pale gray shirt and black sweater and dark gray slacks, one pants leg tucked under him, his shoe shined to mirror black. He has put on his old army hat, and a small American flag pin is secured to his shirt pocket, both taken from the box of memories. He sits upright. Rita is looking on from the kitchen, arms folded over her pale blue Perma Press uniform, watching us with amusement and curiosity. I have put on a white sweater and dressy black slacks and black slingback heels. Willie deserves nothing less.

I present the album to him. He takes it and caresses it, then puts it down on an end table in the living room. He puts a slender finger into his shirt pocket and takes out a gold ring with a blue stone.

"Sergeant Fleischer," he says, his eyes raised to the ceiling, "thank you for saving my life at great risk to your own." He salutes the ceiling. "I have never forgotten what you did. I wish I could do more to show my gratitude."

I take the ring and study it, the first time in my life that I have ever held it. My father's old bar mitzvah ring—*mitzvah* meaning "good deed" in Hebrew—which is what this is all about anyway. It shines cold in my hand, but I can see more in the blue stone than just my reflection.

"Private Jackson," I say. "Thank you for this. You are truly a man of honor." And I salute Willie back.

I shake Rita's hand, kiss Rowena good-bye, and tell her how lucky she is to have Willie, because he is a good, loving father.

Rowena holds me for a moment, murmuring, "The fire that burns the bread, melts the butter." I step back and give her a puzzled look, and she tilts her head and gives my shoulder a little squeeze. "Just so you know," she says, "I also lived with a father haunted by ghosts."

Chapter 44

Any time is the right time to ride a horse, but there is something special about the very early morning. It is the part of the day not yet anchored to burdens, too young, too new to be considered a hard day, a sad day, a difficult day. It is a day still innocently full of optimism and fresh vows.

Lisbon is eager to move toward the woods. I barely touch him with my legs as he trots along the dirt path we have worn through the underbrush. Here and there, the leaves betray the end of summer with traces of orange and red. His hooves beat a tattoo against the earth, the one-two rhythm of the trot, while he tosses his head, impatient to move into a soft canter. I hold him back a little, until we reach a small clearing beyond the trees, and then let him out. His body rocks into the canter, the waltz of the equine—*one-two-three, one-two-three*—and we cover the ground in a dance for two. We have worked it all out. He trusts me not to hurt him; I trust him not to hurt me. It's the best kind of love. I canter along, feeling the balance between us, and I don't have to think, I don't have to plan things, figure anything out. Sandra has taken my mother back to Georgia; David hasn't called. Every ride is between me and my soul and Lisbon. Every ride is new. It has been a hard summer, and I'm not sorry to see it go.

Malachi is slipping away, thinner than a blade of grass, more like a strand of hay. He had been so vital and Willie had been so frail, yet nature sees fit to take what it pleases. Strong trees get felled, slim reeds bend, the reed sometimes outlasts the tree. By the time I got back from Boston, he was a whisper of a man, wrapped in blankets, lying in his hospital bed, a big, soft pillow under his head. I sit by his side every day and watch his nurse adjust the IV that carries pain medicine into his veins.

"How are you doing?" I ask him, even though his eyes are closed. I refuse to ask his nurse; to ask her is to lose the connection with him.

He can barely smile. "I'm all right," he whispers, then adds ruefully, "I could use some Potter's mixture." He takes a pained, coughing breath and says something I can't hear. I bend down to put my ear near him. "You got to grab the brass ring, missy," he whispers raggedly.

"Lisbon?"

He coughs again, and turns his head away for a moment to catch his breath. The nurse steps up to wipe his mouth.

"I'm calling the fence company," I tell him. "I'm putting Lisbon in his own paddock." He nods approvingly.

Sometimes a horse is just a horse, not an issue, not a philosophical commentary. Lisbon will never be brave, and it doesn't matter to me anymore.

I sit for a while, worrying about the way Malachi's breathing sounds. "My sister is going to come presently," he suddenly says. A flash of pain crosses my heart, and I reach out to hold his hand.

I stay with him all the next day, and we talk about the farm. He tells me what he wants me to plant in the spring, what I should do if I get another windswept foal, which horse to sell, which to keep, makes me promise to name a horse after him so that something of him will be left with me. I sit by his bed, stroking his thin arm, afraid to speak, because if I let a word slip out, the tears will follow and I am afraid I would never be able to stop them. I know he can't put the gardens to bed and he won't be here to wake them again in the spring. I want to beg him to stay with me, but I know it isn't up to him. The day, spent like a fast dollar, is relenting its authority to the night; the sun slips from our grasp.

"Lissen up," he says as the night climbs through the window. He raises his head for a moment, then drops it back on the crisp white pillow, closing his eyes from exhaustion.

"I'm listening."

"Open my satchel," he whispers. "It's for you. Everything you need is in there."

The leather satchel is old but well-preserved. Dark brown, wrinkled with patina and shine that says it has been cleaned with saddle soap maybe hundreds of times. It smells warm and comforting in the sun. The tag tied to the handle has my name on it, which surprises me. I thought perhaps it was a plane tag, that perhaps Minnie was going to fly Malachi back to wherever he needed to be. That was before I realized about Minnie. It zips right open. And it is empty. Totally empty. Puzzled, I run my hand through the side pockets and find a piece of lined notebook paper. I turn it over. Malachi's neat cursive, in pen, which is what he used when he wrote me important notes. *Travel light.* That's all it says. *Travel light.*

I sit on the hay bale in front of his cottage and stare at the paper for a long time. A breeze ruffles my hair and brings the smell of horse and woods and fresh hay. I have to think about this, Malachi's last message to me.

And then it is like an eye opening within my heart. The words suddenly startle me. And I know what he means.

There was my father. He had to have been a good man to think and behave the way he did. He had to have been a good friend, a good officer, a good husband, his head filled with little poems and silly pieces of jewelry and riddles and songs for my mother, only to be defeated, destroyed, shattered, by hatred, by senseless rules that everyone thought was just nature's way. He had been decimated by the war. He had given his sanity to it. That really, my father died in the war. He died a hero. A war hero, and they deserve a special understanding and forgiveness.

I think how the injuries filter down to their families, like loose change falling between the sofa cushions. Collateral damage.

I think of Sandra, budgeting for my mother, so that she will have something left in the end, when she'll need more care. Dear Sandra, struggling to find love in a piece of cake, needs me to tell her that she is a good daughter and a good sister, and that I love her, because if I save up all my love, who do I give it to in the end? Who will even be there, in the end, for me to give it to? I will die with a heartful of hoarded love, like preserved crab apples, bitter and shriveled, and lonely. The anger has to end sometime, and as I watch Malachi slip further and further away, I realize I can't be worse off than worrying about living without things that I am already living without.

Malachi is right. It is time for me to leave it all behind. The baggage, the burden, it was all awful and way too heavy to carry with me for so long. A plane, overburdened with cargo, cannot soar. It loses its lift, stalls, and crashes. I realize, when there are no more points to be made, when there are no more hearts to break, when you suddenly see through the clouds and beyond the sky, it's time to drop the cargo and take flight. Travel light.

I call David and he answers.

"Do you love her?" I ask. "Do you love her?" I don't want to know, but it is my charge to find out what I have done to him.

He takes a deep breath. "I just don't know," he says. "She isn't so complicated."

"I am sorry," I tell him. "Please forgive me. I did this to us, and I was very wrong. I was so wrong." The words come from my mouth in chokes. This is a new language for me, a new geography. I am making new rules. "When you are ready to give the ring to someone, I would like it to be me."

"I'll remember that," he says.

"I'm sorry for trying to prove a point every minute of our time together," I tell him. "I'm sorry I hurt you. I can change, I *will* change." I have left myself vulnerable now, a windswept foal slowly straightening its legs to take its first tenuous, normal steps. Anything can knock me over, but I have to try. "I love you," I tell him. "I've always loved you."

"I know," he says and there is a long pause. I hear him breathing on the other end, maybe even crying.

Malachi passes quietly in the middle of the night, like the wisps of fog that hang over the pastures and are gone by morning. He goes so quietly, a breath taken, a breath expelled, soft as a foal's muzzle, and gone. I put my head down against his chest. He wasn't my father, and I'm not sure I need him or anyone, anymore, to be my father. We get what we get and make our adjustments. And when it is over, I suppose we make our peace with what's left, because there is no point in doing otherwise.

And I think if Malachi had a little more time, I might have convinced him that nature is not immutable; she makes and breaks her own rules all the time. She can bring death in the winter and turn it all around in the spring. She can take an unforgiving, stubborn heart and split it open and then close it again, filled with the grace of clemency. She can take a heart that has lived like an empty barrel, echoing angrily with noise from the past, and fill it with hope. Love, even.

I watch the horses eating their hay. The sun lays warm on my shoulders, and there is a slight breeze that comes through the woods and smells like pine, and brushes through my hair like Malachi used to brush the hair from my eyes after I'd ridden. Maybe it will all come to nothing. Maybe love doesn't need to be returned like an envelope with its stamp missing. Maybe it exists for itself and that's fine. I will be all right; I will fight to be all right. I might thrive, even. Overwhelmed, I fold my arms on the fence rail and lay my head down in them.

And weep.

ACKNOWLEDGMENTS

I can never thank my agents, Jane Gelfman and Victoria Marini, enough for always being so supportive of me, always optimistic, and always ready with encouragement and a kind word. I welcome their criticisms and suggestions and am forever grateful that it is because of them that I am able to pursue my passion of writing.

Also, many thanks to my editor, Esi Sogah, for her enthusiasm, for being so exacting, asking for more clarity, for pushing me to write better and better. Her insights and requests brought more dimension and heart to my story, and I am very appreciative.

HOW THIS BOOK CAME TO BE

My father and I weren't mortal enemies, but to say we didn't get along was an understatement. I didn't understand his rage and bitterness, followed by periods of withdrawal. He was a bully; he cried at odd moments; he shunned most social life. What I did understand was that I couldn't live with him. I ran away from home at the age of fifteen, right after I graduated from an accelerated high school program, and never returned. I went to college, I married, had children, divorced, attended graduate school, married again, and had an entire life without him in it.

We didn't speak for a long time. Years passed, and my mother, with whom I had kept in touch, occasionally mentioned some kind of medal she was trying to help my father get from his years in the Army Air Corps. He had saved his men from an explosion. That's all I knew. Eventually I learned that my father had been drafted to serve during World War II. It was 1941; he was a Jewish kid from Brooklyn and had never been out of his element. He was sent to Gunter Field Air Force Base, in Montgomery, Alabama, 58th Air Base Squadron, 66th Air Base Group.

The heart of Dixie. It was his first taste of the South.

He made master sergeant, and was put in command of a platoon of men, all of them black. He and they were assigned to the Housekeeping Squadron, where they took on the maintenance and cleaning of the Vultee BT-13s, the bomber training planes. I want to emphasize that it was the South, 1941, a Jewish sergeant, and an all-black platoon. My father became outraged by the treatment of his men. He had a strong sense of social justice, which stayed with him his entire life, and he wanted his men treated properly. He fought for them, for their rights as United States soldiers, and was treated miserably for it. It culminated in a mysterious explosion that tore their hangar apart. He rescued as many as he could, but was forever haunted by the men he lost.

He was recommended for a medal by his base commander. Time passed, and it was overlooked. On July 12, 1973, there was a huge fire at the National Personnel Record Center, in St. Louis, Missouri, where veteran service records were stored. All his records were destroyed, along with the recommendation for a medal. Years later, in 1997, when he was already elderly, he received a letter from the French government commending him for saving French lives by preventing additional Vultee crashes. He never knew who had written them on his behalf, but he was very proud of being remembered.

It wasn't until I was an adult that PTSD was finally diagnosed in people who had undergone physical and emotional trauma. And there it was. My father was suffering from PTSD. It explained everything. Over a period of time, my father and I reconciled, of sorts.

Just before he died, he was elected into the Arizona Veterans Hall of Fame in 2003, and honored by the Phoenix NAACP the same year. But he never did receive recognition from his government. It embittered him even further.

The events that take place in this book mostly belong to my father's story; all of them are true, but there are a few events I included that I thought were so telling of the culture of that period, so horrific, that it seemed right to add them to the book. Names are changed for the sake of privacy, but the stories are real and heartbreaking.

I needed to write this story. I needed to honor my father and his men by remembering for them these many years later and telling others. There were so many service people like him from earlier wars, and so many who are still returning from present conflicts who are overlooked and need to be understood and helped and honored.

May God bless and heal every one of us.